"Is this your sister, Jane?" asked Amanda.

"Yes, miss."

"So you're Lilith."

Lilith nodded. She was not going to curtsy, no matter what they did to her.

"I hope you'll like it here," said Amanda.

"Thank you, miss," said Jane. "You must forgive my sister, miss. She's shy."

"I'm not," said Lilith.

Amanda smiled. For the moment *she* was Lilith, the poor little servant girl on her first day in a new place. She said: "It must be strange . . . to come to a new house. . . . The first time . . . I mean."

Lilith said: "I'm not frightened."

Jane's fingers dug hard into Lilith's arm as she drew her to the door. Jane was preparing a lecture on how to address the gentry. At the door Lilith turned to look back. She wanted to grimace, but even Lilith dared not do that.

LILITH

Jean Plaidy

FAWCETT CREST • NEW YORK

A Fawcett Crest Book
Published by Ballantine Books
Copyright © 1954 and 1967 by Jean Plaidy

Library of Congress Catalog Card Number: 90-8488

ISBN 0-449-22095-8

This edition published by arrangement with G. P. Putnam's Sons

Manufactured in the United States of America

First Ballantine Books Edition: March 1993

PART ONE

❖ One

It was a wild day in November when Lilith arrived at Leigh House. Amanda, who was at the schoolroom window, kneeling on a window seat and looking out over the damp lawns, saw her—a small, angry figure, with the wind pulling back her short black curls as though it took her part against her mother who was dragging her forward. The schoolroom window looked out from the back of the house over the lawns and stables; and because the schoolroom was at the top of the house, and because Leigh House stood halfway up a hill, Amanda could see beyond her father's grounds to the fields which were part of the Polgard Farm.

Amanda pressed her face close to the glass for, of all the people she knew, Lilith was not only the strangest but the one she felt to be most different from herself. Whenever she saw Lilith or Lilith's grandmother, or whenever she passed their cottage, she would feel apprehensive and excited, as though she were expecting something extraordinary to happen. Once when she had passed with Miss Robinson, her governess, the old woman—Lilith's grandmother—was at the door, smoking her pipe, and Amanda, fascinated and with trepidation, had turned to look back; at which the old woman had taken the pipe from her mouth and moved her head in a beckoning manner, slyly, perhaps malevolently, as Amanda felt sure she would not have dared to do if Miss Robinson had been looking her way.

In that cottage lived a big family of Tremorneys, but the grandmother and Lilith seemed apart from the others; Amanda had seen numerous small children—as well as Lilith's father and mother—barefoot, bareheaded, working in the fields, looking for lance and sand-eels on the beaches when food was scarce, gathering winkles and limpets when the storms were so fierce that the fishing boats could not leave the harbour. At such times Amanda would be sad, thinking of their sharp little faces, and hardly able to eat her luncheon at the table in the dining-room or her supper in the schoolroom. More than once Miss Robinson had found her weeping silently, and it had been impossible to explain how she felt. In any case, she had been told often enough that ladies controlled their feelings on every occasion. "Remember," said Miss Robinson twenty times a day, "that you are a lady." "My darling," said poor Mamma, who spent the greater part of the day on a couch in the drawing-room with her hartshorn within reach, "don't make so much noise. It goes right through my head and it's so unladylike." As for Amanda's father, he was mournfully convinced, she knew, that even the rigid upbringing he had arranged for her might not save her from hell; for, of course, real ladies did not go to hell.

Amanda was twelve years old and tall for her age; her hair was long, fine and silky and the colour of August wheat; she had blue eyes, a short straight nose, a sensitive mouth and a pale, grave face. The golden hair was combed back from her face, and tied with a narrow black ribbon to hide as much of it as possible. Miss Robinson had covered up the mirror in Amanda's bedroom because she had caught her arranging her hair over her shoulders. Vanity, said Miss Robinson, was one of the greatest temptations to sin which the Devil set in the path of the unwary. Amanda knew that the very colour of her hair offended her father, for it was the same as her grandfather's in the portrait which hung in the gallery. This portrait was no bigger than the other family portraits, but it always seemed to dominate the house.

Amanda, who was at the same time alert and fanciful, noted a good deal of what went on about her and guessed much more. They thought her a quiet child whose quietness did not indicate goodness since she was given to outbursts of wickedness such as running when she thought she was unobserved, taking food from the kitchen to give to the children in the lanes, crying in front of the county because she could not endure the sight of a stag with the hounds about it. "Difficult child!" sighed Amanda's mother. "I can't imagine where she gets her oddness. I do wish she would be more normal."

"Quietly wilful," said Miss Robinson, who, as she was wont to say quite often, had had great experience of children . . . *and* children of the best families. Amanda often had the feeling that if it had not been for her fear of Amanda's father and mother, Miss Robinson would have been on her side; and that she was only eager to agree that Amanda was a difficult child in order to cover her own shortcomings. As for Amanda's father, he thought his daughter had been born with more than the usual share of original sin.

All this made Amanda feel bewildered at times, made her feel that she was apart from them all, made her very conscious of her own shortcomings; and because she longed to please them all, her most passionate wish was that she might be the sort of girl they would like her to be. She was argumentative, she knew, for she could never resist saying: "But I don't see that" when all the time she knew it would be much wiser to agree. She could not help being sorry for little creatures, sick and starving animals, stray cats and dogs, the hunted and the homeless, for the barefooted children who ran about the lanes and had so little to eat when times were bad.

"God meant them to be poor, my love," her mother had explained in the days when she had been young enough to ask for an explanation. "There must be some poor people. And if He did not want them to be poor, why should He have made them so? It's therefore silly to think about them; and to *talk* about them is quite uncouth."

Amanda had soon realized that however much she tried to please them she never could; this matter of pleasing had been decided before she was born—by God, she supposed. She could not please Miss Robinson because she had to grow up, and when she was fully grown she would no longer have need of Miss Robinson. Poor Robbie! Amanda called her Robbie now and then—not that she thought of her as Robbie. How could Miss Robinson, with her sharp nose and that thin mouth which never seemed to be pleased or angry of its own accord but only because it would be expedient to be so, with the red hands which always seemed to be cold—how could she be called *Robbie*? But Amanda knew that it pleased Miss Robinson to be called Robbie; and whenever she saw that her governess was particularly worried she used the name as a sort of soothing syrup. Miss Robinson told tales of children who had called her Robbie. "Robbie," they had said, "when we grow up and have children, you shall be their governess. No one else would do but you, Robbie."

So, when Amanda felt that a double dose of balm was necessary she would tell Miss Robinson that when *she*, Amanda, grew up, no one but Robbie should look after *her* children.

As for her parents, Amanda knew that she could never please them either. They had wanted many children, and they had only one. They had wanted a son, and they had a daughter. She had as yet discovered no sedative to offer them.

Perhaps it was because of this life of hers which was ordered by the adults about her, and because she felt that she was shut up in a house from which wickedness was shut out, that she was so interested in Lilith who was all that she was not. Lilith's original sin could never have been curbed; it would have been magnified and multiplied by now. Lilith was wild and free, unlike her sister Jane who worked in the kitchen under Mrs. Derry, the cook. Amanda could see that Jane was little different from Bess, the other maid; she had watched them, giggling together when they were out of Mrs. Derry's sight.

It was only Lilith and the grandmother who were strange. There was a boy, too, about Lilith's age, and he was rather queer, but not in the same way that Lilith and the grandmother were.

And as Amanda knelt there at the schoolroom window, Lilith looked up suddenly and saw her. Lilith put out her tongue, and with her free hand dragged at the flesh of her cheeks so that the red rim round her eyeballs showed; it was a hideous grimace.

For a few seconds she and Amanda stared at each other, Amanda gravely, Lilith insolently; then Lilith was dragged along by her mother.

Amanda climbed down from the window seat and, as she did so, Miss Robinson came into the schoolroom.

"Amanda, what are you doing? You should be at your exercise books. How dirty your hands are. Oh dear, I did hope I was making a little lady of you. After all I've done . . ."

Those twinges of pity—Amanda's greatest weakness—troubled her now. "After all I've done . . ." That meant that Amanda was looking more grown-up than usual or that there had been a veiled complaint from one of her parents. Poor Miss Robinson— perpetually afraid that her good services were going unnoticed and would soon be forgotten. Amanda had heard of people being haunted by the past, but how much more terrifying it was to be haunted by the future! She put her hands behind her back and tried to look like the little lady Miss Robinson longed for her to be.

"Robbie, Lilith Tremorney is being taken to the kitchen. Why?"

"Ladies," said Miss Robinson, "do not concern themselves with the common people. And you must not be so curious. Have you learned those first three irregular verbs? Where is your French grammar? Come along. That will teach you not to be so curious."

"But it won't, Miss Robinson," said Amanda solemnly. "It will only teach me three irregular verbs; it won't teach me not to be curious, for I am. . . ." She sat down silently and resignedly.

She might have sulked. Frith would have done so—at least, he would have been argumentative, for he was not sulky by nature. Alice might have sulked. The rectory children were more normal than she was. Even Mary and Janet Holford, the daughters of the doctor, who were quiet girls, would not have been so meek as Amanda. But how could she be anything but meek with Miss Robinson when she understood so well why Miss Robinson behaved as she did?

So silently Amanda began to learn those verbs, wishing that she could enjoy grimacing at Miss Robinson as Lilith would have done. She wished that she did not have to put herself continually in people's places and suffer their troubles as well as her own. She sighed and tried to replace her curiosity concerning Lilith by a study of the methods in which the French might go, send and acquire.

Lilith, looking at Leigh House, thought of it as a prison, a prison of plenty. She had never been inside Leigh House, but Jane, when she had returned to the cottage with cheese, butter and bread such as was eaten by the gentry and which was quite different from the barley bread which was the staple food of the poor, had told the family of the wonders of Leigh House.

Lilith and her brothers and sisters, who had known little of the years before those which were later to be called the Hungry Forties, thought continually of food; and Leigh House always seemed to them rather like the cottage which Hansel and Gretel had found in the woods; its walls would not be of gingerbread, but of cheese and pastry, and the best room would be made of that greatest of all delicacies—hog's pudding.

It looked gloomy now, but Lilith knew that when the sun shone, the house shone with it; all the diamond panes in the gabled windows twinkled like real diamonds. Even now the diamonds twinkled on the bushes which old Faithful Steert had cut into fanciful shapes—fowls and peacocks, dogs and lions. It was old, this house; it was built in the reign of Queen Elizabeth—not that Lilith knew or cared about that. It was just Leigh House to her, where Amanda Leigh lived, and towards Amanda Lilith felt a particular resentment which, while it angered her, yet delighted her.

Old Grandmother Lil had fostered that resentment. She was a strange one, the old grandmother. Old as she was, she had all her wits about her. She ruled the cottage, even though she brought nothing into it—or so it seemed; but Lilith was wise enough to know that, indirectly, she brought a good deal. When, at Christmas time, the Leighs sent hampers to all the cottagers, that sent to the Tremorneys was bigger than the others. Mrs. Leigh sent a blanket to all the poor families at Christmas, but to the Tremorneys came two blankets. Now that times were so hard, the Leighs and the Danesboroughs at the Rectory sent food at all times of the year; sometimes there would be a bit of salt pork or a great pasty which would provide a meal for the whole family. But more came from the Leighs to the Tremorneys than any of the other families enjoyed; and the family would look at Grandmother Lil then, who would sit smiling and nodding as though she were some old fairy who had waved a wand and produced the food.

Of all the children, Grandmother Lil cared most for Lilith. Lilith, she said, was the image of what she had been at her age. This knowledge pleased Lilith, but the child knew—yet she was too wise to say this—that she was going to be cleverer than her old grandmother. She did not intend to end her days in an old cottage smoking a pipe and talking of the past—queen though she might be of that cottage, and the past had been something to boast about.

The grandmother could tell tales of the past which enchanted Lilith. She remembered how the men of the county had formed into bands when the French were coming, how her mother had tried to frighten her with threats of Boney: "Boney will come and get you. Boney will eat you right up." But she had never been afraid of Boney. "I never cared for God nor man," she said. "Nor will you, Granddaughter, for you're to be your old grandmother all over again."

She could remember the times when they had starved because the tax on salt was so high that they could not preserve their fish and had to dig it into the ground as manure. Not that she herself had gone short; she would close one eye and look sly, as she often did when she told these stories, and Lilith would know that they had reached their climax, for all the stories were stories of Grandmother Lil's cleverness, her ability to avoid the troubles which beset lesser folk.

"I had my friends, my little queen," she would say, fondling Lilith's curls, so like her own had been. "Ah, my handsome, your grandmother was clevèr, her was—just as you'll be, my Lilith."

Grandmother Lil's name was Lilith; and she said that she had recognized Lilith's quality when she had been born and had insisted on her being named after her old grandmother. The boy, who was Lilith's twin, had not interested her. Lilith was her girl, her little queen, her handsome.

So Lilith had known from the beginning that there was about her something which her brothers and sisters did not possess. It gave her confidence, gave her boldness. She cared for no one but herself, her grandmother and her twin brother William.

"Your brother," said Grandmother Lil, puffing out smoke, for she always had her tobacco brought to her—a gift from an old smuggler who, so she declared, had been her lover many years ago—"your brother, my little queen, be a softie. You don't want to be troubling yourself with the likes of he."

But Lilith knew certain things about William which none other knew, and although he was neither sly nor clever as she was, she loved him; and she loved him because of those very qualities which her grandmother despised.

When Amanda Leigh went by the cottages with her governess, prim and neat in her beautiful clothes, Grandmother Lil would laugh so much that she almost choked. Then she would grow fierce and angry, and point after the neat little girl and her governess and say: "That's where you ought to be, my little queen. You ought to be prinking along aside a governess just like that one."

Two days before, Lilith had heard that she was to work at Leigh House. Her mother had told her while they had been spreading the washing on the line between the rows of cottages.

"You're going to work at the House along of Jane."

"I won't work at the House," said Lilith, who hated being told what she must do and always registered her defiant disapproval before even considering the suggestion.

"Don't 'ee be a softie," said her mother. " 'Tis the best thing for 'ee. You'm lucky, I reckon."

"I won't," said Lilith, her slanting black eyes flashing, her mouth stubborn, and her pointed olive-skinned face, with the high cheekbones, flushing slightly.

"You'll be along o' Jane," said her mother. "You'll get plenty to eat."

Lilith considered that, stretching out her long, thin arms that were like brown sticks. Plenty to eat. For years there had been little to eat. These were the days of famine and starvation and the most magical words in the language were: "Plenty to eat."

Lilith laid her hands on her little stomach, which was like a cave. Breakfast this morning had consisted of the usual 'Sky-blue-and-sinkers,' which was nothing more than a little barley water mixed with scalded milk and slops of barley bread; the skimmed milk was blue, and because the bread always sank to the bottom of the dish it was known throughout the countryside by this name. The night before they had had only one pilchard each for supper; and while they had eaten it Grandmother Lil had talked of the feasts she remembered; she had spoken of tables spread with salted pig and squab or lammy pie, with clotted cream and saffron cake to be washed down with a glass of metheglin or parsnip wine; and she had talked, Lilith knew now, for a purpose. It was clear to Lilith that it was Grandmother Lil who wished her to go to Leigh House—the prison of plenty.

Lilith had told William of their plans for her, since she always took her problems to William. He was quiet, and he had not her spirit, her boldness and her courage; but he was sensible in his way and he would know what should be done.

He had known before she had that they would not be allowed to stay in the cottage much longer, as they were the eldest of the children now that Jane had gone. The cottage consisted of one room divided by a partition which did not quite reach the ceiling. Its walls were of Cornish stone—grey as the frequent mists; its roof was of Cornish slate, the colour of rain; and it was built, so it was said, by their great-grandfather—the father of the man who had married Grandmother Lil; and he had built it, with the aid of his friends, during one summer's night, because the law of the land at that time was that anyone who could build a cottage overnight could claim it and the ground on which it stood as his own property. Inside the cottage was an open hearth and at one side of the fire was a cloam oven. There were no stairs, for there were no upper rooms, but boards had been fixed to the walls to make shelves; they were reached by a ladder and called 'the talfat'; and on this the children slept. Lilith and William had known for some time that they were getting too big for the talfat; they slept on it uneasily, with their legs hanging down.

Yesterday they had gone up to the Downs, and had lain there looking below at the river which wound its way between the fold of the hills, dividing the town in two. From where they lay they could see their cottage among the group huddled together on the west quay and close by it the ancient building which had once been the Church of St. Nicholas, but which now did service as the town's Guildhall. Lilith let her gaze wander to the east side of the river, over the hills towards Plaidy and Millendreath. The hills hid Leigh House from view.

As they lay there she told William of her fears. He said little. When did he ever say much? He was not like her—except in appearance. He was small, with that foreign look which many believed to be inherited from the Spaniards who had ravaged this coast in another century.

"To go there!" Lilith was saying. "To Leigh House . . . to wait on people!"

He thought of this for a while; then he said what they all said, what must be the main consideration of those who had known hunger, "There'll be plenty to eat there, Lilith. Not sky-blues or gurts, not just pilchards, but pasties and pies and maybe a hog's pudding now and then."

Then she looked at him and saw fear in his own eyes. They were the same age; he had been born only one hour before she had; and he, too, was too big for the talfat.

"What of you, William?" she said.

He said: "Reckon I'll work in the fields."

They remembered last harvest, when they had worked in the fields from six in the morning till eight at night. They recalled

the weariness, the aching limbs, the sharp eyes of the farmer
and his wife who made sure that they earned the few pence they
were paid, made sure they deserved the scanty food they were
given to eat. They remembered lifting potatoes, cleaning out
stalls and stables. Poor William! That was what he would have
to do again.

"A fisherman's life be a better one," she said, "though there
be the sea to face in all weathers."

"And if you do have your own boat," said William, "you'm
your own master."

Lilith thought: William would never have his own boat; he'd
never be his own master.

"There's the tin mines out to Cheesewring and Caradon,"
she said. "Perhaps there'd be something for 'ee there?"

It occurred to her that smuggling was perhaps the best life for
a boy who was too big for the talfat; had Lilith been a boy, that
was the life she would have chosen. But William was not Lilith.

She said: "I'll come home and see you often, William. And
you shall come to the House."

"They wouldn't like that."

"Then they'll learn to like it."

They were both thinking of Amanda Leigh, Lilith with resentment, William with admiration. William dared not tell Lilith how much he admired the elegant young lady with the yellow
hair and the tender mouth. And as Lilith looked at her brother
she knew that, although she stormed and raged and declared she
would hate Leigh House and all it contained, William's was the
greater tragedy.

So the next day she reluctantly allowed herself to be taken to
Leigh House; and when her mother knocked at the back door,
it was opened by Jane, who looked important and wise because
she had already spent two years in service in this house.

"Come on in then," said Jane. "Mrs. Derry be expecting
you."

Mrs. Derry, large and rosy-cheeked, was sitting at a refectory
table. Her cap seemed of fine lace and she looked very grand,
and would have been alarming, Lilith felt sure, to anyone but
herself who was determined to banish all fear of authority. She
pretended not to see Mrs. Derry; instead she looked round the
kitchen, huge and warm, with red tiles on the floor and a big
fire with a cloam oven beside it; brass gleamed brightly round

this fireplace, and there were pewter plates and jugs on the high mantelshelf; a big clock ticked away there also. The room seemed vast to Lilith, for two cottages would have fitted into it with ease. From the rafters hung hams and sides of bacon, bags of spices and herbs and bunches of onions; a smell of baking came from the oven. The house of plenty! Lilith's mouth began to water.

Two maids who were putting crockery on the dresser were sharply dismissed by Mrs. Derry, who, continuing to sit at the table, bade Lilith's mother approach with her daughter.

Mrs. Derry studied Lilith with a gaze which was none too flattering. She liked to choose her own helpers and not to have them thrust upon her. She had made something of Jane; but this one appeared to be less malleable material. If ever Mrs. Derry had seen defiance, she saw it in that face now, and, considering there were plenty of nice girls in the village who would have been glad to come, she was more than a little piqued. Mistress's orders! And everybody knew that the mistress's orders came from the master.

"Come here, my girl," said Mrs. Derry.

Lilith approached and Mrs. Derry's grey eyes looked into Lilith's black ones.

"I hope you're going to be a good worker," said Mrs. Derry. "Because if you're not I'll not have you in my kitchen."

"Her'll give 'ee every satisfaction, ma'am," said Lilith's mother.

"She'd better! My dear life, she's small for her age."

"She'll fatten up," said Lilith's mother. "She'll grow."

"She's strong, is she?"

"Strong as a moor pony."

"Is she clean? I won't have dirty folks in my kitchen."

Lilith's eyes kindled. If it had not been for the smell from the oven, she would have run out; but the smell fascinated her.

"She'll sleep with Jane and Bess. We'll train her. Now she can sit down and have a bite to eat. You too. Them's the mistress's orders."

"Thank you, m'am," said Mrs. Tremorney.

"Ain't the girl got a tongue in her head?"

Lilith's impulse was to put it out, but for the sake of the oven smell she said: "Thank you, m'am."

"Now, Jane," said Mrs. Derry, "set out the last of that pasty."

Lilith sat at the big table and ate ravenously. Never, she was sure, had she tasted such food. They were right, all of them; the most important thing was to get plenty to eat; when you had that you could think of other things.

When they had eaten, Mrs. Tremorney was sent back to the cottage with a parcel of good things. "The mistress's orders," said Mrs. Derry grudgingly.

"Now, Jane," said Mrs. Derry, "you take your sister up and show her where she'll sleep. You can let her put on those things I set aside for her. Then come straight down. There's the fire to be lighted in Miss Amanda's room; she can help you do that. Then there'll be the mistress's bath water to be taken up."

"Yes, m'am," said Jane. And she led her sister away.

Lilith's eyes were round with wonder, and there was no longer an empty cave in her stomach. The House of Plenty was even more wonderful than Jane had described it; it was more beautiful than Lilith had ever imagined it.

When she exclaimed, Jane looked superior. "This is only the back staircase. Wait till you see the front. Only you mustn't let them see you there. You mustn't never let them see you. They don't like to *see* us. That's what you've got to remember."

"Why not?" asked Lilith.

"The master's very strict. And the mistress can't a-bear noise."

Lilith let her feet sink into the thick carpet; she had never imagined there was such a carpet. In the corridor there was wonderful wallpaper. Lilith touched it wonderingly.

"You wait!" Jane promised her.

On the walls there were pictures of people in beautiful gilt frames.

"The family. They're all over the place. Wait till you see the gallery. I'll show you . . . to-morrow morning . . . before they're up. You mustn't go there in the day-time."

They had reached the top of the house and Jane opened a door, and they went into a room which was even bigger than the kitchen, although the ceiling sloped to the floor and its window looked out from the roof. The boards were highly polished and there were four beds, very clean and very narrow.

"Bessie's, Ada's, mine," said Jane, pointing to each in turn. "And that'll be yours."

A bed! How would it feel to sleep in a bed? She never had before. Her father and mother had a mattress; so had old Grandmother Lil.

She leaped on it and lay stretched out.

"Your dirty feet!" cried Jane.

But Lilith lay there, grinning defiantly at her sister.

"Get up. Get up. If Mrs. Derry were to know . . ."

Lilith said: "You worry too much about Mrs. Derry. She's only a servant."

Jane looked shocked. "She's Cook."

"She's only a servant, I said; and so she is."

"Well, and who are you, then?"

Lilith was silent. Something more than that. She remembered those sly looks of Grandmother Lil.

"Come on," said Jane. "Put on those things. We've got to get the fire going in Miss Amanda's room."

Lilith got up. Miss Amanda's room. She wanted to see that more than anything. She put on the house-frock and the shoes which Mrs. Derry had put out for her. They were too big, but they were finer than anything she had ever had before, and they made her feel like a queen—the queen of Leigh House.

She went to the window, and, standing on tiptoe, she could just see through it. It was a wild and rugged scene that met her eyes; she stood for a few seconds staring at it. She knew that stretch of coast, but she had never before seen it from a top window at Leigh House. She could see the sea breaking about the jagged rocks which to-day looked black, but in sunshine would be pink and purple. The cliff, glistening green to-day, hung out over the grey water. The arm which was Rame Head was only just visible, merging as it did into the haze.

"Come on, I said," said Jane impatiently. "We haven't got all day."

They went quietly down the stairs, and in a short time she was remounting them carrying a bucket of coal.

Amanda's room was beautiful, and Lilith was fascinated by the silken curtains on the four-poster bed.

"It's very old," said Jane as Lilith fingered the curtains. "Everything here's old. It was like this in Mr. Leigh's grandfather's day."

Lilith was not listening. She was running from the bed to the dressing table, fingering the flounces about it; she was daring enough to open a cupboard door and peer inside it. Jane was beside herself with anxiety. "You mustn't . . . you mustn't. . . . Why, if Mrs. Derry . . ."

But Lilith laughed and touched the silks and velvets, and could only be lured from the cupboard to see the ornaments on the mantelshelf.

The fire was drawing up when Amanda came in. Lilith, remembering the grimace she had made at the girl, struck a defiant attitude; but she was excited to be so near Amanda. Her grand new clothes were no longer grand; and all the angry jealousy fostered by her grandmother came back to her.

Amanda said nothing about the face Lilith had made at her. Could it be that she had not noticed? Lilith could not imagine anyone's not taking revenge if they could.

"Is this your sister, Jane?" asked Amanda.

"Yes, miss."

"So you're Lilith."

Lilith nodded. Jane frowned at her sister. Lilith was not going to curtsy, no matter what they did to her.

"I hope you'll like it here," said Amanda.

"Thank you, miss," said Jane. "You must forgive my sister, miss. She's shy. That's what it is, miss."

"I'm not," said Lilith.

Amanda smiled, and a troubled frown wrinkled her brow temporarily while the tender smile was on her mouth. For the moment *she* was Lilith, the poor little servant girl on her first day in a new place. She said: "It must be strange . . . to come to a new house. . . . The first time . . . I mean."

Lilith said: "I'm not frightened."

Jane's fingers dug hard into Lilith's arm as she drew her to the door. Jane was preparing a lecture on how to address the gentry. At the door Lilith turned to look back. Amanda was watching her. Lilith wanted to grimace as she had before, but even Lilith dared not do that.

Laura Leigh was sitting close to the lamp, her embroidery frame before her. In and out went her needle and she appeared to be intent on her work, but really she was only conscious of her husband. When he was in a room she was always aware of him to the exclusion of all else. He sat now, relaxed in his chair, his lips moving slightly as he read to himself from the Bible. He was a very good man, she knew, and she was most fortunate to have married him. She was sorry she was too delicate to bear him the family of children which he should have had. She had had four miscarriages and only one child, and that a girl.

But for that she would have been rather proud of her delicate state of health. It was, after all, rather lady-like to be delicate; she followed the fashion of her day, eating very little at meal-times, and often having trays sent up to her room, for eating was a most disgusting habit and should, she believed, be performed only when necessary and then in private.

Her daughter was a problem. The child had an excellent appetite; moreover, she was too outspoken for gentility. Laura wondered whether the company of the Holford and the Danesborough children was good for her. The doctor's two daughters and Alice Danesborough were nice quiet girls, but Frith Danesborough was noisy; he was a wild boy; he rode madly about the countryside. No one would think that he was the son of a clergyman; although it must be admitted that the Reverend Charles Danesborough was not a typical clergyman. He too was a keen horseman, had a taste for good wine, and was certainly addicted to the pleasures of the table. He was reckoned to be a charming man, and by all accounts Frith took after him in that respect.

All the young female servants were excited when Frith and his sister came over to take schoolroom tea with Amanda. Cook would bake a special coconut cake because Master Frith liked coconut cake; even Miss Robinson would titter a little, and had said that he was a wild boy, but for some strange reason one could not be angry with him for long. If he had not been a Danesborough—Charles Danesborough was a younger son of a peer and by no means dependent on the stipend he received from the Church—Laura would have had doubts as to the suitability of Amanda's friendship with Frith. At the same time, she did wonder if she got that ridiculous outspokenness from him. Then there was that unfortunate habit of concerning herself with stray dogs and barefooted children. Of course, her grandfather had concerned himself with the poor—mostly the *female* poor, it had to be lamentably confessed—but his obsession may have begun in this way.

Amanda was a source of anxiety not only to her mother, but

to that good man who now sat reading his Bible, for they were afraid, both of them, that Amanda was going to take after her grandfather. Her hair was the same colour, and it was said that the colour of the hair often indicated character. Red-haired people were notoriously quick-tempered, for instance.

Mrs. Leigh and her husband never discussed Mr. Leigh's father. It was one of those topics which it was improper to discuss, for Mr. Leigh's father had lived an immoral life and was guilty not only of inebriety, but of adultery.

She knew that her husband nightly thanked God for so providentially taking his father; and because Mr. Leigh was a merciful man, he added to his prayers of thanksgiving a plea for the salvation of his father's soul.

Laura could not pass the portrait in the gallery without shuddering; the eyes were so like Amanda's; the hair grew back from the broad brows in the same manner. Amanda's mouth was soft, it was true, whereas her grandfather's was merely sensual; but Amanda was a child yet, and there was a certain air of self-will about both faces that was similar. The man's said clearly that he did not care what the countryside thought of him, he would have his pleasure; and that very look was in Amanda's face when she was in what her mother called 'her argumentative moods,' when she asked questions and stubbornly clung to the point, refusing to accept explanations which all properly brought up children should and did accept.

Only this afternoon Laura had been sighing over Amanda's rather grubby sampler with the red spot on it where the child had pricked her finger. Amanda would never be a good needlewoman. "This is my mother's sampler," Laura had said. "She completed it when she was six years old—half your age. Aren't you ashamed?"

Amanda had looked critically at the neat cross-stitches which proclaimed that the Lord was the Shepherd of Mathilda Bartlett and that she had finished the sampler on the sixth day of January 1806 A.D.

"Perhaps," said Amanda, "in years to come, mine will be more important because I've left my blood on it."

"That is quite disgusting," Laura had cried, shuddering. "If your father heard you say that he would have you whipped."

Amanda had seemed to be contrite; she did not mean to irritate; she merely did it naturally.

Amanda's sampler was in Laura's work-basket now, and she wondered whether it was her duty to show it to Mr. Leigh. He was very stern, and he would probably order that Amanda should stay in her room until the sampler was finished. He would only be thinking of what was good for Amanda. Yet she hesitated to bring Amanda's faults to his notice; she was afraid that, if she did so, he would be reminded that their only child was a girl, and an unsatisfactory one at that. He prayed each night that they might have a child. Unfortunately, this was one of those things which needed more than prayers. She sighed lightly to avoid disturbing him. She was quite undecided what she should do about Amanda. Her life was made up of such difficult problems; they set wrinkles on her brow; they tormented her perpetually.

Mr. Leigh broke in on her thoughts. "Pray ring the bell, my love. We need more coal."

She rose obediently and went to the embroidered bell-pull.

"I am sorry. . . . I did not notice."

He was silent; his lips moved as he went on reading.

There was a knock on the door and Jane entered.

"Jane, more coal, please."

"Yes, m'am."

The coal was brought by Jane's sister Lilith, the new girl, and Laura was immediately uneasy. When Jane had first come to the house she had felt the same disquiet; she had watched her husband and wondered what his thoughts were every time the new servant appeared. He had said nothing; but it was on his orders that Jane had come; and now again he had commanded Lilith's presence. "We need a new maid, Mrs. Leigh," he had said. "You must get one of the Tremorney girls." It was very uncomfortable having the creatures in the house; but Mr. Leigh was a good man who would never shirk his responsibilities.

And now Lilith was here, and she, Laura was afraid, would never grow like the other girls.

"Put it on the fire," said Laura remotely. Lilith was awkward. There was much she had to be taught. As she put the coal on the fire some of it rattled into the hearth.

When she had gone, Laura said nervously: "She is new. She has not yet learned. I wish that it had not been necessary to have her; there are so many *nice* girls in the village."

Mr. Leigh looked astonished. "I thought you knew my feelings in this matter."

"Oh . . . oh, I am sure you are right . . . but . . ."

"I *know* I am right. We must learn to bear our burdens."

"But . . . after all these years." She was frightened at her own temerity and was trying in her ineffectual way to cover it up. She had dared to criticize his actions. What had come over her?

"My dear," he said sternly, "you may trust me to know my duty."

In the dining-room the family was gathered for prayers. Kneeling at the head of the table was the master; beside him was the mistress, and on his other side Amanda. Next to Amanda was Miss Robinson; and farther down the table, at a respectable distance, knelt Steert, who was both coachman and butler, Mrs. Derry, the groom and the stable-boy, the two gardeners and the three maids, with Lilith.

Mr. Leigh said prayers, his palms pressed closely together, his eyes shut; but it was never safe to presume that his eyes would remain shut; they were liable to open suddenly and notice any misdemeanour on the part of his little congregation.

Amanda's knees were hurting; she found it difficult to keep still and, being so near her father, she dared not move, for she knew that the least offence on her part would be more severely punished than a similar lapse on the part of any of the servants. "Don't forget," she was continually being told, "*you* must show an example."

Her father rose, and the ten-minute sermon which he gave every morning began. He spoke of the meanness and wickedness of human nature—and he meant that of those he addressed, of course; he made continual allusions to the recording angel, who always seemed to Amanda like an omniscient and malicious Miss Robinson. After that Amanda lost the gist of what he was saying, until she remembered, with sudden panic, that she would probably be questioned on the subject at the midday meal. Her father's conversation at the dining table, if it involved herself, was usually about lessons and prayers; it was full of pitfalls, and Amanda never knew which she dreaded more—his conversation or his melancholy silences. She would have to discover from Miss Robinson what had been the subject of this morning's discourse.

After the sermon there was one more prayer. Amanda, cov-

ering her face with her hands, peered through her fingers and
saw that Lilith was doing the same; their eyes met and neither
of them could look away.

Now the prayer was over. "Dismiss," said her father; and the
servants went to their duties, Mr. Leigh to affairs of his estate,
Mrs. Leigh to instructing the cook or working in her stillroom
or at her embroidery, and Amanda and Miss Robinson to lessons.

Amanda took out her history books and said: "Miss Robinson, what do you think of Papa's sermon to-day?"

"Very good, and very necessary."

"Did you think the first part was very good?"

Miss Robinson looked at her pupil with an exasperation not
untinged with affection. Amanda had not been listening. Miss
Robinson could understand that. She had had to force herself to
listen; there were so many things that Miss Robinson had to
force herself to do.

She began to discuss the points of the sermon slowly and
lucidly, that the child might memorize them. Miss Robinson was
fond of her charge, but all her feelings were held in check by
the urgent need to give satisfaction to her employers. She must
always take their side against that of her charges, for it was they
who decided whether or not she should remain in her post.

Now she was most anxious that Amanda should be able to
give the right answers at luncheon if she were questioned on to-
day's sermon, since any deficiency in the pupil must necessarily
reflect on the teacher.

Amanda studied her history book and wept a little over the
Princes in the Tower, who had been about her age when they
had been murdered. They reminded her this morning of poor
Miss Robinson, which showed how odd she was, and how right
everyone was when they said she was ridiculously fanciful. Yet
she was more sorry for Miss Robinson than for the Princes. It
was surely better to be a prince and smothered in the Tower
than, as Antonio said:

> "To let the wretched man out-live his wealth,
>   To view with hollow eye and wrinkled brow
>   An age of poverty. . . ."

Those lines always made her cry because they seemed to fit Miss Robinson. No wonder Amanda could not learn history; she mixed it continually with contemporary life.

"Have you been crying again?" said Miss Robinson uneasily. No one ever asked the reason for Amanda's tears; they seemed to realize that the reasons were too complicated for them to understand. Miss Robinson did not want her to go down to luncheon with a tear-stained face. It might seem that lessons had been difficult, and Miss Robinson was afraid that difficult lessons might suggest an incompetent governess.

Fortunately, Jane came up at that moment to say that Master Frith and Miss Alice Danesborough had ridden over and were asking if Miss Amanda might accompany them on their morning ride.

"Yes; you may," said Miss Robinson. "You have worked well this morning. The wind will wipe away the traces of those tears. And, Amanda, *do* try not to give way to your feelings quite so readily. It's most unladylike."

"I do . . . try, Miss Robinson."

"Go along, then."

Amanda went down to the stables and asked the boy to saddle Gobbo for her. The Danesboroughs' horses were impatiently pawing the cobbles while Frith and Alice were running about the garden.

"Hello!" called Frith. "There's Amanda."

Amanda went to meet them. Frith was tall and very handsome. He was nearly seventeen now—quite a man; Alice thought he was wonderful, for she was a meek little girl of Amanda's age.

"Hail, Niobe!" cried Frith. He was very kind really, but he was careless; he said whatever came into his mind and then thought about it afterwards.

"Niobe?" queried Alice, who, said Frith, was a hopeless dunce except in the feminine accomplishments of the needle and the stillroom. "You mean Amanda."

Amanda touched her cheeks. ."Does it show, then?"

"Never mind," said Frith. "It ceases to startle. And Niobe was wrong for you. You're the least proud person I know, and I don't suppose you've ever sneered at anyone. Did you ask them to get Gobbo ready?"

"Yes."

"Well, let's go."

"Frith said we ought to come and rescue you from that old dragon, Robinson," said Alice.

"She's not really a dragon. She's really very nice. . . ."

"Oh, Amanda," said Frith. "you'd make excuses for the Devil."

They rode out of the stables and took the road downhill to the sea.

It was warm this morning and a soft south-westerly wind was blowing; Amanda smelt with appreciation the mingling smells of the sea—seaweed, tar, salt spray and the perfume that some said was blown all the way across the water from Spain.

Frith rode on ahead of them, leading the way, choosing the most dangerous spots over the cliffs, looking round every now and then to assure himself that they were all right.

He led them on to the beach.

"Race!" cried Frith; and they galloped over the beach, which was sandy this morning although yesterday the cruel rocks had been exposed. "Must have been a high wind in the night," said Frith, "to produce all this sand."

He won the race; Amanda felt that he would always win whatever he wanted.

"The trouble with you girls," said Frith, "is that you don't let your horses go all out. You're scared. You can't afford to be scared."

When Frith was tired of racing, they turned away from the beach and he led the way along the cliff path.

"One false step," he cried with glee, "and you'd go rolling over . . . horse and all, and that would be the end of Miss Amanda Leigh or Miss Alice Danesborough."

He was not really callous, thought Amanda; he was really very kind. It was merely that he wanted to call attention all the time to his own courage, his own leadership.

"There's no need to tell us," she said aloud. "We know."

"You know what?" called Frith.

But she could not answer that; it was too involved, and he was leading them now through Smugglers' Lane, that path cut through the cliffs which was imperceptible from below because it was hidden by foliage. They pushed their way through the branches, which scratched them unless they were very careful, and Alice was very nearly pulled off her mount by one of the

branches which swung back unexpectedly and caught her un-
awares.

Amanda said: "We've got a new girl. She's from the west
quay cottages."

"Not another Tremorney?" said Alice.

"Yes . . . Lilith."

"There's a little dark one," said Frith.

"That's the one."

"They're so dirty . . . all of them," said Alice distastefully.

"She's rather queer," began Amanda.

"Queer? How?" demanded Frith.

But that was another thing which Amanda could not explain.

"Oh . . . I don't know . . . just queer."

They had reached the Kellow cottages, and some of the children came out to look at them and curtsy and touch their hair in
the way they had seen their parents greet the gentry.

Frith threw some money at them. He was like that. He liked
to be admired, but he wanted to be liked at the same time. He
was proud too, and he pretended not to look pleased when the
children shrieked with delight, and he would not deign to look
back at them.

"Frith," said Amanda, "what's the time? I mustn't be late
for luncheon."

Frith took out his watch and looked at it.

"Not much time," he said; and he made them gallop most
of the way back to Leigh House.

Lordly as he was, completely in command, she believed, in
his father's house—for everyone knew that the Reverend the
Honourable Charles Danesborough was an easy-going man who
liked his ease and comfort and peace in his house—he had the
imagination to understand Amanda's predicament and he had
the kindness to be sorry for her.

Even so, when they arrived at Leigh House she saw that there
was only ten minutes in which to get to the stables and back to
her room to change for luncheon.

She went in by way of the paddock and as Gobbo went swiftly
over the long grass she saw a small figure cowering against the
hedge.

She pulled up. She knew that it was someone from the village,
and she was immediately frightened, because whoever it was
was trespassing, and trespassers fared ill if discovered by her

father. Moreover, the servants were in such fear of him that, like all people who lived in fear, they seemed to be perpetually searching for scapegoats whom they could bring forward in order to turn his attention from their own shortcomings.

"Who are you?" she called. But she knew, for she recognized him at once as Lilith's brother.

"You . . . you're trespassing," she said as she rode back.

"Yes, miss. . . . I wanted . . ."

She leaned forward and smiled one of those tender smiles which endeared her to so many people.

"It was Lilith I came to see," he said.

"Lilith's your sister. I know. She came to us yesterday."

"Yes, miss."

"You must be careful. If they found you here . . . they would hand you over to the magistrates."

"I know, miss. You see . . . we be twins. . . . We've always been together . . . till now."

"Twins!" said Amanda. "And you came to see that she was getting on all right here?"

He nodded. "You might think she wasn't the sort to settle, miss. But she will. . . ."

"Oh, yes. She'll settle."

He smiled, and Amanda knew that he was very worried about his sister. He was afraid she was going to be so wild that they would turn her out.

"Does she know you were coming to see her?"

"No, miss. I hoped she'd come out. I hoped I might get a chance of seeing her. . . ."

"I . . . I'll tell her. But you mustn't stay here. You might get caught. Hide under the hedge. I'll tell your sister you're here."

She was aware of the adoration in his eyes, and it pleased her. Perhaps she was a little like Frith, who wanted the admiration and the liking of the village children.

She rode into the stables and handed Gobbo over to the stableboy. As she came into the house she saw that she had only five minutes in which to change for luncheon.

She ran up to her room and put on a dress. The boy would have to wait. But how could he wait all through luncheon? He might be caught if any of the servants went into the paddock.

She grasped the bell-pull and gave it three sharp tugs. Bess answered it.

"I wish to see Lilith at once. Tell her to hurry. It is very urgent."

But Lilith was long in coming and the clock went ticking on. Now grace would have begun in the dining-room.

Lilith came then, slowly and insolently.

"Your twin brother came to see you," said Amanda. "He is in the paddock waiting for you. Be careful. Keep close to the hedge and you will not be seen. It is fairly safe at this time of the day."

Lilith stared at her in astonishment.

"Go quickly," said Amanda. "And be careful."

Amanda ran past Lilith, down the stairs to the dining-room.

She opened the door; her father's voice was raised as he was getting near the end of grace. They were aware of her—all three of them—but they pretended not to know that she was there, for their eyes were closed and they were supposed to be united in thanking God for what they were about to receive.

Steert by the sideboard had his eyes closed too. Bess had half opened hers to throw a sympathetic glance at Amanda.

When grace was over, Mr. Leigh opened his eyes and stared coldly at his daughter.

"Papa," began Amanda, "I'm sorry . . ."

"*I* am more than sorry," he interrupted. "*I* am deeply grieved. What explanation could there possibly be for such conduct?"

"I . . . I'm afraid I stayed out too late."

"You stayed out too late! You were riding, I gather, and so selfishly concerned with your own pleasure that you could not spare a thought for the anguish you were causing your mother and myself. You have led us to fear that we cannot expect you to honour us. That is perhaps of less importance when set beside your sin towards God. I was talking to Him. Your mother, your governess and the servants were all talking to Him. But you burst in upon us. You come late. *You* decided to dispense with thanking our Lord for what is set on my table."

"Papa . . ." she began helplessly.

But he waved his hand. "You are overheated; you are dishevelled and in no fit state to come to the table. Do not imagine that, although I overlook your insults to your family, I will overlook those to God. Go to your room at once. You shall not partake of a meal to which you do not consider it worth while to come in good time. You will stay in your room until you are bidden to leave it.''

Under the reproachful eyes of her mother and the frightened ones of Miss Robinson and the sympathetic ones of Steert and Bess, Amanda walked out of the room.

Miss Robinson came up to Amanda immediately after luncheon was over.

"Your father is very angry," she said. "Your mother is very sad. Not a word was spoken during the meal. I'm sure I don't know what to say. After all I've done . . .''

Amanda put her arm about the governess. "I'm sorry, Robbie. It wasn't your fault. I'll tell them it wasn't your fault.''

"Your father says you are to go to his study at once. I should lose no time. But do comb your hair first. It's like a bird's nest. Are your hands clean? But hurry, child. It will be most unwise to keep him waiting.''

Amanda solemnly smoothed her hair; she did not stop to wash her hands. As she went along the gallery she glanced at the portrait of her grandfather, which she often fancied mocked her a little, egged her on to be bold and not to care because they thought her so wicked. She went down the staircase into the hall and knocked at the door of the room which was known as her father's study.

She disliked the room. It was more gloomy than any other part of the house; the windows were almost completely hidden by the thick curtains of that shade which was not quite grey and not quite brown. There were no bright colours in this room; here there was no memory of other days, no relic of a gaudy past; this was her father's sanctum, furnished by himself.

Amanda was bidden to enter.

He did not look up immediately, but when he did so his gaze was almost warm with contempt. "So . . . you are here. Can you be my daughter? Is it possible?" That was one of his many questions to which he did not expect an answer, so she stood, hands clasped behind her back, her eyes downcast, looking demure in her long dress of blue merino. "Why were you late for luncheon?" he asked.

"I am very sorry, Papa. I forgot the time.''

"You forgot the time! 'Time is the stuff that life is made of.' Sometimes I wonder what will become of you. You are careless of what hurt you bring to myself and your mother. You are wicked, and there are times when I believe you revel in your wickedness. Day after day I see you going almost merrily on your way to Hell. I ask myself what is this monster which I have helped to bring into the world. Have you no responsibility? And if you grieve me, your earthly father, how much more do you grieve your Father which is in Heaven? You say nothing. Are you sullen, then?''

"No, Papa. I am very sorry about hurting you and God. I didn't mean to.''

"I doubt that you are sorry. I doubt that you have even considered the extent of your wickedness.''

He stood up and leaned towards her, his hands on the table. He began to talk about the road to Hell, and how people slipped into it, unconsciously at first, how the Devil was always lurking round the corner, ready to recognize his own.

"You will kneel with me,'' he said eventually. "We will ask God to help you. We will leave no stone unturned; we will defy the Devil.''

She knelt. Even the rugs in this room were harsh; he liked to live like a monk in a cell. He was so good that, to him, everyone else seemed bad. She heard his voice going on and on, and when at last he signed to her to rise, she could not remember what he had been saying, except that it was all about her wickedness.

He pronounced sentence now. "You will go to your room and have nothing but bread and water for the rest of to-day and to-morrow. You will take your lessons in your own room, and you will learn by heart the twenty-fifth psalm, which you will repeat to me to-morrow evening. You will continue on bread and water until you can say it without faltering. Go now. And try to mend your ways. Not only for my sake, not only for the love of God, but for the sake of your immortal soul.''

When his daughter had left him, Mr. Leigh sat down at the table and buried his face in his hands. He could not shut out the picture his daughter had made standing before him; her yellow hair reminded him of his father's hair; those eyes, which she had made to appear subdued, were, if not bold, full of secrets. He remembered his father's conduct after a particular bit of knavery when the whole countryside was discussing the scandal of his latest exploit. He remembered how he would be charming and tender and so contrite, how he would compliment his wife and tell her she was the prettiest creature in Cornwall. He fancied he had seen the same look in Amanda's face. Wickedness had been born in the girl; it had skipped a generation.

He could shut his eyes now and see his father's face—not handsome, but flushed with wine and bloated with lechery as it had been at the end, with the doctors bleeding him, and himself roaring because they had forbidden him his whisky; he remembered how his father had risen from his sickbed to find for himself the bottle which, on doctor's orders, had been denied him. He had fallen downstairs and had lain in the hall with a broken neck and all his sins upon him.

Mr. Leigh knelt and prayed for the soul of his father, which he believed to be suffering eternal torment, prayed for guidance to drive the slyness of Satan out of his daughter.

He had spoken of Amanda to Charles Danesborough, but Danesborough, he had come to believe, was too fond of ease and comfort to be a true man of God. Mr. Leigh distrusted that hearty laughter, that indulgence he displayed towards his own children. "Amanda?" Danesborough had said. "A nice little thing. A quiet little thing. My two are very fond of Amanda." As though because the girl found favour with his two children she must be a model of all the virtues. There was too much levity about Danesborough; the man was a fool. He could be no help.

Mrs. Leigh knocked timidly on the door; he called to her to come in, but did not rise from his knees. He signed to her to join him and prayed aloud once more for the salvation of their wicked daughter.

"Amen," he said eventually.

"Amen," echoed Laura.

"Our daughter presents a grave problem," he said, rising.

Laura was grateful that he should refer to Amanda as their daughter. There were times when he said *your* daughter. She felt this to be a good sign.

"I tremble for her future," he went on.

"It's so easy . . . when one is young and thoughtless . . . to forget the time. I do so myself, I'm afraid."

"She has been taught to honour her father and mother, and she has wounded us deeply. I wish I could say that this is the first time it has happened. She has broken one of God's commandments. 'Honour thy father and thy mother . . .' Do not make excuses for your daughter, Mrs. Leigh. If she be allowed to break one commandment, she may break others. Her wickedness may be aggravated by the fact that she is an only child.''

Laura cast down her eyes. Here was that other shadow which hung over the house. Two miscarriages and then Amanda. Two more and still no son. She was terrified of pregnancy. Nor did she welcome the ritual which must precede those weary months. Every night when they sat together in the drawing-room, she dreaded to hear those words: ''I will come to your room tonight, Mrs. Leigh.''

Yesterday she had looked out from her window and had seen young Jane Tremorney talking to Farmer Polgard's son, who drove round in his pony and trap with the eggs and butter; she had watched the farmer's son, clumsy and shy, while Jane provoked him with that jocular asperity which the female of the lower classes often employed in her conduct towards young men. How could they? If only they knew! They appeared to enjoy it; but they were, of course, not delicate ladies.

''I am sure,'' she said quickly, ''that you have dealt with this matter as it should be dealt with. I am sure that we shall see her footsteps firmly planted on the road to righteousness.''

He bowed his head, while she stood before him, longing to escape and yet not daring to go, dreading his next words, which might intimate that she was to expect his company that night.

It was dusk and Amanda was alone in her room.

'' 'Unto thee, O Lord, will I lift up my soul; my God I have put my trust in Thee. O let not me be confounded, neither let mine enemies triumph over me.' ''

Her enemies, she knew, were the Devil and those agents of his, the wicked people who worked for him on Earth.

She was aware of a sound in the room. She looked towards the door and saw that it was slowly opening.

''Who is that?'' she asked quickly.

The door opened and Lilith stood there. She smiled slowly and advanced; she was holding her right hand behind her back.

''Alone?'' whispered Lilith.

''Yes.''

From behind her back Lilith produced something wrapped in a table napkin. She laid it on the table, and, opening the napkin, disclosed a piece of pastry concealed in which was meat, potatoes and onions. Lilith stood back looking at it with pleasure.

"It's for you," she whispered.

"Did you steal it from the kitchen?"

Lilith nodded, grinning.

"Oh . . . but you shouldn't."

"It's not really stealing," said Lilith impatiently. " 'Twas for you, so how could that be stealing. I thought you'd be hungry."

"I am, but . . ."

"Don't 'ee be so soft, then," said Lilith contemptuously.

Amanda picked up the pastry and her scruples disappeared, for she was very hungry. She dug her teeth into it.

"Don't you fret," said Lilith. "No matter how long they keep 'ee here, I'll get things for 'ee to eat, my poor soul."

"Did you . . . speak to your brother?"

"I did, then. I heard about 'ee in the kitchen. A regular shame, they say. And I says: 'My dear life, she have done that for me and William.' "

Lilith was happy. She realized that the girl whom she had envied all her life was no more fortunate than she was; indeed, she was of so little importance that she could be humiliated before servants, sent to her room, put on a diet of bread and water. To think of them down there eating roast duckling and cheese, pasties and clotted cream, while she was in this room with bread and water! Lilith would never have endured that. It wasn't all honey, then, being a daughter of the gentry. All enmity had vanished as far as she was concerned.

"If anyone had seen you steal this," said Amanda, "you might have been taken before the magistrates."

Lilith nodded gleefully.

"My father is a very good man," said Amanda. "He's so good that almost everybody seems to him very bad."

Lilith nodded again. She lay back on Amanda's bed and looked at the new shoes which Mrs. Derry had found for her.

"Please get off my bed," said Amanda with as much authority as she could command.

But Lilith just lay there laughing. Then slowly Amanda smiled. She understood that Lilith was an ally; she was offering her friendship. The only stipulation was that when they were alone she should be treated as an equal.

✻ Two

A year had gone by since Lilith first came to Leigh House. She was an unsatisfactory servant, always contriving to be out of the way when wanted, performing her duties in a slipshod manner, which, said Mrs. Derry, broke her heart. Again and again had Mrs. Derry complained. "We must bear our crosses," the mistress had told her; and she was quoting the master. It meant that they had to put up with the nasty little creature. One thing Mrs. Derry was determined on: she would not spare the rod; and the rod in this case was her own capable right hand, which often sent Lilith spinning across the kitchen.

She was unnatural, that devil's imp, said Mrs. Derry; she did not care. She would get up again, white-faced and defiant as ever. Mrs. Derry knew that she grimaced at her behind her back, and no one could grimace quite so horribly as Lilith Tremorney.

Mrs. Derry puffed about her kitchen in frustrated anger. She believed she had a weak heart and would go right off one of these days. She liked to say, "When I'm gone, you'll be sorry." She had always been able to frighten the others with that, conjuring up by those words visions of hauntings by the portly ghost of a cook driven to death by the wickedness of her kitchen girls. But Lilith could not be moved by such words.

Lilith was contented in her prison of plenty; she thought little of food now, for food, like money and comfort, she knew now, were only important when you hadn't got them. She was happy because she preferred her own life to that of Amanda. Her contentment circled about Amanda, for the golden-haired daughter of the house was far more a prisoner than Lilith could ever be. Poor little prisoner! Her father, her mother and her governess were her jailers; she had to remember continually that she was a lady; she had to learn from books; she was often sent to her

32

room on bread and water, when she must rely on the good services of her friend and benefactress, the girl from the kitchen.

Life had become richer to Amanda because of Lilith. She was fascinated by Lilith; she must accept the fact that there was knowledge beyond Latin, Greek and compound interest; Lilith's was a different sort of knowledge, sly and subtle.

Amanda knew more of what was in books, Lilith pointed out; but she, Lilith, knew more of what was in the world, and that was the more useful knowledge.

Lilith came to Amanda's room and for the joy of lying on her bed—a real feather bed and quite different from her own—Lilith would tell stories of the strange world of which, until she had come, Amanda had known so little.

Lilith had a philosophy of her own. There was no need for Amanda to fear punishment, she pointed out. If Amanda was shut in her room, Lilith would find some means of coming to her; if they sentenced Amanda to bread and water, she could rest assured that Lilith would bring her some delicacy from the pantry.

"They'd never let you get real hungry," said Lilith. "People die of hunger. I've seen them. Little children from the cottages . . . legs like birds' legs and bellies right out here. They eat the grass, and that be bad for 'em. But they'd never let you go that way. You'm their only child, and gentry set terrible store by children . . . even girls."

Amanda wanted to hear more; she wanted to know about the sufferings of the poor, of the children who ate grass and were ready to risk a public flogging for an apple or two stolen from an orchard.

Lilith herself had known such hunger.

"Sometimes the weather be so bad and there's naught in the cottages to eat, for the boats can't go out. Then you do have one salt pilchard from the bottom of the barrel between two of you . . . and pilchards be terrible salt from the bottom of the barrel. William and me, we worked at Farmer Polgard's. In the fields we was . . . and the sun beating down on us. . . . My back ached so, I felt I'd never stand up no more. William's were the same. And there was an old wolf inside of us . . . making anything what you could eat worth risking your life for. Old Missus Polgard, she's a pig. 'One tatie each,' she'd say. 'And no more. I know you villains. You come to eat at Polgards', but you don't come to work.' And there'd be us sitting at the table in the kitchen. . . . But first we had to wait on the big 'uns and sit down when they'd done. And old Mrs. Polgard she wouldn't give us long sitting there, case we did eat too much. We must cram it in and cram it down . . . afore she'd start shushing us out to the fields and more work.''

''Didn't you hate her?''

''Like to kill her.''

''I wonder someone didn't.''

''You can't. You'd be hung. You get flogged for stealing, but you get hung for killing. Didn't you know that? Don't you know nothing?''

''You shouldn't speak to me like that,'' said Amanda. ''It's insolence. If you are insolent, I shall have to send you away.''

But Lilith went on to tell about a thief she had seen flogged in the streets of Liskeard, smiling and stroking the coverlet as she did so—a small and crafty Scheherazade, a teller of tales which were as irresistible to Amanda as others had been to the Sultan Schahriar.

''Screamed he did, and you should have seen the blood. It was all over the road. He stole a kettle loaf, that's what he'd done, and he'd been seen taking it. William didn't like it; William didn't like to look.''

''So William is kind,'' said Amanda.

''He wouldn't have minded being flogged himself . . . not so much. He just didn't like to see anyone else flogged. He be different. He's got all the soft bits and I've got all the hard bits . . . because we was in the womb together.''

''Where?''

''Before we was born, we grew together. Don't you know? Don't you know nothing? I'll take 'ee to see old Ma Trelaw one of these days. She's mad and they've chained her to the rafters in her cottage. That's 'cause they ain't got room for her at the madhouse. The door be open and you can walk in and look at her. She snaps at you like a wolf and she roars like a lion.''

Her conversation was racy; she declared she knew everything; she knew about birth and death and love; and these mysteries she was prepared to explain for a place on Amanda's feather bed.

''One day,'' said Lilith, ''I'll sleep in a feather bed . . . a feather bed of my own.''

There came a day when Amanda went with Lilith to the cottage of which she had heard so much; she wanted to see for herself the old table where Lilith sat with her brothers and sisters, and the talfat where she had slept; but most of all she wanted to see at close quarters old Grandmother Lil.

It was hot June and the hedges were red, blue and white with campion, bluebells and stitchwort. The melting heat shimmered in the air and seemed to make a lake at the top of the hill.

They went along the high road past the Polgard Farm. Lilith shook her fist at a hayfield bright now with red sorrel.

"See. That be the farmhouse. That's where old Polgard and his ugly missus do live. Pigs . . . swine . . . both on 'em. I hope the piskies get them when it's dusk, I do, and drive 'em mazed. I hope they get carried off by the Little People."

That was more of Lilith's knowledge; she was aware not only of the strangeness of this world, but of the one unseen. She knew all about the Little People in their scarlet jackets and their sugar-loaf hats.

Now she danced along the road, and when they came to St. Martin's Church she took a turn to the left and began to run downhill.

"This way," she chanted. "This way."

She was triumphant. Never before had she taken Amanda to the cottage. When she had gone back there she had told them of her friendship, but she fancied they hardly believed her. "Don't tell such lies, don't," said her mother. "I wonder the earth don't open." Her father was silent, and the little ones listened open-mouthed. William wanted to hear all about Leigh House and everything that Amanda had said and done. Grandmother Lil wanted to know also. "That's right," she said. "That's right. You've as much right there as her."

They came into the town and crossed the bridge to the west side and they ran until they reached the cottage.

Grandmother Lil was sitting at the door, smoking her pipe.

"This be my friend, Amanda," said Lilith; and Amanda looked into the old woman's face.

Amanda had changed during the last year; she felt just as deeply, but she had learned to control her emotions, and the tears did not come as easily as they once had. Knowledge of Lilith's world had widened her outlook, and now she was not sorry for Grandmother Lil, for rarely had she seen such a contented face.

" 'Tis a red-letter day indeed," said Grandmother Lil, "when a fine lady comes to see a poor old woman."

But although the words were humble, Amanda felt that she was being mocked.

"How are you to-day, Mrs. Tremorney?"

"Right well, my handsome queen; and all the better for the kind enquiry from your lady lips. So you're my granddaughter's friend, I do hear. Let me have a look at 'ee."

The old woman gave Lilith her pipe to hold; then she drew Amanda towards her and, taking her face in her skinny hands, looked down at it.

"My dear soul," she said, "you be the spitting image of him."

Then she drew the girl to her and kissed her full and hard on the mouth, so that Amanda involuntarily cried out in horror and wriggled free from the embrace. Amanda stood back flushing while the old woman laughed. Uncertain, Amanda stood still, wishing she had not come, trying in vain to turn haughtily away.

"And how are they all up at the House?" asked Grandmother Lil. "Tell me that, my little queen."

Amanda found her voice. "We're all well, thank you."

"And your poor sweet mother? When is she going to give you a little brother . . . or a little sister, eh?"

"I . . . I don't know."

"Never! says I. Never." The old woman laughed harshly as though it were in her power to command such things. "And your father? How's your holy father?"

"He's well, thank you."

"And taking a different path to what his father did, eh?"

She laughed again, showing the stumps of teeth, nicotine-stained and ugly.

William came out of the cottage. He stopped short and flushed when he saw who the visitor was.

"Don't stand there sheepish," said the old woman. "Bow to the lady. Bow like you was gentry. Kiss her hand and tell her she be a beauty."

William bowed his head and looked more sheepish than ever.

" 'Tis not every day that'll bring 'ee the chance of kissing a lady's hand . . . though you've a right to it. You've a right to it.''

William and Amanda stared at each other shyly. Amanda's heart was beating madly. They were strange, this family, stranger than she had believed them to be.

Suddenly she was filled with pity for the uncouth boy standing before her, just as she had been when she had found him in the paddock. She held out her hand to him; he took it, and she noticed how rough his were, and she thought of the back-aching work in Farmer Polgard's fields and the long kitchen table at which they were not given enough time to sit and eat a proper meal; and instead of being disgusted—as she felt she ought to have been—she knew nothing but pity.

She smiled at him and, flushing deeply, he kissed her hand and then, as though ashamed, he turned and ran as fast as he could away from the cottage and the loud mocking laughter of Grandmother Lil.

Mrs. Derry said: "Jane, you can take that bit of pie home with you . . . and the rest of last Wednesday's baking. You can take your sister, too." Mrs. Derry's glance, which had been benevolent while it rested on Jane, turned to a scowl as she looked towards Lilith. "And it would please me if you left her there," she muttered under her breath.

Lilith grimaced as soon as Mrs. Derry had turned her back, and Jane was terrified that Mrs. Derry would see.

Jane was a fresh young girl of seventeen, inclined to buxomness since she had been working at Leigh House. She was very different in appearance from Lilith and William; her hair was light brown and her eyes grey; her lack of expression made her almost indistinguishable from Bess and Ada. Jane was placid by nature; all she wished for, now that she had plenty to eat, was to live at peace . . . so Lilith thought, and Lilith scorned her. It seemed to Lilith that Jane was perfectly content to be a servant, content to bow and curtsy, to live in fear that she might be turned away from Leigh House. She was always respectful to Mrs. Derry, always trying to please. But Lilith discovered during that afternoon that there were some things she did not know about Jane.

They had left the house, climbed the hill to the high road and had come to Three Acres, the first field of the Polgard farm,

when Jane, swallowing a little, took Lilith by the arm and said:
"Lilith, will 'ee do something for me?"

Lilith turned in surprise. Jane looked excited and secretive,
and Lilith realized that she had never seen her sister look like
that before.

"Well," said Lilith, standing still the better to study her sister. "What?"

"Take this home." She thrust the parcel of food into Lilith's
hands. "Don't tell them I was to come with 'ee; and when you
leave . . . wait here for me so's we can go back to the house
together."

Lilith narrowed her eyes. "Why? Where be you going, then?"

"That's my business."

" 'Tis mine too . . . if I've got to say you didn't come with
me and to wait for 'ee."

Jane was uneasy. Her forehead went into wrinkles as it did
when she was worried.

"Oh, Lilith, won't you do this for me?"

"I've got to know why. Then I might."

"Will you swear not to say nothing?"

Lilith nodded eagerly.

"Not to a soul. Not to Bess or Ada . . . nor to none? Not to
William even?"

"I swear," said Lilith solemnly.

"Well, you know Tom Polgard." Jane smiled rather foolishly
so that Lilith began to guess.

"What you . . . and Tom Polgard?"

Jane nodded. Then she was frightened suddenly. "You mustn't
say a word to anyone. 'Twould be terrible if you did. What
would his father and mother say?"

"Swine!" Lilith spat on the ground as she had seen the fishermen do. "Pigs . . . both on 'em."

"Hush such talk," said Jane.

Lilith looked haughty. Jane must not talk to her like that.
Lilith held Jane's secret; and it was fun holding people's secrets.
It gave one a sense of power. Power! That was what Lilith wanted
more than anything. She had power over Amanda, so that, in
private, she had become her equal. Now Jane's secret was in her
possession, and Jane could no longer give herself airs as the big
sister.

Lilith said again: "Pigs . . . both on 'em! But, Jane, do you want to marry him?"

Jane looked distressed. "Well, that's what we do want . . . but they'll never let us."

"You'll have to run away."

"Where would we run to?"

Lilith looked at her sister obliquely. Run away . . . to the hungry world? Leave those islands of plenty which were Leigh House for Jane and the Polgard Farm for Tom Polgard—for Mrs. Polgard didn't shush her own son from the table, Lilith reckoned; farmers, who were not gentry, but a layer or two above labouring folk, set terrible store on their children, particularly if they were sons, like Tom Polgard.

"Well, what'll you do then?" demanded Lilith.

"That's what we don't know."

"You going to see him now?"

"Yes. We must, Lilith. But we'm terrified someone'll see. The Lord knows what Farmer and Missus would say if we were caught. I reckon something terrible would happen to we two if we was caught. But we've got to see each other, Lilith. That's how it is."

"Go on, then," said Lilith. "I won't tell on 'ee. I'll go home and say you was kept; and I'll wait here for 'ee on the way back."

"That's right. You do that. But remember . . . no talking to a soul. 'Tis terrible dangerous."

Lilith nodded and went on alone thinking of them: Jane and Tom Polgard, alike in a way, quiet people only wanting enough to eat and to live in peace; and now this love had overtaken them so that they wanted something which was going to be terrible hard for them to get.

And why should it be? Lilith was angry suddenly. Because Farmer and his Missus wouldn't think Jane Tremorney good enough for their son. Why? It was all due to the unfairness of life when some were born in cottages and some in farms—and some like Amanda Leigh in big houses. Such thoughts made Lilith hate the world.

When she reached the cottage her mother was there with the small children—only William was out with his father on the sea. The family had just finished a meal of sand-eels which the young children had brought from the beach. That meant food was low.

They were very pleased therefore to see Lilith, and particularly pleased to see the parcel she carried.

She opened it and watched their eyes shine. She herself set aside portions for William and her father; and as she did so she was glowing with the wonderful new sense of power which she was beginning to appreciate.

How glorious to look on food with indifference while the little ones watched her as though she were a goddess, and the old grandmother made gruff little noises which indicated pride.

"And where be Jane?"

"Oh, her got kept."

They nodded. The old grandmother's eyes were shining. Two of the family at Leigh House! It was an achievement which made the rest of their little community envy them; and it was all due to her!

Later she sat outside the cottage with the old woman and filled a pipe for her as she used to do when she was a little girl.

"That's the way, my handsome. Don't be sparing of the baccy. I get it regular, you know."

"From Bill Larkin, that's who," said Lilith. "Him whose father was your lover long ago and always remembered it."

Lilith wanted to talk about love—this thing which had come to Jane and changed her from the placid girl to the one who was ready to risk the wrath of the Polgards for an hour in the fields with their firstborn.

Old Grandmother Lil was ready enough to discuss a topic which was her favourite.

"You'm right, my little queen. Old Jack Larkin, he said on his dying bed, he said to his son Bill, who followed the same trade as he'd brought him up to: 'Bill,' he says, 'see that old Lil Tremorney gets her baccy . . . regular like she did in my lifetime . . . for Lil and me was a lot to each other in the old days . . . and there was never one like her for pleasuring.' That's what he did say."

Lilith looked up into her face. "And now you're old . . . too old for pleasuring?"

"Too old for pleasuring. But that's what comes to us all."

"You were a bad woman, weren't you?"

The grandmother punched Lilith playfully. "Come here and I'll whisper to 'ee. You be a smart one, my pretty, you be. You be myself all over again. You'll be the smart one. When some's crying out because they suffer the gnaw of hunger, you'll be sitting at a table with a great taddage pie afore 'ee . . . and a lammy pie all served with clotted cream like the gentry has. And you'll have wines . . . sloe gin and metheglin to wash it down with . . . just like I had. I was a smart one . . . just like you be, my queen. Oh, they say the wages of sin be death; but 'tain't so. My wages of what they do call sin was a full belly. That's how 'twas with me. Some was sleeping on their straw while I was in my feather bed.''

"I've been on a feather bed.'Twas Amanda Leigh's. I tell her stories and she lets me lie there. Next to plenty to eat, feather beds is the best thing in the world.''

The old woman's claws caught at Lilith's curls, and the girl's head was shaken in an affectionate gesture.

"You're growing up, girl. How old be you now?''

"Nearly fourteen.''

"Why, at fourteen, I was on me road. But fourteen then was different from fourteen now. All things was different then. At fourteen I was a woman, and you be a scrap of a girl.''

"Who was your first lover?''

"The tally-man . . . who come round with his goods. A handsome man, my little one, and travelled the countryside he did. The others must pay for his wares, but not your old grand-mother. See this old shawl? 'Tis one I had of him. Old it be now, but it do keep me warm at night still. I've still got me tally-man to keep me warm, though where he be now I couldn't tell 'ee . . . except that it's out of this world, for he were a man old enough to be my father and I be an old woman now. At night when the windows rattle and the snow falls, I pull my shawl about me and I says: 'This is a fine old shawl you gave me, tally-man.' For I do forget his name now . . . though once it did mean all the world to me. So here's the wages of that bit of sin.''

Lilith took the shawl in her hands and felt it. It had been thick once, and, as the grandmother said, it still had the power to keep out the draughts.

"What I want to know most is . . . what about the man at Leigh House?''

"I'll tell 'ee. I went there, my pretty, when I was fifteen . . . just a year older than you be now. But I was a woman then . . . bigger than you . . . bigger than you'll ever be . . . and I went to the kitchens to work. He was a fine man . . . a finer man than his son, who's naught but a snivelling Puritan too busy thinking of the next world to enjoy himself in this. I dunno whether he be right or wrong. What's God going to say to him when he gets up there? And what's He going to say to me? I dunno. But if He'd wanted us to live like your master does, He shouldn't have made the earth so beautiful. That's what I'll tell Him when I come face to face with Him. Why, I'll say, 'tis like someone as asks you to a feast . . . and there's all the good things on the table and you turn away from them to eat a carrot or a turnip as you claw up from the ground. I reckon He'd be sort of offended with them as turned away . . . after all the trouble He took to make it beautiful. That's why I ain't feared of Him. I reckon Him and me will understand each other a lot better than the snivelling master of Leigh House, I do.''

"Well, tell me about it. What happened when you got there?''

"He was a handsome man—yellow hair, and beard that was more red than yellow . . . and big, flashing eyes . . . like Miss Amanda's, only hers be too soft. His looked out on the world like they weren't afraid of God or man or even woman. That's how he was too. I clapped eyes on him and I knew he were the one for me . . . then and for evermore. And he seed it too; and it wasn't long before I was sleeping in a feather bed . . . his feather bed.''

"What of the mistress?''

"She was of no account. Poor and sick and tired, she were, so that she died and none seemed to mind. And there was his son . . . the master now . . . a quiet, unnatural boy, his mother's boy, so his father used to say. Come here, my love. Come here, my little queen. Now I'm going to tell 'ee a secret . . . something you be old enough to know and something I've been saving up for 'ee. Are you listening?''

"Yes,'' said Lilith eagerly.

"It was when I was nigh on eighteen. I remember it well. I was going to have a child, you see . . . 'twas mine and the Master's. And I told him and he said: 'Don't you fret yourself about that, Lil. It'll be all right, you see.' And it were. Married I were to your Grandfather Tremorney, and your father born in wedlock; and your Grandfather Tremorney was paid handsome to ask no questions. That was how gentlemen were in those days, and that was how Miss Amanda's grandfather behaved to me. It wasn't the same, living in a cottage after Leigh

House, I can tell 'ee. I felt it bad at first. But I'd go up to see him and our cottage was always warm in winter and there was plenty to eat all the year round. I saw to that . . . and your grandfather was wise enough to ask no questions. And now, my handsome, you know the truth. You know why you've as much right to be up at the House as the little lady; you've every right to stretch yourself out on her feather bed, and you've no need to pay for what you enjoy with your tales. You've a right to a feather bed of your own up there at the House . . . and one day, who knows, you may have it.''

"So," said Lilith, "I've really got the same grandfather as Amanda Leigh, because the other one . . . the one you married . . . weren't my grandfather at all. My father is the Master's brother."

"Half-brother be what they call it. Though it ain't quite that. You see, the Master, he's an educated gentleman born in wedlock and all, and your father, he's lived all his life . . . for decency's sake . . . as the son of another man."

"But they be brothers, Grandmother; really they be."

"That's so."

"And I be . . . what be I to Amanda then?"

"Well, you'd be cousins like, wouldn't 'ee?"

"Cousins!"

Lilith stood up and threw her arms about her grandmother.

"I've wanted to tell 'ee time and time again," said the old woman. "Your father, he had naught of his father in him . . . proper little cottage boy he were. But you, my pretty one, you're me all over again; and for all he's so quiet, William might have something in him."

"Yes," said Lilith. " 'Tis so."

"William, he's got gentle ways. He's not like his grandfather; but then again he's not like me . . . and he's no cottage boy. Give him fine clothes and learn him a bit . . . take away his shyness, and there you'd have a gentleman . . . a *gentle* gentleman. I've seen some like that. Why, you'd have a gentleman fit to marry his cousin and inherit Leigh House . . . for looks like there'll be no son to leave it to, and such places be best left in a family."

Lilith sat listening, her eyes narrowed, looking away from the cottage, away from Grandmother Lil, into the future.

* * *

Leigh House was quieter and even more gloomy than usual. Amanda wept and tried to imagine what it would be like without Mamma, for Mamma was very ill. Miss Robinson obviously thought that she was going to die. Amanda could read that in the shaking of her head and the tight pressing together of her lips, the faint grief—and, moreover, the hope that overwhelmed all else and that grew each day with the rapidity of Jack's beanstalk.

Lilith had whispered months ago: "I'll tell 'ee something. You're going to have a baby brother or a sister . . . or perhaps both."

Amanda had not believed it and had not liked to ask Lilith why she thought it, for she hated to provoke that scornful "Don't 'ee know nothing? You'm terrible ignorant."

But before long Amanda had discovered that Lilith was right.

Papa spent more time in prayer than ever; Mamma was frankly frightened; she cried a good deal and prayed for strength to bear her cross. There was no doubt that while everyone pretended that it was a new baby, it was really the death of Mrs. Leigh that they expected.

Amanda, supporting her face in her hands, looked wistfully at Miss Robinson, who had, it seemed, become prettier. Her hair was more fluffed out and she wore new lace collars. At luncheon she blushed when Papa spoke to her; and she always referred to the little sermon he had given at prayer time.

As the weeks passed Laura spent more and more time on her sofa when she was not in her bedroom. She would have Amanda sit near her and would become quite tender to her. Amanda began to feel protective towards her, as thought she were the adult, her mother the child.

One night in August there were sounds of disturbance throughout the house, and Amanda, putting on her dressing-gown, was sharply ordered back to bed by Miss Robinson. The governess's hair was in a thin pigtail, her eyes gleamed with excitement. The next morning there were two nurses in the house and the doctor came again in the afternoon. The news leaked out: there was to be no baby and Mrs. Leigh was very ill.

But she continued to be ill and, thought Amanda, although one wanted to be sad and worried, and could be for quite a long time, it was not easy to stay so when that state was demanded of a person for weeks on end.

With her mother ill, her father quite often not appearing at the luncheon table, and Miss Robinson still impersonating in turns the fond prospective mother and the reproachful governess, it was possible to enjoy a little more freedom; and one day as she sat in the window-seat of the schoolroom, she heard the sound of pebbles on the window and, looking out, saw Lilith below.

Lilith beckoned, and in such a manner as to indicate that something both urgent and delightful was afoot.

Amanda went downstairs.

"Come on," said Lilith. "This be something special. Have 'ee ever been for a ride in a hay-cart?"

Amanda had not.

"Then now's your chance."

"But Lilith . . . where. . . ? I should be in the schoolroom. . . ."

Lilith snapped her fingers. "Don't 'ee be so soft. You can do your educating to-morrow. Ye'll never get another chance to ride in a hay-cart. William, he's got to take a load out to St. Keyne. I'm going with him."

"You go, then. I can't."

"You'm a coward, Amanda. You don't know nothing and you ain't been nowhere."

"I've got my house shoes on."

"House shoes!" said Lilith contemptuously. "It wouldn't do 'ee no harm to go barefoot. Come on. Don't 'ee be such a coward and a softie and a know-naught."

Lilith took her by the hand and darted with her through the shrubs to the hedge that bordered the paddock; she ran with her through the paddock to the road. The cart was there, with William quiet and shy, the reins in his hands while the horse cropped the grass on the roadside.

"Climb up," said Lilith. "William, give her a hand."

That was a memorable day. Sometimes afterwards, Amanda dreamed of jogging along the road, past fields in which the wheat was turning to golden brown, past white oats and yellow barley; uphill, downhill, past woods in which she glimpsed the crimson betony, past orchards filled with ripening fruit. They chattered light-heartedly—at least she and Lilith did; William remained quiet, but there was a look of deep contentment on his face. He had to take a load to a farm near St. Keyne, he explained; he added shyly that he was happy to have a little company.

"He got word to me," said Lilith, "and I thought as you'd like to come with us . . . seeing as you'd never ridden in a hay-cart afore."

"There's some," said William shyly, "that should have carriages to ride in . . . not hay-carts."

" 'Tis best to ride in carriages *and* hay-carts," chided Lilith, "for 'tis best to taste all that's to be had. That's what my grandmother do say, and she knows. . . ."

"Whose load is this?" asked Amanda. "Whose cart?"

" 'Tis Farmer Polgard's," William told her.

"You work for him?"

"Just till harvest."

"And what'll you do when the harvest is over?" asked Lilith sharply.

"That I don't know," answered William.

There were tears in Amanda's eyes; she was picturing him lifting potatoes, weary and hungry, creeping into that farmhouse kitchen where the wicked Mrs. Polgard would be standing over him, allowing him only a few minutes in which to snatch something to eat. Amanda suffered for him, just as she suffered with all who aroused her pity.

"Don't stay there," she said. "Why don't you run away?"

Lilith looked at her scornfully. Lilith had been very arrogant during the last few days. "Where would he run to?" she demanded.

"Well . . . he might be a fisherman."

"And what do you know about fishermen, Amanda?" Lilith spoke almost insolently; previously she had always said *Miss* Amanda when others were present.

"It's surely better than working for the Polgards."

"I don't know that it is," said Lilith. "Think of it . . . think of it when you're in your warm feather bed. . . . Think of the fishermen with the sea all round them and the mist coming up and shutting off the land. Think of the wind and storm rising and the boat tossing this way and that so you're well-nigh flung out . . . and that shine on the water that may be the ghost lights instead of a shoal of mackerel. A fisherman don't never know when his time be come. The storms will keep him ashore and there'll be no fish for weeks. What's he going to do? Stay home and starve or go out and drown . . . or work for Farmer Pol-gard?''

Amanda shivered.

"See?" went on Lilith. "You be a know-naught, that's what you be!''

"Well," said Amanda, "I think I'd rather be a fisherman than work for the Polgards.''

William said: " 'Tis not a matter of what is most pleasant, miss. 'Tis what's there to be took.''

" 'Tis what's there to be took,'' repeated Lilith with angry lights in her eyes. "I know what I'd do if I were a man. I'd care for naught and join the smugglers.''

"And what if you were caught?'' asked Amanda.

"I'd rather be caught by the law than by the sea.''

"What would they do if they caught you?''

"I mind seeing a man once," said William, "when I were a little thing. He'd been to Botany Bay and come back after he'd served his seven years. He was in a chain-gang . . . chained to others night and day . . . and worked on the roads. There was marks on his back where they'd flogged him, and they wouldn't never heal. The maggots had got in and eaten his flesh away. He used to talk about Botany Bay . . . all the bright-coloured birds and the blue sea and the sunshine . . . and all the misery and floggings and starvation.''

"Oh . . . how could they!'' murmured Amanda.

"They don't send men there now, miss. But there's other miseries. That man was a farm-hand and he'd stole a turnip out of the farmer's fields. . . .'' William's eyes were shining and he had ceased to be the cottage boy. Lilith watched him with affec-tion, Amanda with startled eyes.

William went on: "It won't always be so. Us have got to stop that. Us have got to alter things . . . to see as people can't be treated bad because they're poor. Us have got to see that people don't starve when there be plenty.''

"But if the weather is too bad for the fisherman to go out and fish . . . what can be done about that?'' asked Amanda.

"Miss Amanda," said William, "you mustn't take no offence at this. But we've got to make things more equal like. You can't have some feasting and some starving. That ain't right. It's got to be shared. This be dangerous talk. Not long ago men has been sent to Botany Bay for talking like this. They call it a crime, miss. But it ain't a crime. And one of these days . . . one of these days . . .'' He smiled and finished lamely: ''One of these days I'll do something about it.''

They were silent as the cart went on. He had changed, Amanda thought, changed so that one did not notice his ragged clothes; he looked powerful sitting there with the reins in his hands as though he were conducting his oppressed fellow men to a better life, instead of a load of hay and two young girls to a farm near St. Keyne.

He began to talk again and then Amanda wondered why she had ever thought him nothing more than an awkward cottage boy; he talked of the miseries of his kind of people, of hunger and poverty; he talked with anger, resentment and determination. He told them of that party of Dorset men who had talked of their rights and had been transported for their impudence. Eloquently he spoke, and the girls listened in silence.

Then they came to the farm and he told them to jump down and wait in the lane while he delivered the hay; and while they waited they talked of William.

''One day,'' said Lilith, ''I reckon William will be a great man. I've always thought it. William and me . . . we'm close. Just think of it, we've been together even afore we was born . . . cuddling inside our mother's body. Ain't that a wonderful thing?''

''He mustn't talk like that, though,'' said Amanda. ''What if someone was to hear him and he were to be sentenced? What good would that do? What good did those men do?''

''William says that everything that's done do leave its mark. He says they seem to fail and they suffer terrible for failing, but people remember them. It's like as if they've made themselves into a sort of banner for them that comes after to follow. That's what it's like.''

''A banner!'' said Amanda. ''A banner that says: 'Don't *you* try. See what happened to us.' ''

''*I* think you're right. William don't, though. I think William's wrong. I've told him so. He's thinking of others. He'd make himself into one of them banners, he would. But what's the good of that? He needs to make a place for *himself*, I tell him . . . not for others. Who wants banners? What folks want is a good table laden with food and drink, and a feather bed to sleep in. That's what I tell William. But he's a *gentle* gentleman. There are that sort. My grandmother says so, and she do know. William ought to be a gentleman; then he could learn to talk proper and what he said wouldn't get him into trouble.''

Amanda said: "He can't be a gentleman because he wasn't born one, so because he's not a gentleman he ought to be careful what he says.''

Lilith glanced at her with narrowing eyes, but Amanda was not looking at Lilith, for she had heard the sound of cartwheels which heralded the return of William.

When they had scrambled into the cart, Lilith said: "William, go round by the well. I reckon Amanda's never seen the well.''

"No; I haven't,'' said Amanda. "Do let's go by the well.''

"It'll take time,'' said William.

"Ah!'' mocked Lilith. "Are you afraid of old Polgard? You talk fine, but you don't do much. Haven't you earned a bit of a ride? Besides, Amanda wants to, don't 'ee, Amanda?''

Amanda said quickly: "I don't want to if it's going to . . . if it's going to get William into trouble.''

Lilith's eyes flashed scorn. "She thinks you're a coward, William. She thinks you talk bold while there's fear inside you.''

"I don't,'' cried Amanda. "I just don't want you to do anything that might cause trouble.''

But William had whipped up the horse and they went rattling along to the well.

"What well *is* this?'' asked Amanda.

"Don't 'ee know, then?'' mocked Lilith. "You don't know nothing. You're educated every morning and you don't know nothing. You look at maps and even draw 'em and you don't know what St. Keyne's Well's for.''

"Don't you dare talk to me like that, Lilith,'' said Amanda.

But Lilith laughed. "You ain't mistress here. Why, what if William and me put you down here on the road. A nice pickle you'd be in.''

William said: "We wouldn't do it, Miss Amanda. Lilith, you haven't no right to talk to Miss Amanda that way.''

"Hark to him!'' cried Lilith. "He's going to stand up for his rights and the rights of all of us, but he won't forget to touch his cap to the gentry while he's doing it!''

Amanda said solemnly: "Lilith *is* insolent, and one of these days she'll regret it. But never mind.''

Lilith did not care; she snapped her fingers at them both.

They pulled up at the well which was at the fork of the roads and was hidden from view by masses of foliage.

Lilith said: "I'll hold the horse while William shows you the well. It's in there. *You* go round that way to it. William, *you* go that, and see who gets there first."

"No, Lilith, *no*," said William.

But Lilith was laughing, for Amanda had already run off in the direction Lilith had indicated.

"Don't be soft," said Lilith to her brother. "Do as I say. Go . . . there's not a second to lose."

Amanda had reached the well by the right-hand path, which was only wide enough for one, some seconds before William arrived by the left-hand path, blushing and sheepish.

They peered down into the darkness.

"It's a well, nothing more," said Amanda. "It's got an unpleasant smell."

"It's the damp weeds and things . . ."

"Should we wish something?"

William shook his head.

"Then it's not a magic well at all. I wish it was St. Uny's Well at Redruth, William."

"Why do you wish that, Miss Amanda?"

"Because if you dip your finger in that water you preserve yourself from being hanged."

"And *you* want to do that?"

"No. I want you to."

"You think I'll come to that then, Miss Amanda?"

"I don't know. But I'm afraid you'll say something wild and foolish and you'll be punished for it. You're not like the other cottage people. You seem like them, but beneath that . . . you're different."

He put his hands on the wall of the well and said solemnly: "And you're not like the gentry, Miss Amanda. You seem so, but you're different. . . . You're loving and kind and you look at people as though you see them . . . as though you care what happens to them."

"Hey!" called Lilith. "What be doing in there?"

They smiled at each other; Amanda turned to the right and William to the left and they ran back to the road.

"Who got there first?" asked Lilith.

"Miss Amanda."

"William, you great softie!" cried Lilith indignantly. "You should have seen to that."

"It be silly to think of that," said William.

"I had a few seconds' start," said Amanda.

"That don't make no difference." said Lilith. "Well, 'tis done now."

"What's done?"

"Ah, don't you know nothing? When a man and a woman goes to the well for the first time together, the one who gets there first is the one who'll be master in their married life. That's the magic of St. Keyne's."

"How silly!" said Amanda coldly.

" 'Tis not silly. 'Tis magic," said Lilith.

"Give over, do," said William sternly, and he whipped up the horse.

Lilith chattered all the time; she had a fund of stories, mostly those which she had heard from Grandmother Lil. She would not let them forget the incident which had disturbed both Amanda and William and caused such delight to herself. She told them how, when Grandmother Lil had gone to Altarnon with a tally-man she knew, riding pillion with him, she had seen a mad woman dipped into St. Nun's Well. "In she went, screaming like she were possessed with a million demons . . . and out she come sane as you or me. There's magic in the wells of Cornwall because they were blessed long ago by our saints."

Then Lilith began to sing; she had a strong and pleasing mezzo-soprano voice which seemed doubly powerful coming from such a small person. She sang the Furry Dance tune, fitting to it her own words about a pair who had met at St. Keyne's and a man who had let a maid get there before him. Then she went on to the Christmas songs, "As I sat on a sunny bank . . ." and "The mistress and the master our wassail begin." And William and Amanda joined with her in singing these.

At last they came near to Leigh House, where the two girls got down, and William drove on to the Polgard Farm.

Amanda wished to be quiet, but Lilith was still in command.

"You'm cross," she said.

"I'm not."

"You are. And I'll tell 'ee why. 'Twas because of what happened at the well. You beat William to it, and that means if you two was to wed, you'd be the master."

"I forbid you to say such things. It would not be possible for me and William to marry."

" 'Tis possible for any young man and maid to marry."

"You forget who I am . . . and who he is."

"You forgot it when you came riding with us."

"I did not forget it for a minute."

"Then you should. But you ain't any better than we are . . . or not much . . . not enough to make that difference."

"I never heard such nonsense, and I wish you would address me with more respect. In fact, I'm going to insist that you do."

Lilith danced ahead and looked mockingly over her shoulder.

"Amanda, do you know the portrait in the gallery, of the man with yellow hair, and eyes the colour of yours too?"

"Do you mean my grandfather?"

"I do. Your grandfather . . . and mine."

"*Your* grandfather?"

" 'Twas so. My father was his son . . . just as your father was. Grandmother Lil, she worked at the House. He married her to old Grandfather Tremorney . . . but that don't change nothing, does it? He's my grandfather, same as he were yours. . . . And he's William's."

Lilith ran on ahead, laughing, turning to look over her shoulder. Amanda stumbled after her, the rough stones of the road hurting her feet through the thin soles of her house shoes.

Laura Leigh lay in her sick-room. The curtains were drawn; the windows were tightly shut; a fire burned in the grate and she only knew that the late September day was full of sunshine because a little penetrated the room where the curtains did not quite meet where one of the maids had not drawn them properly.

Her head ached; her body ached; but these physical aches were not as bitter as the resentment in her heart.

Her husband was away; he had gone to visit his brother on the borders of Devon and Somerset, and he would be away for some weeks. She was glad he had gone. During her illness, as she had lain in this room believing that she would never leave it, it was as though the truth had refused to be kept out, even as the sunshine of this day, which hurt her eyes, refused to be kept out. It had penetrated that chink in the curtain of hypocrisy, and it was hurtful . . . hurtful as sunshine to her tired eyes.

She reached for her hartshorn. She felt faint when she moved.

But she would get better, just as she had got better after those other ordeals; and in time the command would come again—for it was a command, in whatever gentle terms it was couched: "I will come to your room to-night."

She had heard how he had prayed for her during her illness. Praying for better luck next time? She wondered. Praying that the Lord might see His way to provide Paul Leigh with a son?

Divine omnipotence could supply either: a miracle in the form of a son for Laura, or a natural event like the death of one wife, a discreet interval, then marriage to another to whose room he might go.

Should she be sorry for him? She knew he suffered in his way as much as she did in hers. He had to fight sensuality. She had not been unaware of that. Had he thought differently, he might have been such as his father. Oh yes, he was not without his cross to bear!

So here she was, recovering, with no son to offer him . . . nothing but a body that was a little weaker than it had been before, a body which had still less chance of fulfilling its purposes.

She began to cry because she felt so weak. Then she remembered her childhood and how happy she had been at home. Their father had been a jolly man; their mother had been a little domineering, but loving and tender at heart. Looking back, those days seemed very happy ones—all childhood troubles shaded away; all joys heightened with the clever crayon of memory. There had been three sisters and two brothers. Two of them were dead now. The others were married; her two sisters were in London society, enjoying gay balls, excursions in the Park, seeing the Coronation of the Queen and the opening of Parliament. What lives they had! And she was here in a house made dismal by its master, confronted continually by her own inadequacy to provide him with a son.

If only she were a child again! At this time of the year they would be thinking of going to St. Matthew's Fair. Their father had always driven them in. They saw the bearded lady and the fat man; she remembered the fortune-teller who had said she would marry a lord; she could almost taste gingerbread and sweet drinks; she could almost smell the burning flesh of an ox.

The door was opened and Amanda came into the room.

"Mamma, are you awake?"

"Yes, my love. What did you want?"

"To see you. How is your head?"

"It aches very badly."

"Then I'll not disturb you."

"I wish to speak to you, Amanda."

Did she come reluctantly to the bed? Did she long to leave the sickroom? Poor little Amanda! What sort of life was hers, living in this house?

"I was just thinking," said Laura, "that at this time of the year, when I was your age, I always went to St. Matthew's Fair. It was a great treat. Would you like to go to the Fair?"

"Why, Mamma, yes. But . . . would Papa allow it?"

Laura plucked at the sheet, and her fingers made it into a neat fold before she replied. Then she said: "Go and find Miss Robinson, and when you have found her, bring her here."

Amanda went out and Laura wondered a little at this mood of defiance. Was she just a little mad? They said these things sometimes drove a woman mad. When he came back she would tell him: "I gave Miss Robinson permission to take Amanda to the Fair." She could imagine his astonishment changing to horror. He believed all fairs—in fact, everything that was made for enjoyment—were made by the Devil's imps at Satan's command. Well, for once it would be too late to stop her doing one little thing she wished. And perhaps too, she thought with a return of sanity, it need never be told.

Amanda came in with Miss Robinson.

"Oh, Miss Robinson," said Laura, "Amanda would like to go to St. Matthew's Fair. I don't see why you shouldn't take her. The outing will do you both good. It is the first of October tomorrow, I believe. Get Steert to take you in the dog-cart. Amanda, you can bring me back a comfit. I remember the first one I had. It was a pink heart with a blue ribbon through it."

Both Amanda and Miss Robinson were too startled to speak.

But on the next day, which was the first of October, they set out in the dog-cart for St. Matthew's Fair.

Places, thought Amanda, must vary according to whose company you were in when you visited them. During the first half-hour the Fair was a crowded, noisy place, a little vulgar, not quite what a lady should enjoy; that was because she saw it in the company of Miss Robinson; with Lilith, she was sure, it would have displayed a hundred excitements and pleasures. Miss Robinson held Amanda's hand tightly; she carried her head high and gathered in her skirts that they might not be contaminated by the jostling crowds. Amanda had never seen so many people gathered in one spot intent on one thing—enjoyment.

"Tell your fortune, lady?" That was the old Gipsy woman looking eagerly into Miss Robinson's face. "My, you've got a lucky face, you have!"

There was the fat woman with her mob-cap and her greasy ringlets. "Gingerbread, ladies. Ooo . . . lovely gingerbread. You ain't never tasted the like of it. Gingerbread with currants and nuts . . . lady . . . the best of the Fair."

Amanda watched the barefooted boys and girls pushing their way through the crowd, free from the restraining hands of a governess. A year ago she would have wept for them because their feet were bare and they looked cold and thin; but Lilith had taught her that freedom from a governess and the need to be a lady were blessings; and that the daughters of the gentry were to be pitied for not possessing them.

In the field beyond the Fair they had started to roast an ox; she could see the smoke rising, and she could hear the crackle of flames and the shouts of the people while she smelt the roasting meat. Soon they would be carving off pieces to sell to the crowd. She hoped Miss Robinson would not want to see that. Lilith would have laughed at her fastidiousness.

They were passing a tent at which stood a man with brass rings in his ears and a blue turban on his head. His voice was hoarse.

"Come inside. Come and see Salome. The world's wonder dancer. Three pennies to see Salome dance."

And while he was shouting Salome herself appeared—a girl not much older than Amanda, in a short pink dress with red roses sewn on its skirt, and tinsel about the neck and sleeves. Amanda thought her beautiful.

"Miss Robinson . . . look! Oh, *do* look."

"Come along," said Miss Robinson. "Quite vulgar. A child of that age."

"She's Salome," protested Amanda. "How could Salome be vulgar? She's in the Bible."

Salome knew that they were talking about her; she knew that Amanda was trying to urge Miss Robinson to pay the sixpence in order that they might go into the tent; she smiled at Amanda pathetically, appealingly, and Amanda longed to see her dance. Moreover, she was poor and she danced for a living. Amanda was deeply touched.

"Oh, Robbie . . . please. I do so want to. I want to more than anything."

The man with the earrings came forward.

"You want to see Salome dance, do you, my dear? Bring the little girl in, madam."

Miss Robinson had drawn herself up haughtily.

"Why," he went on persuasively, "you'll enjoy it yourself. This ain't the sort of show your ladyship can see in every booth. Oh, no. This is culture. And you're a lady of culture, a lady of breeding. You don't have to tell me that."

Amanda, who was looking appealingly up into her governess's face, saw it soften. The man laid a hand on Miss Robinson's arm. His eyes showed something which Amanda did not understand. She expected Miss Robinson to throw him off angrily, but she did nothing of the sort.

"You appreciate beauty, lady. I can see that." His eyes travelled lightly over Miss Robinson and he added softly: "Beautiful ladies always do."

Miss Robinson turned to Amanda. "You really want to see it?"

"Oh yes, please."

The lovely girl in the pink frock was smiling at Amanda; the man was gripping her shoulder affectionately. "Of course she does. Don't you, my little one? It's something she'll never forget."

"It's not . . . improper, I hope," said Miss Robinson, in a voice which sounded rather frivolous, unlike the usually severe tone she employed when addressing those whom she considered to be her inferiors.

"Why, bless you, lady, it's . . . *art*!"

Then Miss Robinson paid their threepences and they went into the tent which smelt of damp earth and sweat. They sat on one of the forms, and when their eyes had grown accustomed to the darkness they saw that several other people were waiting there, their eyes fixed on a blue curtain across one end of the tent.

Amanda felt that the dark tent was an enchanted place; the noises in the Fair sounded muffled, heard from within the canvas, and more exciting than they had been outside. She did not mind waiting while the people came in slowly to fill the forms, for naturally, as she explained to Miss Robinson, they could not expect Salome to perform for them alone. At last, when they had waited a quarter of an hour, those people who were already in the tent began to stamp their feet and whistle and shout, so that Miss Robinson was afraid for her dignity and Amanda for Salome.

Then the blue curtain was pulled aside, and there was Salome in the pink dress with red roses; and she danced in the lighted space, twirling on her toes, lifting her skirts and looking so beautiful that all the people cheered and clapped.

Salome stopped suddenly and held up her hand.

"Ladies and gentlemen," she said, "thank you for your appreciation. I am now about to dance the Dance of the Seven Veils. I hope I shall please you."

Then she disappeared behind the curtain until the audience began to stamp and clap to show their impatience; and when she appeared again she was wrapped in what, to Amanda, looked like white muslin, and her black hair was loose about her shoulders.

She bowed and said in that strange voice which was not of the West Country: "Ladies and gentlemen, the Dance of the Seven Veils."

She danced, and as she danced she plucked at the muslin, which came off like the wrapping round a package, to disclose her in another muslin wrapping; and the first muslin she threw behind the curtain.

A red-faced man sitting next to Miss Robinson began to chuckle.

Everyone was staring hard at Salome. Sinuously she danced, twisting, writhing, twirling . . . and then off came another of the muslin wrappings.

Miss Robinson sat bolt upright. Amanda felt her grip her arm. "We will go," said Miss Robinson in a whisper.

But Amanda had learned defiance from Lilith. "*I* shall stay," she said; and she fixed her eyes defiantly on Salome.

The red-faced man turned to Miss Robinson. "That's the fourth," he said. "There be seven. What then, eh?" And he dug his elbow into Miss Robinson's side.

She recoiled from him haughtily. "I insist . . ." she hissed in Amanda's ear.

But Amanda drew away from her; she could not take her eyes from the twirling figure. The fifth piece of muslin came off. The red-faced man was so delighted; he turned to Miss Robinson. "Would 'ee believe it?" he demanded. "Would 'ee believe it?"

The sixth veil was off and Miss Robinson had risen.

"Sit down!" commanded those in the rows behind her. "You be blocking the view. Sit down, I tell 'ee."

Crimson with anger, Miss Robinson sat.

The seventh veil was removed and there was Salome in flesh-coloured tights that fitted so closely that they looked like her own skin. She wore a tunic which started a long way from her neck and ended where the tights began.

She bowed. The red-faced man whistled; and it seemed that the tent was filled with shouts and the sound of clapping.

Then Salome ran behind the curtain and came out in what looked like a cloak of black satin covered in glittering sequins; this she held about her, taking care not to hide her pretty legs in the flesh-coloured tights.

"Ladies and gentlemen," she said, "thank you for your appreciation. If there are any of you who would like to see the performance again, pray keep your seats. I will come and collect the small charge of threepence from you."

The flap of the tent opened, letting in the sunlight and the noise.

"Come on," said Miss Robinson. "Let's get out of here . . . quickly."

They came out into the sunshine, but the magic of Salome stayed with Amanda.

"It was quite disgusting," Miss Robinson was saying. "You must never tell your mother. She would be quite ashamed. Did you see that man beside me . . . molest me?"

"I don't think he wanted to molest you, Miss Robinson. He was just happy and wanted to tell you so."

"And did you see the way in which that showman in earrings looked at me?"

"That was because he admired you. He said you were a lady of breeding and culture. And he thought you were beautiful too, didn't he?"

"He did *not*!" said Miss Robinson with a pleased smile. She was now quite good-humoured, Amanda noticed.

Amanda knew that the showman had not really thought Miss Robinson either cultured or beautiful, but that he had merely been trying to lure them into the tent with his compliments as Salome had with her beauty; but it gave Miss Robinson such obvious pleasure to believe him that Amanda wished to foster that belief. She was happy to-day; she loved the Fair and this was one of the most exciting days of her life.

"You don't think," said Miss Robinson, "that that man in the tent was trying to scrape an acquaintance?"

"He might have been," said Amanda.

"The impertinence!"

Oh, what a joyous day! thought Amanda. Miss Robinson was happy, without a thought of the future; and all because of the insolence of a red-faced man!

"I do believe," said Miss Robinson, "that he tried to follow us when we left. I do hope we have lost him in the crowd. It would be most unpleasant."

Amanda did not say that she was sure he had not followed them and that she had seen him getting out his money to pay Salome in order that he might see her dance once more, for she knew that Miss Robinson was so happy imagining herself to be pursued.

With Miss Robinson in her present mood it was possible to persuade her that they should have their fortunes told. They found the old Gipsy who added to their happiness by promising Miss Robinson a husband in the very near future. Amanda had a future too—a handsome husband, a fortune and a trip across the water.

After that they bought the comfit for Mrs. Leigh—a heart of pink sugar on a blue ribbon with the words "The Faithful Heart" inscribed on it in yellow letters.

Miss Robinson seemed to have become so much younger and better-looking that Amanda reflected that if she could live at a fair she might grow so much more attractive that she would find a husband.

The comfit stall was near the edge of the Fair, and close by, standing on a raised platform, were several men and women.

"What is this?" asked Amanda. "Who are they?"

Miss Robinson looked and answered: "Oh, they're serving-girls and men . . . hiring themselves out."

"Hiring themselves out!"

"They want someone to take them . . . as servants."

"Selling themselves!" cried Amanda. "Like the woman sold comfits! Like they are selling pieces of the ox!"

"How ridiculous!" said Miss Robinson. "Let us go back to the heart of the Fair."

But Amanda stood firm. She wanted to know more of these hirelings, for she could not prevent herself thinking of herself standing there, asking people to hire *her*, begging for work—not knowing what sort of work, what sort of people she would go to.

She felt now that she had been wrong to be so happy a little while ago. Some of them looked frightened. There were two young girls—not more than ten years old—clinging together, trying not to cry. There was a big man showing the muscles on his arms; there was one girl, plumpish and black-eyed, with her hair hanging about her face, who was giving saucy smiles to a man who was standing close to her asking questions. Amanda watched the man pinch her and saw the girl laugh.

"What are you staring at?" asked Miss Robinson. "Come along at once."

But Amanda's gaze had gone from the girl to a boy who was standing awkwardly there, wretched, detached, because while most of the others seemed to be showing their powers with eagerness he was hanging back. Indignation, anger and despair smothered all Amanda's pleasure, for standing there, forlorn and disconsolate, was William.

Miss Robinson was tugging at her hand. "Come on. We'll go and try the gingerbread."

He would not want me to see him, thought Amanda as she was pulled away. That would only make him more unhappy.

There was no more pleasure for her in the Fair. Life was not beautiful; it was ugly. All the excitement of the day, all the enchantment of Salome had vanished—shattered by the look of misery in William's face.

The gingerbread stuck in her throat. What was happening there at the hiring stand? Who was hiring William?

"Don't you want your gingerbread?" asked Miss Robinson. "How perverse you are!"

"Miss Robinson, let's go this way. . . ."

"But that's the way we've just come. We don't want to go back there."

"But *I* want to. . . ."

"I never heard such nonsense. We'll have to find Steert soon. It's almost time we started the journey back."

But Amanda had to go back to the hiring stand. She had been a coward to run away. She should have waited to see what happened; she should have spoken to him, told him how she suffered with him.

Miss Robinson was examining some ribbons on a stall. Amanda turned and ran, tears blinding her as she pushed her way through the crowds.

When she reached the hiring stand she stared at it disconsolately for William was no longer there. But almost immediately she saw him. He had his back to her, yet she knew that he was infinitely sad, infinitely dejected. He walked behind a man whom Lilith had pointed out to Amanda as Farmer Polgard.

Amanda stood looking after them as William followed the farmer to a waiting gig. There was a woman sitting in the gig. She was small and shrewish; and under her black bonnet her face looked cruel. Amanda knew this must be the farmer's wife who had shooed Lilith and William away from the table before they had been able to eat their fill.

William climbed into the back of the gig.

Miss Robinson was calling her, but she did not hear her and was astonished to see the governess, flushed and indignant, beside her. Miss Robinson took her by the arm and shook her. "What came over you? To run off like that! I just saw you in time. What is it? What is it?"

Amanda lifted her melancholy eyes to Miss Robinson's face, but she could not explain to her.

"I don't understand you. To run off like that! So . . . so pointless . . . so quietly wilful. Come along at once, miss."

They went to find Steert, and when they were in the dog-cart Amanda discovered that in her flight to the hiring stand she had lost the comfit her mother had asked her to buy for her.

"What carelessness! What ingratitude! Oh dear, what a difficult child," sighed Miss Robinson.

But Amanda was not listening; she was crying quietly as the dog-cart carried them through the lanes.

Three

The Polgard Farm was one of the biggest in the neighbourhood; it was also one of the most prosperous. Some said this was due to the skill of the farmer, Jos Polgard; others said it had its roots in the niggardliness of Annie.

The Polgards had been lucky. They had two daughters to work in the farmhouse and do the women's jobs on the farm; and they had three sons towards the necessary masculine labour. Annie grumbled perpetually; she had wanted another daughter for the dairy; and if she had been able to bear two or three more sons it would not have been necessary to hire any men.

She was a little woman, this Annie Polgard, while her husband Jos was a big man, slow to think and quick to anger—and when his anger was roused it was mad and violent, so that he resembled his bulls. Everyone on the farm, except Annie, was afraid of him; but they all knew that he was afraid of Annie. It was not that his sons, Tom, Harry and Fred, could not have stood up to him. Tom and Harry had their father's ox-like strength, and Fred was thin and small like his mother, but strong and wiry. As for the two hired men—Jim Burke and William Tremorney—if they lacked the fighting qualities of the Polgards, they were as strong. It was the knowledge that if they did not please Jos Polgard they could be turned off the farm, which made them accept his blows. Nobody—unless they had an income of their own—could calmly face a workless future which meant a breadless one; and in these days of hardship any work that was available, whatever the disadvantages that went with it, was quickly taken up.

The Polgards were fully aware of this, and they took the utmost advantage of it.

Jos, therefore, had to be endured, but it was a great satisfaction to all to know that his anxious moments were provided by his little shrew of a wife. The power of Jos was easy to understand. He was six feet tall, of great girth, a swarthy man with a crop of thick black hair that stood out straight from his head because it was too coarse to lie down. The black hairs seemed to sprout everywhere on his body; they pushed themselves up at the neck of his shirt; they sprouted from his nose and ears; his spatulate hands were covered with them. When he snorted about the farm—for he breathed heavily through his mouth—he was like one of the animals, a wild animal of a strange and terrifying species. He would ride or walk about the farm with his riding-crop, which he took a delight in using on his horses, his dogs and his men and women. It was very pleasant to know he went in fear of Annie.

And more terrifying than the farmer was the farmer's wife. This might have been because her power came from a mysterious source. Jos was an example of brutish man; but Annie, it was believed, had the devil in her. Her shrill voice could be heard coming from the kitchen and the dairies—her own particular domain. If the Polgard Farm was a purgatory, the kitchen and the dairy were the bowels of hell.

There was a legend about Annie: She had come to the farm twenty-five years ago with her father, a casual labourer of no substance who roamed the countryside picking up odd jobs. Jos had been a young man then and had just inherited the place from his father. The story went that they came to the Polgard Farm and Jos gave the man a few days' work outside, saying that Annie could make herself useful in the house. They slept in one of the barns—at least the old man did—so said Millie Tarder, who was housekeeping there at the time and hoped to marry Jos; but it was not long before Annie seduced Jos. Millie was indignant. Annie! A scrap of a thing with no beauty, no grace, and all her shrewishness there on her face for any man to see if he had the sense. Not that Jos had much; but he should, said Millie, even with his little bit, have been able to see what was so clear. " 'Tweren't natural,'' Millie often said even now. "Her weren't Jos's sort. And even if he did get up to his larks he could have brought them to a proper conclusion like. No, 'tweren't natural. She had some hold over him. She said: 'Jos Polgard, I belong to be missus of this farm.' And Missus she was within two months.''

But she did something to the farm when she came. Their butter was richer; their cows gave more milk. There was an influence at work, said Millie; but Millie was prejudiced, for she had been given her marching orders the day Annie became the mistress of the farm.

She was mean, watching every mite of food that went into their mouths. " 'Tis a wonder," said Millie, "that she didn't make 'em scrape the mud off their boots and find a use for it."

Jos worsened after his marriage. It seemed as though, because she ruled him, he had to revenge himself on others. He had not her tongue, but he had a strong arm and a fist like a club; he had the strength of an ox even if he had the brains of an ass. And if he had the finest farm in the neighbourhood, the less successful would laugh behind their hands and say: "That may be, but Annie Polgard goes along with it!"

To this farmstead came William on that October day. It was solely in order to escape working on this farm that he had set himself up for hire at the Fair, and it was ironical that the Polgards should have taken him after all. He was sensitive and nervous and he felt dejected and degraded. Yet the knowledge, which Lilith had passed on to him, that he was the grandson of old Mr. Leigh sustained him through the terrible months—that and his friendship with Tom Polgard the eldest of the farmer's sons.

The long working days began before the first streaks of dawn were in the sky, so that work could start as soon as it was light enough to see. Napoleon, the boy from the Workhouse, who was worse off then any of them, had the job of rousing them. Napoleon had been so called as a joke; there had been so many Wellingtons in the Workhouse. He was now eleven; he slept in a hut which was inferior to the barn of the hired men. Annie Polgard, who arranged such matters, believed fervently in dividing the classes. She was the queen of this hive of industry; the farmer was a consort of great power, but controlled by herself; her sons were next in rank, but powerless against her and their father; then came the daughters; and very far down the scale the hired men; and something lower than the animals was young Napoleon.

Napoleon was said to be half-witted, which was not true; it was merely that when confronted by anyone in authority he could not speak, so great was his fear. His life had been one of misery, starvation and physical violence ever since he could remember, and he had acquired the perpetual look of a sick animal expecting a blow. He was fond of anyone who showed him kindness, and he adored William because William had compassion and sympathy to offer and was the first person to teach poor Napoleon that these feelings and emotions existed in a bitter world.

Napoleon worked for nothing but his keep; this he must do for three years; 'on apprenticeship,' it was called; then he was entitled to threepence a week. He would never get it, he knew; because when the three years had expired he would be sent out into the world, and Annie Polgard would ask the Workhouse for another boy 'on apprenticeship.' Napoleon was never allowed to sit at the table; he crouched in a corner, and when the feeding was over the scraps would be collected on one of the plates and given to him. William had on more than one occasion slipped a piece of barley bread into his pocket and given it surreptitiously to the boy.

It was Napoleon's duty to wake at cock-crow and rouse the hired men. They must milk the cows before breakfast, which consisted of 'sky-blue-and-sinkers.' Lately Annie Polgard had added a piece of barley bread because Jim Burke had fainted from hunger in the middle of the morning, and although it might be expected that Annie would say, "We'll get a man who's got more sense than to faint in the middle of the morning," she was wise enough to know that workers, like dogs, had to be fed.

There was no letting up on the work—Jos saw to that—which continued all the morning. Then there was the break for the midday meal and on again until four, when they drank home-brewed ale and ate dry bread. For supper the men had a pasty and a tankard of cider each.

William lived through those days in a haze of misery; it was not the work that hurt him so much as the indignity. No man, he reflected, had a right to treat other men as Jos Polgard did. He never forgot that, if his own sufferings were great, Napoleon's were acute. He himself suffered humiliation, but what Napoleon had to endure was utter degradation. There were times when William thought of leaving the farm, of running off to another part of the country. In the meantime he tried to make Napoleon's life tolerable.

Tom Polgard chatted to him as they mended the hedges together or made preparations for the lambing season. Greatly daring, William talked to Tom of the thoughts that came to him; he even mentioned those men of Tolpuddle who had so stirred his imagination. Tom listened—or seemed to. He would nod from time to time and say, "That's so" or "You'm right there." But William fancied that his thoughts were far away.

One day William discovered the real reason for Tom's friendship.

It was December and they were breaking the ice on a cattle trough when Tom said: "Bide here awhile. If me father do ask you where I be, tell him I've gone up to Five Acres to get a rabbit, will 'ee?"

He went off with pleasure on his face, but a few hours later when William saw Tom again there was a weal there, and he looked sullen. William had often seen him bruised from his father's fist or cut from his whip, but had never seen him in that brooding angry mood before.

Napoleon brought the news to William.

"Reckon they'll be blaming you for this."

"What do you mean, Nap?"

"Well, 'twas your sister Master Tom were caught with."

"Which sister?"

"Her as is at Leigh House. The big 'un—Jane."

"Jane . . . and Tom?"

" 'Twas so. Master found 'em together. He flicked his crop about them. She ran off . . . but Tom couldn't do that."

Now William understood that Tom had singled him out for friendship because he was Jane's brother.

When he went in for the meal, Annie Polgard looked at him scornfully; she had been working herself into a passion. When the others were seated at the table, she said to William: "Go and bring me a basket of taters. Here . . . fill this."

He took the basket and went out into the yard, past the pigeon lofts and the harness house to the potato house. While he was filling the basket he heard her coming after him.

"Some of them taters is rotten," she said. "Just take 'em out. We'll have it spreading."

And, hungry from the morning's work, William thought of the kitchen table and the food he was missing, for he would have to start work with the others, he knew.

Then she began to say what was in her mind; she could never control her tongue.

"So your sister's after our Tom. That be like her impidence. She'll have to think again. Won't be no good her coming here and saying our Tom's got to marry her . . . that won't do, Will Tremorney. I wouldn't have my boy marrying the likes of her, that I wouldn't. So you be telling her to take a bit of care what she's up to. I never heard the like! She'd like to be mistress of Polgards', would she? She'd like to step in my shoes. Just let her try and she shall feel the Farmer's whip, she shall. When you see that slut of a sister of yourn, tell her not to raise her eyes to her betters. Tell her to look where she likes, but not at Tom Polgard." She came close to him and leered up at him. "I reckon you fixed this. I reckon you said to Tom: 'I've got a sister . . . a willing sister. . . .' " She began to laugh while her little ferret eyes grew lewd and malicious, and there flowed from her lips a stream of obscenities. She spat as she talked and little drops of moisture clung to the hairs about her mouth. "Does she think she's coming to my house . . . to take my place? My boys will marry when I say so . . . and not else . . . and they'll marry who I want . . . their own kind, not anybody's slut from them quay cottages."

William went on sorting the potatoes, and the expression on his face did not change. He would fight for his rights when the time came, but that time had not yet come, and there was no sense in getting wounded before the battle began.

"Mild as milk . . . that's you," she said. "Not a word to say for yourself. Well, you've got some sense. Get back to the kitchen, and take the basket with 'ee. You won't have much time to eat, will 'ee now?"

He went. He did get a mouthful or two before work started again, but, although he went back to work hungry, he did not seem to notice his hunger.

It was dark in Amanda's room. There was no night-light. That was forbidden by her father.

When she heard the door of her room opening she was not in the least startled, for she guessed who was paying her a visit. Lilith had never lost her desire for a feather bed, and often came to enjoy the comfort of Amanda's.

On this evening she had news, and as she lay stretched out on the bed she told it to Amanda. " 'Tis Jane. She says her heart be broke, and it's all along of Tom Polgard."

The name Polgard made Amanda shudder; this had been the case since she had seen William get into the farmer's gig at the Fair.

"Does Tom Polgard love Jane?"

"He do indeed. 'Twas yesterday. They met in Five Acres like they've been doing on and off for months, and while they were kissing and cuddling there, who should come along but Farmer himself. Jane came home crying; she said she had to run for her life. She's scared he's well-nigh murdered poor Tom."

"Polgard Farm is a terrible place, Lilith."

" 'Tis truly. The old Farmer has the devil in him, and old Missus is worse than Farmer. Jane says she'll never let them marry."

"They ought to run away. So ought William."

"You don't know naught. Where would they run to?"

"Couldn't Grandmother Lil do something for William?"

"She could, but he won't have nothing done for him. He could join in with Larkins if he had a mind to. William won't run against the law. 'Tis mazed he be. For what have the law done for him? I'll tell you what, Cousin Amanda, I've made a promise to Jane. I'm going over to Polgards' and I'm going to see Tom . . . or I'll see William, and I'll pass on messages between 'em, that's what I'll do."

"What if you're caught?"

"You don't think I'm afraid of they Polgards . . . Farmer or Missus?"

"Lilith, you must be careful not to get caught. I shall never forget the farmer's face . . . nor that of his wife . . . that day when I saw them in the gig."

Lilith nodded. They had cried together when Amanda had come home and told Lilith what she had seen at the Fair; and that was the first and only time Amanda had seen Lilith shed tears.

Lilith kicked at the curtains of the bed. "Amanda, *Cousin* Amanda, when I do take a message from Jane to-morrow, you come with me. You see if you can talk to William. He sets terrible store by you. I reckon it would make up for a lot if you was to have a word or two to say to him."

"Oh, Lilith, I will. I will."

                          * * *

Miss Robinson's fingers were trembling as she stitched the lace collar on to her black velvet dress. Her mother had said: "You should always have an evening dress in case you should need one suddenly. You never know. And black velvet is *so* serviceable."

It was. This black velvet looked as good as it had ten years ago; there had been very few opportunities of wearing it.

But this morning Mrs. Leigh had come to Miss Robinson's room and had said: "Miss Robinson, I wonder if you would join us for dinner to-night. Mr. Danesborough is coming, but his sister is unable to accompany him."

Miss Robinson had expressed her willingness. There was an air of conspiracy, she had thought, about Mrs. Leigh, as though she were hatching some plot in which Miss Robinson was to play a part.

Could it be? Ever since the death of the Reverend Charles Danesborough's wife, Miss Robinson had had hopes. After all, she herself was a clergyman's daughter and Church of England, so it did not really seem as though her hopes were so very wild. Mr. Danesborough needed a wife; and Amanda would soon no longer be needing a governess. Could it be that the Leighs, knowing they must soon decide to dispense with her services, were thinking that, since they must deprive her of a pupil, they might provide her with a husband?

How very happy she would make him! The Gipsy at the Fair had said that she would have a choice of two men. One would be enough if he were as eligible as Charles Danesborough!

She was sure she would get on very well with his family; they were such nice people. And she would not interfere with Miss Danesborough's running of the house; they would be the best of friends. She had always admired her—far more than she had the somewhat frivolous Mrs. Danesborough, who she was convinced had been most unsuitable.

As for Frith, who must be nearly nineteen now, he was a pleasant young man, although rather high-spirited. Then there was his sister Alice, about Amanda's age—a quiet, pleasant child. How glad she was that she had always shown the greatest eagerness to help in church affairs.

She was glowing with excitement and apprehension when Amanda, looking disturbed, came into the room.

"Miss Robinson, I'm to go down to dinner to-night."

"You?" said Miss Robinson.

Amanda nodded gloomily. "Yes. Mamma has just told me. I'm to wear my new blue silk. She said, would you look at it to make sure everything is all right? Why do they want *me* to go down? Do you know?"

Miss Robinson's lips tightened and her red hands trembled a little. "I suppose they think you are growing up and it is time you took your place in such affairs."

"Shall I always have to go down to dinner, then?"

Amanda was visualizing two ordeals at the dining-room table every day, instead of one.

"It might be that this is a special occasion. You are as yet only fifteen, and that is rather young. I should not have thought your father would have wished you to join a grown-up dinner party just yet. But I suppose he has some reason. I too I am going."

"Oh . . . Robbie . . . you want to go! *Why* do you want to go?"

"My dear child, it will make a change. It is rather pleasant to meet people now and then."

"Whom shall we meet?"

"It is quite a small and informal dinner party, I gather. Just the Rector and his son, I believe."

"It will be the first time Frith has come to dinner. What about Alice? Why is she not invited?"

"My dear, I do not know why she is not asked. Now, let me look at your dress."

The blue dress was spread out on the bed, and as she examined it Miss Robinson said: "You will soon have a real ball dress, I suppose. I expect your father and mother will be making plans for you."

Amanda flung her arms about her governess—not that she wished to embrace her, but because she wished not to see her face.

"It'll be years and years, Robbie . . . years and years. . . ." She withdrew her arms. "I'm glad you'll be there, Robbie. It's certainly strange . . . both of us having to go."

"I am going because Miss Danesborough is unable to come. She is slightly unwell, I understand."

"Poor Miss Danesborough! I thought she was never ill."

Miss Robinson smiled secretly. Could it be that Miss Danesborough had arranged this? Could it be that she thought it was high time her brother had a wife? Miss Danesborough had managed the affairs of the parish so efficiently—for poor Mrs. Danesborough had been quite hopeless at the task—that it was possible she might wish to carry her efficiency even farther. After all, one never knew what unmarried men would do—even rectors—and it might be that Miss Danesborough thought it would be advisable to choose the second Mrs. Danesborough quickly, before the Rector committed the folly of choosing for himself.

Such thoughts were pleasant; they carried Miss Robinson gaily through that December afternoon.

At dinner Miss Robinson found herself on the right hand of the Rector, who was charming to her in his rather boisterous way. How pleased he must be to find her so conversant with church matters. Laura Leigh looked quite attractive in her plum-coloured silk; and even the master of the house appeared less sombre than usual. He said a very special grace which was longer than the one he usually said.

Steert stood waiting to serve, with Bess beside him, and Ada and Jane came back and forth from the kitchen. Amanda wondered what Lilith was doing, and she was certain that she would put in an appearance sooner or later, because Lilith had been very eager to know about the ways of the gentry ever since she had learned of the relationship she bore to them. She would come in on some pretext during the meal, Amanda felt sure.

Frith was smiling at Amanda, looking older than the boy with whom she rode and who had, the last time he had come to tea, shown her the body of a rabbit which he had dissected. He wanted to be a surgeon, he had confided to her and to Alice; and there might be some trouble about that, for naturally his aunt—the more forceful of his guardians—wished him to go into the church. But Frith was the sort of young man who would do what he wanted, thought Amanda; there was a look about his mouth which indicated that quite clearly.

The pheasant-flavoured soup was being served and conversation between Paul Leigh and the Rector was mostly of parish matters, the fury of the gales which had been fiercer than usual this October, and the many signs that the coming winter would be a hard one.

The fish was crimped soles and turbot served with lobster sauce.

"This," said Laura when they had all been served, and it was almost as though she had received a cue from her husband, "is our daughter's first dinner party."

Mr. Danesborough raised his glass. "Congratulations, Amanda my dear."

"Thank you," said Amanda.

"And what do you think of your first dinner party?" asked Frith. His eyes twinkled: he had changed; now that she saw him among adults she realized that he was really one of them. He went away to college, out into the world; he was growing bold in readiness for the battle he would have to wage with Miss Danesborough and perhaps his father. He had travelled far from this little corner of England.

"I am enjoying it very much, thank you," said Amanda demurely.

She felt that her parents and Miss Robinson were listening to every word she said, every inflection of her voice; she felt as though she were repeating a lesson which she should have prepared. How could she have prepared it when she had no warning of the test, and had no idea why it was being made?

"My daughter," said her father, "is now fifteen years of age. We feel it is time she made a few excursions from the schoolroom, so that she will be prepared for the battle of life when she has to face it."

Amanda was silent; she was blushing; she felt so inadequate, not understanding why they had wanted her to come to dinner to-night. Frith was smiling at her, and the wine was making her flesh tingle. If her father had not been there it might have been true to say that she was enjoying herself.

Conversation was taken over by the men once more. It was about the war which America was waging against Mexico; and by the time the lamb cutlets were appearing they were discussing the great topics of the day—the repeal of the Corn Laws and the merits of Free Trade and Protection.

Now and then Miss Robinson put in a word just to show that, although she was a woman, she, as a governess, was in a class apart; she was, it must be admitted, a little clever, but she was careful to agree with everything Mr. Danesborough said while she made sure of never going against Mr. Leigh.

"I do so agree. My father was of the same opinion as yourself. He was, of course, also in the Church."

"That's interesting," said Mr. Danesborough, who was always courteous to everybody. "And what part of the country was that?"

"In Berkshire," said Miss Robinson, glowing. "A small place not far from Wantage."

"Now I wonder if it would be the James Robinson I knew . . . why, it must be forty years ago. . . .' "

Miss Robinson's father was not, unfortunately, that James Robinson, but how comforting it was to be talking thus to Mr. Danesborough—not at a jumble sale, not in the church as pastor and parishioner, but at the same dinner table.

Frith was talking to Mr. Leigh, and it was clear from Mr. Leigh's expression that he did not greatly like what Frith was saying. Listening, Amanda marvelled at Frith's courage; he did not seem in the least afraid of her father.

They were discussing a Mr. Charles Dickens—a most unpleasant man according to Mr. Leigh, a most interesting one according to Frith.

"I would not," said Mr. Leigh, "allow my family to read anything the fellow writes."

"But why not, sir?"

"Why not, indeed! Because, my dear boy, I consider what he writes to be unfit for females."

"But, sir, compare him with Balzac and—er . . ."

"I do not wish to compare him with any, and I certainly wish still less to waste my time with a French teller of tales, who, I gather, is even more unpleasant than his English counterpart."

"Sir, if you will forgive my saying so, you are missing a good deal."

"I do forgive you, Frith," said Mr. Leigh with dignity. "I forgive you on the score of your youth, inexperience and irresponsibility."

Frith shrugged his shoulders and smiled suddenly at Amanda.

Mr. Leigh went on: "Although I do not wish to sully my mind with the works of this Dickens, I did read something about him the other day which convinces me that I am not alone in my opinion. It was in the *Athenœum*, I believe. 'A meteor,' said the writer, 'which we have seen darting across the sky and which has fallen limply to the ground without even exploding into coloured lights . . .' or some such phrase. Have you such a high opinion of your Mr. Dickens now, Frith?"

"Quite as high, but a very low one of the critic."

Mr. Danesborough gave one of his booming laughs. "Frith is young yet," he said. "He is fierce in all his loves and hates. That is youth."

"It sounds distinctly radical to me," said Mr. Leigh severely.

Laura changed the subject as the chicken was brought in. "I have heard," she said, looking at her husband so that Amanda understood at once that it was from him that she had heard this, "that Peel has committed political suicide over the repeal of the Corn Laws."

"That is undoubtedly a fact," said Mr. Danesborough.

"He should have realized that when he removed the tax," said Mr. Leigh. "And what is going to happen to our farmers, do you think? What price will they get for their corn now that there is all this competition?"

"The main thing is," said Frith, "that the poor will get cheap bread. The farmers will look after themselves, I don't doubt."

Mr. Danesborough threw an amused glance at his son, and Laura said quickly: "I don't know what the world's coming to. With income tax sevenpence in the pound . . . I really don't know. . . ."

"We live in sad times!" said Mr. Danesborough in a merry tone which indicated that he thought them anything but sad.

"And not," added Mr. Leigh sternly looking at Frith, "made any better by this radical fellow Dickens's playing on the feelings of the illiterate."

Frith was argumentative by nature, and to-night he seemed particularly so. "Not the illiterate, sir," he pointed out, "but the literate. It is the sufferings of the illiterate that he wishes the literate to understand."

Amanda felt excited. It seemed to her that Frith was of the same mind as William. Perhaps all young people were; perhaps this was not so much a fight between the rich and the poor as between the old and the young.

"Frith," said his father with a smile, "has become a member of his college debating society; and it is a fact that whenever an opinion is stated in our house, he must immediately take the opposite view in the hope of luring us into a debate."

"Ah," said Laura, "I guessed something of the sort. Why, if you do that, Frith, people will take you for a very argumentative young man."

"And that," said Frith, "is what I believe I am."

The lemon pudding had been brought in, and Amanda was aware that Lilith had entered the room; she was carrying the almond sauce. Steert was glaring at her. He knew that Lilith had contrived this to satisfy her curiosity. She had no right to be in the dining-room.

Amanda looked at Lilith and flushed slightly; Frith noticed the flush and looked at Lilith, trying to ascertain the cause. Lilith met his gaze. She could hardly believe that he was the Rector's son. She had thought of him as a rather haughty boy who gave himself airs. He had never given her a glance before, although she had sometimes helped with the schoolroom tea which he had attended with his sister.

But now that he was in dinner dress he no longer seemed a boy. He was so handsome compared with the melancholy master and his big, red-faced father. Lilith, with her quick intuition, knew why Amanda was at that dinner table in her beautiful blue silk dress. It was because the Leighs and the Danesboroughs wanted Frith and Amanda to marry.

Lilith ignored the disapproving glances which her presence had evoked. She did not see the glass and the cutlery and the elaborate centre piece of flowers; she saw only Frith Danesborough, handsome, debonair and outrageously bold; and she was conscious of a jealousy towards Amanda more bitter than that which she had felt in the old days before she had come to the house and Amanda had become her friend.

"Get out into the kitchen," hissed Steert; and Lilith went.

Mr. Danesborough said that the pudding was delicious; and he added that he did not know when he had tasted such a delicious pudding—unless it was the last time he had dined with the Leighs.

Conversation was general after that, and although the men returned to politics, Frith did not intrude. Instead, he talked to Amanda, asked her what she did all day; and Amanda answered shyly, wondering whether her father would be annoyed with her for speaking while he was speaking; but she had to answer Frith's questions. Then her mother and Miss Robinson joined in and she felt relieved.

Laura eventually gave the signal and the ladies rose, leaving the men at the table.

"Frith is a little captious," said Laura as they entered the drawing-room. "I suppose it is his age."

"Perhaps he feels the lack of a mother," suggested Miss Robinson.

"I think it is that college of his. Young men . . . they leave home and then feel they are no longer boys. They must have ideas of their own."

"The young will always voice their ideas," said Miss Robinson.

"I am afraid that Mr. Leigh may be a little cross with him. I suppose *you*, Amanda, agree with everything he says?"

There was an archness in Laura's voice, in the glance she threw at her daughter, which gave Miss Robinson a clue to the meaning of Amanda's presence at the dinner party.

Miss Robinson, in spite of what she believed to be her success with Mr. Danesborough, felt a sick panic within her. So they were thinking of marrying Amanda already! But she was only fifteen. Miss Robinson understood. Despairing of ever having a son, they wished for a grandson. Frith Danesborough was eligible in every way. The Danesboroughs were a moneyed family. If Frith went into the Church and took over his father's living, he and his wife could live in the neighbourhood, and his children could be brought up in the shadow of Leigh House. Miss Robinson's knees began to tremble—a silly habit of theirs lately. In this instance they did so because she knew that her days as Amanda's governess were numbered.

Amanda was remarking that she did not know enough to say whether she agreed with Frith; but if the repealing of the Corn Laws really meant that the poor would have more to eat, she was sure that Peel . . . and Frith were right.

"Do not tell your father so," said Mrs. Leigh with a laugh.

Miss Robinson did not speak, and Amanda noticed the well-remembered look of fear on her face.

Later, in the drawing-room, Frith said to Amanda: "This is past your usual bedtime, I suppose?"

"Much past it."

"Are you tired?"

"No. Although I go to bed early, I am rarely asleep at this hour."

"You look just as childish as ever. Putting on a blue frock and wearing your hair in a new way does not alter that."

"No. I suppose not."

"I hope I haven't offended your father. Have I, do you think?"

She was silent, and he laughed in the booming and infectious manner in which his father did. "Oh well, we can't help it, can we? The older generation always thinks that, although they themselves were mature at sixteen, we are so retarded that we remain at the mental age of six all our lives."

"Do they?"

"They do. Don't let them bully you, Amanda. Stand up for your rights. That's what I'm going to do. Like to hear a secret?" He leaned forward, his eyes sparkling. "They're watching us, you know. It's rather amusing to appear to be talking about trivialities, but to be talking about the most important things. Amanda, listen. I am definitely not going into the Church."

"They'll make you, surely."

"Make me! They couldn't. You can lead a horse to the water, but you can't make him drink. Ever heard that, Miss Amanda?"

"Yes; I have indeed."

"It's true."

"You can drive the horse into the water."

"That wouldn't make him drink."

"You can keep him from drinking until he's so thirsty that he'll rush to do so."

"You're a philosopher, Amanda. These analogies never work out. I'm not a horse and the Church is not a pond. I'll tell you this: I shall never go into the Church. Here's another secret. I have already started on my medical career. I've told the aunt. That's why she is unable to come to-night. She is prostrate with grief, disappointment and so on. To-night I shall tell my father."

"Oh, Frith, that's splendid. No one will be able to stop you. They'll never understand, though, why you should prefer a medical profession to the Church."

"They should, then. It's simple enough. I'm more interested in people's bodies than their souls."

"It's a great profession, healing the sick. I think it's the greatest of all professions. . . ."

There were tears in her eyes and he laughed at her. "Dear Niobe! But don't cry now, for Heaven's sake. They'll think I've been bullying you. Do you cry as much as ever? Alice could always make you cry when she sang that old ballad about the girl going out into the falling snow to freeze to death. I'm going to lecture you, Amanda. You're too sentimental. You want to save some of those tears for your own troubles and not fritter them away on other people. Everyone is not as nice as you are, you know. *I* don't think about removing people's sufferings. I'm interested in cutting them down the middle to see what's inside. Who was the black-eyed witch who made an appearance at dinner?''

''Lilith. . . . You know Lilith.''

''Lilith . . . of course. She looked different to-night. I've never noticed her before.''

Laura came over to them. ''I think it's time you said good night, dear,'' she said to Amanda. ''It's the first time she has been up so late, Frith. I'm going to ask Miss Robinson to take her up now.''

''Good night,'' said Amanda to Frith.

Frith took her hand and bowed over it. ''I hope that when you attend your next dinner party I shall be a member of the company.''

When Miss Robinson helped Amanda to unhook her dress, she noticed that the governess's hands were trembling. She turned to her suddenly in an access of pity, and, putting her arms about Miss Robinson's thin shoulders, she said: ''Robbie, when I marry, I shall have no one . . . no one but you to look after my children. It is a solemn oath. I swear it.''

Lilith watched them ride out from the stables—Amanda, Frith and Frith's sister Alice. Lilith had eyes for none but the young man. He was nearly six feet tall and his sleek fair hair was almost hidden by his hard hat. In his riding clothes he looked as handsome as he had at the dinner table—in fact, the most handsome man Lilith had ever seen.

Oh, if only she were riding on a horse with him! She saw herself in a neat riding habit, her horse galloping and Frith in pursuit, laughing, saying her name in that drawl of his which she had once mocked and which she knew she would never mock again; for in future she would never mock anything that he did.

Mrs. Derry sent Bess out after her.

''What be doing?'' demanded Bess. ''There's the taties to peel. What be garping at?''

She had never before felt so conscious of the unfairness of

life. The dirty brown water ran up her arm as she jabbed viciously at the potatoes and she thought of Amanda on her horse, cantering, galloping with him beside her.

She had lain on Amanda's bed on the night of the dinner party and she had made her tell everything that had been said that evening; and she had been listening all the time for what *he* had said and done. Since that day when Amanda had been to the Fair and seen Salome dance, Lilith had dreamed of wearing a pink dress trimmed with red roses, of dancing as Salome danced, of throwing off her muslin veils to stand before an admiring audience in flesh-coloured tights. Now she had another dream to evoke alternately with that one.

The potatoes were done and in the pot. They were all busy now, so Lilith slipped out of the kitchen. She had to get away from the house; she did not care what the consequences were.

She ran as fast as she could down the steep, rough hill past the Barbican Farm right down to the town; she sped across the bridge and did not stop running until she reached the cottage on the west quay. She was delighted to see Grandmother Lil at the door.

"This be a surprise, my handsome."

Lilith flung herself down beside the old woman; she was panting, and her eyes glistened with the tears she would not shed.

"You been running away?"

"I wanted to come home. I wanted to talk to 'ee."

"Well, and what's been happening at Leigh House then to make 'ee do this? Tell your old grandmother."

"They'm thinking of marrying her," said Lilith.

"Well, that don't surprise me. She be growing up. Nigh on sixteen her be. 'Tis time she was married."

"They be going to marry her to Mr. Danesborough's son."

Grandmother Lil nodded. "Reckon it don't need a lot of brains to guess that. They was always meant for each other."

Lilith was silent.

"Ah," went on the old grandmother, "I do know what you be thinking. You'm of an age . . . you and she. If her's to be a wife, why not you? You says to yourself . . . I've just as much right to have a husband found for me, that I have. But 'tain't so, my pretty. You see, her be the rightful daughter. Her father was born in wedlock and though yours were too, 'tweren't the same thing, as I did tell 'ee. She be an educated young lady and you ain't that, my little 'un. Her do know what be in books, and there's some as do set terrible store by what be in books. You want to look for a husband . . . if 'tis a husband you'm wanting . . . and you want to mark him down, and then you want to set out and get him. Now, there's Tom Polgard. He's a fine figure of a young man, and he'll have lands and wealth coming to him when his father goes.''

"Polgard!" cried Lilith, spitting as the fishermen did. "Pigs . . . swine . . . I hate 'em. Look at William and the way he lives. Do you think I'd have aught to do with Polgards?''

" 'Twould be different, my pretty, if you was mistress of the farm like. Why, think on it. You could look after William . . . and he needs looking after.''

"And what about Farmer and Missus?''

"You'd be a match for 'em, my queen; and they won't live for ever.''

"Tom wants to marry our Jane.''

The old woman laughed. "That won't be. Old Polgard do want to marry his eldest to the daughter of a farmer out Barcelona way. Jane'll never get Tom, because there ain't that in her what would get him. And Tom, though he may have the strength of his father's bullocks, ain't got no will of his own. And it's *will* you need if you're to have your way. Now, if it was you instead of Jane . . . I reckon you'd find a way, I do. I reckon you'd have the will. Haven't you a fancy for him?''

"I hate all Polgards.''

"Well, what's wrong with Jim Larkin? He'll follow the steps of his father and his grandfather. You'd have all the rory-tory hats and shally-go-naked gownds in Cornwall if you was to take him. You'd have plenty to eat and a feather bed to sleep on.''

"Plenty to eat is good, and feather beds is the next best thing. But I wouldn't take Jim Larkin, not for roast peacock every day and a feather bed each night of my life.''

"What's come over 'ee, my little 'un? Has someone caught your fancy?''

"No. . . . *No!* But I won't have any that don't.''

"Ho! That's brave talk. I'll tell 'ee what you'd do if you was clever. You'd be looking round for a nice *gentleman* to give 'ee a bit of comfort.''

The old woman thrust her hands into her granddaughter's curls. But there was no comfort for Lilith, even in her grandmother. She was afraid suddenly that if her flight was discovered she might be dismissed, and if she were she would not see Frith when he came to the house.

She jumped up. "I must run back. They'll be terrible put out if they find out I went."

And she would wait for no more, but sped back the way she had come, thinking all the time of her grandmother who had ridden to Altarnon with her first love, the tally-man; and as Lilith felt the wind in her curls *she* was riding pillion, not with a tally-man, but with Frith Danesborough.

It was a cold January day and the east wind was howling down the chimneys. Luncheon was over and Mrs. Derry drowsed by the fire. Lilith seized the opportunity to escape. Jane would see that her work was done for her by the time she returned, and that her absence was not discovered by Mrs. Derry. Bess and Ada knew of Lilith's mission; they would help too. How did any maid know when she might have a lover of her own and need similar assistance?

Before setting out to find Tom Polgard and tell him that if he would go to the spinney at the back of Leigh House that night he would find Jane waiting for him there, Lilith sought Amanda; for she wished Amanda to accompany her to the Polgard Farm.

Some time ago they had talked together while Lilith lay on Amanda's bed, and Lilith had spoken, not only of the sufferings of William, but of those of Napoleon also.

"You must take some food to them," Amanda had said.

And Lilith, who had desired Amanda's company on her proposed trip, had answered: "Then you must bring it, for if I were caught I'd be had up for stealing."

Amanda had agreed to do this and had been collecting food from the kitchen over the past few days.

Amanda was ready to leave with Lilith. Lilith looked at her in her thick cloak and the boots which would keep her feet snug. She was two inches taller than Lilith, although they were of an age; she was beautiful in her rich clothes; and Lilith contrasted her own small pale face with Amanda's rosy one, her own thick black curls with Amanda's sleek golden mane. She decided that it was only Amanda's clothes that need make her jealous.

"Have 'ee got the parcel of food?" asked Lilith.

"Yes."

"Then wait for me at the paddock, and don't 'ee be long about it. 'Tis time we was away."

As they came out to the high road and the east wind tugged at their skirts, Amanda said: "Lilith, something's happened to you. You remember how you were always dancing . . . how you were going to dance the Dance of the Seven Veils one day? You used to say you would be a dancer, and you looked as if you would, when you said that. I used to think you were planning to run away."

Lilith said: "I hate this wind. Where did you ride to this morning?"

"Over to the Rectory. Alice wanted us to try some of the elderberry wine her aunt has taught her to make."

"I reckon you'll only have Miss Alice to ride with soon. Her brother'll be going away soon, I reckon."

"Yes. Lilith . . . there's a bit of trouble at the Rectory. It'll soon be common knowledge, so it doesn't matter about my telling you. Frith's not going into the Church. He's going to be a doctor."

"What do you do when you learn to be a doctor?"

"You pass examinations and go to a hospital to work for a bit, I think."

"I reckon a doctor is a very grand thing to be," said Lilith.

"Yes. I think so too."

"Where will he learn it?"

"In London, I think . . . or perhaps at his University."

"He'll come back here when he has his holidays?"

"Oh yes."

"So it'll be just the same as if he were going to be in the Church with his father?"

"I expect so . . . until he's qualified, of course. Even then he might live here. That will be a long time yet, though."

Lilith ran on ahead; she was thinking of Amanda and William, and herself and Frith. Suppose Amanda married William and made him master of Leigh House; and suppose Frith became the doctor here and surprised the neighbourhood by taking wild Lilith Tremorney to be his wife.

"Let 'em lift their eyebrows," he said in Lilith's imagination. "Let 'em talk all they wish. There's no one as will do for me but you, and there's no one will do for you but me."

But that was Lilith's voice, not his; and that was a wild dream of hers—the wildest she had ever dreamed.

Yet Lilith believed that dreams could come true. She lifted her face to the dark sky, across which the wind was driving the grey clouds like a shepherd gone mad.

"Listen," said Amanda. "I can hear someone calling to the horses."

Lilith stood still listening. "I believe it be William's voice I hear." She led the way through the hedge.

"Keep yourself hid, Amanda," she whispered. "Don't forget we be on Polgard land now."

They crossed the field cautiously, keeping close to the hedge, and in the next field there was William ploughing, and Napoleon was helping him.

"William," called Lilith; and William turned and saw them.

He told Napoleon to look after the plough while he came over to them.

"Amanda have brought you something to eat," said Lilith.

"It's not much," said Amanda. "But we'll come again."

"Where be Tom?" asked Lilith impatiently. "I've got to find him."

"That I couldn't say. He be somewhere about the farm."

"I've got to find him, then. I'll leave you to talk to William. Wait for me in the road, Amanda."

She ran off, leaving Amanda with William.

"William," said Amanda, "we haven't brought as much as we should like to. But we'll come again in a little while. There's just something there for you . . . and Napoleon. Oh, how are you, William? Are they still as cruel as ever?"

William seemed tongue-tied; he looked at the food Amanda had thrust into his hands, but made no attempt to eat it. "They don't mean to be cruel perhaps, Miss Amanda," he stammered at length. " 'Tis just . . . 'tis just that they're natural . . . what's natural to them, you do see."

"Oh, William, couldn't you do something? Couldn't you get away?"

He looked over his shoulder. "That's what I plan, Miss Amanda. I save my money. I save it every week, and when I've got enough I'm going away from here to seek my fortune. I'm getting wages of a shilling a day—although there's generally some excuse to be made about paying all that. But what I do get be money, and I'm saving it. I tell no one. . . . I reckon if Farmer and his wife knew I had that money they'd find some way of taking it from me."

"Are you afraid they'd steal it, William?"

He nodded.

"William, let me keep it for you. I'd mind it very carefully. I've got a little box of mother-of-pearl, and only I have the key. Would you trust me to look after it for you, William?"

"I'd trust you with my life, Miss Amanda. I keep it tied up in a bit of rag and sewed in my coat." He began ripping away the stitches.

She said: "Oh, William, where have you thought of going?"

"That I can't say. Travelling like. Perhaps like a tinker . . . going over the Tamar. We'm in a backwater here, Miss Amanda. I thought I'd like to travel through Devonshire to Dorset, say." He handed her the money. "There be twenty-one shillings there, Miss Amanda."

"I'll take the greatest care of it. I'll lock it up as soon as I get home. And if you ever want some of it . . . or all of it . . . you must tell me. I know now that you won't go away without telling me."

"I wouldn't go away without telling 'ee, Miss Amanda, if I did think you'd be wanting to know."

They smiled at each other, forgetful of the biting east wind.

Lilith kept close to the hedge. It would not do for her to be caught. Old Farmer Polgard would suspect that she had come to steal something—the old rogue. The cows in the field looked at her, as she approached, with bold curiosity.

"Heigh oop!" said Lilith. They waited until she approached, and then began to move slowly away.

The wind was bitter; and she was startled by the sudden, jesting laugh of a woodpecker. She looked about her urgently. Where was Tom Polgard? Where was he likely to be at this time of day?

There was a barn in the next field; she made her way towards it and, gently pushing open the door half an inch or so, peeped in. She caught her breath, and even in that first second of surprise she rejoiced that she had been so careful. The barn, she reckoned, some distance from the farmhouse, would naturally provide cosy shelter on such a day for those that needed it.

She drew back hastily and ran as fast as she could round the barn. She stood leaning against it, poised, ready for flight in case someone should appear round that side. Her cheeks were flaming; her heart was pounding. Then she heard a voice say: " 'Tis all right. 'Twere only the wind.'' The barn door was shut with a bang. And after a second or so Lilith began to run as fast as she could away from the barn.

Laura sat at her embroidery in the drawing-room. It was the after-dinner hour which she dreaded most. Mr. Leigh was seated at the table; he was reading his Bible.

He had just spoken and his words had terrified Laura: "You seem to be quite your normal self now, my dear.''

She had put her hand to her heart and answered: "I still feel very tired.''

"You should take more exercise.''

"I suppose I should, but that seems to make me more tired.''

Then he had returned to his reading.

Was he thinking of trying the experiment once more? He was restless, she knew. Last night she had heard him come to her door and she had lain cowering in her bed until he had gone away. Yes, he was certainly restless. He knew it was dangerous for her to attempt to have another child, yet he was trying to convince himself that this was not so. When he prayed, as she knew he did, for a son, she believed he was trying to convince himself that the attempt would not be dangerous. If he had been like his father, there would have been other women. His father's wife had been delicate, but how much more peaceful than Laura's her life must have been; and how ironical it was that a good man could not give his wife the peace and comfort that a bad man could.

Strange thoughts had come to her lately. She had even thought of running away, of going to one of her sisters in London. But how could she leave Paul? She would be penniless. The little fortune which had been hers when she married was his now. Life was so unfair to women. Why should marriage put a halter round a woman's neck? Why should she not, if she found it intolerable, be able to go away from it?

She was becoming frantic.

Mr. Leigh was watching her, and when he spoke she started

violently. "I have decided that young Frith Danesborough is something of a disappointment."

"Have you?"

"Yes. He is arrogant, irresponsible and disobedient."

"Do . . . do you think so?"

"Indeed I do."

"You . . . you have decided . . ."

"I have decided, my love, that the plans I had for him and our daughter shall be put aside."

"Oh! But . . . he . . . he . . . he is a rather charming young man."

"A charming young man! What do you mean?"

"Only that . . . he is very pleasant . . . and Amanda seems to have become so fond of him."

"I assure you that *I* find him far from pleasant. His behaviour at dinner the other night could scarcely be called pleasant, I should have imagined, even by the most empty-headed woman. As for Amanda, she will, I hope, not be so unmaidenly as to become fond of any man but the one she is to marry."

"I . . . I am sure. . . . Yes . . . You are right, of course."

"He has decided against the Church, I hear. Did you ever hear such arrogant nonsense? He will choose his own way of life, he says. He will take up a medical career. If he were my son . . ."

Laura shivered, as she did whenever he talked of a son.

"If," he went on sternly, "I had been *blessed* with a son, I should have turned him out of my house had he shown such disobedience."

"Mr. Danesborough seems to be reconciled . . ."

"Mr. Danesborough is a fool, my dear. He lets his son and that sister of his rule his life. I shall be beginning to think his children are having a bad influence on Amanda."

"Do you mean that they are not to be allowed to come here any more?"

"You take me too literally, Mrs. Leigh. How could we close our doors to the Danesboroughs? Our family has been on friendly terms with theirs for generations. No. I merely wish you to know that I frown on the furtherance of our plan. There must be no understanding between Frith Danesborough and our daughter."

"I . . . I hope it has not gone too far, as we have rather encouraged . . ."

"Mrs. Leigh! What are you saying?" he thundered. "Too far? We encouraged . . . *what*? Pray be explicit. I await your answer in trepidation."

"Oh, nothing . . . nothing at all. I just thought that they might have grown fond of one another."

"As I told you before," he said in exasperation, "I hope no daughter of mine would be so unmaidenly as to let any affair of this nature go, as you so graphically describe it, 'too far.' I will acquaint you with my plans, which are these: When I was visiting my brother in Devonshire, I talked with him. *He*, as you know, has *six* sons."

She blushed hotly, like a little girl at the bottom of the class who is shown the top girl's marks.

"Yes, I know. They . . . they must be very happy."

"Six sons and three daughters. 'Happy is the man who hath his quiver full.' "

"Happy indeed," she said dutifully.

"Well, this is what I have in mind: I wish our daughter to be married as soon as possible. I had, as you know, selected Frith Danesborough. He is a neighbour; he is of good family; and he will be comfortably off, so that with Amanda's inheritance, they would have been able to have lived graciously. But the young man disappoints me, and God has mercifully opened my eyes to his shortcomings. Now it has occurred to me that although my brother is not a poor man, all his six sons cannot be as rich as he is, since his fortune must necessarily be divided among them. I have had this in mind for some time; indeed, I must have been inspired, because I hinted it when I last visited my brother. You must know that it would be a great sadness in my life if I were forced to believe that in the future there would be others than Leighs in this house."

Laura wanted to cover her face with her hands and burst into tears. Now it seemed that the whole line of Leighs, from the days of the Tudors when they had built this house, were accusing her: "Always Leighs at Leigh House until *you* failed to produce a male heir."

"I propose to bring our daughter's cousin, Anthony Leigh, here on a visit, and before he has left I hope to announce his engagement to our daughter."

"She . . . is very young."

"She is sixteen. You were married when you were seventeen."

"Yes . . . but children seem younger now."

"What nonsense! Amanda is marriageable. She shall marry her cousin, Anthony Leigh. They will live here and I trust before long, as I am denied a son, I shall see my grandson at Leigh House. Now! You know my wishes."

"What . . . what am I to do?"

"Discourage Mr. Frith Danesborough from calling too frequently. Prepare the girl by talking of her cousins and their excellent qualities. Try to imbue *her* with a sense of her duty."

"I will try."

"Very well. I shall write to my brother, and I think in the spring Anthony might visit us. He is a young man of twenty—pleasant and God-fearing. Our daughter will find herself most fortunate."

Laura nodded and began to ply her needle.

Lilith could not sleep. She lay in her narrow bed and watched the shadows in the room as the clouds chased one another across the face of the moon. Now it was light; now it was dark. Now she could see the faces of the sleeping girls; now they were just vague figures in their beds.

The wind shook the branches of the tree outside the window and the twigs scratched the panes. There was a pattern on Jane's face; it moved as the tree swayed. It was as though the mischievous old moon was laughing because the wind was playing tricks and using the tree branch as a pencil to draw wrinkles on Jane's face, like a child defacing a picture in a book and with a few deft touches turning a young woman into an old one.

And she'll get old too, thought Lilith, afore she gets Tom Polgard. That farmer's daughter over to Barcelona would get Tom. He was such a softie. He was like one of his father's sheep. "Baa! Baa! I want Jane. But I'll go which way I'm pushed."

Fools . . . all of them . . . all except Lilith.

It was a pity she was so young. If only she were a little older. If she had had more experience of the world she would know what to do. She burrowed under the bedclothes and thought of that moment when she had opened the barn door; she saw again vividly what she had seen then and she felt excited and powerful. Yes, that was what had been given to her: Power! But she was not sure whether she was old enough . . . strong enough to use it.

It was a long time before she could sleep, and when she did she dreamed of Frith Danesborough. And in the dream she said to him: "You must obey me. You must do just as I wish, because I have the power to make you."

She could not have slept long, for when she awoke again there was the moon still making patterns on Jane's face. Old . . . young. . . . Old as she'll be afore she gets Tom Polgard!

Sometimes Jane cried in the night—silly, frustrated crying. What was the good of crying? If you want something you should go out and get it. Crying in bed at night helped no one.

She slept at last and they had to shake her to awaken her in the morning, and when she rose her dreams were still with her. She hardly recognized that slim slip of a girl in the old mottled glass as the powerful person she had dreamed she was.

Going about her work, she was thoughtful. Once she almost confided in Amanda. But Amanda was ignorant, except for book-learning; and what Lilith had seen in the barn was quite outside book-learning.

It was two days later when she made up her mind what to do.

She was strong enough to do it; she knew she was. She knew too that if she failed in this she would lose her faith in herself. Why should she be afraid? It was not for her to fear anyone. That was for others.

She hung about the Polgard Farm until she saw him. He was carrying one of the lambs and he was even uglier than she remembered him; perhaps because he was carrying a lamb, like Jesus carried in the pictures, he seemed all the uglier, for there was nothing of the Good Shepherd about Farmer Polgard.

It was near the barn that they saw each other. She stood stock still staring at him, and he was so astonished that he just remained where he was, gaping. He was a slow-thinking man and he could not speak for a moment; he was bewildered to see a trespasser on his land who did not turn and fly in terror at the sight of him.

It was Lilith who spoke first. "Farmer Polgard, I do want a word with you."

The hair in his nose seemed to vibrate; his lips were drawn back in a snarl.

"You . . ." he stammered. "You . . . you . . . imp!"

Lilith kept a comfortable distance between them. She was four feet ten inches tall and slim as a wand. He was six feet tall and correspondingly broad. She imagined that he would have no chance if it came to a chase; but if those great hairy hands were to seize her, he could kill her as easily as he killed a rabbit.

She kept her eyes on him, alert, waiting. Her voice was high-pitched with nervousness and defiance. "You'd better be careful how you do talk to me, Farmer."

She paused, waiting for the effect of these words to show itself, but it was obvious that his slow brain was numb with bewilderment. No one had ever spoken to him like that except his wife.

"But if you listen to me," went on Lilith, "and if you do as I say, you won't have nothing to fear."

He spluttered. "You . . . you . . . I'll have you flogged . . . you brat. I'll have you . . . locked up. I will. I'll kill you with my own hands."

"You won't. People gets hanged for killing. You'd better have a care. You've got to be very careful, because I know something about you. 'Tis something you wouldn't like your missus to know. I saw you in the barn with that fat dairy maid of yours, Dolly Brent. 'Twas three days ago. I looked in and saw 'ee. My word, wasn't no mistaking what you was up to."

He lumbered forward, but she had stepped quickly back.

"Don't you go making no fool of yourself, Farmer. You've got to listen to what I say. I saw you . . . and I saw Dolly too. I could go and tell Mrs. Polgard. And I will . . . unless you stop me."

"I . . . I'll stop you. I'll break every bone . . ."

"No, you won't, then. For one thing, you won't catch me. And if you don't stand still and listen to me I'll run screaming to your house and tell 'em you're after doing to me what you do to Dolly Brent."

She was triumphant now, enjoying this. She was a young David—small and lithe, ready to conquer this hairy Goliath. He had the strength, but strength was not much good against brains . . . particularly when the brains could be swiftly carried away to safety.

"Don't you go thinking you can save yourself by getting rid of me. 'Twouldn't do. I'll tell 'ee about that. But first hear what you've got to do if you want to go on meeting Dolly in the barn and don't want Missus to know. You've got to do what I say. You've got to let your Tom marry our Jane and you've got to treat William right.''

He was staring at her as though he did not understand her words.

"Keep your distance," she warned. "Take one step nearer to me and I'll run screaming to the farmhouse. I reckon that wouldn't be nice for you. I reckon Dolly would be sent off. I reckon . . ."

"You shut your mouth," he growled. "I'll kill you." But she noticed with satisfaction that he was obeying her orders. He was keeping himself under control; his right foot was ready, but his slow brain was controlling it, was urging caution.

"That's all you've got to do. Let them two marry, and treat William right. 'Tis only what you ought to do."

"You . . . you . . ." He was almost sobbing in his rage.

But she laughed, and her laughter sounded to him like the laughter of demons.

"You wait . . ." he said. "You wait . . ."

She was suddenly frightened. The lamb in his arms began to bleat as though it were aware of the anger in the man who held it; a chaffinch began to try out a few notes; and the wind made a singing noise in the hedges. Lilith thought: If I cried out now, no one would hear me. He was powerful, this man. He would think of some means of destroying her. Perhaps one night, if she ventured out, he would creep silently upon her and she would feel those hairy hands about her throat. Perhaps he would catch her in a lonely lane when he was driving his gig, and drive right over her. Perhaps he would take her in his strong arms and crush her, and throw her over the cliffs.

He was dumbfounded now because his brain could not work quickly, but when he had made up his mind what he could do, he would dash at it like a mad bull.

But her fears disappeared and she felt powerful, as she had in her dreams.

"Now listen here, Farmer. Don't you try nothing. 'Twould be worse for you if you did. You've got to do what I say, unless you want your wife to know about you and Dolly. It ain't so hard, is it? Jane's a good worker. And you've only got to treat William right. That's all you got to do, and it ain't no more than you ought. You needn't think you can hurt me either, because I ain't the only one that knows. . . .''

He clenched his fist and she saw how it was shaking, shaking with rage which he longed to let loose and dared not.

"It's that brother of yourn," he growled. "By God . . ."

She shook her head. "No, it ain't then . . .''

"It's that sly sister of yourn, that's who 'tis. You've made this up between you."

"No. 'Tain't that. Perhaps there's others on this farm as knows about you and Dolly. I don't know nothing about that. But there be one other as I told this to, and one as you dursn't touch, because her be quite out of your reach. I've said to her, 'If aught happens to me, if harm comes to me, you'll know who's done it, 'cause I know what he's been up to with Dolly in the barn.' You don't know who that be. Well, I'll tell 'ee. 'Tis Miss Amanda Leigh. And if aught happened to me, Miss Amanda Leigh would know who's to blame. They hang you up, Farmer Polgard, for breaking people's bones. 'Twould be folly, when all you has to do is let your son marry where he's a mind to . . . and to treat my brother as he's got a right to expect.''

As she spoke she was backing away; the distance between them was growing; then swiftly she began to run; and having reached the edge of the field, she looked back. He was still standing there, the lamb in his arms, a bewildered and worried shepherd.

Nobody understood why the Polgards suddenly decided to allow their son to marry Jane Tremorney—no one but Lilith, that is to say. As for Lilith, a smile of delight would involuntarily spread itself across her face whenever the coming wedding was mentioned, and she gave herself such airs that she became almost intolerable, even to Amanda. Jane was the only one who would put up with her, but then Jane was so happy that she could see nothing wrong in anything about her.

In the Polgard farmhouse great preparations were being made for the wedding, because, mean as Annie Polgard was, she was now a conventional woman, and when her eldest son was married it must be a proper wedding that she might show the whole neighbourhood that the Polgards were people of substance.

She herself set to preparing the feast. She was not going to have her son's wedding celebrated in some dirty little cottage on the quay, home of the bride though it might be—she was not as conventional as all that. No, the wedding of Tom Polgard should be celebrated in his own home, and his own mother would preside over the occasion.

She was an obstinate woman, but if she could be shown a way of saving money she would always be ready to alter her views. She had been set on that girl from Barcelona for Tom, but Jos had won her round to his way of thinking.

"What do 'ee think I heard about her?" said Jos. "Maid! She be no maid. Why, if our Tom did marry her, he'd be the laughing-stock of the countryside."

Annie Polgard did not see that Tom's being the laughing-stock of the countryside was important if the girl inherited a nice bit from her father.

However, Jos went on: "She do think more of dancing and making dresses for herself than of making cream and butter, Missus."

That *was* a matter for consideration. Flighty girls were no use to Annie Polgard.

"There be sommat else I thought of, Missus. People round abouts don't like their neighbours to marry foreigners. I reckon folks wouldn't like Tom to marry a girl from the other side of the river. Barcelona do belong to Polperro more than to Looe, and as you do know, Missus, there be terrible bad blood between them two. Why, if our Tom was to marry that wanton, be sure there'd be bad feelings. Remember how they set fire to Fisherman Penrose's cottage when he did marry the girl from Pelynt."

That was true, Annie had to admit.

She thought of ricks and barns blazing, and sticks and stones breaking her windows. Neighbours never forgot. They'd never take kindly to a stranger from Barcelona. Was it worth it for a flighty girl who thought more of dancing and dressing herself up than making cream and butter?

"He's had his eye on Jane Tremorney, Missus. She's only a cottage girl, I know, but I think of the training she's had up at Leigh House, I do. I reckon a girl couldn't get better training than at a house like that. She do know how to look after a house, I reckon, better than most. She'd be a great help to 'ee, Missus."

At last Annie had been won over. She had Jane brought to her, and Jane answered questions in a right and proper manner.

She showed Annie how gentry put cream between the layers of apples, bacon, onions, mutton and young pigeon when they made a squab pie. She had a light touch with pastry; Annie tested her. She was strong too. So Annie decided that Jos was right; and preparations for Tom's marriage to Jane went ahead.

The young couple seemed almost dazed with delight; they were kissing and cuddling in the open now. Jane sang as she worked, and had to be suppressed by Mrs. Derry, for the master did not like singing unless it was hymns, and they must not be sung in the way Jane was singing now. Mrs. Derry herself was tolerant; she liked a wedding as well as anyone else. It meant she was going to lose a good girl in Jane, but she would choose her own maid this time, as none of the Tremorneys was old enough to come. Bess and Ada were envious—in the nicest possible way. They whispered and giggled together in corners. It seemed that miracles could happen; and if they could happen to Jane Tremorney, why not to them?

Even on the Polgard Farm, life had taken a turn for the better. The farmer used his whip less frequently. He seemed a quieter man, less prone to violence; and Annie, busily preparing for the wedding, did not notice what the farm hands ate; and as the spring crept across the land life became comparatively easy and pleasant.

April came and the meadows were golden with cowslips and the hedges white with hawthorn; the wild violets, wet and sweet-smelling, mingled with the wood sorrel, and the banks looked starry with stitchwort.

In the kitchen, Annie Polgard, with her servants about her, sweat running down her face, her arms covered with flour, her face hot from the oven, shouted her orders. Pies and pasties, bursting with good things, lay on the table; cakes—saffron and fuggan—were to be prepared last thing. The drink had already been made. Annie herself made the shenegrum, stirring the home-brewed beer with her own hands, licking her lips while she added the Jamaican rum, the lemon, the sugar, the nutmeg. The metheglin and the dash-and-darras were ready.

"Oh, there ain't never going to have been a wedding like this. It has cost money . . . but 'tis money well spent, for all the world will know we Polgards for what we be."

She would look at the cider barrel in which the live toad dwelt. He had purified their cider time and time again, for everyone knew that cider was purer for being drunk by a toad and passed through his body.

"You be all right in there, little toad?" she called. "Do your work now . . . and see that Polgards' cider for the wedding be better than any other."

And so, all through those first weeks of April, Annie Polgard prepared for the wedding of her son.

There were gigs and traps outside the church to take the wedding party back to the farm that they might celebrate the occasion.

Mr. and Mrs. Tremorney were proud of their girl who had done so well, who had risen in the social scale and become a farmer's wife. Grandmother Lil was proud. It seemed to her that quiet little Jane had done better than any of them, and that was surely something of a miracle. Jane was proud too, but in such a daze of happiness that she could feel little else. Annie Polgard, all through the service, was thinking of how she was going to surprise them when they saw all the good things there would be to eat and drink. But proudest of all was Lilith. She was the anonymous fairy who had waved her wand; she was the magician.

When the guests reached the farmhouse there was nothing to think of for a while but eating and drinking.

Lilith kept close to her grandmother, longing to tell her of all she had done; she felt that if Grandmother Lil kept looking at Jane with such wondering admiration she would be tempted to do so. But Grandmother Lil forgot even what she presumed to be Jane's cleverness in her admiration for the food.

"Why, I'd forgot there was such food," she said to Lilith. "Taddage pie, eh? That was my favourite in the old days . . . taddage and nattlins. My dear life, Mrs. Polgard do know how to cook . . . no mistake about that. I do wish there'd be a wedding like this every day, that I do. Hey, my queen, you ain't doing justice to all this here. Do they feed you too well up to Leigh House, then? Don't 'ee turn your nose up at food like this. Here be a hog's pudding!"

Annie Polgard watched how much her guests put away. She was half proud, half exasperated. She had made them open their eyes all right, but what it had cost her to do it! At one minute she wanted to press food on her guests; at another to snatch it away. She congratulated herself while she told herself she must have been mazed to lay out so much on good food just because Tom was marrying a cottage girl. Then she reminded herself that she would be turning off one of the dairy-maids and Tom's wife would do the work for naught but her keep, as well as doing a good deal in the farmhouse kitchen. They weren't turning off Dolly Brent. Jos had said that, although she might not be any better than the other dairy girl, she knew how to make herself useful outside, and of course Jos would know about that. Annie reckoned he had noticed her with the cows. So she was taking his word for it that it should be the other that went, not Dolly.

The girls were filling up the glasses and some of the guests were getting a bit boisterous. The drink was going to their heads.

Then they all went into the kitchen, which had been cleared for dancing, and there they sang the old songs, and the bride and the groom danced the old fandango which they said belonged to Spain. Jane danced well and Annie hoped uneasily that she was not going to be too fond of dancing. Not that Annie would allow that.

While the bride and groom were dancing, the guests stamped their feet and made merry jokes about brides and grooms, and Tom and Jane looked so bashful and showed the whole world how happy they were.

Lilith felt it was all oddly unreal. This feeling was due to her secret knowledge that she had brought it about, as well as to the potency of Annie Polgard's shenegrum. Jos Polgard was close to her and when their eyes met she thought his looked murderous. He dursen't hurt me, though, thought Lilith; and she smiled at him recklessly.

" 'Tis a fine wedding, Farmer Polgard," she said slyly.

Others had joined the dancers now, but Lilith did not dance. Her head felt too dizzy and she wanted to do nothing but to sit still and watch it all and remember that she had brought it about.

She wished Amanda could be here to see it all, but poor Amanda was barred from excitement such as this.

The fiddler was playing a merry tune and Lilith's feet seemed to dance in spite of her. But she would not dance. She felt that there was only one person with whom she could dance on an occasion like this; and of course he was not here, because some people were too grand to come to a farmer's wedding.

She watched them twisting and turning, twirling on their toes, bowing, clasping hands, swinging in the dance—sweating, clumsy country folk. Yet none of them was enjoying the wedding as much as Lilith. This was as important a day in her life as it was in that of Jane, for in it she had learned that she could have anything she desired if she were only bold enough and clever enough to get it.

"Shallal!" Lilith heard the word whispered among the guests.

They had left the farmhouse and were standing outside, whispering and laughing among themselves. The bridal couple had retired to their room. Everyone knew which room in the farmhouse had been assigned to them, because it was not possible to keep such an important matter secret; there were the servants to give that away.

Shallal! That was the last ceremony of the wedding day, the ritual to which all—except perhaps the bride and groom—looked forward when they had had their fill of food and drink and dancing.

It had been a grand wedding and it must have a grand finale. The crowd was very merry on Polgards' shenegrum, and metheglin, dash-and-darras and cider. There must be a shallal to round off this wedding.

They were laughing now because they could see the flickering candle in the bridal chamber. Jim Larkin stood facing them and held up a hand; he gave the signal and they began to chant: "Be you in bed yet, bride and groom? Be you in bed?"

There was a pause and the chanting began again: "We be coming to find 'ee."

Lilith was with them, dancing now, dancing like a sprite among the crowd, singing as loudly as any of them.

"All ready?" cried Jim Larkin.

"We be ready!" chanted the crowd; and they marched in an orderly fashion through the porch of the farmhouse chanting: "Shallal. Shallal." Through the hall they went and up the wide staircase, chanting all the time.

Annie Polgard shouted after them: "You'll pay for what you break. Remember that . . . with your shallal."

The crowd was indifferent to Annie. "Be you there, bride and groom?" they chanted as they went up the stairs.

Lilith was the first to reach the corridor. She was at the door when it was burst open. Tom was in his shirt and trousers; and

Jane was not undressed, but her hair was hanging about her shoulders. They were waiting. They knew that after the wedding feast and so much to drink, there was certain to be a shallal; and they were not going to be caught in bed, as some had been before them.

Jane screamed when she saw the crowd, and the crowd shrieked its delight.

"Shallal!" cried the crowd.

Lilith—more gay than any, still intoxicated by success and shenegrum—leaped madly on to the bed shouting "Shallal!" and feeling that she was the leader, the queen, for without her there would be no shallal. How could there have been, since without her there would be no wedding?

Lilith jumped off the bed, for Jim Larkin, who was carrying a stocking filled with sand, had come forward and with the others had seized the shrieking bride and bridegroom. They beat Tom with the sand-filled stocking while he lashed out with his great fists and floored two of them. Jane ran shrieking from the room. While Tom was held down on the floor, young Harry Polgard slipped the furze bush into the bed.

Lilith, caught up in the excitement, felt that if she stayed in that room a moment longer she would shout to them, telling them how she had brought all this about.

She pressed her lips tightly together and pushed her way out of the room; she ran down the stairs and out into the yard; she did not stop running until she had reached the road.

The moon was nearly full and Lilith stopped to look up at it. She was intoxicated with moonlight, life, success and shenegrum.

And as she stood there, she was aware of a movement close behind her. Her heart seemed to leap into her throat and threaten to choke her. She was terrified that Jos Polgard had followed her and was standing behind her, his hairy hands ready to fasten themselves about her throat.

"Hello," said a voice. "It's Lilith, I believe."

Lilith smiled secretly and turned slowly. It was not Jos Polgard who stood there watching her, but the young man who had, for some time now, haunted her pleasantest dreams.

"I thought you were a pisky at first," he said. He came closer. "Have you been to the shallal?"

"Yes."

"You look as if you've enjoyed it."

She began to walk along the moonlit road, her heart capering within her, while she tried to think of words to say to him.

He walked beside her. He put a hand on her arm.

"I'm glad I saw you to-night," he said. "I've been wanting to talk to you . . . alone . . . like this, for a long time. It's a queer thing, Lilith, but it's only lately that I feel I've begun to know you."

Still she said nothing; she stared towards the gloom of the woods ahead of her.

"Haven't you anything to say to me, Lilith?"

She looked at him, and that look must have told him a good deal, for he caught her curls and pulled back her head so that the moonlight shone full on her face.

He was laughing; and she laughed too—intoxicated by she-negrum and moonlight and the sudden understanding that another of her dreams was about to come true.

☒ Four

Lilith was lying on Amanda's bed.

What had changed her lately? Amanda wondered. She was different—quieter at times, and at others wilder than ever.

Yesterday had been Amanda's sixteenth birthday. Some parts of a birthday could be a little more tiresome than other days. The prayers were longer. At breakfast she had solemnly been presented with her parents' gift—a book in a soft, dark purple cover with a purple bookmark; it was a companion to her Bible and Prayer-book, and it was full of advice to a young girl printed under a text which headed each page. Miss Robinson had given her six handkerchiefs; Alice Danesborough a musical box in the shape of a piano which played "Sweet Lavender" when opened; and Frith had given her a copy of *The Pickwick Papers*. This last, Amanda knew to be a defiant act, for she remembered her father's saying at her first dinner party, that he would not have Mr. Dickens's books in the house.

She hid the book and decided that if asked what the Danesboroughs had given her she would show the musical box and let it be believed that it had been a joint gift from Frith and Alice.

She told Lilith this, and Lilith nodded her approval.

Lilith was now fondling the book as she lay on the bed.

"It's the best of all your presents," declared Lilith.

"Why do you like it so much, when you can't read?"

Lilith opened it and frowned at the words. She smiled suddenly: "No. But I can see the pictures. I can see this fat man and the coach, and the man cleaning the shoes, and the lady in curl-papers."

"Would you like me to read some of it to you?"

"No. I'll look at the pictures. I'll hold it . . while you tell me about your birthday."

"I think I'd rather have an ordinary day than a birthday, apart from the presents, of course. They're lovely. But prayers were so long, and Papa talked all about my growing up and the duties of an adult. That was not very exciting. I just sat there, not knowing whether I ought to look pleased to be growing up or solemn about all the new duties. I looked solemn, because I thought that was safest. Then he asked me how I liked the present—his and Mamma's. I said it was beautiful; and he said I would find it a guide in after-life as well as now. I was terrified that he was going to ask about Frith's present. I wondered what I should say if he did."

"Why wouldn't he want you to have a present from Frith?"

"It's not Frith he minds. It's this Charles Dickens . . . the man who wrote the book. Papa thinks he is wicked."

Lilith laughed and held the book against her as though it were a baby whom she loved. "Is it a wicked book?"

"I don't think so."

"Is is just because it's nice and you enjoy it that he thinks it's wicked?"

"I expect so. Then, of course, I believe it's about the poor. That's what Papa thinks makes it so unpleasant."

"He likes the poor . . . Frith, I mean."

"I think he does. He talks like William sometimes . . . in a way. That's what makes Papa rather angry with him. And Frith doesn't care. He just goes on saying things which he must know Papa doesn't like."

Lilith laughed.

"And then," went on Amanda, "I had tea with Papa and Mamma in the drawing-room instead of with Miss Robinson in the schoolroom. I hated that. They talked to me while we were having tea just as though I were grown up. I suppose it was because I am sixteen. Mamma said: 'We have a surprise for you . . . a pleasant surprise . . .' And they both looked at me . . . oddly, Lilith, as though they were considering . . .'"

"Considering what?" asked Lilith.

"How big I was . . . how old I was . . . how *bad* I was, I suppose."

"Did they look angry?"

"No . . . not exactly. Mamma looked a bit frightened and Papa was just a bit stern. Then he said: 'This is the surprise, Daughter.' And when he says 'Daughter' like that I always know something very solemn is coming. He said: 'Your cousin, Anthony Leigh, is going to pay us a visit.' ''

"Anthony Leigh," repeated Lilith. "Has he been here before?"

"No. He lives a long way off. On the borders of Devon and Somerset. His father is Papa's brother, and that means he is my cousin."

"He's my cousin too, then," said Lilith.

"He's got a lot of brothers and sisters, and Papa visits them now and then. Mamma told me afterwards that he was about twenty-one."

"Grown up, then."

"Yes; and then they said a strange thing, Lilith. Papa said it and that makes it important. He is not like Mamma. Everything he says means something. He said: 'Daughter . . .' Still 'Daughter,' you see, so I know it must be very solemn and important. 'We, your mother and I, want you to do everything *you* can to make his stay a happy one.' He said it very slowly, pausing at the *you*, as though *I* had suddenly become quite important and could make people's stay a happy one if I wanted to."

Lilith grunted.

"He's coming in a week or so. He's travelling some of the way by railway. I wonder what he'll be like."

"I don't like foreigners," said Lilith.

"Don't be silly. He's my cousin."

"*Our* cousin," scowled Lilith. "But he's still a foreigner." Then her face lightened. "I can tell 'ee why he's coming. They've chosen him for you. That's what 'tis. You'm sixteen and 'tis high time they found a husband for 'ee. He be twenty-one, so 'tis high time he were married. You be sixteen. That's what he's coming for—to ask 'ee to marry him."

"You're quite wrong, Lilith. I know you're wrong. They've already decided who my husband's to be."

" 'Tain't so. This be the one for you."

"No. It's Frith. They want me to marry Frith. Miss Robinson said so. She said that was why I went down to dinner that night he was asked. She said she believes it had always been a fixed thing between his family and mine."

Lilith's eyes were black with sudden rage. " 'Tain't so!" she murmured angrily.

"What's the matter with you? Why do you mind?"

Lilith bit her brown fist and looked at the mark of her teeth. "I know it ain't so. I know this new one's for you. You wait. It's this new one. Here, take the book and read a bit to me. Read about the man that's polishing the shoes; read about him."

Amanda looked sharply at her; she took the book, but as she read Lilith was not listening; she was thinking of the damp, mossy woods and the night of Jane's wedding. She had gone back to those woods the next day; she had lain in the same spot and kissed the damp earth. And that night she had gone again to the woods, but there had been no one to share them with her.

She broke in on the reading. "Do you want to marry Frith?"

"Frith's nice," said Amanda. "I know him better than anyone else, I suppose. I'd rather have Frith than this new cousin, I think."

Lilith laughed with bitterness. "You don't know nothing; you never did."

"And what do you know about this?" demanded Amanda.

"What do I know? I know a lot, Amanda. I do know a terrible lot."

Amanda sat primly in the drawing-room, working at a piece of embroidery. With her were Miss Robinson and her mother; and at any moment they could expect to hear the sound of carriage wheels on the drive, for Mr. Leigh was driving Anthony Leigh on the last stages of his journey to Leigh House.

Amanda knew that both Miss Robinson and her mother were acutely aware of her—of her appearance, of her posture, of the grace a young lady should display when plying her needle. Amanda felt that she lacked those qualities for which they looked. It was not easy to look graceful, doing something which she hated doing as much as she hated working on this embroidery. She was frowning over it; she could not get the roses all the same size; and they looked like cabbages speared on sticks.

She was alarmed. There was tension in the house, and she was the centre of it. She was on show. She was like a prize cow at a cattle show or perhaps in the market-place. "Bend your head gracefully. Show how obedient, how docile you are. For here comes a bidder."

Lilith had told her that they intended to marry her to this cousin of hers whom she had never seen, and she feared that

Lilith was right. Miss Robinson had hinted it too; and Amanda knew that Miss Robinson was making enquiries in various quarters where she thought a governess's services might be required. Change had not yet come, but it was looming.

Amanda, bending over her embroidery frame, listened with apprehension for the first sounds of horses' hoofs, while her mother and Miss Robinson kept up a light conversation.

"He will be very tired after his journey," said Laura. "I wonder whether I should order tea to be sent into the drawing-room or whether he would prefer a tray in his room."

Miss Robinson said: "Railway journeys terrify me. One never feels safe. Besides, there are so many dreadful people on the trains."

Amanda went on with her own thoughts. What would happen if she said: "I do not wish to marry. Least of all do I wish to marry my cousin!" Would they punish her? Would they whip her, send her to her room, keep her on bread and water? She could exist like that indefinitely . . . with Lilith's help. They could make her life miserable, but they could not make her marry. People like Frith and Lilith did what they wanted to; but she was different. She wondered how long she would be able to stand out against the demands of her parents, the sermons, the reproaches.

"Listen," said Laura.

There was a silence broken only by the clopping of horses' hoofs on the road.

"Yes; they are turning in at the drive," said Miss Robinson.

Laura was flustered immediately. "I'll go to greet them. No, no, Amanda. You stay where you are. You and Miss Robinson stay here. I shall bring them straight into the drawing-room. Be bending over your embroidery . . . and look surprised to see us . . . as though you were going about your ordinary duties and have been disturbed by the unexpected arrival of visitors."

She hurried out, and Amanda looked at Miss Robinson.

"Miss Robinson, how can you look surprised when you are not in the least surprised?"

"Just bend over your work . . . and then when the door opens, count three before you look up. Then open your eyes very wide and rise slowly to your feet, but be careful not to let the frame fall."

"Wouldn't he be more pleased if he thought we were eagerly awaiting him?"

"Perhaps it would be wiser not to please him . . . too soon," said Miss Robinson archly.

"It's very mysterious," sighed Amanda. "I think it's a little silly. He must know the whole household is expecting him."

"*I* think," said Miss Robinson, "that this is a very untimely and unnecessary conversation."

As she stopped speaking, they heard the carriage draw up and the sound of voices drifted through the open window. Now Steert was driving the carriage round to the stables and Mr. and Mrs. Leigh were coming into the house with the visitor.

"Look down at your work!" hissed Miss Robinson as the door was opened.

"One, two, three," counted Amanda obediently. Then she looked up.

A young man was coming towards her; he was short and rather plump; he had light sandy hair and hardly any eyebrows or eyelashes; his eyes were small and light brown; he was chubby, rather like a baby whose body had grown up while his face had remained the same as it must have been when he was a year or two old.

"Daughter," said Mr. Leigh; and Amanda rose.

"So this is Cousin Amanda."

Amanda's hand was taken in his fat, white one; he stooped over it and kissed it.

"I am delighted to make your acquaintance, Cousin Amanda. I have heard so much about you and have been longing to meet you."

"I am glad to meet you too, Cousin Anthony."

Mr. Leigh was looking at Miss Robinson in a way which conveyed to her that when she had greeted the visitor her presence would be no longer required. She therefore greeted him and, saying that she had work to prepare, slipped out of the room.

"And have you had a pleasant journey?" asked Amanda.

He raised his eyebrows, but they were so faint that it merely seemed as though he opened his eyes wider.

"Those railways!" He shuddered. "I confess I was glad when I took to the road. Your father was kind indeed to come so far to meet me."

"Well, now you are here," said Mr. Leigh, "we hope you are going to enjoy your stay."

"Would you care for tea here . . . in the drawing-room?" asked Laura. "Or would you prefer a tray in your own room?"

"I should be delighted to have it here in the drawing-room, but I beg of you, dear Aunt, let me put you to no inconvenience."

"I am delighted," said Laura, "that you will have it with us. Would you like to go to your room first? I will have hot water sent up. Perhaps you would like to wash your hands."

"You are very kind, Aunt."

"Well, take my nephew to his room," said Mr. Leigh. "And, Daughter, you go too. See that he has everything he will need."

Amanda was not sorry to go. She had for a few terrible moments believed that she might be left alone in the drawing-room with her father.

"What a delightful house!" the new cousin was saying as they left the drawing-room. "I declare it is even more beautiful than I was led to believe. I long to see more of it, and I shall insist that my cousin gives me all its history."

"Father would do that better than I," said Amanda.

He smiled at her and laid his hand on her arm. "Nevertheless, I hope *you* will," he said.

She drew back in alarm. But he had turned almost immediately to her mother. "What a wonderful old staircase! Sixteenth-century, I imagine. I know my stay here is going to be very pleasant and interesting."

Amanda tried to step behind him and her mother as they started up the staircase, but he took her arm and gently pushed her ahead of them.

"Lead the way, Cousin," he said.

She felt his eyes on her as she mounted the staircase. He was watching her as they watched horses showing their paces at the shows.

Here was his room—long and lofty with a great fireplace and diamond-paned windows, dark as were all the rooms in this house. The furniture—apart from the heavy four-poster bed—showed the dainty elegance of the eighteenth century.

"Wonderful! Wonderful!" he murmured; and although he pretended to be looking at the furniture, he was really studying Amanda. He was appraising her, no doubt thinking her shy, gauche, easy to manage. She wanted to escape from this house because now, not only did it contain her father, but her cousin.

"Ah!" said Laura. "I see the hot water is here. Would you care to join us in the drawing-room when you are ready?"

"I shall look forward to our reunion," he said, smiling at Laura, but his quick glance was for his cousin.

Amanda found that she was shivering as she went downstairs.

"My dear," whispered Laura. "I think you made *quite* an impression."

Mr. Leigh was looking pleased when they returned to the drawing-room.

"A very pleasant young man," he said. "Very much a Leigh. Don't you think so, my dear?"

"Very much," agreed Laura.

"He has been telling me that it has always been his ambition to visit us. His father assures me that he is a very serious young man, intensely religious. I think, my dear, that when you know him better you will agree with me that he is a very pleasant young man."

"I'm sure I shall. He seems to have taken to his cousin immediately. You will be able to show him the countryside, will you not, Amanda?"

"He is very fond of riding, he tells me," went on Mr. Leigh. "I gather he is an excellent horseman. I wonder if our horses will satisfy him. I'll give Steert instructions that he is to have the chestnut mare. She's the most suitable mount for him, I imagine. Daughter, you say nothing. You will be pleased to have a cousin to whom to show our beauty spots, eh?"

"Yes, Papa."

"I shall expect you to do everything you can to make his stay a pleasant one."

As tea was being brought in, Anthony reappeared.

"You must be hungry," said Mr. Leigh.

"I do confess that the sight of so much excellent fare makes me believe that I am."

"Then let us have tea at once."

While Mr. Leigh said grace, Amanda noticed how deeply absorbed Anthony seemed, how grave, how solemn.

They sat down and were served with boiled eggs and bread and butter. How different, thought Amanda, from schoolroom tea, which consisted of bread and butter with jam or honey and milk; sometimes a slice of seed cake was permitted, saffron or the raisin cake, which was called fuggan by the cottage people. This was far more elaborate, but how she longed to be in the schoolroom with Miss Robinson!

Conversation progressed during the meal. It seemed to Amanda that in her father's eyes Anthony must be nearly perfect. He was like her father in all his thoughts and ideas; he addressed him with the utmost respect, and yet he was not afraid to speak; he showed no hesitancy, yet Amanda had the feeling that, like herself, he knew there were often two answers to her father's questions, and that, unlike herself, he never failed to give the right one.

They were halfway through tea when Frith was announced.

Amanda felt a lifting of her spirits at the sight of Frith. He had ridden over, he told them, guessing he would be in time for tea. They must forgive his coming without an invitation, but he would be leaving for London to-morrow. He had really come to say goodbye.

His eyes were mischievous, and Amanda guessed that he had come to see the new cousin as well as say goodbye, for he would have guessed that the newcomer was to be offered to Amanda in place of himself.

How I wish he was not going to London! thought Amanda. I could tell him how I feel, and he might advise me.

A place was made for him at the table.

"So *you* are going away just as *I* arrive," said Anthony.

"Alas! yes. I wonder if that is a tragedy or a blessing. You can never tell."

Frith was determined to be flippant—careless, as Mr. Leigh would be thinking, in his arrogant youth, very sure of himself since he had got his own way with his family.

He was eating with great enjoyment, realizing that his presence was not very welcome—except perhaps to Amanda—but not caring in the least for that.

"Mr. Danesborough," said Laura, "is going to London to study. He is going to study for the medical profession."

"How interesting," said Anthony.

"Do you propose to do anything?" asked Frith.

"My nephew," said Mr. Leigh severely, "does not work. He is a gentleman."

"Don't you find that a little dull?" Frith did not wait for an answer. "Are you staying long?"

"I hope my host will allow me to."

"I'm sure he will," said Frith.

"My nephew tells me he has long looked forward to his visit. I hope it will be a long one. The distance between our two families is too great for us to pay short visits."

"Mr. Danesborough will be making an even longer journey," said Laura. "All the way to London. I wonder your father is not beside himself with anxiety. Miss Danesborough also."

"They know I'm a match for any smart Londoner. Have you ever visited the capital?"

"Never," said Anthony. "I might add that I have no wish to."

"All the evils of England are drawn to its centre," said Mr. Leigh. "I must say I wonder at your father's giving his permission for you to go there."

"I fancy," said Amanda, speaking for the first time, and realizing as soon as she had done so that she had spoken without due consideration, "that Frith does not *ask* permission."

Her father and mother were looking at her in dismay, Anthony with astonishment, Frith with approval.

"Amanda, my *dear*!" said Laura in trembling reproach.

"She's right, of course," said Frith.

"You seem surprisingly pleased about it," said Anthony. "I should have thought you would have been remorseful at the thought of going against your father's wishes."

"Neither my father nor I are prone to remorse or gloom of any sort. My father has the good sense to see that taking an important step in life is mainly the concern of the one about to take it."

"That seems a very revolutionary doctrine," said Mr. Leigh severely.

"Revolutionary indeed!" cried Frith. "But revolution is in the air, for this is a revolutionary age. There is revolution on the Continent. Will it come to England? Think of all the crowned heads that are falling. What of the Queen? Will she survive the *débâcle*?"

Laura said: "Anthony, we don't take Mr. Danesborough too seriously. He likes to joke."

"But indeed I am not joking. I mean it. It is true. Revolution *is* in the air. You see, it's inevitable. There's too big a gap between the rich and the poor. Trouble simmers . . . boils up . . . boils over. Something will have to be done or it will happen here.''

''You seem to have some unusual ideas, young man,'' said Mr. Leigh.

''Not so unusual,'' said Frith, taking a spoonful of Laura's home-made strawberry jam and heaping it on to a piece of raisin cake. ''These ideas of mine have been held by greater men than I. Have you read Kingsley's *Alton Locke*? What of Mr. Dickens and Mr. Jerrold?''

''Paid journalists!'' snorted Mr. Leigh. ''England will be in a fine state if we continue to allow such fellows to encourage sedition.''

Laura was frightened, as she always was when anyone expressed an opinion different from that of her husband. Paul was, she assured herself, the most tolerant of men, except when he was contradicted over matters which he *knew* to be right. She said uneasily: ''I think this income tax is pernicious.''

That was safe. Even Frith must agree about that. But it seemed that Frith was determined to argue.

''A necessary evil, dear Mrs. Leigh.''

''I echo my wife's words,'' said Mr. Leigh ominously. ''A *pernicious* evil.''

''It should never have been introduced,'' said Anthony.

''It had to be. How could Pitt have financed the wars without it? I thought you were a Tory, Mr. Leigh. It was the Tories, remember, who brought it back seven years ago.''

''I do not in every instance agree with the Party.''

''Ah! Would you support the Whigs then, sir?''

''It seems that you, whom I understand to be a Whig supporter, are now on the side of the Tories.''

''Not I!'' cried Frith. ''I'm neither Whig nor Tory. I'm a Radical in some ways; but you know the Whigs, who were all for freedom from the tax, just did not understand finance. If the country's in debt we've got to have some tax to get it out of its difficulty; and in my humble opinion Peel was right to bring it in when he did. Sevenpence in the pound . . . but only on incomes over one hundred and fifty pounds a year. We don't like it, but it's reasonable.''

"That may be your opinion," said Mr. Leigh, "but I could hardly call it a humble one."

Anthony laughed, and Amanda hated his laughter. She had ranged herself on Frith's side as surely as Anthony had ranged himself on her father's.

"All this," said Laura with a sigh, "is quite beyond us poor ladies, eh, Amanda?"

"No, I don't think so, Mamma. I think that Frith is right. Neither side is wholly right in everything it does; neither side is wholly wrong. Therefore you can side at one time with Lord Russell and at another with Sir Robert."

She trailed off, having caught the look of cold disapproval on her father's face.

"Ah," said Anthony affably, "so my little cousin is interested in affairs of state. Brains and beauty, I see. What a rare combination!"

Frith looked at Amanda helplessly.

"Shall we make ourselves more comfortable?" said Laura, rising from the table.

They sat looking over the lawns while Steert and Bess cleared the table.

Frith glanced at Amanda with sympathy; he was even a little contrite because he felt that his reckless conversation had lured her to make a little speech for which she would later be reprimanded. He tried to make amends by putting the old man into a good mood; he talked of the countryside, those beauty spots which Anthony would see. He knew a good deal about the ancient lore of Cornwall and, when he wished, he could be very entertaining. There was great charm about Frith, Amanda realized. He could, even after arousing such antagonism as he had at the tea table, put her father quickly into a good mood. Now he talked of the old days and the superstitions of the people, of the various healing qualities which the wells of Cornwall were supposed to possess. From Cornish customs he went to Cornish food. "Our cream is the same as that you Devonians called Devonshire cream. But you learned it from us. We were the first in this country to make it, and we learned it from the Phoenicians." This was the sort of rivalry to which Mr. Leigh did not object, and in this case he could side with Frith. The two young men argued a little in favour of their respective counties and Mr.

Leigh looked on benignly, while Laura smiled and Amanda watched them silently.

"There was a shallal here the other night," said Frith.

"A shallal?" said Anthony.

Amanda saw her father's frown and admired the deft way in which Frith said quickly: "Oh, just a little wedding celebration. Very quaint." For, of course, shallals did not provide material for polite conversation.

Amanda's thoughts went then to the Polgard wedding. Theirs was the shallal of which Frith had spoken. Lilith had been present; she had talked of it a little, but not with her usual gusto. She had come in late that night and had not come immediately to tell Amanda about the wedding. Amanda had been rather hurt, for she had been very eager to hear of it, and she had thought that Lilith would have been eager to tell.

When Frith left he managed to whisper to Amanda: "So he's the consolation prize. Don't accept him, Amanda . . . unless you want to. Be bold. Choose your own way. Think of me . . . the shining example."

He insisted that they must not come to the stables to see him off.

"Adieu. I shall see you when I return—which I suppose will be within a few months."

"A very wild young man," said Mr. Leigh when he had gone. "And one, I fear, who will bring sorrow to his family."

Meanwhile, Frith was whistling as he slowly made his way to the stables. Lilith came out by the back door as if by chance.

She stood still, looking at him.

"Lilith," he said, "I came to see you . . . not the family. To-night? In the woods . . . at eight?"

Lilith nodded. With the joy and eagerness about her, she was very beautiful.

It was quiet in the woods.

Now and then the lovers spoke; they marvelled at their pleasure in each other. Lilith was fearful as the time for parting grew near.

"Where'll you be this time to-morrow? Far away from me."

"You talk as though I were going to the other side of the world."

"And so it might as well be, for I'll be here and you'll be far away in England."

He kissed her and said: "It won't be for long, Lilith. I'll come back."

"What's it like to London?" she asked.

"Wonderful, Lilith. More wonderful than any place you've ever seen. One day you'll come to London."

"When?"

"When I'm settled there. I'm going to live there altogether one day. I won't stay here. I want to be out in the world. I want to be in the centre of life. You understand that, Lilith? That's where you want to be too, I know."

"I'd want to be with you."

"Oh, Lilith," he murmured, "how small you are! Like a little statue. I wish I could turn you into a statue . . . a little stone statue so that I could take you to London with me wrapped up in a silk handkerchief, and turn you into flesh and blood whenever the fancy took me."

"Could it be done?" she asked eagerly. "Is there a spell to make it so?"

He laughed. "Lilith, what things you say! And if it could be done, would you let me do it? Suppose I forgot the spell that would make you breathe again?"

"I wouldn't mind . . . if you carried me wherever you went."

They were quiet for a little while, then he said: "You shall come to London, Lilith. When I'm ready, you shall come."

"When? When will that be?"

"When I'm ready. When I'm qualified."

"Next time you come back?"

"Not as soon as that. But there'll come a day when I shall meet you here and say, 'Lilith, I'm a doctor now.' And then . . . when I leave for London that time, you'll go with me. I'll manage it, Lilith, because you love me. How much do you love me and for how long?"

"As much as any could," she answered, "and for ever-more."

Lilith sat beside the old grandmother. The smoke from her pipe went up in spirals which spelt contentment; Lilith had always known her grandmother's mood by the way in which she smoked.

The old hand caressed Lilith's curls.

"Don't think 'ee could keep it from me," she said. "I do know. I do see it. It's like a light about 'ee. 'T'as made 'ee beautiful, my queen. You was spry and you had your pretty curls, but you was never beautiful till now."

Lilith was silent.

"Ah, you don't deny it. 'Twouldn't be no good. You can't keep a thing like that from old Grandmother Lil. Jane, her's done well for herself. Her's the farmer's wife, and when old farmer dies, our Jane will be mistress of a nice bit of property. I do call that doing well. But that wouldn't have done for you, my pretty. You ain't the sort to live quiet on a farm. You've got to have change in your life. That's what you've got to have. You've got to live like your old Grandmother did. A farmer wouldn't be good enough for you. 'Tis the gentry for you . . . as 'twas with me."

Lilith took her grandmother's hand and laid it against her cheek. "Did you ever want to go abroad, Grandmother?"

"Oh, I travelled a bit, as I told 'ee. I've been to Altarnon and to Launceston along of my tally-man."

"I mean a long way . . . right out of Cornwall."

"No. I ain't never been to foreign parts and I ain't never wanted to."

"Didn't you? Didn't you really?"

"No. Me own country were good enough for me. Nor would I stray for long from these here parts, for I feel lonesome if so be I can't feel the sea-wind on me face and watch the masties on the water. There's English on t'other side of Tamar and they say they be a terrible people . . . sharp and sly . . . and thinking a power of themselves."

"But didn't you ever want to see London, Grandmother? It's the most wonderful place there is."

"Who told 'ee that? Did he tell 'ee that?"

Lilith nodded.

"Well," said the grandmother smiling, "if that's what the gentry thinks, then I reckon 'tis so. 'Tis a big place, I reckon. Like as not 'tis another Liskeard or Plymouth."

"It's bigger than they, Grandmother. The Queen lives there."

"Does her, then?"

"Yes. Amanda showed me a picture of where she do live. It's

in London. But she don't live there all the time. She do go to other places in the country.''

''Well, if it be so grand, why don't her live there all the time?'' demanded Grandmother Lil triumphantly.

''Well, her do like a change, I suppose.''

''I never wanted a change. This place be good enough for me, and I reckon if that place were good enough for the Queen she'd bide there. Tell me, my pretty, did he say he'd take you there?''

Lilith nodded.

''Well, then, I reckon 'tis good for 'ee to go. Does he love you dearly, my queen?''

Lilith nodded again.

''And so he should, for you'm worth it, and if he do want to take you to London, then London be the place for you. I see'd 'un riding past here the other day, and he called to me and waved his hand. He's a fine young man, and as he passed, I thought, He'll love the women and they'll love him, for believe me, my love, the women love those that love them . . . just as the men do . . . and that's natural enough. He might be the son of your grandfather instead of the parson's son by the looks of him. He'll not be the faithful sort, I reckon. He's too gay and too handsome, and there'll be too many to love him. And don't you ask him to be the faithful sort. Men is made up of different parts, my pretty, and one man can't have all the qualities we'd like 'em to. You be content with what is there and don't try no grafting on of what you'd like 'em to be, for that's the surest way to lose 'em . . . least, so I found. Now, the master at Leigh House . . . he'd be the faithful sort. He's not the sort to stray far afield. Because why? Because there'd be no one to beckon him, that's why. Now you be happy; you be content. You've got a fine gentleman and he'll take 'ee to London, I don't doubt . . . and if that's where you're happy, that's where you belong to be.''

It was pleasant there in the hot sunshine, leaning against her grandmother's skirts just as though she were a little girl again. She sat dreaming of a future of love and contentment, recalling the damp earthiness of the woods, the freshness of wild violets, and hearing his voice talking of love and the future, while the grandmother was assured that this granddaughter was such another as herself, and, happy that this should be so, puffed contentedly at her pipe.

* * *

Amanda was frightened. There seemed no escape from her fate. *He* was always there, it seemed. Even when she was at her lessons she would see him from the schoolroom window; and if ever she stood close to the window, he would be aware of her; he would turn and bow. He was like a spider sitting at the edge of the web, and she was the fly who was just beginning to feel the sticky substance which would eventually hold her fast.

When they rode together he kept his horse close to hers. At meals—and she had them all with the family now—she was aware of his eyes watching her all the time; his voice caressed her when he spoke—soft, tender, yet somehow authoritative; sometimes his plump white hands would linger on her arm; they reminded her of a slow-worm on which she had once laid her hands involuntarily before she turned shuddering away.

She had not been to the Polgard Farm since he had come to the house. It was impossible to do so, because she knew that he would follow her. Once when she had joined Lilith he had overtaken her.

"And where are you going?" he had asked.

"Oh . . . we were just going to visit some poor people . . . to take them some food." She had flushed as she spoke, remembering that if he had told her parents they would want to know to which family she was taking food.

"May I come with you?" He had turned to Lilith. "You may go," he had said.

Amanda had thought then how like her father her cousin was. He said, "May I come with you?" and without waiting for permission proceeded to do so.

There had been only one course to take then. She had said quickly: "Lilith, you go alone. Let us go for a ride, cousin. I will take you to Polperro. You have said you wanted to go."

He had bowed his head then. "I am yours to command, dear cousin."

But he had meant, of course, that he was in command. He wanted her society and, because he would prefer to have it during a ride rather than on a visit of mercy, he had agreed to her suggestion.

There was no escape from him.

Lilith had changed and no longer seemed to display the same vital interest in everything that went on. Lilith was remote, joyous and melancholy in turn. Frith was in London; Alice was visiting her aunt at St. Austell; and there were times when Amanda felt desperately alone.

Even Miss Robinson's thoughts were far away. She was too deeply concerned in what was going to happen to herself to think very much about Amanda's problems. Amanda was too worried about her own future to think very much about Miss Robinson, for marriage to Anthony seemed to her a more terrible ordeal than anything which could happen to Miss Robinson.

One day the governess was quite pink with excitement.

"I have had a letter from my married sister," she explained, "who tells me that she has heard Lady Egger is looking for a governess for her youngest daughter. The Eggers are a very great family. I remember they had a place not very far from my father's parish in Berkshire. It would be rather wonderful to visit the old haunts again. I shall write to Lady Egger immediately."

"Miss Robinson, have Papa or Mamma told you that I shan't be needing you?"

"You are growing up." Miss Robinson was arch. "When a young lady has admirers . . . when her parents have *plans* for her . . . it becomes obvious that she will soon be out of the schoolroom."

"Then they have spoken to you!"

"They have hinted that I should be looking out. Your Papa has said that if I found a suitable position he would be delighted to let nothing stand in the way of my taking it. He said I must think of myself . . . and I must not consider any inconvenience I might cause to the family. And so . . . in view of that, I don't see that I am being in the least bit premature in writing to Lady Egger."

"No, Miss Robinson." Amanda stared blankly before her. "Oh!" she burst out suddenly. "Robbie . . . Robbie . . . I don't want you to go."

Miss Robinson put her arms about her. But what could they say to comfort each other? Miss Robinson, for all her high hopes, was afraid, afraid of a new house, the new ordeals which would have to be faced, the continuous control she must keep on herself, subservient yet genteel—the lot of the governess who spent her precarious existence between the gentry and the servants, herself neither one nor the other, always watchful of charges' growing up, always fearful of the future when she would be too old for even that joyless life. And what comfort could Amanda offer now? She could not say, as she used to: "Robbie, when I marry I will have no one but you to look after my children." She could not bear to think of her children, for how could she think of them without thinking also of her cousin Anthony, the smiling jailor whom her father had chosen to guard her future?

Slowly and solemnly the bearers were carrying the coffin to the church. William was one of those bearers, and behind it, with her family and some of their friends and neighbours, Lilith followed.

Grandmother Lil had gone to her mattress one night just as she had for many years, and when they had tried to waken her in the morning they had found that she was dead.

"Smiling in her sleep, she were," said Mrs. Tremorney, "just as though she were happy to make the journey."

"We shall miss her," said Mr. Tremorney, "but us do know her's at peace; and that's a terrible good thing in this sad world, I do say."

The children were excited; it was not every day that they attended a funeral. They had spent the morning gathering flowers from the woods and hedges that they might decorate Grandmother Lil's coffin for the last journey.

Lilith felt bewildered. Too much was happening all at once: the great acquisition of power over Farmer Polgard made her feel strong, the love for Frith Danesborough made her feel weak, and now the loss of her old guide and comforter made her feel defenceless. She did not weep as the others did.

Her be terrible hard, thought her mother. Our Lilith were the one Grandmother Lil loved the best and Lilith don't shed a tear for her.

Lilith was thinking: She'll never be there no more; she'll not sit at the door puffing at her old pipe, fondling my hair, boasting about how much cleverer she was than other folk. I can't go to her no more.

The way was steep and the bearers had often to stop that others might take their places.

Oh Grandmother Lil, thought Lilith, you be having a fine funeral. 'Tis a funeral you'd be proud of.

The silence of the graveyard seemed unearthly to Lilith. The old tower of the church with its grey stones, washed by the rain of centuries, looked cruelly indifferent, seeming to suggest that it had stood for years and would stand many more, and what did it care for one more poor body brought home to rest? The bees were busy on the privet hedge. They haven't no right to go on like as nothing's happened, thought Lilith, when Grandmother Lil be dead.

William touched her hand and they both stared down at the coffin as it was lowered into the grave.

Nearby a cuckoo stammered; he had lost the first rapture of the spring. Tears came into Lilith's eyes for the first time since she had heard that Grandmother Lil had gone away, away from the cottage and the sight of the masties dancing on the water.

It was over now. The last words had been said and the earth had rattled on the coffin. They filed out of the churchyard and walked solemnly down the hill.

Everyone was talking of Grandmother Lil, how she had been a fine old lady, how she had brought up her family and done her duty all the days of her life. She was a good wife and a good mother, they said. And Lilith wanted to shout at them: "Her wouldn't want for you to say that. Her'd want for you to say she was a bad one . . . and that she was smart and sly and knew how to make a soft place for herself."

William whispered to her: "Her was old. Her wouldn't have wanted to go on much longer . . . her wouldn't have wanted to get deaf and blind. . . ."

Lilith turned to him. " 'Tis not to hear her voice," she murmured. " 'Tis not to sit there beside her. 'Tis not to fill her pipes and sit there watching the smoke. . . . Never . . . never no more."

Miss Robinson said: "Such news! I have heard from Lady Egger. She tells me that she has considered my application most favourably. 'Providing,' she says, 'your present employer can give a satisfactory reference, you may consider the position yours; and you may come to take up your duties at the beginning of next month.' "

"Will Papa give you the reference?" asked Amanda.

"He has said he will."

"I hope you will be very happy there."

Amanda felt that little by little the past was disintegrating and the future was forming.

"Cousin," said Anthony one morning, "will you ride with me? I want you to show me Morval Woods."

There was a gleam in his eyes. He had been at Leigh House three weeks now, and each day his attitude towards her had changed a little, had become slightly more possessive. He never made a false move with her father; always he deferred; always he agreed; he was always deeply grateful and determined to be worthy of his uncle's belief in him. It seemed to Amanda that her father was happier than he had ever been; he treated Anthony as though he were a son, and Anthony behaved like her father's ideal son.

They rode out side by side, up the steep Hay Lane and along the high road until they turned off to the woods.

"I hear there's a blacksmith's shop in the village," he said. "I think the chestnut has a loose shoe by the sound of it."

It was necessary for them to ride in single file, for which Amanda was glad. She led the way through the woods, where the branches grew so low that it was often necessary to bend their heads in order to avoid them. She had always enjoyed riding through the woods when her companions had been Frith and Alice. This morning the foxgloves under the trees, and the deep pink rose-bay willow-herb seemed more beautiful than usual; and she thought: If only he were not with me.

They rode past the kissing gate, past the lawns of the big house and the church where the old yews seemed to stand guard over the graves, past the ancient cottages.

The hammer had a merry ring that morning, and the blacksmith himself came to the open door to touch his cap.

Haughtily Anthony gave his orders. How different he was now from the deferential young man who talked to her father! Frith was careless and quick to anger, haughty and arrogant often, but he was the same with anyone. It was Anthony's cold arrogance to some and his studied way of pleasing others that alarmed and nauseated her; it seemed so hypocritical; moreover, she knew intuitively that all his polite attention towards herself would disappear if she married him.

She smiled at old Reuben Escott.

"And you'm well, Miss Amanda?" he asked. "You'll take a glass of cider while you'm waiting?"

It was the custom that, when the horses were brought to be shod, a glass of Reuben's cider should be drunk. He always said that there was no cider like his in the whole of the country; and he would be delighted for the rest of the day with a compliment on its flavour.

"We shall return in an hour for the horses," Anthony told him.

Reuben's face fell, and Amanda said quickly: "I couldn't go without a glass of Reuben's cider. I've been looking forward to it ever since I knew we were coming here."

Now the old man's face shone with pleasure. "Aye. You do know good cider, Miss Amanda. No mistake about that."

"Do you really want the cider?" asked Anthony. His lips were drawn back over his teeth to represent a smile, but his eyes remained hard and angry.

"Of course. So will you when you've tasted it."

Reuben was rubbing his hands. "I'll get 'ee a glass. 'Tis extra special, this lot. This cider be the best I did ever make."

Anthony said: "I wished to talk to you, cousin."

"You can talk here."

"What I have to say is for your ears alone."

"Well then, you can say it another time. Old Reuben won't hear in any case. He's a bit deaf, though he won't admit it; and when he shoes a horse he's always so intent on the shoeing that he hears nothing at all."

The blacksmith came back with two brimming glasses on a tray. He stood back watching them while they drank.

"There!" he demanded. "How be that then?"

"Better than ever," said Amanda.

"Very good," said Anthony perfunctorily.

They stood watching the shoeing of the chestnut. Amanda felt triumphant; she had successfully avoided the walk with him which he had no doubt planned. He drank his cider quickly and looked impatiently at her glass; but she was not going to be hurried. She stood enjoying the smell of burning hoof, watching the glow from the furnace, listening to the ring of the anvil, savouring the atmosphere of the blacksmith's shop, thinking of the many times she had been here with Frith and Alice.

"My dear cousin, how you linger over your cider!"

"One should, in order to savour it."

"It is unusual for a lady to be such a connoisseur of such a drink."

"But I've had the privilege of tasting Reuben's cider since I was very young and first brought my pony to be shod."

He smiled, but the angry gleam was still in his eyes.

That was the first victory, for when they rode away from the blacksmith's shop it was necessary to go straight home or be late for luncheon and that, of course, was something which Anthony would not allow, for his uncle had made it perfectly clear that he considered unpunctuality a major sin.

They were in the woods, side by side, walking their horses, when he pulled up his horse and laid his hand on her reins.

"Amanda," he said, "I meant to speak to you this morning, and speak I will. I want to marry you."

She was unprepared. She had known there must be a proposal but she had imagined it differently. She had believed she had successfully avoided it this morning.

"But," she stammered, "I . . . I had not expected . . ."

"You need have no fear. I have spoken to your father and he has given his permission. So that is settled."

"But it is my permission you are asking," she reminded him.

He smiled indulgently and took her hand. She tried to withdraw it and was frightened by the firmness of his grip. The horses were at a standstill now; it seemed to her that the woods were silent, alert, all the insects and birds, all the trees and flowers, every blade of grass . . . waiting to see if she had the courage to say what was in her mind.

"Of course it is, my love. But, as I say, your father wishes it, so you need not be afraid."

She was praying now, praying for the sort of courage which had been denied her and given to Frith, praying for the boldness of Lilith.

She took refuge in the remark: "I did not expect . . ." And she took this, of course, for maidenly modesty; his arm shot out suddenly and he seized her by the shoulders. Before she knew what was happening she was almost pulled off her horse and she felt his lips on hers.

Frantic, feeling now only the need to escape from him, she touched her horse with her riding whip so that he moved forward and Anthony had to release her. She saw that her cousin was smiling, smug and self-satisfied.

Her face was flaming; there was violent anger within her. That caress, so odious to her, had given her the courage she needed.

She would rather die, she felt now, than endure more of that. She looked over her shoulder.

"I do not wish to marry," she said.

"My dear little cousin, I have taken you too much by surprise."

She threw all hypocrisy to the winds. "I am not surprised. I knew what they were planning. I knew why you wanted us to leave the forge while the horse was being shod. So it is no surprise. I know why you're here. And I know this: I don't want to marry you."

"Ah!" he said lightly. "So she wishes to be wooed."

"I do not. I want none of that."

She pressed her horse into a canter. "I don't want to marry," she called over her shoulder. "Not for years. . . ."

"You'll change your mind."

"I never shall."

He was beside her now and his lips were drawn back across his teeth in his forced smile, while his eyes glittered.

"Then, my little cousin," he said, "we shall have to *make* you change your mind."

Laura said: "But, Amanda my dear, have you considered what this means? Your father has set his heart upon this marriage."

"I think it is for me to set my heart on it, Mamma."

"My dear, what objection can you possibly have? Your cousin is a delightful young man. He is young and handsome . . . and in any case, it is the wish of your father and myself."

"But it is not mine, Mamma. It is not mine."

"*Your* wishes, Amanda? But they hardly come into this. Your *father* has decided."

Laura's lips began to tremble; she wanted to take the child in her arms and weep over her; but she dared not. She must be firm; she must support her husband. Amanda was a wilful girl, quietly stubborn.

Laura could not trust herself to stay with her daughter. She said: "You are very obstinate, Amanda. Sometimes I think you behave as you do in order deliberately to pain us."

"That's not true, Mamma. I want to please you and Papa. But this marriage . . . it is asking too much."

"How can anything a parent asks a child be too much?"

"Marriage could be."

Laura sighed. Her daughter could be very disconcerting.

Miss Robinson talked to Amanda.

"You are not being a credit to me, Amanda. After all I've done to teach you to honour your father's wishes!"

"Miss Robinson, this marriage would be for the whole of my life. How can I enter into that lightly?"

"Your father has arranged it for you. Do you then doubt his wisdom?"

"Yes, Miss Robinson, I do."

"I beg of you, control yourself. Do not let him hear you talk in that way."

Poor Miss Robinson! Even in her own distress, Amanda could spare time to think of her. Miss Robinson, who had battled so long alone, felt that any marriage was better than no marriage; but Amanda knew that she would rather face a future of poverty and hardship—anything rather than marriage with her cousin.

The days passed—two days of apprehension. Anthony was always with her when she rode out; he sat close to her when they were in the drawing-room; she believed he had begged her father not to be too hard with her, to give her a chance to be brought to reason by means of tenderness and gentle persuasion. He would bend over her embroidery frame and admire the colours she was using; he always seemed to be hovering over her, breathing on her neck, touching her hair, her arms, her hands, his brilliant, kindling eyes frightening her.

In her bedroom she told Lilith of her fears, but Lilith nowadays was abstracted. Like Miss Robinson she seemed no longer vitally interested in the affairs of Leigh House. She was for ever asking questions about London; her great ambition now, it seemed, was to go there.

"Now that Grandmother Lil be dead," she said, "there's naught to keep me here. I've a fancy that she died contented, knowing that I'd be took care of. It was like as if she knew it . . . and then . . . she died."

"Well, she knew you were all right when you first came here surely!"

But Lilith just looked past Amanda.

She said suddenly: "You hate him, don't you? You hate this cousin?"

"I think I do. At first I didn't mind him. If he had gone away after a short visit I might even have liked him. It's only now that I dislike him. Lilith, I'm frightened, because every day I seem to hate him more and more.''

"Is it that you love someone else?'' asked Lilith. "Is it because you have another in mind as you'd like to be your husband?''

"No, Lilith. I don't want any husband. I want to wait . . . for a long time. Lilith, what shall I do if they make me marry?''

"You could run away to London.''

"Lilith, how could I do that?''

"Other people go. You get on the railway. Then it don't take long.''

"Lilith . . . how *could* I run away? Where should I go? You can't live in London alone.''

"I'd come with 'ee. You'd have me to look after 'ee.'' Lilith's eyes were shining. "We could ride there on the railway. I reckon Frith would let us be with him.''

"I don't know where he is.''

"You said he was to London.''

"So he is. But I don't know where.''

"We could ask when we got there.'' Lilith was smiling.

After that she talked continually of going to London, and Amanda encouraged her; she found that discussing such an absurd proposition helped to direct her thoughts away from the miserable prospect before her.

A week had passed since Anthony's proposal, and Amanda had known by the cruel look in his eyes at breakfast this morning that he was getting impatient.

When prayers were over he had asked Mr. Leigh if he could have a word with him in his study. That request had been granted, and as a result, Amanda was summoned to her father's presence.

She entered the room in trepidation.

"Daughter,'' said her father, "I have sent for you in sorrow when I hoped to send for you in gladness. Tell me this: Do you enjoy wounding your parents?'' There was no need to protest that this was not the case, for he did not expect an answer. "My dearest wish is to see you happily settled, leading a good and useful life. You know this, but as you have consistently through your childhood, you flout my wishes; you bring sorrow to your mother, wretchedness to us both. I have prayed God to soften you, to endow you with a little of that filial duty which you sadly lack, but so far God has not seen fit to grant my request. Your cousin has asked my permission to make you his wife. I gave that permission most joyfully. He is a young man whom I have known all his life; he is my brother's son. There is not another to whom I would more happily see you united. He is a Leigh—of our own flesh and blood. Your marriage to him would bring me that son which God has seen fit to deny me. I knew that, when the idea occurred to me that this match might take place, God had put the idea into my head. This was God's answer to my prayers. This was why my earnest plea for a son had not been granted. 'Here is your son,' said God. 'Take him and unite him with your daughter.' Gladly would I obey God's will as I have ever striven to do. But you have decided once more, not only to defy me but your Heavenly Father.''

The discourse was taking its usual line. How many times had she heard the same phrases, the same sentiments? God was always on her father's side, always leading him whither he had decided to go.

"Papa," she said, "I feel I am too young as yet."

"That is a matter for me to decide. You are turned sixteen. Your mother was married just before her seventeenth birthday, and I see no reason why you should not be."

"If I could wait a little while, and perhaps meet other people . . ."

"Are you presuming to tell me that I do not know what is best for my own daughter?"

"Yes, Papa, I suppose I am."

He started with astonishment; then he closed his eyes and pressed the palms of his hands together. "Oh God," he said, "what burden is this that You have put upon me? What cross is this I have to bear . . . and what more bitter cross could there be but an ungrateful, disobedient daughter? Forgive me. I know not what I say."

Amanda had always found her father's conversations with God embarrassing. For all his feigned humility, he seemed to be continually reproaching God for something He had done or not done, trying to guide Him in the way He should go. She planted her feet very firmly on the carpet and put her hands behind her back. She tried to imagine Frith's laughing face and take courage from it.

Her father had opened his eyes.

"You are defiant," he said.

"I am afraid so, Papa."

"Yet you know that I have decided you shall marry your cousin?"

"Yes, Papa."

"And you still say that you will not?"

"Yes, Papa."

"You may go to your room. We will announce your engagement formally at dinner."

"I beg of you, do not force me into this, Papa."

She knew this was weakness. This was not 'I will not'; it was: 'I beg of you, do not force me.' There was all the difference in the world between the two. She had recognized defeat, and the habit of a lifetime was making her accept it.

"I shall insist," said her father; he smiled benignly, for he had been quick to see the slackening of defiance. "And," he added, almost gently, "in after years you will fall before me on your bended knees and thank me for what I have done. Go now, my child." He came to her and patted her shoulder. "A little reluctance is perhaps natural at first. You feel we have hurried you into this. Now to your room. You are a fortunate young woman. I congratulate you on acquiring a charming husband."

She went out; it was useless to argue. This was just another task which had been set before her. Already she was placating that other defiant self. I'll get used to it perhaps, she thought. Perhaps it is not so bad. Everyone has to marry, and if they do not—like Miss Robinson—they seem to spend the rest of their days regretting it.

She was very pale when she went down to dinner, very subdued.

It was to be a very solemn occasion. Mr. Leigh had all the servants brought into the dining-room.

"My daughter is engaged to be married to Mr. Anthony Leigh. We will drink to their health and their happiness. Steert, fill a glass for everyone."

And Amanda stood beside Anthony, who took her hand and kissed it before them all.

Lilith was there. "Coward!" signalled Lilith's eyes.

Later, when Amanda was in her room, Lilith came and lay on her bed.

"You're a coward," said Lilith.

"Yes, Lilith, I am. I knew suddenly when I was in Papa's study that I had to do this . . . that there was nothing else. It was like learning one of the psalms . . . something that had to be done because there was no way out."

"There's always a way out."

"There's not. You talk about running away. What could I do if I ran away? Where should I go? You can't just run away. If I could be a governess like Miss Robinson, I would."

"Perhaps you could."

"How? You have to have references. Where would I get them? You don't know anything about these things, Lilith. You can't run away . . . you can't! I'm Papa's daughter and I've got to do what he says."

"Only cowards do what they'm made to."

"Lilith, what can I do? What *can* I do?"

"You can run away, I tell 'ee. You can run to London."

Amanda turned away from her impatiently.

The wedding of Amanda and Anthony Leigh was to take place in four months' time.

"That," said Laura, "will give us time for all the preparations."

Miss Robinson had left for her new position. She had wept bitterly at the parting and had presented Amanda with a keepsake—a little book-mark of silk with a sprig of flowers embroidered on it, which Amanda might have thought were almost anything if Miss Robinson had not pointed out that it was rosemary. She gave her address and begged Amanda to write and, whenever she looked at the book-mark, which she hoped she would always keep, to think that rosemary was for remembrance.

"Dear Robbie, I will!" cried Amanda; and almost forgot her own predicament in the contemplation of poor Miss Robinson's.

"If you ever need me," said Miss Robinson, flushing slightly, feeling, now that Amanda was engaged, it would be a little improper to mention the family she might have, "write to me. You would have first claim on me, Amanda dear. Now that I am going I don't think there can be any harm in telling you that you have been my favourite pupil."

"Oh, Robbie!" Amanda was weeping bitterly, not only for

Miss Robinson, but for herself and all the sadness which so many like themselves, who had not the strength of Frith and Lilith, must be forced to suffer.

Anthony, as the acknowledged fiancé, was strangely enough more tolerable. He smiled with his eyes as well as his mouth now, and that was an improvement. At least he was no longer angry. She avoided him when possible; and when he announced his decision to go back home for a month or so to settle his affairs there, she felt a good deal happier.

It was a warm August day when, with her father and mother, she drove with him on the first stage of his journey; and as the carriage went along past wheatfields which were beginning to turn a golden brown, Amanda felt her spirits rise. They were driving him to the inn where he would pick up the coach which would take him out of Cornwall by way of Gunnislake. Once in Devon he would travel by rail.

"Coward! Coward!" the clopping hoofs of the horses seemed to be saying to Amanda, but all the same she felt a lightness of heart. He would be away for six weeks—probably two months. A good deal could happen in that time.

They were silent driving back. Her father and mother pretended to think that her silence meant she was grieving for Anthony. *Pretended* to think! It was all pretence . . . everything in their lives. She realized this now. Her mother was afraid of her father, although she pretended not to be; her father pretended to protect her mother when all he did was command her obedience. Amanda was in revolt. I will not marry Anthony! she thought. I will not be a coward.

But it was easy to say that now he had gone. Soon . . . all too soon . . . he would be back; and when he came back the wedding would take place.

It was getting dark when they came along the high road, and they were all drowsy with the heat, the monotonous clop-clop of the horses' hoofs, the jolting of the carriage. As they came close to St. Martin's Church they heard shouting, and very soon a small procession came into view from the direction of Polgards' Farm. This was led by a crowd of people who danced and shouted and screamed; there followed a donkey cart, pulled by some of the crowd; and in it were two effigies.

Amanda was alert immediately; she wanted to know what was happening.

"Some of the townspeople behaving with their usual folly," said her father. "If they would only worship God as zealously as they remember their old customs . . ."

"I wonder what custom this is," said Amanda, breaking in on his sentence—a thing which she had never done before and which, surprisingly, did not astonish her. She had changed. Something had happened on the road. She was not going to be a coward any more.

"I have no idea," said her father remotely; but she noticed gleefully that he did not reprimand her.

They drove on.

Lilith will know, she thought; Lilith will soon discover.

Lilith had discovered. She was one of the crowd. She had known at once that it was a 'riding,' for she had seen this particular ceremony enacted before. In the donkey cart were two effigies which represented two people known to them all. They were sinners, guilty of that sin which, when discovered, aroused more indignation than any other. Cruelty could be looked upon with equanimity; adultery and fornication, which, Lilith knew, many of them had committed in secret, were, when discovered—but only when discovered—those which aroused the most righteous indignation.

Here in the cart were the effigies of two adulterers.

The crowd chanted horribly; stones and mud were flung at the pair. On the quay a fire was already burning and the cart was being slowly trundled towards that fire.

Who? wondered Lilith.

The crowd was shouting obscenities; she could hear only a confused gabble of voices, but as she drew nearer to the cart someone shouted: "Come then, Dolly my dear. 'Twas time you and me was together again like."

The crowd shrieked; then there was silence.

An imitation of a high-pitched, simpering female voice followed: "Well, Jos, me dear, I be willing."

Dolly! Jos! Lilith stood still, holding her breath. Dolly Brent! Jos Polgard!

There was no doubt now as to the identity of the pair represented by the two figures in the cart. The adultery of Jos Polgard

with Dolly Brent was no longer Lilith's secret, to wield as a
queen wields a sceptre of power. The whole neighbourhood
would know now.

She turned away, sickened and frightened. What now?
What if Jos thought she had betrayed him? What when he
realized he need no longer fear what she might do? What
of William? What would happen to him? He had never been
whipped since the day Lilith had faced Jos Polgard in his
field. What now? In her mind's eye she saw that brutish
hairy face, livid with anger, eager for revenge. And how
could he take revenge but on William? Jane was all right.
She was married to Tom Polgard. She was happy in the
farmhouse, for Annie had taken to her on finding her a good
and willing worker, ready to learn her thrifty ways. She
need not fear for Jane. But what of William?

She sped away from the fire; she ran as fast as she could up
the Barbican Hill, and she did not stop until she reached the
Polgard Farm.

She was fortunate in finding the boy Napoleon in his hut.

"Find William," she panted. "Don't lose a minute. Go . . .
and bring him to me."

The boy ran off. William was his god. William had helped
him with his work, saved him many a whipping; William
had fed him when he was hungry and had made his life
bearable, because he had put something into it which the
boy did not understand, but which gave him a shadowy hope
of better things. He was like a dog; he would go straight to
his master.

"William," cried Lilith as soon as her brother arrived,
"something terrible have happened."

She told him everything, right from that time when she had
peeped into the barn and seen Jos Polgard and Dolly Brent making love.

William listened in astonishment. "So, 'twas you . . . you
who got Jane married!"

She nodded, proud even in her terrible fear.

"But 'tis no good now, William. Others have discovered. The
whole town knows about Jos and Dolly. I reckon before morning
Jos'll know . . . and so will Annie Polgard. I wouldn't like to
be here then. I reckon he'll just on kill me . . . and you too,
William. Your life wouldn't be worth living. He'll make it hell

for you . . . and for me if he gets a chance . . . because Annie'll be making it so for him.''

William saw the truth of this. ''Lilith, you'm a terrible meddler.''

'' 'Twas for good I meddled. 'Twas for you and Jane.''

''Yes,'' he said, '' 'twas for me and Jane. But what be going to do now?''

''Let's run away, William.''

''Run? Where'd we run to?''

''To London.''

''To London? But that be a terrible long way.''

'' 'Tis not so far as you do think. London be a wonderful place. I do know, because Amanda have shown me pictures of it. You've got money. I've got some too. I've been waiting to go to London for a long time. William, we've got to go *now*. You get everything you've got. Don't lose a minute. For all we do know, he might have heard there's a riding in the town. I reckon he'll kill you, William. I reckon he'll kill us both. Get everything you've got and come away. You hide . . . hide in Morval Woods, and I'll get your money from Amanda. I'll bring everything I've got . . . and we'll go together. We'll go to London. 'Tis the only thing we can do now.''

He was staring at her with dawning assurance. She was so vehement, so sure of herself. He was aware of the power in that small, childish body—the little girl who had stood up to the mighty Jos Polgard and forced him to allow his son to marry his own choice of a maiden.

''Lilith,'' he said, ''you'm right. I do believe you'm right.''

Lilith stood in Amanda's room.

''Amanda, give me William's money. I have come to say goodbye.''

''Lilith! What do you mean?''

''We'm going away. We'm going to London.''

''How can you?''

''I don't know, but we'm going. With William's money and what I've got we'm going. We'll be killed if we stay.''

''Lilith, have you gone mad?''

''I'm not silly. I know what we've got to do. In the town they'm having a riding. They'm burning 'em now . . . two bundles of straw dressed up like people—Jos Polgard and Dolly Brent. . . . They'm giving them a riding and a burning.''

''I saw them on the road.''

In short, breathless sentences Lilith told the story of her discovery of Jos and Dolly in the barn, and the subsequent blackmail and its results.

''Now the whole world do know and there'll be nothing to make him give William a softer life. He might think I told. . . . He'd kill me. He said he would, and it was only his fear that stopped him. He'll flog William to death.''

''He wouldn't dare.''

''Wouldn't he? He wouldn't be the first one to have done it.''

''It would be murder.''

'' 'Tain't murder if 'tis the likes of we who gets killed, as you do very well know.''

Amanda pressed her hands to her burning temples. ''So . . . you're going away?'' she said slowly. She could not bear this. She could not go on living here without Lilith. She thought cynically that if her father had been in her place he would have said that God was showing him the way. It was bold and it terrified her; but why should she be more afraid than Lilith? The answer was simple: She lacked Lilith's courage.

''Lilith,'' she said breathlessly, ''could I come to London with you?''

Lilith stared at her.

''I . . . I've got some money . . . quite a lot, I think. It's in my money-box. It has not been banked yet. I can bring clothes for us both. Oh, Lilith . . . I'm coming . . . I'm coming with you to London!''

Lilith smiled slowly; then she did what she had never done before; she ran to Amanda and put her arms about her.

PART TWO

❈ One

Light was beginning to show in the sky. Amanda, lying on the floor of the attic which she shared with Lilith, watched it as it filtered through the tiny window. The life of freedom had begun a week ago.

It was a draughty attic; the wallpaper was peeling off the walls and there were patches of damp on the cracked ceiling; the one small window was difficult to open and, once open, it was difficult to shut. The furniture consisted of two mattresses—hers and Lilith's—a small wash-handstand and two chairs. It was very humble, yet she was not unhappy, for each day brought a new excitement; she could never be sure what would take place. Since she had arrived in London, she had been alternately enchanted and disgusted; secure in her freedom, yet terrified of it.

She could just make out the shape of a parcel on the floor, and she smiled as she looked towards it. She was longing for daylight so that she could open that parcel; she wanted to show the others that she could become one of them.

This capital city was, as Frith had said, a truly wonderful place; but Amanda knew that she and William saw it differently from the way in which Lilith and Napoleon saw it. To Amanda it was like a woman with ugly sores on her face, yet opulently dressed and sparkling with jewels; it was those contrasts, which never seemed absent, which fascinated and horrified her.

Lying there, waiting for the daylight, she thought of the week of freedom which had begun with flight from Cornwall. She relived that escape as she had many times during the last week: the gathering together of clothes and what money she could, writing a note to her parents, explaining why she must go, meeting Lilith and finding William, with Napoleon, waiting for them in Morval Woods. They had walked for some hours, and it was

137

not until they had put a good many miles between themselves and Looe that, weary and tired, they persuaded a wagoner to give them a lift which took them to where they could pick up 'Kellow's Fairy,' the working man's conveyance, to take them out of Cornwall.

How exciting it had been to ride on the railway for the first time! Lilith's eyes had been like black stones that sparkled as they caught the light; perpetually she had talked of London, with exhilaration, with reverence; so that, oddly enough, she reminded the fanciful Amanda of one of the knights in search of the Holy Grail. The boy Napoleon had been almost as happy as Lilith, although he was so quiet. He might meet hunger and hardship in the city, but he was already on familiar terms with those two, and familiarity bred contempt. He was like a slave who had cast off his fetters and was at last free. William was too serious to share his sister's lighthearted optimism; he had been worried on account of Amanda. How could they know what awaited them in the city? And what would happen there to a lady, such as Amanda, who had been bred to luxury? Amanda had known how concerned he had been on her account.

How they had laughed as the railway wagons jolted them! And how cold they had been, unprotected as they were from the wind! For, although there was a roof over the wagon, which was like a cattle-box, the sides were open. Amanda, stiff with cold, thought fleetingly of how Frith and Anthony would travel on the railway; they would have gone first-class, sitting on cushioned seats with plenty of space to stretch their legs. That was how she would have travelled if she had been with her parents or Anthony. But what were cold limbs compared with that cold fear that her father had always been able to arouse in her? What was a little jolting compared with the terror Anthony had inspired?

"Free! Free! Free!" said the train; and freedom was wonderful; it was something to make you joyful.

As soon as they had arrived in London, Amanda had been struck by the contrasts in everything she saw—luxury and poverty, grandeur and squalor, the abundance of food in the shops and people starving in the streets. Amanda herself must feel contrasting emotions—pleasure and horror.

It was the year of the Great Exhibition, and the streets were thronged with foreigners from all over the world: Indians in turbans which were studded with gems, Chinese with pigtails, Africans in flowing robes. In the streets the carriages would be drawn up while well-dressed women and dandified men, on their way to the Crystal Palace in Hyde Park, enjoyed their picnic luncheons of chicken and champagne. Watching them were the poor—bare-footed, ragged and lousy—catching the bones which were thrown from the carriages, fighting over them and the privilege of holding the horses for a penny if they got the chance. Bunting adorned the windows of all the buildings, and all roads seemed to lead to that thoroughfare on one side of which were the great mansions, Ennismore House, Park House and Gore House, and on the other the vast and glittering palace of glass. All along the route were those who sought to profit from the great occasion in English history. Stalls and barrows were overflowing with fruit and ginger beer; beneath them the urchins scrambled in search of what they could find; between them pickpockets lurked and confidence tricksters waited for the unwary. Barrel organs played; costers danced, children cried for a red, white and blue button to be worn on the lapels of the coat or gay pictures of the Exhibition to take home as mementoes. They saw the lower middle classes sitting on the grass before the palace enjoying their picnics, or going into the grounds of Gore House for a rest, or making their way to Batty's Hippodrome, which had been set up near the Broad Walk in Kensington Gardens; and they saw the fashion parade on a late Saturday afternoon when the Exhibition was closed to all but those with five-shilling tickets or season tickets. In London, as in Cornwall, there must be sharp dividing lines between the classes, and they must be kept rigorously apart. Never had Amanda seen anything like the streets of this capital with their colour and squalor, their riches and poverty; that perpetual contrast lifted her spirits one moment, and the next made her feel utterly depressed, for then she would feel that this great city itself was like a crystal palace built over a cesspool.

Amanda remembered now the slight shock she had experienced on arriving at the London station, that shock which brought with it the realization that she had stepped from one class to another. There had been a notice on the platform which announced that: "The company's servants are strictly ordered *not* to porter for wagon passengers." She had been glad that she was the only member of the party who could read that. It was significant. It was her welcome into the new class to which she now belonged; it was the rule of the day. Riches were honourable and poverty disgraceful.

They spent their first night in London at an inn near the station, but it was clear to them all that they could not continue in such extravagance. They were fortunate for, on the day after their arrival, they found cheap rooms; and it was only after they had begun to learn something of the city to which they had come that they understood what good luck was theirs on that day.

It began when, as they wandered out into the streets, Amanda had seen a blind man trying to make a perilous journey through the traffic. William had hurried to help him across, and the man had become excited when he heard them speak. They were from the country, he said. He was interested to hear who they were and what they were doing here. They had taken him to his pitch in Oxford Street, where his wife was waiting for him. She had brought flowers for him to sell, sprays of roses and forget-me-nots, which she had made out of silk.

She, like her husband, was interested in them, and when she heard that they wanted somewhere to live she became more excited than ever.

She lived with her family—mother, father, husband and sister—in a cottage not far from Tichfield Street. They had two beautiful attics. The rent was cheap—not more than three and sixpence a week. There couldn't be anything cheaper than that, could there?

And so, within a short time of their arrival, they found adequate lodgings which would not make too great a demand on their small capital.

The flower-maker and her husband had proved the best of friends. The woman sat in her room most of the day, for she must put in fourteen hours each day at her work so that, if the weather was good, she and her husband might earn ten shillings a week between them. Most of her work went to the shops, who, so she told Amanda, paid sevenpence a gross for violets although she could get up to three shillings a gross for a good rose.

If Amanda had been deeply moved by the poor of Cornwall, how much more so should she have been by the poor of London; but she found it was impossible to be entirely sorry for these people, because they defied pity. There was a quality about them which scorned it; it was a defence against the world, a pride, a sense of the ridiculous that was infectious and irrepressible. Laughter followed quickly on tragedy in these London streets. Even the beggars at the street corners, with their swollen feet, sore and bruised, and their skin bearing the grime of years, huddling in their rags, were not wholly sad. The costers, trying to force their wares on passers-by, had a merry chatter; even those drunken people who reeled out of the gin- and beer-shops, which were open all day, invariably had a song on their lips. The children, waiting for their parents outside these places, would hop, dance, fight and laugh, whatever the misery they had to endure.

It was the same with the people who shared their new home. Apart from Dora, the flower-maker, and her husband Tom, there were Mr. and Mrs. Murphy, Dora's parents, who by selling ballads, water-cress, fish and fruit pies earned a few shillings a week, and Dora's sister Jenny, who was a shirt-maker. This family was piteously poor, but in them all was that quality of the streets—courage, endurance and the desire to laugh at life.

The need to earn money was apparent. What could Amanda do? She could sew. How she wished now that she had worked harder at her needlework as her mother and Miss Robinson had said she should!

Well now she was going to earn money. The parcel on the floor was a parcel of shirts which Jenny had brought for her. She must sew the buttons which were in the parcel on to the shirts, and when she had sewn on one hundred and forty-four and carried the parcel back to the factory, she would be paid three-pence for her pains. She was lucky because Jenny had been working on shirts for years, and there was no deposit needed before she could bring the shirts away.

"I'm responsible, you see," said Jenny, proud of the responsibility.

There had been moments of sheer delight in this wonderful city. They had seen the Crystal Palace, although they could not afford to pay a shilling to go inside on those days when the lower classes were allowed in. But it had been wonderful to stand outside it and look at it; to lie on the grass and watch the people. They had all four spent some hours on Saturday night in the nearby market, which had seemed a fantastic place in the glow from gas lamps and grease lamps and with candles casting a glow over the stalls. The shouts of the costers were like a foreign language to them and it was impossible to be there and not to sense the excitement, to enjoy the fun of seeing something so strange for the first time, to get a bargain. Fish for sale; hot pies; apples; crockery; saucepans; old clothes; butchers' shops, grocers' shops; and the chemist's shop with the bottles of coloured water. There were beggars everywhere—blind, crippled or merely ragged. There were sellers of watercress, oranges, wallflowers and sweet lavender. There was the joy of drinking a cup of coffee and eating a ham sandwich at a coffee-stall, and amusing the coffee-stall-keeper with their quaint accents, and listening to his lecture on the wickedness of those who frequented a great city.

The others had had luck, besides Amanda with her shirts. Napoleon had been given a shilling for carrying a parcel for a gentleman at the railway station. He brought it home and it seemed like a fortune. William had heard a Chartist speak in the park and that had set his eyes shining; Lilith, hearing a barrel organ playing in Kensington Road, close to the Crystal Palace, had danced to the music and several people had stopped to watch her and to laugh and throw her some coppers. So it seemed to them all that the streets of this city might after all be paved with gold; if you worked hard to find it, you might do so.

"If," said Lilith, "we got very poor, if we were starving, I expect Frith would help us."

"But we don't know where he is," answered Amanda.

"You could write to Alice. It do only cost a penny to send a letter. You be able to write a letter."

"I wouldn't think of writing to Alice. I ran away from home. I've cut myself right off."

"Not from Frith, you ain't. You write to Alice. I reckon her'd like to know where you were."

"I shall do no such thing. It would embarrass her. Besides, it would tell her where we are. What if my father came here?"

Lilith had to admit that might make a difficulty. Jos Polgard might hear and make a journey to London. Lilith had stopped talking about her writing to Alice then, but Amanda knew that she still thought of it.

And now the sun was up and it was time to wake to a new day. This was the first day when Amanda would not go out with them. She felt proud and happy because she had work to do.

The others talked about what they would do, while they ate breakfast—a slice of bread and a cold baked potato each—in the girls' room.

William had some watercress to sell. Amanda guessed he would go near the park in the hope of hearing more speeches.

Lilith began to sing one of the ballads she would try to sell. She made up her own tunes and she danced while she sang them. The Murphys had told her where to get them at a farthing apiece; they sold theirs for a halfpenny. Lilith had daringly asked a penny for hers, for she said she did a song and a dance as well; and surprisingly she had often got it, and was already earning more than the old man who had instructed her. Her droll grimaces, her odd accent, her liveliness, her *gamin* charm attracted people; it made them laugh, and there was nothing that was so welcome in these streets as laughter. People were ready to pay for their laughter, and Lilith realized she had the trick of luring money out of their pockets. She was already the main breadwinner in the little group. She found that she could earn ten shillings a week—earn it easily and pleasantly—a sum which was as much as the skilled flower-maker and her husband could earn between them. Lilith gave herself airs. *She* was in command of the party. She had known that, in spite of her foreign-looking little face, in spite of her accent, she was very close to these people of London. She could pit her wits against theirs, for she had a sharpness to match their own, which the other three lacked; she was immediately at home in this warren of streets and they were already becoming as familiar to her as the lanes among which she had been brought up.

Napoleon had a broom, and he was happy enough. He was not a recognized crossing-sweeper yet with a crossing of his own, but an ancient crossing-sweeper of Regent Street had allowed him to use his crossing when he himself was absent, which was for two or three hours each day. This was an exciting game for Napoleon; he never knew when he would be paid for his work, but he never forgot the man who had given him a shilling, and such was his nature that he believed every day when he set out that he would have the joy of bringing home another shilling to add to the exchequer, and that by some miracle he would that day acquire a crossing of his own.

Amanda was not sorry when they had eaten their breakfasts

and gone their separate ways. She then went to the parcel, un-wrapped it and began to work.

During the morning, Jenny looked in to see how she was getting on. Jenny grimaced a little over the buttons.

"You mustn't pucker it up, dearie. They don't pay for puck-ers. They take off for them. You've got to be neat. Look. Let me show you."

So she sat awhile, sewing on the buttons withe deft fingers, and her speed shamed Amanda, reminding her of the sampler of Martha Bartlett which had been completed in 1805 and held up as an example for her to follow.

"You must not leave your own work," she said.

"That's right, dearie. Mustn't lose the daylight. You just let me see the shirts when you've done and I'll tell you where to take them. Put them puckered ones in the middle. They mightn't see them then. Though they'll be partic'ler with a new 'un."

"I shall never be as quick as you."

"Lord bless you, it comes. Crystal Palace wasn't built in a day, lovey."

"Could I . . . bring them down to your room and work with you? We could talk while we worked. I'd like that."

"I'll come up here," said Jenny. "It's lighter up here."

"Please do. I should so enjoy it."

So Jenny brought her work to the attic, and while Amanda sewed Jenny gave reminiscences of her past. She told how she had been apprenticed to a tailor's shop.

"That were a hard life, dearie . . . though I thought it would be a good 'un when I started. Lived in, I did. There, I said to meself, you'll be sure of your dinner, Jin, *and* a bed to sleep in. But it was this here piece-work. You see, when there was a rush job they'd have ten of us working on it. They'd only have wanted about five . . . but for the rush. Then there'd be no work after that, and we'd have to pay rent for our bed and food . . . so that when there was work again we was still paying for the food and lodging what we'd had when there was no work, so you didn't get no wages at all, and that was like working for nothing. That was a hard life. Why, says I to meself, you'd be better on your own, Jin. And so I have been. But this shirt work . . . you've got to stick at it to make anything."

"It's so wrong!" cried Amanda. "So unfair."

"Well, dearie, so it is, I reckon . . . but as the tailor used to say, he'd got to have the goods at the right price or he wouldn't sell 'em. And if people wanted their things quick, there was no two ways about it, they'd got to have them.''

Jenny stitched away with resignation while Amanda talked as William would have talked.

''If people could only get together. If something could only be done. . . . If people want things made quickly they should pay more. And they should put up prices so that people who worked should be paid enough to buy their food and a decent lodging.''

''Hey, dearie, you've pricked your finger. Look! You've put blood on that shirt. They don't like that. I've knowed 'em not pay for shirts that go back with blood on them. It's on the tail. I'll show you how to fold it so it's not seen. Oh, Gawd love yer, don't get no more on . . . or you'll work for nothing.''

Sewing buttons on shirts, it seemed, was a skilled occupation. Amanda worked industriously. The money she received for the shirts would be the first she earned, and she alone of the party had so far brought nothing in. She could console herself with the fact that she had brought more money with her than the others; she had also brought clothes which kept them warm at night and which Lilith was glad to wear by day; but all the same she longed to earn money, to be one of them.

It was four o'clock before Amanda had sewn on all the buttons.

''I'll tell you where to take 'em,'' said Jenny. ''I'd take 'em back meself, but I'm all behind. Go straight out of the alley to Tichfield and on to Oxford Street, turn left and cross the road and go on till you come to Dean Street. Go down there, first left, then right again. You'll see Fiddlers' Court and there's the shop. It's a tall building . . . tall and narrow. You can't make no mistake.''

So Amanda wrapped up her parcel and went out.

The streets were busy, but not so busy as they would be a little later on when the shop-girls and apprentices came out to stretch their legs, when the clerks would leave the warehouses and join the streams of traffic and pedestrians that were flowing as usual towards Hyde Park.

Following Jenny's instructions, she soon arrived at Fiddlers' Court, a small and frowsty spot with tall houses that seemed to meet overhead, almost as though determined to let in as little air as possible. There were a few dirty children squatting on the cobbles, and some more were swinging on a rope which they had attached to the lamp-post.

She recognized the shop immediately because there were shirts piled up in the window. She approached timidly and looked down the area into the basement, where she could see women working at the tables. It was dark down there and some held the coarse, limey stuff close to their noses. Amanda shuddered. She could already smell the odour of sweating bodies mingling with the limey smell of the shirts.

She walked down three stone steps into a small, dark passage, in which was a door on the right with the word "Enquiries" painted on it. She knocked diffidently; there was no answer, so she knocked again.

"Come in!" called a deep voice and she entered.

In a small room, surrounded by piles of shirts, sat a fat man. He wore a dirty shirt open at the neck. It was very hot in this room and flies cruised over a plate on the table which had contained a meat meal. Some of the food was on the man's shirt, and the porter—a half-filled tankard was still beside him—was glistening on his whiskers.

"Ha!" he said at the sight of Amanda. "So the lady's brought back some shirts, has she?"

He grinned and, repelled as she was, Amanda felt relieved that he was going to be friendly. Before he had smiled he seemed a very angry man.

He patted the table at which he sat. "Put 'em down, lady. Put 'em down."

She laid the parcel on the spot he had indicated.

"First time 'ere, eh?"

She nodded.

"So you brought some shirts back, eh?" he repeated unnecessarily, and then almost incredulously: "And you want me to pay for 'em, eh?"

She nodded again. She was very much afraid of him. She felt that the room was too small and too hot.

"Ain't you got a tongue in your head, eh?"

"Yes," she said, timidly. "I . . . I have brought back the shirts."

Something seemed to amuse him; he leaned back, so that the

chair supported him by its two hind legs only; he rocked a little, looking at her slyly.

"Little Miss Goldilocks!" he said.

"Will you please give me the money for the shirts," said Amanda. "I'm in rather a hurry."

"Ho!" he cried; and he began to laugh. He turned to the shirts and addressed them in a manner which she realized was meant to be an imitation of her own. "Little Miss Goldilocks his hin a hurry. Little Miss Goldilocks wants her money. Little Miss Goldilocks ain't got the time to say a civil word to poor old Jimmy."

There was something ominous in the way he kept repeating the name he had given her. "I'm sorry," she began.

"Ho!" he went on, still addressing the shirts. "Little Miss Goldilocks is sorry. All right. Never mind." He stood up slowly and came round to the other side of the table; then he sat on it, still looking at her.

"We'll look at the work," he said. "We'll see if little Miss Goldilocks has done her work proper, shall we? We'll see if little Miss Goldilocks *deserves* her pay."

He opened the parcel and began to examine the work.

"Ho! She's a bit of a cobbler, little Miss Goldilocks his. Little Miss Cobbler, eh? She ought to go and work for the snob down the street." He tugged at one of the buttons.

"That . . . that's not fair," said Amanda.

He wiped his nose with the back of his hand. Then he turned to her grinning. "Don't you upset yourself, little Miss Cobbler. You give me a nice kiss, eh, and we'll say nothing about bad work." He winked at her. "We won't pass on no complaints. We'll say there ain't no Miss Cobbler. She's little Miss Goldilocks what's earned her pay."

She stepped backwards, terrified of him.

"Give me my money!" she said. "Give me the money I've earned."

He sat on the table, shaking his finger at her. "You ain't earned nothing yet," he said. "All you done is ruin this lot of shirts, that's all."

He gave the shirts a push with his hand and they were scattered all over the floor.

"You come here. You give me a nice kiss . . . then we'll see."

He stood up, but she waited for no more. She turned, pulled open the door, stumbled up the three steps to the street, and ran.

Lilith was glad it was a fine day. On fine days the streets were crowded. Her great plan each day was to earn her pennies with her ballads and spend the rest of the day walking in the grand streets looking for Frith. He would never venture near the warrens and the rookeries. She laughed to think of him there. He belonged in the wide streets; he belonged in a carriage. She vehemently believed that she would find him. He was here in this city, so she must meet him.

Here was the street she had decided to try to-day. It was between Covent Garden and the new statue of Lord Nelson in the square. She thought of it as a lucky street. It was not squalid, yet it was lively; it was neither a poor street nor a rich one. In it were two rival supper-rooms, Sam Marpit's and Dan Delaney's.

As she came into the street she saw that the old man with the barrel organ was already there. They had been together only yesterday at this very spot; she had sung to the tunes he had played—songs which she quickly learned; and when she had not known the words she had substituted her own. People did not mind; the organ-grinder did not mind. More crowds had collected about his organ, and if some of the pennies had gone to buying her ballads quite a few had gone into his cap.

The organ-grinder had taken his stand outside Marpit's to catch the people as they passed, for Marpit's remained shut at this hour. Later on, when the supper-rooms opened, the old organ-grinder would be nervous. He had told Lilith in his broken English that Sam Marpit did not like their taking a stand so near his premises.

Lilith had seen Sam Marpit yesterday when he had come out to look at them. He was a man in his late twenties, very grand—so Lilith might have thought if she had not been acquainted with the dress and manners of the real gentry. Sam Marpit wore a fancy waistcoat embroidered with tiny scarlet flowers, a large cravat, a flower in his buttonhole and a well-greased lock of hair over his forehead.

To-day the organ-grinder said: "This is bad day. On such days money it stay in pocket."

"Don't 'ee believe it!" cried Lilith. "We'll make it a day for getting it out of their pockets."

The organ-grinder's repertoire was limited. It consisted of a few popular songs of the day and some Rossini tunes.

"Play up!" commanded Lilith. "And we'll start."

So he played the tune of the Ratcatcher's Daughter, and as Lilith had never heard of the lady who was not born in Westminster, but on the other side of the water, she hummed and sang her own words and danced as she sang; and very soon the people began to gather round.

The sun came out and the crowd grew. Some applauded and the pennies began to come in—some went into the organ-grinder's hat, some in exchange for ballads.

The organ played a Rossini tune, gay, frivolous and sensuous, and Lilith danced the Dance of the Seven Veils which she herself had arranged from Amanda's description of what she had seen at the Fair, throwing aside the imaginary veils, to the amusement of the watchers.

"Buy a ballad. Buy a ballad," she cried as she made her way through the crowd. She stopped as she put a ballad into a man's hand for, as she looked up into his face, she saw that he was none other than Sam Marpit. His expression told her nothing. He must have come out of his supper-rooms to stand at the edge of the crowd.

"Thank 'ee, sir," she said with an air of defiance.

He answered: "When this show's over, young 'un, you pop into Sam Marpit's Supper-rooms, will you? I've got a word to say to you."

"I might," said Lilith.

"If you're smart, you will," he answered.

She had six ballads in her hand. She said: "Now if you was smart you'd buy these, then I'd come right away. I'll stay here till I sell 'em . . . and then I might have to go into another street, and there'd be no knowing if I'd come back."

His eyes twinkled, or so she thought.

"Smart girl, eh?" he said.

She was learning the jargon of the streets and it mixed rather becomingly with her Cornish accent, and it never failed to amuse those who heard it.

"They be smart where I do come from, mister."

"Right you are, Miss I-tal-i-an. Here's your tanner. Hand over them ballads first. This is a deal."

"Six ballads sixpence," she said, her eyes gleaming at the sight of the money. "And I'm no Italian."

"All right, you Spanish monkey. Come on in and have a talk with me."

She was a little afraid of him. She had heard tales of girls who had been lured into dangerous places by strange men, and although there was something about Sam Marpit which made her feel he was not that sort, he was a business-man, first and foremost, and when a businessman paid sixpence for a set of ballads that he could not want, you could be sure he wanted something.

He took her into a big room which was full of tables and chairs; the chairs were standing on top of the tables; there was sawdust on the floor and a piano in a corner of the room.

"Sit down 'ere," he said.

And she sat. He sat opposite her and leaned his elbows on the table.

"Will you have a cup of coffee, little 'un, while we talk business?"

"Well, I wouldn't say no to that."

"Right you are. And what'll you eat with it, eh? A nice ham samwidge . . . with or without mustard?"

"With mustard, please."

"Go on!" he mocked. "I should have thought you wouldn't 'ave needed mustard." He laughed and repeated the joke. "Shouldn't have thought you'd have needed mustard. 'Cos why? 'Cos you look warm enough without it!"

"It's the dancing," she said. "It do make you hot."

That made him laugh more than ever.

"Here, Fanny," he called. "Bring two cups of coffee and hamsams for the lady. See that she gets a dollop of mustard. She likes it."

He patted his thigh—quick little pats as though it were responsible for his jokes and he were congratulating it.

Coffee. Sandwiches with mustard. This, thought Lilith, must be the road to sin. She would take them, but she was going to give nothing in return. There was no one for her but Frith, and when she compared him with this man in his flowered waistcoat and flowing cravat, his lock of hair glistening with Rowland's

Macassar Oil, she was not disgusted by his possible intention, she merely wanted to laugh.

"Now I'd say," he said slowly and significantly, "that you was a little 'un that knowed a big lot." He began to laugh again, patting the thigh, that source of his wit.

"I won't say no to that," she countered.

He pointed a finger at her. "So you know it all," he said, his voice losing itself in a wheeze of laughter.

"Not all," she said, with an air of modesty. "Only some."

The sandwiches had arrived and were put before her by Fanny—a young woman in her early twenties with a large bosom, large hips and a velvet band in her frizzed hair.

"Thanks, Fan." He jerked his hand at Lilith. "Don't mind me. Carry on with the stuff, little 'un."

Lilith tackled the sandwiches, determined to eat them as fast as she could, before he made some proposition which would demand her immediate withdrawal.

"Now," he said, and the word was long drawn out and it came through his nose, "here's what. I've had me peepers on you ever since you started singing in my street and started to draw 'em. Do you know something? You could do better than selling ballads, you could . . . a little 'un like you that knows a big lot."

Here was the old joke. He must spend his time, thought Lilith, making jokes and congratulating that old thigh of his.

Lilith went on placidly eating her sandwiches. She would buy something good and take it back to them; she would sit and watch them eat, as she used to when she took a parcel from Leigh House to the cottage.

He took out a toothpick and started to pick his teeth.

"You could do better for yourself," he said. "Barrel organs! Ballads!"

She waited.

"How'd you like to come and sing in here?" he asked.

Lilith stopped eating to look at him.

"Sing here?" Her eyes went to the piano.

"People like a bit of music. It's like mustard. 'Elps the digestion." He began to laugh again.

Lilith brought him back sharply to the point. "Do you mean you'd *pay* me to sing here? I'd belong to be paid."

He struck his fist on the table. "Ten bob a week," he said, "and your supper."

Lilith's heart was fluttering, but some instinct warned her to say: "Fifteen bob a week and my supper."

"Sharp!" he mused. "Sharp as they make 'em. Twelve and six and your supper."

Twelve and six! Every week! The flower-maker and her husband thought they were lucky if they made ten. This London was all she had believed it to be, if people were ready to pay you twelve and six and your supper just for singing a few songs.

She thought of Amanda, who could sing very nicely and had had singing lessons. "I do know someone who can sing beautiful," she said. "She's a real lady."

"Don't want ladies in this place. The customers don't like 'em. I'll tell you something. You've got what they like. Don't know what it is . . . only know it fetches 'em. Look at the way they was round that barrel organ. For what? The Ratcatcher's Daughter? Don't make me laugh. Them Italian tunes? Not *it*! No. I know what. It was to see you dance; and the way you dance is too good for the streets. That's why I'm offering you ten bob—half a jimmy o' goblin . . . *and* your supper, just to give a little song and dance o' nights."

"Not ten," she said. "It would have to be twelve and six."

"All right. All right." He looked sly, winked and patted his thigh even though this was not a joke. "You get it. Twelve and a kick. And we'll have that dance with real veils . . . that'll fetch 'em."

"I'd have to have tights on and a tunic that starts here and finishes where the tights come up to."

"All right. All right." He winked again. "This is a respectable house, this is. We'll get the costumes and you'll dance, eh? Got a family?"

"Yes."

"Live with them?"

"Yes."

"You could live in, you know. Better for you. Don't want to go through the streets the time you'd finish."

"I'll go through the streets when I finish."

"Six in the evening till two in the morning . . . and you get your supper."

"All right. Shall I start to-night?"

"No. Monday. We'll start off then. You come in here tomorrow, and we'll see about the dances, though. We'll see what you're to sing . . . and about clothes. We'll have some rehearsals."

"There'd be none of them unless I was paid."

"You'll be paid. I'll give you seven and six at the end of this week . . . and you start twelve and six at the end of next. How's that? And you get something to eat after rehearsals. You want a bit of fattening up."

He patted her hand and she shook him off.

"Ooh!" he said. "Be careful, Sammy boy. Behave yourself."

She waited for him to finish his laugh and his congratulatory pats before she stood up. She longed to go back to the attic to tell them what had happened, to explain to Amanda that it did not matter now if she did not go back to that beast at the shirt shop. Nothing mattered any more. Lilith was going to be rich. She was going to be a real dancer, just as she had always longed to be.

They had been a whole year in London, and they were as familiar now with the city as most of its inhabitants were; they knew where to get a bargain in the markets, how to answer sharply when spoken to; they had paid a visit to Cremorne; they had eaten oysters in an oyster room and saveloys and faggots from a stall. They no longer stared in horror at the churchyards where the rats prowled among the exposed bones of the ancient corpses; they accepted London just as though they had lived there all their lives.

Amanda had discovered that she was not so inadequate as she had at first believed herself to be. She had never gone back to the shirt shop, but Jenny had brought work home for her, and she had graduated from the sewing-on of buttons to the actual making of shirts. It was hard work and she was tired out with it by the end of the day and not a little dispirited to discover that her earnings were very poor indeed. She grew pale from long confinement in the house; her hair shone less than it had when she came to London; her eyes were often shadowed; but she was happier than she had been in Cornwall. She felt independent—at least, she earned her share of the food; she did not know where this life was leading her, but she did not think very much about that. She was now seventeen, and she told herself again and again that even if freedom meant stitching shirts for hours and hours until her fingers were sore and her eyes and back ached and she was worn out with exhaustion, it was worth the cost.

William was the least happy member of the party, for he knew himself to be a misfit. He lacked Lilith's spirits, Amanda's ability to appreciate her surroundings by setting them side by side in her mind with a prospect which had terrified her, and he lacked Napoleon's simple optimism. William was concerned with the wrongs of the poor and oppressed, and nobody else wanted to hear of these matters which tormented him; people wanted to laugh.

Lilith would dance about the attic, mimicking the people who came into Marpit's Supper-rooms, all the ladies of the town looking for custom, all the dandies and mashers. William told himself that he was disgusted with Lilith's way of life, but in truth he was a little envious, for Lilith had taken that position of guardian of the group which William felt should have been his.

Even Napoleon was happy. Poor, simple Napoleon, going out every morning with one hope in his mind—that he would meet a gentleman who would give him a shilling!

It astonished William that Amanda could have adapted herself so readily to the conditions of this life. Her rosiness had gone and she was like a pale primrose, ethereal, her hair a dull gold now. He loved Amanda, and it was largely for her sake that he wished to be a man of dignity, for dignity was what he needed more than riches. He was just past seventeen and he found it difficult to understand his own thoughts. He could not admit to himself that it was his own sad case which at times enraged and at others depressed him; he wanted to be noble, so he told himself it was the fate of all poor men that tormented him, and that his own dissatisfaction had nothing to do with his state of frustration.

He had failed in all his endeavours to earn money. He went to Billingsgate with Mrs. Murphy, but he could not sell his herrings quickly enough, so they went bad. He became a pieman for a few days, with meat pies, fish pies and fruit pies in his basket, but he had no more success with them than he had had with herrings. People recognized the voice of the countryman in his cry, "Toss or Buy." No pieman could do business without acceding to this ancient custom. The costers tossed with him, and if they won they had a pie for nothing, and if they lost they paid him a penny and received no pie. William found that he always said 'heads' when 'tails' were uppermost and vice versa. He lost most of his pies before he realized that these people had learned how to toss a coin in order to cheat a country pieman.

But one day William found someone to whom he could talk, someone who altered the whole course of his life. It was a young man a few years older than himself who addressed a crowd in the park. William, delighted with this young man's theories, had often listened to him. He was astonished that the young man had noticed him.

"I have seen you often," he said one day.

"I do like to listen to you," said William. "You seem to say all that be in my mind."

"What part do you come from?"

"From Cornwall."

"That's a long way. Came to London, I don't doubt, hoping to find a fortune?"

"Hoping as I'd be able to earn a living."

"From the green fields to the sewer, eh?"

"Well, 'tweren't all that good in Cornwall."

"Nowhere in the country is good for the poor!" said the young man vehemently; and this filled William with admiration, for this young man was expensively—in fact, almost elegantly—dressed.

"That be so."

"And what are they doing about it?" demanded the young man with the fierceness he used when addressing his audiences.

"I'm thinking you'm showing them what they could do."

"Will they listen to me? No! They're lazy, these people. On the continent of Europe crowns are being trampled in the dust. And what happens here? When the Queen steps out they—this starving population—stand and cheer their silly heads off."

William nodded.

"Come and have a drink with me and a bite to eat."

William's new friend took him to an eating-house, where they had eggs and bacon and hot coffee which was like nectar to William.

The young man told him that his name was David Young and

he had for a time been a reporter on the *Daily News*. His name suited him; he gave the impression of youth; he was all fire and enthusiasm; he was determined, he said, to make conditions better for the poor of London. His people were against what he was doing. They were rich; they had no need to care. They lived in Surrey; the family had lived there for a century or two. "Comfortable country squires!" said Mr. David Young with scorn. He was no longer with the *Daily News*; he wished to be free for his work, so he accepted an allowance from his father which enabled him to do this.

He talked eloquently of the evils of the day, which he considered had been largely caused by the springing up of new industries. "Trade . . . trade . . . trade . . ." he cried, his eyes flashing in his face. "England grows richer . . . worshipping the idol of prosperity and gain. Do they realize that that idol has feet of clay? Do they know that those riches and that prosperity are built on the sufferings of the poor? It is our task to bring that great idol crashing to the ground."

To his new friend William was able to talk of his own aspirations; his tongue was loosened and his eyes shone with a fervour similar to that of Mr. David Young.

"You must speak some time. You must tell the townspeople of the sufferings of the countryman. We will meet again. Here . . . to-morrow."

And so William found, in London, something which the country had been unable to give him.

Sam Marpit's Supper-rooms were just becoming lively. Sam was at the door in his elaborate evening attire, his white waistcoat sporting blue as well as red flowers, his cravat more flowing than ever, a great carnation in his buttonhole; his snuffbox in his hand, he welcomed his clients, offering to the most respected, a pinch of his expensive snuff.

Sam was pleased with himself. Marpit's Supper-rooms was doing a flourishing business. Many patrons came because the food they got here was of the best—Sam saw to that—and many came to see the quaint little girl who had, as Sam acknowledged, a little talent for doing a dance, a little talent for a sing-song, and a lot of talent for drawing them in.

Lilith and the Seven Veils! That was what brought quite a lot of them in. Sam patted himself congratulatorily a hundred times a day. He knew a thing or two. He had seen something in her when she had danced out in the street with the Italian organ-grinder. "It's drawing 'em in that counts!" said Sam.

Lilith! The name itself was God's gift to a supper-rooms' proprietor, for who would have thought of 'Lilith' in a month of Sundays? It was somebody in the Bible, he believed . . . not one of those common characters like Eve or Delilah whom everyone knew about, and which less discriminating supper-rooms men might have dubbed on some Jane or Sally. No! Lilith was *ex*clusive, the sort to appeal to the nobs. Nobody knew much about this Lilith in the Bible, and they did not like to say so, so they looked mysterious. Lilith was mysterious. That was the word. And to see Lilith do that Seven Veils dance of hers with the lights low—well, that was, in Sam's opinion, the milk in the coconut. Of course, if there could have been *nothing* on under that seventh veil . . . well, then you'd be talking. That was the sort of thing which would have to be done in a cellar, and this was a respectable house. "I keep it clean and respectable," he had said to the old gentleman with the eyeglass who had suggested a little enterprise in a cellar. But it was Lilith who had decided that; to tell the truth, Sam would not have been averse to doing a little cellar business, for there was no doubt that it brought in the money.

Sam liked money—not only what it bought and what it did. He just liked money; he felt sentimental about money.

"I just like it," he said to Fanny. "I like to feel it in me hands. I like to see it coming in."

And so he stood at the door of the Rooms murmuring "Good evening" to his customers, caressing first the lock of hair plastered on to his brow with macassar oil, then the carnation in his buttonhole, flourishing the gold snuffbox, calculating the money that was coming in, sniffing the anchovy toast, which was a speciality of the supper-rooms, as well as the odour of the richer food. He was not really so carefree as he appeared to be; he was worried, and he was worried about Lilith.

Dan Delany had just come in; he was smoking a cigar and looking very business-like; in fact, he was almost certain to be here on business, for why should he leave his own establishment at such an hour to patronize a rival's unless it was on business?

Dan was a smart man, a man who liked money as much as Sam did, and perhaps, thought Sam virtuously, not quite so particular as to how he got it. There was, so he had heard, a very cosy cellar below Delaney's Supper-rooms; and it was patronized by the wealthy.

Sam knew therefore that some business project had brought Dan to Marpit's, and, as Sam said to himself, he'd bet the week's takings at Delaney's to a penny pie that it was something to do with Lilith.

That was it; Dan wanted Lilith for Delaney's.

Lilith was on the floor now; the lights were low, but not so low as they would be later when she did the Veils number. She was singing one of those funny old Cornish songs in that funny way of hers, about a girl in a 'rorytory hat and a shall-I-go-naked gown'; and Lilith herself wore her red dress with the roses round the skirt and there was a red ribbon in her dark hair. She had insisted on that costume and Sam admitted that it was All Right. Now she had gone on to another song; it was sung to the tune of a dance that was danced in her native parts, and she had put her own words to it. She was clever at putting words to tunes; and this was all about the supper-rooms and the regular clients. They lapped it up like a starving kitten lapped milk. Sam believed she was worth the pound a week she got out of him now.

She had finished the song and gone into the little room just behind the bar where she did her changing.

He waited and then slipped unnoticed out of the main room and round by the passage which led to another door of Lilith's room.

He knocked, and she said "Come in then!" in that queer sort of way of talking which was foreign and yet not quite foreign, and which played its part in 'bringing 'em in.'

"Oh," she said, looking at Sam. " 'Tis you then."

"Yes; it's me all right," answered Sam.

She looked very pretty with the red dress and the red ribbon in her unruly hair.

"Filling up out there," he said with the characteristic little pat.

"Yes," she answered, her complacency matching his. "They'm come to see the Seven Veils."

Sam was a cautious man. He said: "Yes, and to taste Fan's anchovy toast or one of her steaks or chops . . . *and* to have a few drinks. I'll bet you to-night's takings to a penny pie that you wouldn't find anchovy toast like Fan makes in the whole of London.''

She laughed scornfully at that. She was cheeky, sure of herself, fully aware of that indefinable power in her that 'brought them in.'

He was excited. An idea had been forming in his mind for some time, and now it was taking a very definite shape. It had started when he had tried to kiss her on such an occasion as this and had been sharply reproved by a kick on the shin. She never used her hands; it was always her feet; she was a kicker, not a slapper; and he reckoned he had never seen a girl with such a pretty face capable of making such ugly ones.

It seemed pretty silly to him—a girl like Lilith and a man like himself not to be a bit more friendly. It wasn't natural. When he greased his hair and adjusted his cravat, when he fixed his buttonhole and looked at himself in the glass with his snuffbox in his hand, well, talk about the Prince Regent! There were still people who remembered the Prince, and once it had been said to him: "Sam, if you had a bit more of the avoirdupois, you'd be the spitting image of the Regent . . . and I mean when he was Regent . . . before he was King and got so ugly.''

Yet Lilith was aloof; moreover, she would have nothing to do with others who ran after her. It did not make sense. It wasn't as though she were one of the languishing sort who couldn't abide men near them for fear of their evil thoughts. There was nothing like that about Lilith. What she might be came out in her dancing; it was one of those things that brought them in. Promising! That was what Lilith was. It just did not make sense that these promises should not be fulfilled.

Sam thought he understood. Lilith was after something more than a temporary hold over Sam and Marpit's Supper-rooms.

"Well, Lilith,'' he said; and he always had to suppress his desire to call her Lil, which would be bad for business. "Well, Lilith, I won't deny that you're a help when it comes to bringing 'em in. Do you ever think of the way I found you dancing round a barrel organ?'' Her scornful eyes watched the patting hand, as though to say that as long as it was his own thigh he patted she would not complain. '' 'Sam, me lad,' I often says to myself, 'but for you that little girl would be starving when she couldn't sell her ballads.' ''

"Someone else might have seen what you did, Sam. You do never know."

"Look here, Lilith, I've got the Seeing Eye."

"Well, I'd be glad if you'd turn it the other way while I do my changing."

She was getting too smart—too much of the Londoner. She had been born sharp enough without that being added.

"Gratitude," he said sadly; "that's something a man never gets. You raise them up, and what do they do! Do they thank you? No; they turn and bite the hand that feeds 'em."

"Or they kick the shins of them that gets wrong ideas in the head."

"Lilith," he said earnestly, "who else would have done for you what I have?"

She appeared to consider this. "Dan Delaney?" she suggested.

He was filled with panic. "Him! Why, Lilith, I wouldn't like to see you fall into his hands. He's got a bad reputation. You can say what you like about Marpit's, but it's respectable."

"There was a time when you was thinking of doing something else. Remember how you thought of turning that cellar of yours into a . . ."

"Oh, I wasn't serous about *that*! Lilith, I've been thinking a lot about us . . . you and me, I mean."

"Serious? Or the way you thought about that cellar?"

"Very serious. It's over a year since you first came here. You've changed a lot, you have, Lilith. When I think of what you was like when I first picked you up out of the streets as you might say . . ."

"And you looked after me so well, and paid me so well, and never did try any larks. Go on. I've finished that for you."

"Well, it's true. I know . . ." He smiled down at his carnation. "I know, Lilith, there have been times when thoughts have entered my head. I'm natural. I'm human. I don't deny it."

" 'Twouldn't be no good. You going to offer me more money?"

"More than that, Lilith."

"More than money!"

"Myself," he said dramatically. "Lilith, I offer you myself. How would you like to be Mrs. Sam Marpit?"

"Well," said Lilith, temporarily off her guard, "I hadn't thought of that."

He approached her and laid his hands on her shoulders; he was beaming with beneficence. "Why not? Perhaps I had this in mind the day I saw you with the organ-grinder. Perhaps I said to myself . . . 'That's the girl for me!' "

"And perhaps you didn't," said Lilith.

"Well, you don't seem very pleased. Ain't that a good offer?"

"I don't know. You might not be talking serious."

"I'm always serious."

"Like you was when you wanted that cellar."

"A flight of fancy, that's what that was. Me . . . run a cellar like Dan Delaney? Not me! I've got too much respect for them that works for me. I built up this business in the honest way and it's going to stay . . ."

"Respectable!" said Lilith.

"You take the words out of my mouth, that's what you do, Lilith. Well, what's the answer? When are you going to name the day?"

"I'd need time."

"Time!" he spluttered.

"Didn't you know? A lady always has to have time to consider a proposal."

She whipped off the red dress and stood there in her tights and the flesh-coloured tunic which fitted so closely to her figure that she seemed to have nothing on. He had seen her thus many times, as the patrons saw her in the half-lighted room; but as he looked at her now, he realized that being married to Lilith would mean something more than saving himself twenty shillings a week and the fear of Dan Delaney's stepping in.

"Lilith," he said emotionally, "you're sort of different. I don't know how to say it."

"Fancy that!" she mocked. "There be something Sam Marpit don't know how to do! Who'd have thought it!"

"Now look here, who was it who . . . ?"

"Brought me in from the streets? You!" she answered; and she twirled round to give him a view of herself from all angles as though to say: Just see what you might have and what you don't know yet whether you can! She was a born teaser, Lilith was; and teasing was something he had always told himself he would never put up with. Yet he was putting up with it now, from her.

She fitted the words to one of her tunes.

"Brought me in from the streets, that's what you did, Sam Marpit, that's what you did. But there's others in this town, Sam Marpit, who'd be glad to take me in . . . who'd be glad to take me in."

"You stop that," he said. "Save your songs and dances for the patrons. That's what you're paid for."

"Well, I'm giving 'em to you free of charge, Sam, to show how grateful I be because . . . you brought me in from the streets, Sam Marpit. That's what you did. That's what you did, Sam Marpit. That's what you did for me . . ."

He strode towards her; she had stopped, her eyes flashing and her foot raised to kick.

"This is a nice thing!" complained Sam. "A chap proposes, asks you to marry him, and you can't give a civil answer."

"You'll get a civil answer all right . . . only civil answers take time."

She began winding the muslin about her. She looked as pretty as ever, he thought, with the flesh-coloured tights showing under the muslin for all the world as though she had nothing on. A regular draw that veils dance was; and Dan Delaney was out there ready to offer—only he knew what!

"I've got to have my answer now . . . *now*!" he shouted.

She curtsied. "Sorry, Sam. Sorry, Sammy me boy. You brought me here from sorrow to joy . . ."

"Lilith!" he cried.

"Samuel?"

"What's it to be?"

"Wait and see."

She began to sing: "What's it to be? Wait and see. . . ."

There was no sense in Lilith to-night. She knew all about his fears, all about his desires. She knew what he had really felt about that cellar too; and above all she knew that Dan Delaney was sitting out there to-night.

She had the last of the veils about her now.

She said: "I'll let 'ee know, Sammy. All in good time. You should know it takes a bit of time. I'd still want my money every week, and I'd have to have my family here with me. This sort of thing ain't to be rushed, you know."

He softened as she stood before him—flushed, eager, all ready to go out there and give them what they wanted to see—because in his heart he knew it was Lilith they came to see. There were plenty of places they could get supper.

"Give us a kiss, then," he said. "Give us a kiss to go on with."

"Well, if you was to do as I say . . ."

"And what might that be?"

"Take your snuffbox in your hand. That's it. Now hold fast to it and hold it as though you'm offering a gentleman a pinch. Now put the other hand on your cravat. That's beautiful. That's grand."

She came to him and kissed his cheek.

Then she stood back laughing. "That's all, Sam Marpit, for the present."

Then she ran out, and he heard the murmur and the applause as she appeared. She was what they had come for, all right. No doubt about that.

He went into the darkened room and watched her. He watched Delaney too.

One move ahead of you this time, Dan! he thought; and he smiled complacently, thinking of Lilith in all the veils and in no veils, and not any flesh-coloured tights either.

He thought of the money coming in to-night, and he reckoned Sam Marpit was pretty smart.

Napoleon set out with his broom. He had a beautiful new broom, a present from Lilith. It was a special sort of broom, he reckoned; and this was surely due to the fact that Lilith had given it to him. Everything about Lilith was special. Amanda was kind to everybody and Lilith was not always kind. Napoleon had had a wonderful time since his friends had brought him to a wonderful city; he loved all his friends, but it was Lilith who had his special love. It was exciting to watch Lilith. She had fine clothes and she danced and sang in the attic when she showed them how she had become rich in the supper-rooms. Napoleon felt that Amanda was so beautiful that he should not look at her; but Lilith was so beautiful that he could not stop looking at her.

Lilith would cuff him when she was angry; he did not mind that. A cuff was better than no notice at all. Sometimes she would smile at him and even kiss him. "Poor old Nap," she would say. "Here's a penny. Go out and toss with a pieman; and here's another penny in case you lose."

She had now given him his new broom, which he would treasure; he was ready to fight anyone who attempted to take it from him.

He set out on that day, very proud and happy. Who knew, this day he might meet a gentleman who would give him a shilling. That day when such a wonderful thing had happened seemed very far away, so it was surely time that it should happen again. To-day. He was sure it would be to-day.

He had his own crossing now and he felt important. The old man who had allowed him to have his place on occasion had now given up; and the policeman who was stationed nearby, and who was amused by Napoleon's quaint way of talking and his devotion to his profession, was friendly.

It was beginning to rain and Napoleon could have sung for joy, for what was better for a crossing-sweeper's business than a rainy day? Crossings were swept at great speed on wet days. Here a penny; there a halfpenny; there nothing at all. But only the really hard-hearted could resist the shining optimism in Napoleon's face.

And then the miracle happened.

He was a tall man with fair hair—a gentleman, Napoleon made no mistake about that; and sweeping crossings taught you to pick them out.

"Crossing, sir? Be you wanting a crossing?"

The fair man stopped and looked at Napoleon. "I say, what part of the world do you come from?"

"Cornwall, sir."

"What part of Cornwall?"

"Well, sir, I were to the Workhouse up to Bodmin before I did go to Farmer Polgard nearby Looe."

"Well," said the man. "That's queer. I come from those parts myself. Polgards, eh! I know that place well. And what made you come to London?" He smiled. "I know. It was to make your fortune."

"Well, yes, sir."

"Then sweep me a crossing."

Napoleon did so and when they got to the other side of the road, the tall man said: "Here's something towards the fortune."

When he had gone, Napoleon stared in stupefaction, for it was a half-sovereign he was holding in his hand. He could not believe it.

Obviously he could sweep no more crossings that day. He called to the poor little boy who took over crossings when their owners wished to go off duty; then he went straight home.

Both Lilith and Amanda were in the attic, and Lilith was just preparing herself to go off to the supper-rooms.

"You're early," said Amanda. "Something must have happened. You look as if you've found the gentleman who gave you a shilling."

"I have . . ." stammered Napoleon. "Only not so . . . But 'tis even more. Look."

The coin shone in his grimy palm.

"Half a sovereign!" said Amanda. "Whoever gave you that, Napoleon?"

Even Lilith was impressed, Napoleon was delighted to observe. She picked it up.

"It's a true one," she said.

"I knew it were," said Napoleon smiling radiantly. "He were a real gentleman as gave it to me. He said to I: 'And what part of the world do 'ee come from then?' And I did say, 'From Cornwall, sir.' 'Well,' he did say, 'that be queer for I do come from those parts meself. Polgards . . . I do mind them well . . .' "

"Someone from Cornwall," said Amanda. "Someone who knew the Polgards. I wonder who that was."

"He were a proper gentleman," said Napoleon. "He said, 'That's towards the fortune . . .' 'Cos he did ask me if I were seeking me fortune like."

Lilith was standing very still and her face had grown quite white. She said slowly: "Nap . . . you must think . . . you must remember. What were he like . . . this gentleman?"

"Oh, he were tall."

"As tall as who?"

"Taller than William. Taller than anyone I can think on."

"Was he fair or dark?"

"He were fair. Golden like."

"And did he speak like a gentleman . . . a real gentleman?"

"Oh yes, he were a real gentleman. No mistake about that."

"Speaking a bit slower than most with a sort of laugh at the end of it, as though he were making fun . . . but nice sort of fun?''

''That be it.''

Lilith clenched her hands. ''Did he say it like this: 'I say, what part of the world do you come from? That's queer. I come from that part myself.' ''

''Well, now, that be just how he said it. It might have been him talking.''

''Frith!'' cried Amanda. ''It was Frith.''

Lilith's eyes were larger and darker in sudden anger. She took Napoleon by the shoulders and shook him.

''You didn't tell him where we were! You let him go!''

''I don't know. I don't know what you do mean. Did I do wrong?'' He turned appealing eyes to Amanda, who came to his rescue at once and snatched him from Lilith.

''What are you doing to him? Have you gone mad?''

''Don't 'ee see?'' cried Lilith, lapsing into the old way of speaking, as she did in moments of emotion. '' 'Twas Frith who spoke to him. . . . 'Twas Frith. . . .''

She was silent then. She turned away broodingly. He was in London and it was because of that fact that she had longed to come here. Every day she had hoped that he would find her; it was necessary, she had believed, that *he* should find *her* . . . not she him. She had learned a great deal since she had worked in Sam Marpit's Supper-rooms. Often she wondered whether Frith would be as pleased to see her here in London as he had been in Cornwall. She could not have borne to see him embarrassed if confronted with her; he must be delighted, enraptured, as she would be. That was why, when they met, it must be by chance. It must not be as though she had sought him.

Yet if she could aid that chance . . . subtly, so that he would not know she had aided it, how willingly would she do so!

She said no more until she was alone with Napoleon; then she laid her hands on his shoulders and said: ''Nap, when you're sweeping crossings, you've got to watch for that gentleman. No matter what you're doing, you've got to leave it. You've got to bring him to me. Do you understand that?''

''Yes, Lilith.''

''No matter what you be doing!''

''No matter what I be doing. If I be sweeping a crossing for the Queen, I'd leave her to walk across and get herself splashed

I would . . . even if she gave me half a sovereign, like the gentleman. And I'd bring him to 'ee, Lilith.''

After that Napoleon had one ambition. It was not to sweep a crossing for a lady or a gentleman who would give him a shilling or even half a sovereign; it was to bring that one gentleman to Lilith.

The year faded and a new one began. It was their second in London, and a year of frustration for Lilith, Napoleon and Sam Marpit.

Napoleon went out each day feeling certain that that was the day he would find the fair gentleman; but each day passed without reaching a successful conclusion. Napoleon did very well; he was one of the more prosperous crossing-sweepers. The ladies liked his way of talking and the gentlemen the eager way in which he studied their faces. The little crossing-sweeper from the country had become quite a well-known figure; but in vain did he await the return of the fair gentleman whose appearance would have meant so much to Lilith . . . and therefore to Napoleon.

Lilith was alternately hopeful and depressed. Sometimes she thought she saw Frith in the dimness of the supper-rooms, and she let herself imagine his coming there and taking her away. At others she was certain that she had lost Frith for ever.

"Strike me with forked lightning," cried Sam. "But I don't know what's the matter with you. I offer you a good home and a good husband, and you can't make up your mind to take 'em. Suppose I was to change *my* mind? Suppose I was to marry Fan, what then?''

She looked at him scornfully: "You'm forgetting. 'Tain't the anchovy toast that brings 'em in . . . and anchovy ain't so much the fashion now. Her steaks ain't all that good. They say there be better to be got at Delaney's. I'm the one that brings 'em in, and you know it. If I went to Delaney's he'd take most of your business.''

"He ain't been making advances to you, I hope. He ain't the man I am. I ought to warn you he's a man of very shady reputation, that's what I ought to warn you.''

"Someone should warn you you're a man who thinks too much of himself.''

But she liked Sam; she longed for Frith, but she liked Sam.

Sometimes she was so weary of waiting that she almost said: "All right then. Let's get married." Sometimes she thought of this place as Sam's and Lilith's Supper-rooms. No! Lilith's and Sam's. Sam . . . well, he was not a gentleman but he did look rather grand in his fancy waistcoats, and if they were not the sort a gentleman should wear, Lilith liked them all the same. Grandmother Lil had made her set such store by gentlemen; but she believed that she would have married Sam by now if Napoleon had not seen Frith in London.

But if Lilith and Napoleon were frustrated, William was more contented.

He had had many meetings with David Young and his friends during the past months. On one or two occasions he had actually spoken to the crowd. He had found that if he did so naturally, they listened to him. He only had to tell them of the hardships he had endured in Cornwall and to repeat some of those things which he had heard his new friends say so often that he knew them by heart.

He was growing bolder, less humble; and as he did so he thought more and more of Amanda.

One spring day David Young told William that he was going away for a little while.

"Things are getting a bit difficult. We're being watched. The authorities. They call us agitators . . . and they don't like agitators. Young Milbanke's father has been warned. He's a lawyer, you know . . . and he knows everybody. He's been told that if we go on . . . stirring up trouble, they call it . . . they'll have to take action. We're what they call disturbing the peace and they could arrest us for it. So we've decided to lie low. It's the wisest course. No more meetings for a while. Milbanke and I thought of going out of London for a bit. I'll go and stay with my people. But we'll be back in a few weeks when things have quietened down."

So William's new friends went out of London and he missed them very much. There were times when he almost told Amanda of what was in his mind concerning their future, but his courage always failed him. When he was with Amanda he could not see her except as the daughter of Leigh House.

One day he went to the ballad shop to buy himself some stock, and the one-eyed man who sold the bundles of ballads gave him a quick and conspiratorial look.

"Why," he said, scratching his head, "you've bin coming on and off for some time, ain't you?" He winked. "I reckon it's about time I put you on to something a bit more profitable than these 'ere ballads. Ballads is all right . . . all right for the amateurs, as I call 'em. But when you get an old pal—well, then you want to do something special for him. Here. Look what I've got." He produced a sheaf of papers from under the counter and flourished them in William's face. "Now these is something I can let a pal have. 'Cos why? 'Cos it's a special favour, that's why. Royal Litterater, that's what we call it. Sell? You won't be able to get enough of this. Royal Litterater, that's what you call it. And they'll come for it like flies after jam."

William looked at the papers; they did not appear to be very different from the usual ballad sheets, except that there was more printing on them and he could see that the writing was not set out into verses.

"Just take 'em . . . and see. You won't lose by it. Gawd Almighty! You'll be coming back and begging for more. Why, if you had a few hundred gross of these you'd be a rich man. That's why it's a special favour I'm offering you."

William took the papers and went away with them.

"Royal Litterater," he shouted. "Who'll buy a sheet? A penny a sheet. Royal Litterater."

Someone smiled slyly and bought one. Another came and bought.

The man was right. It was easy to sell. He would sell out quickly and go back for more if it were available. *He* would go home rich for once. Perhaps it was at last his turn to have some luck.

The people were buying his papers quickly. He was dreaming as he sold them, seeing himself making so much money that he might save some, and perhaps start a little shop somewhere.

"It's not good enough for you, Amanda," he was saying in his daydream. "But I'll work hard, and we'll get on, and perhaps we'll have a carriage one day. Perhaps . . ."

"I'll trouble you to step along of me."

William turned sharply. A member of the police force stood on either side of him and even as he turned they laid hands on him.

"What . . . what have I done. . . ?"

One of the policemen took the papers from William and flourished them in his face.

"You're arrested on a charge of disturbing the peace by circulating literature which is an insult to the Crown."

William stared blankly at the papers which were to have made his fortune.

"But . . . I didn't know. . . ."

It was useless to protest. They would not listen. This was more humiliating, more degrading than hiring himself at a Fair.

Amanda never forgot that night of anxiety which followed William's arrest.

She could not understand why he had not come home; and she was certain that only some dire calamity would have prevented his return. Her first thought was that he had met with an accident. She pictured him lying crushed and bleeding under an omnibus. Then it occurred to her that he might have been set upon by rogues and murdered.

Eagerly she awaited Lilith's return from the supper-rooms.

Sam had now taken to escorting Lilith home, for he declared she would never have reached her lodgings safely night after night if he had not. Continually to make that journey alone, he said, was tempting Providence. Lilith was glad to have his company, although she protested that she was capable of looking after herself.

When she heard that William had not returned her anxiety was as great as that of Amanda. Knowing London as she did, she could imagine several reasons for his failure to return.

It was Mr. Murphy who discovered what had happened. A friend of his—another seller of ballads—had seen William arrested.

"Two peelers took him off to jail," said Mr. Murphy gloomily. "Like as not he'll be in Newgate."

"In Newgate!" cried Amanda in horror.

"Yes, lady; in Newgate Jail, I reckon. He was selling Royal Litterater. He ought never to have handled the stuff. Leastways, if he had he didn't ought to have gone selling it where he did sell it. Talk about asking for trouble!"

Lilith demanded further explanations.

"Well, it's like this here," went on Mr. Murphy. "He got hold of the wrong sort of litterater. There's some he could have sold without trouble. Love stories and . . . meetings between the quality and little milliners and sewing girls. That's all right. You can sell the latest about the horrible murders and all the blood and mess of 'em. That's all right. But it's this *Royal* stuff. I wouldn't touch it, with all me experience.''

"What Royal Literature is this?'' asked Amanda. "I have never seen it.''

"Of course you ain't. It's about the Queen and the Consort, and how much she loves him and how they quarrel about this and that. Disrespectful to Her Majesty, that's what it is. Treating her like she was one of them little milliners, and the Prince a Duke who comes a-courting her.''

Amanda said: "But William would not know. He can't read.''

"There ain't so many of us as can, but we knows the Royal Litterater when we sees it. And if the bobbies like to be smart they can run you in for selling it.''

"We'll have to explain,'' said Amanda. "We'll have to tell them he can't read and he didn't know.''

Lilith looked scornful; the ballad-seller shook his head.

"Do you think,'' said Lilith, "that they'd take any notice of you? You don't look quite the lady you did two years ago when you were Miss Amanda Leigh of Leigh House. You're just a poor shirt-maker now. You haven't got the influence behind you. You're poor, don't 'ee know that yet?''

"But we must *do* something,'' said Amanda. "We must explain that he is innocent.''

Lilith said no more. This was Amanda who couldn't get the money due to her from a lecherous old man at the shirt-shop. Amanda knew nothing! She never would, it seemed to Lilith; and in the meantime, Lilith was very worried indeed.

"People's been taken in for it before,'' said Mr. Murphy soothingly. "They don't stay long. They can't fine him because he ain't got no money. They'll keep him for a week or so as a warning, and then they'll let him go!''

But William stayed three months in Newgate Jail. He was said to be a person whose character needed investigation; not only had he sold disgusting literature concerning Her Majesty, but he was known to belong to a group of agitators who had made attempts to break the peace.

He grew thinner in prison. He was bewildered and deeply

wounded by what had happened to him; he brooded continually; he was in turns angry and desperate, depressed and resigned. Amanda and Lilith, who visited him whenever possible, were alarmed by the change in him.

The nightmare of those months stayed with Amanda as well as with William for a long time. Amanda thought she would never be able to get the smell of the prison out of her nostrils. In her dreams she heard the clanging of the gates which were shut and locked behind her when she visited William; she saw the dismal stone corridors, the gratings high in the wall, the turnkeys; and everywhere there was that inescapable odour of disease, decay and human sweat, which seemed to Amanda the very essence of hopelessness.

She visited the prison as often as was possible. She talked to William through an iron grating. This presented great difficulties for there were always other prisoners present being visited by their friends, and all must talk through the grating. It was impossible to take food to him, for nothing could be handed through this grating; and so, Amanda and Lilith, Napoleon and David Young—who was deeply moved by what had happened to William—visited him and tried to cheer him with talk of his almost certain speedy release.

David Young came to the attic to talk of William. He was fiery and indignant, feeling more than a little guilty. He would walk about the attic, or stand by the table and beat on it with his fist while he talked.

"They've had their eyes on him for a long time. It's not for selling those papers that he's been put in prison. It's because he was working with us. They've been watching us. We were warned. But I suppose they thought they would arrest William as an example to the rest of us. Our families would have protested if they had taken us."

Amanda felt quite angry with this young man. "You should never have led him into this."

"My dear Miss Leigh, we have to fight for our rights."

"Why should William have to suffer when you and your friends are responsible?"

"Because of the system. It's that which we want to alter."

He was a very serious young man, genuinely idealistic, genuinely distressed that this had—as he was sure was the case—happened to William through his association with himself and his friends; and all through the months of William's imprisonment he called regularly at the Murphys' house.

Lilith said that he came to see Amanda. "If you were wise," she told Amanda, "you'd marry him."

"Marry him! He has suggested no such thing!"

"Oh, but he could be led to it. A man likes to be sure of a sociable reply before putting a question like that."

"I'm sure you're quite wrong," said Amanda.

"And I'm sure I'm quite right. What's going to happen to us, Amanda? Have you ever thought of that? We can't go on like this all our lives. What's going to happen when you're too old for shirt-making?"

"But I couldn't marry just like that. It was to avoid that sort of marriage that I ran away from home. And why don't you follow your own advice? Why don't you marry Sam Marpit?"

Lilith gazed at her and marvelled that she did not know. She shrugged her shoulders, and for the moment became the very young Lilith who had scowled at Amanda from a feather bed.

"You," she said scornfully, "you'm a terrible know-naught. That's what you be!"

It was winter before William came home. David Young brought him in a cab, treating him like a martyr.

The change in William was more apparent in his attic than it had been in prison. There was now about William a burning fervour; if he was physically hurt, he was mentally elated. He had suffered, and he found that he was glad he had suffered; for there was more dignity in the role of martyred prisoner than in any other that he could assume.

"Soon," he said, "I shall be earning again."

But his health did not improve; instead, it deteriorated.

David Young's visits were as frequent as ever.

"You will not be forgotten," he told William. "One day it will be known that you were sent to prison, not for selling those silly sheets—which hundreds have sold without much notice being taken—but because you dared to speak out."

Up and down the attic he would pace, his eyes flashing, his fists clenched. Amanda listened to him as she sewed.

"We've got to get the vote for the working classes. Why shouldn't every man have a chance to choose who shall represent him in Parliament? The first Reform Bill was not enough. We've got to get the vote for the people who do not pay ten pounds a year rent, as well as for those who do. We've got to achieve the equalization of the standard of living."

William listened with shining eyes, and Amanda felt that he was better for David Young's visits. She herself was interested in David's doctrines: he seemed such an admirable young man, so selfless, not seeking to enjoy his life but to dedicate it to the service of others. She wished that she could have kept that view of Mr. Young; she wished she could have felt for him as William so obviously felt.

There came a day when David persuaded her to abandon her work and take a little pleasure trip with him to Cremorne Gardens.

"Amanda," he said as they walked through the avenues, "you ought not to be living in that place."

"None of us should be there," she said.

"In your case it's different."

"But you say we are all equal. Why should it be different for me?"

"You know why. You weren't brought up to that sort of thing. Come and stay with my people in the country."

"If I visited your people, that would not solve my problem," she said. "I should have to go back to the attic and shirt-making."

"Perhaps you need not go back to the attic," he said.

Then she thought of living in a comfortable house again, of privacy and the hundred and one privileges of civilization which she had taken for granted until she had lost them. Briefly a temptation came to her. He was not arrogant, nor possessive like Anthony; but she did not love him. If she sought an easy way now, hers would be only a half-victory.

"Think about it. You shouldn't be there. It's not the place for you."

She smiled. "You are very kind, but I think you too have one law for the rich and one for the poor . . . at least for those who have been rich."

He flushed. "That is quite different," he said.

William was going to die. He knew it; so did Amanda and Lilith.

It was because he knew it that he told Amanda of his feelings for her. It was one afternoon when he lay on his mattress in his attic and she had taken her work in there that she might talk to him as she stitched.

He recovered from a fit of coughing and he said: "I shall never be well again."

She protested but he shook his head. "No," he said, "I shall not. Miss Amanda . . . I hope you done right to come to London as you did. I get to wondering what'll happen to you."

"You mustn't talk like this, William. You're going to get well. We're going to be all right."

"I love you, Miss Amanda," he said. "I wouldn't have said it but . . . for this knowing . . . what I know. I would have minded my place. I've known it was wrong of me. But there's no going against it. 'Tas always been this way since I first saw you. But I never thought to tell 'ee so."

"William," she answered, "you've a right to say what you feel."

" 'Tis not so. When I think of other people, I think 'tis wrong that some should be called gentry and be bowed to and treated with respect while others be of no account. But with you, I know, 'tis right and proper that it should be so." She looked down at her fingers, pricked and roughened with the needle. She said nothing, but the tears were falling down her cheeks.

William watched her, ashamed yet exalted, feeling humble yet proud.

Lilith felt angry because William was dying. The doctor had told her that he was in an advanced state of prostration. She could think of nothing but William now; she remembered the days of their childhood and how they had been together in their mother's body; and she longed above all things to give him some great happiness before he died.

What did he most desire? She knew. It was to marry Amanda. He should marry Amanda. She determined that he should.

Lilith talked to Amanda as they walked in the Park. She was more variable in her moods than usual, it seemed to Amanda; at one moment she was sad and subdued, at another fiery and indignant; almost commanding at one moment, pleading the next.

"William's going to die. You know that, Amanda. How long can he live? One month? Two months? What has he ever had from life but hard work . . . and being treated bad? You was

born a lady. Oh, don't turn away. It's a great thing to be born a
lady. You had plenty to eat and a feather bed to sleep in. That
don't seem much. But that's because you had them. And I was
born with the power to get them. We're lucky. William's not.
William, he's one of the unlucky ones. There's only one person
who could do something for him now—and it's something that
I reckon would make up for everything—and that person's you,
Amanda. You could give him such happiness as he never
dreamed of. You could make everything he suffered worth while.
You . . . *you* could do that.''

People looked at them curiously as they walked from the Park
through the streets; Lilith's eyes were blazing, her curls elabo-
rately dressed now, herself daintily clad; Amanda looked so
different, with her pale golden hair and her eyes a vivid blue in
her pale face, large, sorrowful with the tears shining in them.

''Why don't 'ee do it?'' demanded Lilith. ''It wouldn't be a
proper marriage. He's dying. Don't 'ee know that? It would be
just to give him the knowledge that you were his wife . . . that
you had some love to give him. What harm would that do? No
lovemaking . . . if that's what you'm scared of! He's too ill, and
I reckon if he weren't, a look from you would stop all that. He
worships you. It wouldn't hurt you much to give him all the
world. Why don't you?''

''Stop it, Lilith. Stop it.''

''You don't like to see yourself as you be. You're a coward.
You always were. You cry for nothing . . . and you think you'm
awful good because you do cry. Here's William who'd die for
'ee, and you can't forget you'm a lady, and you can't give him
what he do want more than all the world, though it wouldn't
cost you nothing!''

''I said, stop it, Lilith. I've made up my mind. I'll marry
William.''

Lilith smiled, marvelling at her own power. Everything fell
into her hands. She had longed, years ago when Grandmother
Lil had talked of such things, to make Amanda marry William.
And now this was to be achieved. In the Bible it said that faith
could move mountains. Lilith began to believe that, had she
wished, she could have transported Brown Willy to London.

And so they were married.

Amanda regretted nothing. She knew that as long as she lived

she would remember the joy on William's face as he lay back
on his mattress.

He would talk of the future.

"When I'm well, I'll do something great, Amanda. It be a
strange thing but I have that feeling inside of me. I know that I
be destined for something, Amanda. Do 'ee understand? I felt
it when I stood by Mr. Young and talked to all those people,
talked of the terrible differences between rich and poor. They
listened to me, Amanda. When I close my eyes I see 'em . . .
all round me . . . their faces lifted, their eyes rapt-like. I knew
then that there was something in me . . . something that's God-
given, Amanda. I knew it as though it had been shown me in a
vision."

She was afraid as she looked at him; she was afraid of the
burning flush on his cheeks, the brilliance of his eyes. How
could she feel regret when she saw such happiness in his face;
she had put that there when she had come in from her walk with
Lilith and said: "William, you'll never ask me to marry you,
so I'm going to ask you to marry me. I love you, William; and
I want to feel it's right for me to look after you and be here with
you . . . and to nurse you so that you'll get well."

He had kissed her hands, his lips burning with fever.

Lilith and the Murphys had arranged for the ceremony, con-
ducted by a clergyman, to take place in the attic. It had to be a
bedside wedding, for William had not the strength to get up
from his mattress; and everyone but William knew that he never
would.

Lilith had bought the ring; and it was now on Amanda's finger.

They were peaceful days which followed the ceremony. William, it was obvious, had never been so happy in his life. He
felt that a miracle had happened. He had wanted to be a martyr,
and it seemed to him that he had become one; he had not dared
seriously to think of marrying Amanda, and he had married her.
He was a sick man, but what did sickness matter? If he knew
that it was through this very sickness that he had realized his
greatest desires, he did not admit it even to himself; but he
suffered his illness patiently, almost as though he loved it. It was
the martyr's crown.

Sometimes he lay on his mattress too weak to do anything but
dream; at others he would talk to Amanda while she sat and

stitched; he would talk of the future when he would be strong again, of what he would do, of the life they would have together. He thought of the children they would have; but he did not speak of them.

Then Amanda would talk to him of her plans for the future.

"We'll go back to the country, William," she said. "That will be best for you. Life is easier in the country. We'll have a little cottage and a bit of land . . . our own land. And we'll have cows and pigs. We'll take Napoleon with us. He'll be a great help on the farm."

Amanda painted beautiful pictures of a future in which she did not believe. But he believed in it; he lay there listening to her gentle voice, and as she stitched at the shirts she made a picture of the cottage in such detail that he saw it clearly, and each day she told of the things that would happen to them, building up a life which they could share together.

It was real to him; he saw it all: the thatched cottage with the water-butt outside and the sweet-smelling cabbage roses and the lavender bushes in the garden. Amanda looked after the flowers while he worked on the land; and they sat at the table with the window wide open through which came the mingling smells of newly cut grass and the honeysuckle which grew about the porch.

And eventually Amanda began to talk of their children—several boys and girls, so that they had to leave the cottage, which had become too small for them.

He lay there and listened in deep contentment, living in dreams the life which could never be his in reality.

One summer morning when Amanda went to see William, she found that he was dead. Yesterday when she had talked of that other life he had not always seemed to hear her. He had wandered a little, had talked of the old days, of humiliations, degradations and aspirations; and that incoherence had been surcharged with his desires to do something worth while, his love for Amanda.

She had sat stitching, and she had felt a sense of peace because she had helped him to achieve his desires. There was his martyr's crown—such a little one that no one except those who had known him, would remember his name; and the life with Amanda, for which he had yearned, she had given him—not in reality, but in the mind. Yet he had lived it so intensely during those last months of his life that it had been more real to him than the attic in which he lay.

William . . . dead. She stood looking at him, seeing him in a hundred different pictures—kissing her hand on the instructions of Grandmother Lil; standing with her, one of them on either side of St. Keyne's Well; at the hiring stand; in Newgate. But she would remember him during the last weeks, happy, living with her that life of unreality.

Lilith rose and came to stand beside her. They were dry-eyed, silent.

❈ Two

A year had passed since the death of William. The girls were now nineteen and Napoleon fourteen.

Napoleon would have been quite happy if he could have forgotten William, but, as he explained to Amanda, "That's something I can't manage to do. I keep thinking that if it hadn't been for William I'd still be in that terrible place, with the farmer always there to whip me, instead of me going out every morning with me broom to earn money and to find the gentleman. Then I think of him being gone and I'm sad."

"You must remember, Napoleon," said Amanda, "that William is not sad now."

" 'Tis I that be sad," said Napoleon, "because he be no longer with us."

He loved the two girls devotedly and his love for them was a source of delight to him. If he could serve Amanda in any way he did so; when a pieman who had sheltered with him under a porch during a rainstorm gave him a fruit pie he carried it carefully home for Amanda; once he found a bunch of violets which a lady had thrown out of a carriage because they had begun to wilt; these he brought home for Amanda, and that was a great joy for him; but the greatest joy he would know would be bringing home the fair gentleman for Lilith; and he was convinced that one day he would do so.

David Young still called, and now made no secret of the fact that it was Amanda whom he came to see. He brought presents of flowers and food.

"Sure signs that he comes a-courting," said Jenny apprehensively to her mother.

If Amanda married Mr. Young, Jenny reckoned, Lilith would marry Sam Marpit, and one of them would take Napoleon with her. But it seemed that neither Lilith nor Amanda was in any hurry to marry.

Amanda enjoyed her conversations with David Young. She enjoyed leaving behind the streets of London with those contrasts which had never ceased to astonish her, and to walk into the pleasant groves and paths laid out in the pleasure gardens. David insisted on showing her another London—London at play. They went to Greenwich for the famous Fair and ate the traditional whitebait and drank iced champagne at one of the taverns at Blackwall. There was hardly a pleasure garden to which they did not go. They visited the Bayswater Tea Gardens; they had a shrimp tea at Rosherville; they went to St. Helena's in Rotherhithe, where they danced together. This was daring, of course, but, as David pointed out, Amanda was a widow now and not a young girl in need of a chaperone. At Highbury Barn they danced on the Leviathan dancing platform, looking up at the sky as they did so, and afterwards sitting out in a sheltered alcove; they walked in the gardens about Copenhagen House, and sat at one of the little tables drinking tea and looking out over the fields of Highgate and Hampstead.

Amanda liked David Young, liked his earnestness and sympathy with the poor which she herself had felt even in those days when she had not understood what it meant to be poor. She tried hard during those outings to fall in love with him as he wished her to, but she could not; he seemed younger than she was—although this was not so; he seemed slightly illogical in his ideas.

He wanted equality for all, he assured her; but she must point out to him that this was not entirely true. And how could there be equality when some were educated and some were not? The man who held the horses, who sold pies, could never be as important to society as great statesmen like Pitt or Peel, as great doctors like Jenner; and until they had been educated to that level and their brains had developed accordingly, so that they might stand comparison, equality was impossible.

He would take her scarred hands in his and frown over them. "Making shirts . . . spoiling your hands . . . ruining your eyes . . . it's ridiculous. Come and stay with my family in Sussex."

"You have told them about me? How I ran away from home? That I am a widow?"

"I've told them some things."

"Ah!" she had said. "That is like you. That is like everything you do and everything you think. You tell what you think is good for people to know . . . and you suppress the rest."

"There is no need to tell too much."

Listening to him, watching him, desiring so earnestly to please him, she could not help being aware of a change in him. He seemed less politically earnest; he was abandoning his old friends; he rarely spoke at a meeting; he was shedding his love of equality as a grub sheds its cocoon; and he was emerging, growing up. She realized that what had been the most serious thing in the world to William had been an interesting and amusing game to him. She knew that in a little while he would do what his parents would doubtless call 'settle down.' He would become a man of property, a Sussex squire; and his only concession to the old ideals would be the vote he gave to the Whigs instead of to the Tories; and those days of meetings and righteous anger, of enthusiasm and deep pity, would become to him an adolescent fever which had attacked him in his youth, something which he had caught because he was young and had seen only one side of a problem.

She knew this, and she had known it would be so since he had suggested that *she* should visit his parents, when such an invitation—although it could not have saved William's life—if given to him and accepted might have prolonged it.

Perhaps this was one of the reasons why she could not love him. She, too, was an idealist; she, too, looked for perfection.

Lilith told her she was a fool. "What are you waiting for?" she demanded. "Love? Where do you think you'll find it? Will it be in the eel and pie man at the corner? Are you going to make shirts all your life?"

"What will become of *you*? Are you going to sing at Marpit's all *your* life?"

Lilith looked away, trying to see into the unknown future. Sam was getting restive; she still had the power to 'bring them in,' but how long would it last? She was nineteen, no longer the precocious child; and precocity had been one of her greatest assets, she believed. Sam was not the sort to wait for ever, and he and Fan had resumed a relationship which had been theirs before the arrival of Lilith. Fan was a comfortable, easy-going sort; she had that special kind of repartee which Sam called 'giving change.' She had not that sublime quality which was

Lilith's. But there was such a thing as waiting so long that all the chances went by.

So Amanda gave no definite answer to David Young, while Lilith meditated on Sam Marpit. They were both waiting, so thought Lilith; Amanda, like the little fool she always had been, was waiting for something which she was hardly likely ever to find. Amanda as usual did not know what she wanted; Lilith knew all too well.

And then came change.

It came through Napoleon. He had gone off with his broom. It was a sunny day—perhaps not quite so good for business as those when the roads were muddy or snowy—but even a sunny day meant there was plenty of rubbish and horse-dung to be swept out of the path of ladies and gentlemen.

He was looking idly about him, thinking of William in Heaven, wondering if he were getting enough to eat up there; he had heard more stories of God and from the way in which some of them talked of Him, He seemed like a bigger, fiercer Farmer Polgard. Napoleon was fervently hoping that William was happy in Heaven when, on the other side of the street, he saw the fair-haired man whom Lilith so much desired to meet.

"Mr. Danesborough!" murmured Napoleon in great excitement, for that was the name Lilith said he must remember.

This then was the great moment for which he had been waiting; this was going to be the most wonderful day of his life.

He said the name again; this time shouting it. The man was becoming swallowed up in the crowd and naturally he could not hear Napoleon's voice above the street noises. Napoleon started to dash across the road shouting: "Mr. Danesborough! Mr. Danesborough! Stop! Stop!"

The driver of an omnibus cursed as he darted in front of it.

"Mr. Danesborough! Mr. Danesborough!"

The fair-haired man had stopped and looked round.

But just in that second a brewer's dray which had been coming along on the other side of the omnibus caught Napoleon.

He heard the far-off voices of people, very dimly, very hazily as he lost consciousness.

Amanda said: "Lilith, I'm frightened. What does it mean? Where is Napoleon? Two whole days and nights and he has not come home. Have they sent him to prison as they sent William? What does it mean?''

Lilith was silent, lying on the mattress, thinking of Napoleon.

What did it mean? It could mean that the boy had had an accident and been killed.

She and Amanda went to Regent Street to look for Napoleon, for they knew where he had had his crossing, and here they learned from a policeman that there had been an accident on the day Napoleon had disappeared. He could not say whether or not it was Napoleon, because he had come along when it was all over, but he had heard that it was a crossing-sweeper.

"There must be some way of finding out," said Amanda. "He may be needing us."

"It's queer," said Lilith. "First William goes . . . now Napoleon. Amanda, what are we going to do?"

"It's an accident. There must be something we can do. I'm going to David. He'll know what can be done. He'll know if there's some way of finding where Napoleon is."

She put on her cloak and went out. David would know. Already she was turning to him. Soon she would marry him. Lilith was right, and even Amanda was beginning to see that they could not go on as they were for ever. Lilith was thinking this as she lay on the mattress in the attic. What was the use of trying to rest? She shuddered, thinking of all the terrible things that might happen to the defenceless in a big city.

And as she lay there brooding, Jenny called to her that a gentleman had come to see her and Amanda.

Lilith ran to the door and opened it; her heart began to pound and her knees to tremble, for coming up the stairs to the attic was Frith.

"Lilith!" he said.

"You . . ." she stammered. " 'Tis you. . . ."

Frith had shut the door and was leaning against it. He said slowly: "It's all right. The boy will be all right. He'll live, though it was touch and go. I've only just discovered why he wanted to see me. He's at my place. I'm looking after him."

Lilith was not really listening; she did not mean to be callous about Napoleon, but she could think of nothing but the glorious fact that Frith was here.

"Frith!" she said; and she heard the queer little laugh in her throat which she could not control. She wanted to run to him, to fling herself against him, but she was afraid. He had changed a good deal; she must have changed too. Perhaps she would have to win him all over again.

"Lilith," he said, "how wonderful to find you! Where is Amanda? Not here . . . not *living* here?"

Then she realized that the Murphys' house would seem very mean and humble to him.

"Yes," she said.

"It's incredible. Not *Amanda*!"

"Yes, Amanda," she said, and added reproachfully: "And *me*!"

He laughed suddenly. "And you, Lilith. Strange . . . I might have seen you long ago. Fancy! That boy was here with you. I recognized his accent and when he told me he came from our neighbourhood, it didn't occur to me that he would be with you."

"Won't you sit down, Frith?"

He did not answer that. "You . . . you sleep in this attic?"

"Yes."

"You . . . and Amanda?"

She wished he would not continue to speak of Amanda; he was not disgusted that she, Lilith, should live in such a place, only that Amanda should. She was frightened; she feared Amanda might come back too soon. How she had longed for this meeting, and how difficult it was to say what was necessary! How had she pictured this scene? Herself and Frith coming face to face as they had now and, without a second's hesitation, being in each other's arms. But there was a bridge to cross before they reached that old relationship and she was afraid to cross it.

"Yes, Amanda and me . . . we both sleep here."

"What do you do?"

"She makes shirts and I sing in supper-rooms."

"Amanda makes shirts!" That hurt him; she could see it did, for his face wrinkled up oddly and all the laughter went out of it; it flushed with disapproval.

She said proudly: "We're comfortable . . . considering. I do very well in the supper-rooms."

He laughed then. "Oh, Lilith . . . you would!"

She had to stop his talking of Amanda.

"Napoleon . . . ?" she began.

"Was knocked down in the street when he was running after

me. I heard him calling me. I turned just in time to see him go down. I took him home with me. He's very ill. Very near thing it was. I thought I should not be able to save him. He's been delirious. He kept talking about 'the gentleman.' I presumed that meant me as my name occurred again and again. Then he said 'Lilith' and 'the lady.' It was not until to-day that he was well enough to tell me where you were and why he wanted me. I came at once.''

She advanced towards him a few steps. She said: ''He'll get well . . . poor Napoleon?''

''Yes. He may be crippled. One of his feet is rather smashed up.''

''Oh,'' she said, ''so Napoleon had to be crippled so that I could see you again.''

Her voice broke; he put his arms about her and kissed her.

''You're still the same,'' she said.

''Yes,'' he said. ''I think so.''

Then she laughed aloud for happiness. What did anything matter now that she had found him?

Amanda soon returned, as she had failed to find David.

Lilith stood back, watching them, seeing their delight in the reunion. Amanda's appearance shocked him; he was touched, hurt and very affectionate, all at once.

''Frith!'' cried Amanda.

He went to her swiftly, took her hands in his and kissed her first on one cheek then on the other. He looked long into her face.

''Amanda! How could you? How *could* you?''

She laughed. ''Oh, Frith, how wonderful to see you! What brought you here? How did you know?''

''Napoleon.''

''Napoleon?''

She did the right thing, of course, thought Lilith bitterly; she showed at once her concern for the boy. Her anxiety for Napoleon was greater than her joy in seeing Frith again. It was so easy to do the right thing when you did not care with all your being.

''It's all right, Amanda,'' she said quickly. ''Napoleon's safe.''

''Yes,'' said Frith. ''There was an accident. He was running after me and not looking where he was going. He has been with me for two days. I've only just realized why he wanted me and that he had any connection with you. I came immediately.''

"But, Napoleon, is he . . . ?''

"He'll get better. He's been rather knocked about, poor little fellow. Don't worry. I'll look after him.''

"We must go to see him.''

"Of course you must." He looked round the room. "Amanda, *you* . . . making shirts! What would your parents say?''

"Would they be interested?''

Frith did not answer. He did not tell her that her father had disowned her when she ran away from his house; there was no need to tell her that. She knew it was the only course he would take. She was disgraced, dishonoured in his eyes; therefore it was logical to presume that she was no longer his daughter.

"Something must be done," he said.

Lilith watched him uneasily and she wondered if Frith's return was going to bring her happiness after all, and whether her slightly contemptuous affection for Amanda was going to turn into a bitter jealousy.

They went at once to see Napoleon. How strange he looked in a little bed of his own! He was shy, wondering if it was not all some fantastic mistake. He could not help stroking the sheets every now and then in amazement; he had never before slept between sheets. It was obvious that he had discovered a new god and that that god was Frith. As Amanda and Lilith stood by his bed, he saw from Lilith's eyes that he had done a wonderful thing in finding the gentleman.

Amanda kissed him. "Napoleon! Poor little Napoleon! How glad I am that you came here.''

"It's a real bed," he said. He looked round the room with pride. "It's a real looking-glass on the table. You see yourself in it . . . beautiful. I never seed such a place as this.''

"You're very happy, Napoleon?''

He nodded. "But what about my crossing? I wouldn't want for to lose it. Others will be working it now.''

Frith laid a hand on his head. "Don't think about the crossing. You're not going back to it. When you're better you shall learn to be my tiger.''

"Your tiger, sir?"

"A groom for my carriage."

Napoleon was beginning to understand that there were even better things in life than sweeping a crossing.

"Lilith," he said, "I found him. I found him, didn't I, Lilith?"

Then Lilith knelt by the bed and, before she could stop herself, burst into tears—not the sort of tears which Amanda shed so charmingly, but wild, passionate sobs that shook her.

"Oh, Lilith," cried the boy in fear, "didn't I do right, then? Did I do wrong?"

"No!" sobbed Lilith. "No. Oh, Napoleon, you got hurt . . . and I hadn't been kind to 'ee."

She felt Frith's hand on her neck, and she took it and kissed it passionately, there before them all. Then Amanda knew what she ought to have known long ago: Lilith loved Frith. The knowledge disturbed her.

"It's all right, Napoleon," said Frith. "It just means she's glad you've got well. We're all glad of that. And don't forget. You're going to stay with me and you'll learn how to drive my carriage. You have nothing to worry about. You'll be here always."

"Shall I?" said the boy wonderingly. But he wanted reassurance from Lilith before he could be happy. "Lilith, did I do right?"

"Yes, Nap. Yes. But I didn't want you to get hurt."

"Get up," said Frith to Lilith, and he pulled her hair, as though . . . thought Amanda . . . as though what? She did not know.

Lilith gave a short little laugh and stood up. "I'm sorry. It was silly. I didn't ought to have done that." She was looking at Frith, talking to Frith.

"Let's have some tea," said Frith. "They'll serve it in the drawing-room. Yours will be sent in to you, Napoleon."

Amanda and Lilith kissed Napoleon before they left him lying in his bed, staring up at the wonderful white ceiling, marvelling at the beautiful world.

Tea in the drawing-room! How like home this was! Although the furniture was the very modern, very heavy type, still Amanda could not stop thinking of the drawing-room at Leigh House.

Lilith was silent during the meal, watching for any slight from the servants which she would recognize at once. Hadn't she been a servant herself to know how such things should be done?

They talked about Napoleon's injuries, about the strangeness of finding each other, about his life and theirs.

Lilith said it was time she went to the supper-rooms, and Amanda felt relieved when she had gone. Frith also seemed more at ease; and they talked about Cornwall then.

"There was such a fuss, I can tell you. Alice says your mother nearly died of the shock, and as for your father, he shut himself up for days and would speak to no one. He would not have you back, Amanda."

"I should never want to go."

"I have a piece of news for you. Alice is married."

"Whom did she marry?"

"You'll never guess, so I'll tell you. Anthony Leigh, your cousin."

"Poor Alice!"

"She wouldn't agree. When I last saw her she was very happy at Leigh House. Your father has made Anthony his heir. I'm afraid you're out of it, Amanda. When I spoke of you to your father, he said, 'My daughter? I have no daughter!' Just like that, very dramatically. I can't tell you how glad I am I have found you. Shall I tell them, when I go back?"

"No, Frith. You mustn't."

"I'd like to be able to tell them you had married a Duke. Wouldn't that be fun?"

"Fun for whom? Them? Me? Or the Duke? As far as I'm concerned, so much would depend on the Duke."

"I was as usual thinking of myself. I meant: to go to your father and say, 'I was talking to the Duchess of M—— the other day. Do you know the Duchess? She was a Miss Amanda Leigh of Leigh House. I might have thought she was your daughter, but, you, of course, have no daughter.' "

"I suppose he would be more likely to forgive a duchess than a shirtmaker?"

"Undoubtedly a coronet would cover all your sins."

"Frith, it is wonderful to see you again."

"What maddens me is to think we've been in London all this time and haven't met."

"Lilith wanted me to write to Alice and tell her where we were."

"Why didn't you?"

"I couldn't. How did I know how you would feel about knowing me now?"

"Amanda, you are an idiot. I can see who was the brains of the party. Thank God you had the good sense to take her with you."

"She's very clever. She's brave too. She seems wild and outrageously ill-mannered sometimes, but beneath all that . . ."

"I know," he said. "I know a lot about Lilith."

"She's been magnificent . . . keeping us all, really. Do you know how she got to Marpit's?" She told the story as she knew it. "You should hear Lilith's version, of course. She tells it very amusingly. She makes you see Sam Marpit. He's a very prosperous man and he wears such waistcoats! He is also in love with Lilith and wants to marry her."

"Wouldn't that be good for Lilith?"

"It would. But she keeps saying 'No.' She laughs at Sam, but I think she is quite fond of him. He's rather coarse and a little vulgar, but I think he has a good heart."

"Poor Lilith!" he said.

"Rich Lilith!" she corrected him. "Lilith would never be Poor Lilith. She loves life too much."

He seemed to want to change the subject. "What about you, Amanda? What are you proposing to do?"

"I shall go back to Mrs. Murphy's and get on with my shirts."

"You can't do that."

"Why not? I've done it for three years."

"You wouldn't go on for another three."

"Why not?"

"In that place! You'd die of malnutrition before that time. You look as if you need a bit of fresh air and some nourishing food. Three years in that attic have changed you, Amanda."

"Three years would change anybody."

"You were stronger . . . healthier in the country."

"Well, I'm happier here."

"You're a queer creature. You always seemed so soft. Those continual tears! Remember them? And then suddenly to run away like that. It seemed incredible to me when I heard it."

"I suppose I am soft. I suppose I'm a bit of a coward. But everything worked out so that it seemed inevitable. Flight was the only course if I was to escape my cousin."

"I shall never let you stay in that attic."

"Then where shall I go?"

"I'll think of something."

"What? Can you find me a post as governess, such as Miss Robinson had? How odd to think of myself becoming like Miss Robinson. But I suppose when she was nineteen she never thought of becoming like that."

"I'll think of something," repeated Frith.

Sam watched Lilith dance that night. He had never seen her dance quite like that before. She seemed hardly human. There was tension in the place, thought Sam, just like she'd got something about her . . . well, he couldn't say what, except that it was hardly human.

That veils dance never seemed to pall. Once he had thought there should be a change. But no! The people wanted it. They asked for it. "No veils dance, Sam! Why, that's just what I came to see!"

So back came the veils dance; and there was nothing to touch it. That coloured singer he had brought in was good, but it was Lilith they came to see.

She maddened him. Talk about not being human! He wanted to show her that there were other fish in the sea. There was that girl Betty Flower—a nice dancer, nice, plump figure and a lot of red hair. They had liked Betty just as they had liked the coloured singer; but just let him try to cut out the veils dance, and then they all wanted to know why.

Why? he wondered. What was it? She made them hope every night that when she pulled off the last of the veils she'd be standing there with nothing on at all; they knew it couldn't be so; they knew they'd be in a cellar if it was to be so; and yet they hoped. That was Lilith's power; she could make people hope when there was no hope.

He looked at Fan, leaning her elbows on the counter, watching. Fan wasn't bad . . . in the dark. Nice and warm and loving without that sharpness of tongue—a grateful sort, Fan. Like a nice spaniel—though perhaps even spaniels bit if they were teased too far.

She had a way with anchovy toast, and that was not to be despised. He reckoned he was lucky to have a girl like Fan on the premises. But what was the use of counting up the virtues of Fan when it was Lilith's vagaries that tormented him?

There was a newcomer at one of the tables to-night. A regular toff, Sam called him. And he had come to see Lilith. Sam was wily. Sam was sharp. He had seen the glances she had thrown at him. He had something to do with this mood of hers. He, Sam, would have to warn her. After all, she was just a girl from the country, and toffs like that meant no good to girls like Lilith.

She had been late arriving; and there had been something strange about her even then. She was wearing a new bonnet—and she must have bought it on her way, because she was carrying the old one in a paper bag. It was a very elegant bonnet, of black velvet trimmed with pieces of jet and coral-coloured ribbons.

"We've found Napoleon," she had said.

"Gawd save us!" he had retorted. "I thought you'd found a fortune."

She had smiled and looked quite meek. He had tried to take advantage of that meekness.

"I reckon you was fond of that kid. Why, if you was to marry me I'd start looking for a job for him in the Rooms." He had put an arm about her shoulders, but she had thrown him off—even more touchy than usual.

"Save your eyesight," she had said. "There's no need to look, because I ain't going to marry you."

"Well, what are you driving at? You ain't reckoning to marry someone else, are you?"

"I ain't reckoning on telling you what I plan."

But the softness in her eyes belied the sharpness of her tongue.

And now, there she was, seeming more provocative out there, and that man was watching her. Sam reckoned he knew enough about human nature to see the connection.

She went to her room. The company applauded and whistled, which meant they wanted more of Lilith. Sometimes she danced again or sang something; but she never did the veils dance twice in one evening. Once he had wanted her to, but she had refused, and he believed she had been wise in that. "You don't want to let them get tired of it, Sam," she had said. "They see it once. They've got to be here at a certain time to see it. You can't have them thinking they can come in any time. Make it a bit difficult and they'll like it all the more." And she had been right.

He went out of the Rooms and to her room by that other door.

He knocked. There was no answer. He knocked again and as she still did not speak, he opened the door and went in.

"Didn't you hear me knock?" he demanded.

She nodded.

"Well, why didn't you tell me to come in?"

"P'raps because I preferred you to stay outside."

"Look here, I'm getting just a little tired of these airs and graces of yours."

She merely smiled vaguely.

"Here, Lilith, what's up? What's up?"

She regained a little of the old sharpness then. She looked wonderingly up at the ceiling.

"One of these days," he said, "I'll beat you black and blue."

"Wouldn't be good for business," she said. "They like me the colour I am. You have to think of that, Sam."

"What's the matter with you? Who's that fellow outside?"

"There are lots of fellows outside."

"You know who I mean. Him that was staring at you all the time. Haven't seen him here before."

"Was he watching me all the time! I wonder if he came to see me or try Fan's anchovy toast."

"They're clapping for you. You'd better put on your dress and go out and sing something."

"I'm not going to sing any more to-night. I'm going home now."

Sam's face went purple, matching the flowers embroidered on his waistcoat.

"You're *not*!" he said.

"I am."

"Look here, what do I pay you for?"

She made a face at him. "To bring 'em in . . . which I do."

"Look here . . ."

"Where?"

"Now don't you be saucy!"

"I'm going, Sam."

Sam was generally good-humoured, but, as he said, when his temper did rise, it rose hot and strong; and he had stood just about as much as he could stand from her.

He said: "If you don't go out and sing to them now, you're finished here."

"All right, Sam. Goodbye."

She was mad to-night; she did not seem to hear half he said.

"Do you hear?" he cried. "Did you hear?"

She nodded. " 'Go out and sing or go!' That's what you said. All right. I'm going. I won't go out and sing any more . . . not after that dance."

She was dressing for the street, putting on the new bonnet with the black jet and coral ribbons.

He stared at her.

"Look here," he said, "have you taken up with Dan Delaney?"

She shook her head.

"After all I've done for you . . ." he stammered.

"It wasn't for me, Sam. It was for yourself."

"I've been a father to you."

"A funny sort of father!" she scoffed.

That was the old Lilith and he was glad to see her so.

"Don't you know what a fellow like that's after? Would *he* offer to marry you? Don't you want to be respectable? When I think of all the trouble I took to make you into a real singer!"

But she had walked out into the supper-rooms. He heard the hush of surprise as the patrons saw her in her outdoor clothes, and he was furious. Was she running this place or was he? Let her go, then. Good riddance! He'd get on without her. He would find someone who would do that veils dance; and do it as it was meant to be done too!

Lilith joined Frith at his table.

He said: "Let's go."

They left and everyone watched them as they did so. Sam came out just as they were disappearing through the door.

They walked along in silence for a few streets; then she said: "So you came to see me dance?"

"Amanda told me about Marpit's. I wanted to see it for myself."

"Where is Amanda?" She could not keep the laughter out of her voice as she spoke.

"I took her home."

"You'd like her to stay at your house," said Lilith. "But that wouldn't be right. That wouldn't be proper. So you took her home and came out to enjoy the night life."

"I came out to see you."

She threw away her caution then; she did not care if he saw her happiness and knew the cause; in any case it was now quite impossible to hide it.

"Frith, are you glad we found each other?"

"What do you think?"

She laughed. He would not say how glad he was, because they were in the streets; he said such things in the darkness when they were alone.

"Yes," she said. "I think you are."

"We'll get a cab," he said and hailed one.

When they were inside he put his arms about her and kissed her. The bonnet was crushed, but she had forgotten her pride in the bonnet.

"You're just the same as you were in Cornwall," he said.

"Oh, no, I'm not! I'm grown up. The only thing that's the same is my love for you. And that'll stay the same for evermore."

"Yes," he said. "I remember. You always say such delightful things delightfully."

They were silent for a while. She lay against him thinking that the clopping of the horses' hoofs and the gas-lit streets were more beautiful than the Cornish woods. In those woods there had been ever present the thought that happiness was fleeting, that separation was looming; there had been the continual fear that she would lose him. But she would not lose him now; they were grown up. Oh yes, the gas-lit streets of London were happier than the woods of Morval.

He said: "Do you always leave at this hour?"

"No. Much later."

"Then why did you leave early to-night?"

"Because you came for me."

"So on other nights you would be much later?"

"There won't be no other nights. I was told if I left now I need not come back."

"Lilith! Why did you do it?"

"Because you were waiting for me."

"Do you mean you've lost that job?"

"Don't speak of it. I shall be with you now."

He was silent and she went on: "No matter what I do . . . I don't care. All I care for is to be with you."

The cabby had pulled up in Wimpole Street, outside his house. She looked at him in astonishment.

"Here . . ." she said, and she was laughing softly. "I thought you were taking me home . . . back to Amanda."

"How could we be together there?"

"Here . . ." she said. "In your house . . . wouldn't that be . . . improper?"

He did not answer and they went up the steps.

He opened the door with his latchkey and they went into the hall, where a gas jet burned low in its globe of frosted glass. He turned it out.

He said her name and ran his fingers through her hair. She said nothing because she was too happy for speech. And after a while they went quietly up the stairs.

Three weeks passed; they were weeks of passionate love-making for Frith and Lilith, of convalescence for Napoleon and of uneasiness for Amanda. Understanding the relationship between Frith and Lilith, Amanda was worried. Lilith did not return to the Murphys' house until the early hours of the morning, yet Amanda knew that she had left the supper-rooms. Amanda asked no questions because she knew what was happening. Lilith was not behaving with her usual cleverness. Neither Frith nor Lilith seemed to be aware of the fact that they were acting strangely. They seemed bemused.

Frith called often to see Amanda, and Amanda went to his house in Wimpole Street, ostensibly to visit Napoleon. Often she took tea in Frith's drawing-room; Lilith accompanied her.

Frith was worried on Amanda's account.

Continually he said: "Making shirts! It's ridiculous. Of course you can't go on like that."

"Lilith," he said one night when she had come secretly to his house to visit him, "we can't go on like this indefinitely. I think the servants are already suspicious. Servants have sharp ears for such things. I've got an idea."

"You're not going to send me away?"

"Now, that's ridiculous. As if I would! And as if you'd let me if I wanted to!"

"No," she said. "You're right there. I never would. I'd follow. I'd run after your carriage until I dropped dead."

"Don't talk of dying."

"I won't. Except that I hope I die before you . . . because I couldn't bear to live without you."

"Lilith," he said, "don't say such things. I want to be practical. You must have an apartment where I can come and see you."

"Every night?"

"Every night I possibly can—you can depend on that."

"It *will* be every night," she said blissfully. She was quiet, contemplating this; then she said: "I shall have to tell Amanda, shan't I?"

"N . . . no, I don't think so."

"But what'll she think? What'll she do?"

"Let her think you have a friend . . . that man at the supper-rooms, perhaps."

"Oh!"

"It would be best."

"But what will she do? She can't live at Murphys' without me."

He was silent for a while, and then he began to speak as though he were choosing his words very carefully. "Lilith, I think there might be a solution. I think it might be a good thing if I . . . As a matter of fact, I think it's the only solution. You see, I feel responsible in a way for Amanda. In the old days when they were urging her to marry her cousin, I told her to be bold. I did not think her boldness would end in her running away. It's on my conscience. When I saw her in that attic I felt deeply my own responsibility."

"Yes?" said Lilith faintly.

"I think there's only one way out of this. Amanda could marry me."

Lilith could not believe that she had really heard him say that. This was a nightmare. She was not awake. Marry Amanda! But it was Lilith whom he loved.

He went on quickly: "It wouldn't make any difference to us. It's you whom I love. I wish I could marry you, but you're clever enough to see the impossibility of that."

Still she did not speak. There was a pain in her throat which was preventing her, and she did not know whether it was misery or just blind anger.

"I knew you'd understand, Lilith. Unfortunately for us both, you were not born in the right place. If necessary, we could explain to Amanda how things are, but perhaps that would not be wise. You see, Amanda needs protection. She can't stay in that place. But where can she go? I can't have her here. I've thought about this a good deal, and it seems the only solution. Lilith, why don't you speak? What's the matter?''

She sat up suddenly, clenching her fists and pressing them against her breasts as though by doing so she could hold in her violent emotion.

"I'm not good enough to marry," she said. "Then it seems to me I'm not good enough to be here."

"Lilith," he said, "it's not like you to be so silly. You know perfectly well how things are. It's regrettable, but there's nothing we can do about it. We've got to accept conventions. Picture yourself here . . . as my wife. It would just be impossible."

"Why?" she cried. *"Why?"*

"Why? Oh, surely you don't want me to go into that. I wish we could get right away . . . to some desert island."

"Yes," she said savagely. "I'd be good enough on a desert island, wouldn't I . . . like I was in Morval Woods? It's only here that I'm not."

He took her by the shoulders and forced her down.

"Lilith, be quiet. Someone will hear you."

Then she began to laugh quietly, and because it was dark he could not see the tears on her cheeks.

Now that he had prepared the way with Lilith, Frith decided to speak to Amanda.

He did so during tea, when she had called to see Napoleon. He was feeling rather pleased with himself. He had managed this well, he told himself. Amanda would be just the wife for him—pliable, easy-going and grateful because he would have reinstated her. The perfect wife, gentle, charming and undemanding. And Lilith would be the perfect mistress. He considered he had reason to be proud of his handling of a delicate situation.

"Amanda," he began, "I want to talk to you about the future."

"Well, Frith, as a matter of fact, I did have an idea. I think you might help me."

He listened a little complacently, holding back what he was

about to offer her, like a benign parent at a Christmas party, saving the fairy doll at the top of the tree until the last.

"I think often of Miss Robinson. I could do what she did. I thought that if I taught children or became a companion . . . to read to someone, an invalid perhaps. . . . Something like that. I should be quite fitted for it. I know I can't go on shirt-making for ever, and I don't want to be separated from Lilith. She's been wonderful. I realize now how wonderful. And sometimes I think—but perhaps this is flattering myself—that although I need her very much, she needs me a little."

"Lilith will be all right. She can look after herself. It's you I'm thinking of."

"You have friends, Frith. Perhaps you could recommend me to them."

"That's no life for you, Amanda. A sort of higher servant! Nonsense!"

"Don't forget I've been a humble shirt-maker."

"I remember it with deep regret. No, Amanda, you've got to cut away from all that, and I suggest . . . you marry me."

"Marry you, Frith! Why, that's the last thing I should have thought of, especially as . . ."

He interrupted her. "You must have contemplated it at one time. Remember, our parents planned it. If you married me there would be a reconciliation with your family, I don't doubt for a moment."

She stood up. "Frith! What about Lilith? You and she are lovers, I believe."

"She told you that?"

"She told me nothing, but I am not so blind that I cannot see things that are so very obvious. What would she feel if I married you?"

"Lilith is a very clever girl, although completely uneducated. She would accept the situation as inevitable. She knows she and I could never marry."

"If you think she would accept such a situation as inevitable, you don't know her."

"My dear Amanda, I know her very well. She will accept what is inevitable."

"And afterwards? What do you propose to do? To continue with Lilith . . . as your mistress?"

He was silent.

She went on: "You don't know either of us very well, Frith."

"You are shocked. You are disgusted with me. Dearest Amanda, you have led such a sheltered life. What do you know of the civilized world? Nothing at all. You look upon me as a monster because I am fond of both you and Lilith . . . in different ways. Believe me, it is not a very extraordinary situation."

"I don't look upon you as a monster. I look upon you as just Frith . . . an old friend who has asked me to marry him. But I don't want to marry you, Frith. I want you to help me to find some work that I can do. If you do that I shall be very grateful."

"You are being foolish, Amanda. You are asking me to help you to a life of drudgery when I offer you . . ."

"I know. You offer me a life of honour, of prestige in a kind of *ménage à trois*. It's very kind of you, but I can't accept. You must let me do what I want to with my own life."

"Oh, Amanda, always sentimental! If only you were as sensible as Lilith! She understands. I've explained to her."

"You explained to her . . . before you proposed to me!"

He nodded complacently; but Amanda was sure that he did not know Lilith as she did, and she believed he had little reason for complacency.

Sam Marpit was sitting at one of the tables disconsolately going through accounts when Lilith walked in. He pretended not to see her; he wanted to control his features; it would be a mistake to let her see how elated he felt at the sight of her. Receipts had been falling off since she had gone. People asked where she was. They had come to see the veils dance and they went away disappointed. He'd bet they would be drifting over to Delaney's if he didn't get someone alluring enough to take the place of Lilith and her veils.

Now here she was, creeping back, rather humble, wanting her job back, he supposed, realizing that she had made a mistake, that she ought to have listened to him.

She sat down opposite him; he was reminded, as she was, of their first encounter, when she had sat in this room among the upturned chairs with the blinds down and the floor covered with sawdust.

"Oh!" said Sam, making his voice sound as blank as he could. "Who's this?"

"The Queen of Sheba," said Lilith with more cockney accent

than he had heard from her before. "Who are you? King Solomon?"

He wanted to laugh, to pat his thigh. It was not the joke—much as he liked a joke—but it was having Lilith back that pleased him.

"Solomon," he said, "that's me. You ought to see my wives and conkerbines."

He resumed his study of the accounts.

"I've come back," she said.

He nodded. "That's a pity. I mean it's a pity you walked out like you did. I've got a new singer. She's a corker. She knows how to bring 'em in. I'm very sorry, Lilith."

"Don't be sorry, Sam. I just thought of giving you the first chance. Delaney's waiting."

She got up, and he let her walk three paces towards the door.

"Don't be so sharp," he said. "Sit down. No need to run away just because we can't do business. Let's have a little chin-wag for old friendship's sake."

"Well, Sam, I'm busy. I've got to see Delaney."

"Now, look here. I wouldn't like to see you fall into the hands of a man like that."

"Why not?"

"That cellar of his!"

"I wouldn't work in his cellars. I'm able to state my own terms. Goodbye, Sam."

"Here, come back a minute. You don't want to take me too serious. I got this singer and she's a draw, but . . . well, I might find room for you . . . just for old time's sake. I couldn't be offering you what I paid you before. I'd give you fifteen bob a week . . ."

"That's no good. If I'm to stay away from Delaney's, I'd want what I had before. . . . And there's another thing . . . I'd want to live in."

He could scarcely prevent himself from laughing with glee. "It might be arranged. But we can't do this too fast. You're asking a lot, you know. Business is business. But I've got a soft spot for you, Lilith."

"Never mind about your soft spots. If you want me back, it's because I can draw people in better than any of your singers, coloured or not. Business ain't been so good since I left, has it?"

"That's what you might call a mighty fabercation—a great exaggeration. In me own words—it just ain't true. You're not all that much of a draw."

"Well, if that's how you feel, Sam Marpit, I'll go to Delaney. I fancy he thinks I *am* something of a draw."

"You was always touchy, Lilith. You look worn out. What about a nice hot whisky? Do you good. Fan!" he called. "Fan!"

Fan came. She was a placid girl, but she looked a little put out by the sight of Lilith.

"A nice hot whisky, Fan," said Sam. "Lilith's come back."

Fan brought the whisky, and Sam watched Lilith while she sipped it.

He said: "Things didn't work out right then, eh? Wasn't I right when I told you so?"

She swallowed the lump in her throat. "Perhaps you were, Sam."

"I could see he was a wrong 'un. Them toffs always are. What do they want from the working girl? I always asks meself."

"And you've got the answer to that all right. The same as you want, Sam Marpit."

"Didn't I make an honest offer? Didn't I say I'd even marry you?"

She nodded.

"Of course," he said cautiously, "that was before. . . . That ain't now."

"Don't you worry, Sam. Nobody's falling over themselves to marry you. Unless it's Fan."

"You take me up sharp, don't you? All I want is to help . . . and all you do is take me up sharp."

"I've come here to talk business. If you want me back, say so, Sam. If not . . ."

"All right. All right. I want you back. I look on you like a daughter."

"I'm glad of that, Sam," she said, melting suddenly and looking pathetic and tender, so that Sam Marpit felt the tears in his eyes. "That's just how I want it to be."

Sam nodded. But you wait, he thought. Already he was planning the notice he would put outside the supper-rooms: "The Return of Lilith." They might have eight veils instead of seven, just to make a change, to keep them in suspense a bit longer; or perhaps clients would prefer six and a speedy dénouement. It did not matter. Lilith was back. They would be coming to see her. Living in, too! Wasn't that what he had always wanted? He saw her as mellowed by her experiences, realizing what a good fellow Sam was compared with gentlemanly seducers. She could have that little room at the top. She would be penitent, not quite the haughty piece she had been. She shouldn't set such a store on her favours now, should she? She could hardly expect him to marry her now. She'd be changed. That always changed them.

Sam smiled blissfully, seeing himself mounting the stairs to that little room—which would be Lilith's—over Sam Marpit's Supper-rooms.

Frith was not worried. He had no doubt that he would be able to lure Lilith back to the old relationship. His plan of marriage with Amanda had merely seemed expedient—not only for himself, but for Amanda. He was an easy-going, good-natured man who liked to do a good turn when he could; he was, however, disappointed and piqued that his well-laid plans had been frustrated by two women. He had learned from Amanda that Lilith had decided to move to the supper-rooms, as she had said Amanda would no doubt soon be leaving their room at the Murphys'.

So to the supper-rooms went Frith in search of Lilith.

He sat watching her dance with her veils; she reminded him of many an intimate moment; she was completely sensuous—so much herself in the dance. Why had she not been born in his social sphere? Watching her, he felt tempted to marry her in spite of everything. That, of course, could be social suicide. Working at all was bad enough, for society considered that by working the status of gentleman was forfeited. He had felt he could overcome that. He had wit and charm—enough of these qualities to carry him wherever he wanted to go; but the wrong sort of marriage would mean the end of that particular career which he planned for himself.

He could not marry Lilith; but he had no real fear that she would not continue to be his mistress.

She was dancing, he felt, for him alone. He was sure she had seen him, although she pretended she had not; the change in her was obvious. He smiled, well contented. He knew she would come to his table after the dance, and they would go back together; and to-morrow he would see about the lease of a house somewhere—not too far from Wimpole Street.

Lilith danced until she stood there with the veils all discarded—enchanting in the dim lights; then, acknowledging the applause of the customers, she bowed and with a graceful movement gathered up the veils and disappeared.

Sam followed her into her room.

He was uneasy. This was just like that other night, when that man had come in and she had refused to go on again.

He stood by the door, watching her; she was excited. The man had that effect upon her.

Since her return she had been what Sam called "as spiky as ever and just as haughty." She had made sure that there was a lock on the door which led to her room, and a good key to fit it; and she made him keep his distance. He was still worried on account of that man out there.

"They're calling for you, Lilith," he said. "You go back and sing a little song. Wrap your veils round you. . . . Go on."

"All right," she said. "All right."

So far so good.

He waited in her room, heard her singing, heard the applause. When she came back she said: "You still here!"

"Look here," said Sam, "don't you go walking out like you did that other time. You could strike me with forked lightning before I'd have you back a second time."

She did not answer; but she put on her dress with the red roses and the sequinned top; and she fixed a red rose in her hair.

"Where are you off to?"

"To make myself sociable with the customers. That's my job, ain't it? I'm going to make them buy more brandy and champagne. I'm going to make them eat more steaks and anchovy toast."

"Look here . . ." he began, falsely belligerent and helpless, because she was fully aware of his fears.

In the supper-rooms she sat and chatted with some of the regular clients. Frith watched her, his eyes begging her to come to his table. She enjoyed keeping him waiting. If she did not belong to his world, he did not belong to hers. If she was not good enough for his friends, at least she was Queen of Marpit's Supper-rooms.

At last she went to his table and sat down.

"Lilith!" he said reproachfully.

"Order champagne," she said. "It's expected."

"Who expects it?" he asked. "That oaf . . . with the greasy hair?"

She was quick to defend Sam. "I'd be glad if you didn't talk against him. He's a friend of mine . . . and a good friend."

"Friend? Is that all?"

"He's my friend all right. He's asked me to marry him, so I say he shouldn't be run down." She signed to one of the waiters. "Champagne," she said. "Champagne, Jack."

Frith said: "Have you accepted his proposal of marriage?"

"I might."

"I shouldn't, if I were you."

"But you're not me."

"Lilith, come out of this place. I don't like to see you here."

Her eyes were hard. "Don't you? Why not? Because it's low? Because it's vulgar? But then I'm like that, you know."

"Don't be absurd."

"So I'm absurd, as well as low and vulgar and. . . . Thank you, Jack. You pay him now," she added, while Jack poured out the wine.

When he had gone, Frith said: "For God's sake be reasonable."

"What's being reasonable?"

"Come back with me now."

"What for?"

"I've found a charming house. In fact, there are two of them. I want you to choose. Neither of them is very far from Wimpole Street."

"But not *in* Wimpole Street."

"Don't let's go into all that."

She smiled at him over the top of her glass. "I don't know why you came here."

"To try to persuade you to be sensible."

"To try to persuade me to be sinful, you mean?"

"Sinful, Lilith! You talk like a prude. It's a bit late for that."

"It's a bit late for you to come here."

"I want to explain to you, Lilith. You'd hate being married to me."

"I be best judge of what I do like and hate."

"It wouldn't be you . . . your style. You'd have to meet a lot of tiring people. If you would only look at these houses . . ."

"I don't have to look at houses to know what I want. Houses don't make no difference to me."

"I understand how you feel, Lilith. There's nothing in the world I'd rather do than marry you . . . if it were possible. It simply is not. Anything but that, Lilith . . . anything . . . anything. You see, my darling, it would be so wrong . . . from your point of view as well as mine. My people would not approve. . . ."

"You didn't care about your people when you decided you were coming to London to be a doctor, did you?"

"That's quite different."

"There was no need for you to come here to-night," she said sadly.

"What are you doing here . . . living in this place? What about that dreadful . . . common creature? What is your relationship with him?"

"It ain't what it were with you. He's not a gentleman, you see, so he can ask me to marry him."

"You're being rather silly, Lilith."

"I'm being myself; and if you don't like that you didn't ought to have come."

"You know I like it. I like it better than anything in the world. I love it, in fact."

" 'Tain't no good . . . saying things. I don't want to see you no more. And when you and Amanda's married . . . then I don't want to see either of you again."

"I'm not going to marry Amanda."

"You're not?"

"No. I asked her and she refused. Do you know why?"

She did not answer, and he went on: "I think it's because she knows about us."

Lilith stared at him incredulously, and for the first time since she had sat at his table her eyes softened. "She knew then. She's growing up. And she said, 'No,' did she? My dear soul, you be turned down all round. First me. Then Amanda."

"So you see, Lilith, you wouldn't have to see us together, would you?"

"No. You'd have some time to spare, wouldn't you, for that little house that's near Wimpole Street and not in it."

"I love you, Lilith. I can't think about anything else but that. I've come here to-night. . . ."

"It was terrible good of you to come to a place like this here. You . . . a gentleman!"

"I shall take you back with me to-night."

"No, you won't."

"Yes, I shall. I shall wait until this place closes if necessary."

"Sam has a very good thrower-out. He was a pugilist . . . a champion at the game."

"Don't think you can put me off."

"I'm going to say good night now. I don't have to stop with one customer too long. Sam don't like it."

"Do you think I'll take 'No' for an answer? I'll give you no peace."

"Perhaps," she said, "the days be over when you can interfere with my peace."

"You don't change as quickly as that."

"When I change I turn right round."

He began to talk to her in a low and passionate voice, recalling experiences they had shared, reminding her of how she had longed for him, thought of him continually.

She lifted her glass, and as she sipped she smiled; he did not recognize the complete egoism of Lilith, the pride in her; he only saw her as the yielding mistress who had not hesitated to declare her desire for him.

She listened almost half-heartedly, her eyes straying about the room as she nodded to people or acknowledged their greetings.

"I shall be back again and again," he declared. "I'll make you see reason."

Then she got up and went to another table, but he was still confident that all would go as he wished. He knew that she had been unable to sit there any longer, that she was afraid of giving way.

When she went back to her room to take off the red dress with the roses and sequins, Sam was there.

"Still here?" she said.

"Well, I saw you talking to him."

"What harm was there in that? He bought a bottle of champagne."

"You're not going to try any of your tricks again, are you?" demanded Sam.

"Depends what you mean by tricks, Sam Marpit."

"No more walking out."

She did not answer, and, maddened suddenly by the fear of losing her—herself, he realized suddenly, not her power to 'bring them in'—he went to her, took her by the shoulders and shook her.

The rose fell out of her hair. She said: "You're too rough, Sam Marpit. No wonder I won't marry you."

He picked up the rose. "Me?" he said. "Me rough?" Then he began to laugh with excitement and administer those little pats to his thigh—not with amusement this time, but from sheer nervousness. "You know," he went on in a voice which was a key higher than usual, "you know I wouldn't be rough. I'd be all right . . . I reckon."

"Well," she said, "in that case perhaps I might."

Then he put his arms about her and kissed her, and she was passive—sweet and still, he thought. And he loved her—Lilith—just like that, all for herself and nothing more.

Amanda was dressing for dinner. She was wearing a dress of black velvet, most becoming to a widow, said Frith, who had lent her money to buy the dress. "You can pay me back if you have any scruples, as soon as you are earning money, which you will be soon. To-night is important. It is your first interview."

He had been mysterious. "I don't want you to come to dinner like a young girl—you know you don't look like a widow—a young girl who is about to meet her prospective employer. Remember the dreary Miss Robinson! Always trying to please! Is there anything more unpleasing than a person who goes to such pains to please? No. I want you to meet my guests . . . and if one of them has a post to offer you, then you may graciously decide to take it."

Frith was strange lately—brooding at times, even melancholy, which was odd for him to be; and then at others he would break out into gaiety and be very like the young man she used to know.

As for herself, she was uneasy, wondering what her future would be, thinking more and more of poor Miss Robinson; she was also uneasy about Lilith. She had visited the supper-rooms one morning—because as a lady she could not go there in the evening—and Lilith had received her in the big room among the upturned chairs and tables and the sawdust on the floor which was just as it had been on the day of Lilith's first visit. They had embraced warmly; it had been one of those occasions when Amanda had seen Lilith really moved.

"You've got to meet Sam," said Lilith. "You know we're getting married. I'll want you to come to the wedding. It's going to be a proper one. Sam will insist on that, because it will be good for business. A lot of the customers will be here, but you don't want to worry about that. I'll look after you."

"Lilith . . . is it all right, do you think?"

"Is what all right?"

"Your marrying Sam."

"I'm best judge of what's right for me, Amanda, and you don't think I'd do what's wrong, do you?"

"I suppose not."

"So you're not going to marry, then?"

"No."

"Amanda, what are you going to do? That's what worries me. Napoleon's all right. As for me, I'll be Mrs. Sam Marpit. But what of you?"

"I think I'm going to get some sort of job. Frith is going to help me. A sort of governess and companion or something. That's all I can do apart from making shirts, and it was really you who kept me going there. I realize that. I'm not clever like you, Lilith. You were strong. I couldn't have lived without you."

Lilith nodded. "I reckon that's so. Well, now I'm doing pretty well for myself. Sam's not a poor man, and I'll see he gets richer."

"You'll always be all right, Lilith. You've got that about you which tells me so."

"You'll be all right, too. I'll see to that. Remember how I used to bring you up bits from the kitchen when they shut you in your room? I looked after you then, and I'll look after you now. If this governessing be unbearable, you come to me. You can live here."

"Oh, Lilith, you're good . . . so very good."

"Now don't start crying. Tears never helped nobody. And here's Sam come to see you. Sam, this is my cousin and my sister-in-law. 'Tis about time you began to know my family."

"It's a pleasure I'm sure."

"It is," Amanda had told him. "I'm glad to meet you at last. Lilith had talked a lot about you."

He slapped his thigh. "So she has, has she?"

He had put his arm about Lilith, who wriggled free of him.

What was going to happen to them all, wondered Amanda; herself setting out on a new life which would at best turn her into another Miss Robinson; Lilith, loving Frith, but marrying Sam Marpit?

At the informal dinner party which Frith had arranged there were two guests only: a Mrs. Gillingham, a middle-aged and garrulous widow, and Dr. Stockland, a man of about thirty, quiet, tall, spare of figure, with sad eyes and an air of melancholy.

All through dinner Mrs. Gillingham talked of her house in the country, of her house in Town and of her dogs. Frith was amused by Mrs. Gillingham. He was charming to her, and Amanda, in her new assessment of Frith, guessed that he considered Mrs. Gillingham might be a useful person. He teased her, mocked her affectionately, flirted with her; and she seemed to enjoy that. In fact, thought Amanda, this Dr. Stockland and I might not be here for all the contribution we are making.

She caught the doctor's eyes and he smiled at her; she fancied that he shared her thoughts.

When they had coffee in the drawing-room, Frith kept close to Mrs. Gillingham, leaving Amanda and Dr. Stockland together.

He bent towards her and spoke in a low voice. "Frith tells me that you have been left in straitened circumstances since the death of your husband."

She could not help smiling inwardly at the neat way in which Frith had put that. She could not let him down by telling Dr. Stockland the truth. She nodded.

He went on: "He tells me you are looking for a post of some sort . . . something which would be congenial to a young lady like yourself."

"That is so," she said.

"Did he tell you anything about my circumstances?"

"Nothing at all."

"I suppose he thought it would be better if I told you myself. I live in this very street. I specialize in diseases of the heart."

"I see."

"My wife suffers from a disease of the heart and is therefore unable to lead a very active life. She needs a companion. She

needs someone young like yourself. Someone interesting . . .
to read to her and talk to her and to be with her. I think you
would get along very well together. You see, she was once very
full of vitality, very lively. It is a terrible ordeal for her to be so
ill. Would you come along and see her?"

"You are offering me . . . a post?"

"Yes, if you and my wife can decide that you like each other
and can be happy together. Will you come along and see her?"

"It is most kind of Frith to do all this on my account." The
tears sprang to her eyes; he saw them and looked quickly away.

He said, staring at Frith's very ornate and modern overmantel:
"I know you will be sympathetic. It is not easy, you know. I am
sure my wife would be delighted to make a friend of you. In
fact, as soon as I saw you I realized that if only you could be
persuaded to take this on, it was going to be very satisfactory
from our—my wife's and my own—point of view."

"I can only hope your wife will like me. I very much need
something to do. I am so grateful to you. . . ."

"May I tell her that you will come and see her to-morrow?"
he asked. "Come to tea with her. You could then settle matters
between you."

"Thank you. I shall be delighted to come."

She smiled, for Frith was looking her way. He raised one
eyebrow comically.

Amanda called next day on Mrs. Stockland.

It was a tall house, much larger than Frith's establishment.
As she mounted the steps and rang the bell her heart was racing.

A manservant opened the door.

"I am Mrs. Tremorney," she said. "I believe Mrs. Stockland
is expecting me."

"Please come this way, madam."

She was taken to a drawing-room on the first floor. The man
knocked and Amanda heard a voice—a high-pitched, almost
girlish voice—call "Come in."

In a few seconds Amanda was aware of the luxury of the
room; the carpets and rugs were thick and the room was full of
heavy modern furniture. She quickly noticed the dainty china
articles displayed on a table, the loaded what-not, the ornaments
of bronze, jade and ivory that stood about the room. A great

gilt-framed mirror hanging over the mantelpiece reflected the room as well as the gilt clock and figures on the mantelshelf.

"Forgive my not rising, Mrs. Tremorney. This is one of my bad days."

The voice came from the armchair, and in it Amanda saw the doctor's wife. She was a large woman in her mid-thirties, rather inclined to plumpness, rather over-dressed, with her front hair cut to form a bang and her back hair piled high on her head; earrings swung from her ears, and her blouse had many frills of lace and many bows of pink satin; rings shone on her fingers, bracelets on her arms, and there was a glistening aquamarine pendant about her neck.

"How do you do?" said Amanda, taking the outstretched hand.

"Please sit down. You are very young."

"I am twenty."

"You look younger. And you're a widow, I hear."

"Yes."

"Your husband must have died very young. How sad for you. You must tell me all about it. I love to hear of other people's troubles. Of course, I'm very ill myself. I expect Hesketh has told you. It's my heart, you know. That's really how me met. His father was called in to see me. He specialized in hearts then. That was years ago. . . . My trouble was hardly noticeable then. I was just a bit breathless. It was thought that I had been lacing too tightly. Of course, I was by no means *ill* then. *That* has come since my marriage."

"How very sad."

"Will you ring the bell, please? I hope Shackleton has told them to send up tea. I ordered it to be brought as soon as you came . . . but then"—her face became almost sullen suddenly—"then they don't always take notice of what *I* say. Do please ring. Thank you. Do sit down. So you want to be my companion? A sort of nurse as well, Hesketh said. You nursed your husband, he told me. I need a nurse sometimes. I'm very ill, you know. You wouldn't believe it, would you? It's always like that with hearts. You're up one minute and down the next. And you don't really look ill. I inherited it. My father died of it. Oh . . ."

A maid came into the room.

"You rang, madam?"

"Tea . . . *tea*!" said Mrs. Stockland impatiently. "I ordered it to be sent up as soon as Mrs. Tremorney arrived."

"It will be here very shortly, madam."

Mrs. Stockland tossed her head; the earrings flapped against her neck and the veins showed at her temples. "All right. But don't keep me waiting any longer. I will not endure it."

Sarah went out, and the doctor's wife turned to Amanda. "You must tell me all about yourself. You can imagine how sad it is for me, how wretched . . . to be unable to go out as I used to. When I was a few years younger . . . before my marriage . . . I used to go to balls and the gayest parties. I was always in the centre of things. Just imagine what it's like now . . . to be cut off . . . to go out so seldom. And then it's only for a drive round the Park. Oh, here comes the tea."

She looked sulky while it was brought in.

"You need not wait, Sarah. Mrs. Tremorney will pour. You will, won't you, Mrs. Tremorney? Then we can talk. I am longing to hear *all* about you. I'm afraid you will find me rather inquisitive. I love hearing all about people's lives. What else is there for me . . . shut off as I am from the social round?"

"Do you take sugar? Cream?" asked Amanda.

"Sugar, please . . . and plenty of cream. Oh, they have sent up only Indian. They know I sometimes like China. Mrs. Tremorney, I believe they do it to plague me. I'll tell you. . . . But never mind. You might think we were a strange household and refuse to come. . . . I do want you to come. You're going to read to me, Hesketh says. That'll be delightful. And you're going to be a nurse-companion. That will be delightful also. One gets so lonely. People don't visit you if they know you're ill. People are hideously selfish . . . everybody . . . *everybody*! Oh, please give me one of those scones. They have no currants! Well, never mind. I hope you don't hate scones without currants."

"These are delicious. Mrs. Stockland, please tell me what my duties would be if you decided to give me this post."

"Duties? Oh, looking after poor me. We'd be together. After all, I only have the servants. Hesketh is always busy . . . so he says. There's never time to be with me." Again Amanda was aware of that sulky expression. "Patients, you know. They are so demanding, he says. And he is always reading too . . . studying. All about the heart. I think he hopes to cure me." She shook her head and the earrings sparkled as they swung. "There is no cure. I saw what happened to my father." Her face was dark with depression. Never, thought Amanda, had she seen so many emotions expressed in such a short time.

"Are you fond of reading?"

"I think I might be more interested in books if I were read to. I get so tired reading by myself. . . . My eyes . . . Ah, I see you are looking at my portrait."

Amanda had not been looking at anything but her prospective employer, but she now understood her enough to realize that her attention was being directed to a picture. This was a painting of a beautiful young girl, and it was just possible to recognize that the woman in the armchair had been the model for that portrait. How could she bear to look at it, wondered Amanda, since she obviously set such store by her appearance! The face in the portrait was rounded—perhaps a little too full, showing a threat of future fleshiness; the reddish hair was parted in the centre, smoothed down on either side of the face and worn in a knot at the nape of the neck. The beautiful, rounded shoulders were bare, and the blue-green of the evening gown toned harmoniously with the reddish hair.

"It's very lovely," said Amanda.

"You recognized me? So I have not changed so very much."

"I could see immediately who it was."

Amanda realized that she had said the right thing, and that if she came to work at this house her most arduous task would be the choice of her words.

Mrs. Stockland had changed suddenly and had become more like the young girl in the picture.

"I remember sitting for that portrait. He was not very well known at the time. That came afterwards. I do believe my portrait helped a little. It was hung in the Academy. I remember how it was admired. He was in love with me, of course. I remember the crowds about that picture. . . . It was the picture of the year."

"I can well believe it. It is very arresting."

"Arresting! What a lovely word! I can see you are going to be amusing. Hesketh tells me that you have lived in the country. Oh dear, so boring, don't you think? I could not endure the country. And you're a friend of Frith Danesborough. Such an amusing person! You must tell me all about your life in the country, although I suppose it was rather dull. Almost as dull as being here. . . . Yes, please, I will have another cup. It is weak. They know I like it strong. I think they do it on purpose. Perhaps when you have been here a while you will be able to manage them. Servants are so sly, I think. Particularly when they know there's an opportunity of being so . . . and nobody is going to protest.''

"Oughtn't we to discuss terms and such things?'' suggested Amanda.

"Yes; I suppose so. You'd live here, of course; and I'd want you to have a room near mine. After all, you'll be a companion to *me*, won't you? And you'd have your meals with us . . . and be like one of the family, I suppose.''

"I shouldn't want to intrude on your privacy. I could have my meals on a tray sometimes . . . if that was more convenient. You wouldn't want me always with you. . . .''

"I dare say the servants would decide. They seem to decide everything in this house. Do give me my fan, Mrs. Tremorney.''

Her face had become very flushed and she began to fan herself with the ornamental Japanese fan which Amanda had handed to her. Watching her, Amanda felt a sudden desire to escape from this overcrowded room, from the woman whose face repelled her; she had already surmised that life as nurse-companion to this woman was going to be full of difficulties.

Mrs. Stockland lay back in her chair, fanning herself and talking about salary and privileges, offering what was, after life in Mrs. Murphy's attic, a very comfortable existence; yet Amanda could feel no pleasure in the prospect before her and was beginning to doubt the wisdom of accepting it.

"That's better,'' said Mrs. Stockland. "I feel overcome by the heat sometimes. I'm always afraid that I'm going to have one of my bad attacks. I must not get excited. That's the whole point. I have to keep calm. People don't remember, you know. They upset me without thinking what harm they might cause.''

A depression came to Amanda then. This woman alarmed her, and yet what could she do? Frith had arranged this for her, and she should be grateful. She must take it. She should at least try it. Mrs. Stockland was an invalid—a fretful invalid, no doubt. What was it that made her long to escape? The overheated room? The portrait? The strange glitter in the woman's eyes, the self-pity, the continual reproaches against people who were not there to defend themselves? She had been imagining a gentle invalid, and she had not had time yet to adjust her thoughts.

Mrs. Stockland had dropped her fan and was looking at it helplessly, so Amanda picked it up; when she gave it to Mrs. Stockland their faces were close for a moment. Amanda looked at the flushed cheeks and glittering eyes, and as she did so she detected the smell of spirits, and she knew that her prospective employer must have been drinking rather heavily for this to be apparent after she had had her tea; and she guessed that a form of intoxication must be the reason for the strangeness of her mood.

Intoxication! Amanda thought of the people she had seen sitting on the pavements outside the gin palaces, of the queer, lost, depraved look on their faces, of the flushed excitement of some, of the pale depression of others. Why had she not recognized it in this woman at once?

I can't stay here, she thought. It would be impossible. I should never get on with her.

And then Dr. Stockland came into the room. She understood now the meaning of his tiredness, his air of melancholy. It was this woman who had made him thus.

"Ah, Mrs. Tremorney," he said. "I guessed I should find you here." He took her hand and held it. His eyes were anxious. He seemed a different person from the man whom she had met at Frith's house on the previous night. He was on edge.

"Mrs. Tremorney has been telling me *all* about herself," said his wife. "How she nursed her poor sick husband and lived in the country and was so bored with living there. She's going to love being with me. I'm sure it's going to make things a little more pleasant for me. I need them to be." She was malevolent now and the malevolence was for him.

I cannot live in this household, thought Amanda. I can see that it would be impossible. I should not please her; nothing would ever please her. And she hates her husband.

"Is there any more tea?" he asked, smiling at Amanda. "I am glad you have been getting on well together."

Amanda poured out a cup of tea, and she noticed that her hand was a little unsteady.

"Mrs. Tremorney is going to have the room next to mine," said Mrs. Stockland. "We've arranged it all."

"I'm so glad."

"Well . . ." began Amanda.

He looked at her anxiously and she was more moved than the occasion warranted.

"We shall do everything possible to make you comfortable," he said. "My wife, as you have no doubt gathered, needs companionship. She needs intelligent companionship, Mrs. Tremorney. I am so glad you will come to us. You *have* made up your mind, haven't you?"

Now was the moment to say that she had not, and that she needed a little time to consider. She looked from one to the other; both pairs of eyes were urging her to come, the woman's wide and bleary, the man's sad and melancholy. She was aware of the weakness in herself which amused Frith and Lilith.

"We rely on you to come," he went on. "It will make such a difference to us both."

He looked so earnest, so tired, so eager. It was as though he said: "Help me. Amuse her. Take her off my hands a little each day. Take her off my conscience."

She heard herself answer weakly: "Why, yes . . . of course I will come."

PART THREE

※ One

Amanda lay in bed unable to sleep. A comfortable room had been assigned to her in the house in Wimpole Street. It was on the second floor immediately above the drawing-room and next to it was Bella Stockland's own bedroom.

"I want you," Bella had said, "to be within calling distance. That gives me a nice cosy feeling."

The room was richly furnished, as were all the rooms in the house. The carpet was thick, the bed of carved mahogany, the curtains of dark blue velvet. On the heavy dressing table was a big mirror reflecting the room with its lofty ceiling and the ornamental centre-piece; and when the weather was the least bit cold there was always a fire in the grate.

The servants were attentive to her. Hers was a very different position from those Miss Robinson must have had. Everyone in this house, including Bella, realized how important Amanda was, for she had a quality which, it appeared, no one else in the house possessed: it was a quality to soothe Bella's tantrums and restore peace. Everyone else, including her husband—and perhaps indeed he more than any other—could, with the most casual remark, infuriate the mistress of the house; and when she was angry, when she stormed in rage or wept in self-pity, life in that house seemed intolerable.

The fire was dying in the grate and it must be past midnight. Amanda felt exhausted—for her days were exhausting—yet she could not sleep.

She knew why it eluded her on this night. It was because the doctor was away from home. It was the first time since she had come to this house, six months ago, that he had been away; and she felt a sense of insecurity because that room at the end of the corridor was unoccupied.

I believe, she pondered, that I ought to get away from this house.

It was a house of shadows. Its stately and magnificent furnishings gave it an air of solid respectability, and that was misleading. There was hatred in this house. The servants hated their mistress. She was so unaccountable, so impossible to please. Their meekness was assumed and they hated Bella Stockland. But they were sorry for her husband.

And the doctor himself? He was brave and gentle; always he soothed his wife and never did he allow himself to retort in anger.

There had been an occasion when Amanda was on the point of telling him she must go, but he, seeming to sense what was in her mind, had said to her: "Mrs. Tremorney, it's difficult to thank you as I would like to. You have a soothing effect on my wife. She has been much happier since you came. I hope you will stay with us for a long time."

That had been the beginning of a new uneasiness. She had felt that his gratitude was out of all proportion to what she had been able to do.

In his helplessness in dealing with his wife he seemed doubly pitiable when it was remembered that he was clever and that his work was of great importance. Frith had told her that Hesketh Stockland was one of the cleverest "heart" men in London, and that his services were in constant demand. His large practice and his work in a big hospital in the East End of London kept him perpetually occupied. How strange, and how sad, that a man who could do so much for suffering humanity should be unable to deal with one ailing woman.

Why had he married her? That was a question Amanda was continually asking herself. The marriage seemed incongruous. He was so serious; she was so frivolous. Then Amanda would look at the picture in the drawing-room and realize that that gay young girl was not the same person who now employed her. Time and suffering had wrought this terrible change.

In the night it seemed easier to appraise the situation.

Was she disliking Bella more and more every day, and did her dislike grow in proportion to the pity she felt for Bella's husband?

There were times when Bella dined in her room and Amanda and the doctor had a meal alone together. On such occasions he would be relaxed, more at ease, free from the tension which Bella's presence always created. Then he would encourage Amanda to talk, and little by little he had heard the story of her life. She had not meant to tell him, yet somehow he had drawn it from her. He knew now of her life at Leigh House; she re-created for him the atmosphere of dread which had oppressed her childhood. He could understand that readily, for he felt another kind of dread in his house. She told him of Lilith and how they had left Cornwall; she told of their adventures in London. He was astonished, shocked and filled with admiration at the same time.

He never sought her company; yet she could not but know of his pleasure when they were alone together. That, she reminded herself, was due to the absence of his wife rather than to her own presence. How sorry she was for him! He would live in a perpetual dread of what his wife would blurt out. When she was present he seemed to be on edge, waiting for some outburst, which he pathetically tried to prevent.

Amanda had learned a good deal about the affairs of these two people through Bella, for Bella talked continually about herself—but her husband must necessarily be involved in these reminiscences. Little reading was done, since Bella could not concentrate on anything but herself, and it seemed that, whatever the book was, it always contained some incident to remind her of an occurrence in her own life. She would say: "That reminds me . . . Put the book away and let us talk. . . ."

Then would begin one of those excursions into the past which excited her as much as the spirits which she kept in her bedroom cupboard, producing the same exhilaration, which would, after a time, pass into melancholy or, worse still, violent anger ostensibly against some member of the household, but actually against Life for inflicting on such a lover of gaiety, sickness which must result in early death.

Amanda learned of the house in the country in which, it appeared, there had been perpetual entertaining. Bella had been the adored child of indulgent parents, brought up to believe that everything she desired was hers for the asking.

She must have been very pretty in those days—the picture bore evidence of that. There had been many suitors, and they had begun to assemble when she had been barely sixteen. "Like bees," as her father was reputed to have said, "round the heliotrope." "Ah, if only you could have seen me then! I would dance all through the night and be up early ready to hunt all through the next day."

One of her favourite diversions was to contemplate what might have happened if she had married Lord Bankside or Sir Gerald Thor or one of those men who had sought her in marriage. "I might have married quite twenty times, I'm sure. Oh, more than that." She would start counting on her fingers. "I was engaged four times. My father used to say I would hesitate too long. And then my parents were afraid that I had his heart trouble. I remember how they used to watch me. I started to get breathless and one day I had an attack. They called in the doctor. . . ."

"Was *he* in love with you?" asked Amanda with a faint touch of irony.

"Well, in a way he was. He was about sixty, but he used to say such charming things. But they weren't really satisfied with him and that was when they decided to call in a specialist. Hesketh was that specialist's son. He was learning to be one then. We got to know each other's families. Perhaps I shouldn't have married. Or if I did . . . someone different. Hesketh is always saying 'You mustn't do this. . . .' 'You mustn't do that. . . .' And of course 'this' and 'that' is everything I want to do. 'That would excite you too much.' 'This would be too much for you.' Sometimes I think I'd rather be dead than go on living drearily as Hesketh wants me to live."

"It's only because he's so careful of you, because he wants to keep you well," soothed Amanda.

"Oh yes, I know. But who wants to be well just to live this dreary existence?" Her eyes would fill with those tears which were dreaded as much as her rages, the tears of self-pity. "Sometimes I wish I was dead. Sometimes I think I'll give a ball and I'll dance and dance . . . just as I used to . . . dance and dance until I drop down dead."

"But you would not dance until you dropped down dead," said Amanda practically. "That's a romanticized picture. You would become breathless . . . unable to dance. You would collapse and have an attack. You could not dance until you neatly and charmingly dropped down dead."

"How unkind you are!"

But she would take such 'unkindness' from Amanda, though from no one else. Amanda's quiet common sense did not anger

her. Perhaps because it was accompanied by a pity and understanding which was greater than that which she received from
anyone else.

Yes, thought Amanda again, looking towards the dull glow in
the fireplace, I ought to get away from here.

Six months in the house had been enough to show her that
she must leave, and that the longer she stayed the more difficult
it would be to get away, not because of her pity for the invalid,
but for the invalid's husband.

There were alternatives: She might marry Frith. She was sure
that with a little encouragement from herself he would ask her
again. She might marry David Young. She thought of life in a
pleasant country house—a return to that life in which she had
been brought up.

There was Lilith who might help her. Amanda visited Lilith
now and then, and Lilith liked these visits to take place when
Sam was out of the way. She never asked about Frith and Frith
never spoke of her. Amanda guessed that they often thought of
each other. They should have married. But should they? It was
the old problem of class; there was no escaping it. One either
belonged or one did not. And Lilith and Frith belonged to two
different worlds. Would it be possible to combine those two
worlds? Perhaps some people could do it. Amanda saw Frith's
point of view, but she was equally sympathetic towards Lilith's.
That was why she found it difficult to give whole-hearted support to one side or the other; that was why she could never be
so whole-hearted in her devotion to a cause as William had been,
as David had wanted to be. She could not give her allegiance to
one set of combatants only. Nothing in the world was clear-cut
enough for that. There were too many shades between black and
white, too many degrees between good and evil. She was sorry
for Hesketh; she was sorry for Bella. And there she was, back
to the doctor and his wife again.

As she lay there she heard a movement in the next room.
Bella was walking about. She heard the sound of the cupboard
door's being opened, followed by that of the clink of glasses.
Bella could not sleep, then, and her consolation for sleepless-
ness was in her cupboard.

Amanda shivered. Bella had had three glasses of port after
dinner. When the doctor was there he always saw that she was

moderate, and he kept wines and spirits locked up as much as possible.

Amanda had often seen Bella look slyly at him when he locked the sideboard, and she guessed that Bella was thinking of the secret store which she kept in her own cupboard.

That cupboard in the bedroom was replenished through the servants. Bella believed herself to be clever and cunning. She would send out each of the servants in turn to buy her gin or whisky, preferring to believe that they kept this information to themselves. There were times when, finding the wine cellar unlocked, she would gleefully bring up a bottle of something for her store cupboard. In this house the skeleton was undoubtedly in Bella's cupboard.

Often Amanda had heard the doctor go into his wife's room; she had heard the protesting voices—his alternately authoritative and pleading, hers high-pitched and querulous.

But to-night he was not there to stop her drinking.

She pictured him on those nights when he would be in his room on the other side of the communicating door. They had had separate rooms for years, so Bella had told Amanda. He would be lying awake as she lay now, listening for the sound of the cupboard door's opening, for the clink of glass against glass.

I *must* get away! thought Amanda for the twentieth time that night.

She was startled by the tinkle of breaking glass, and, getting out of bed and wrapping her dressing-gown about her, she went into the corridor. Outside Bella's room she paused, hesitating for a second or two before she knocked.

There was no answer.

"Mrs. Stockland," she asked, "are you all right?"

As there was still no answer, she opened the door and went in.

Bella was in the armchair. The broken glass lay at her feet, and she smiled and waved her hand at Amanda.

"I was just having a little drink. Felt thirsty . . . terribly thirsty. Got out of bed and got something to drink. . . ."

Amanda picked up the pieces of the broken glass.

"I'll mop it up," she said. "There must be a cloth somewhere."

Bella nodded. Her eyes were glazed and she was laughing.

She was not in a violent mood, which was something to be thankful for.

Amanda found a cloth and mopped up the mess on the carpet. She caught sight of the cupboard, the door of which was open. It contained several bottles and glasses. Bella followed her gaze.

"I've got the key . . ." she muttered. "He'd like to have it, but I'd never let that go. While the cat's away . . . what is it? The mice play! I'm the little mouse. Mouse! That's what my father used to call me. Said I was his little pet mouse. But the little mouse got caught by the cat and the cat wouldn't let her have any more fun. Wouldn't let her dance . . . wouldn't let her have her friends to stay . . . tried to take away the key of her cupboard. . . ."

"You ought to get to bed," said Amanda. "Let me help you."

"Whisky . . ." murmured Bella.

"You've had enough."

"That's what *he* says. . . . Tried to take my key. Why shouldn't I have a drop of whisky when I want it, eh? Tell me that."

"It's bad for you," said Amanda. "Come. Let me help you into bed. Then perhaps we'll get you some hot milk."

"Hot milk! Hot milk! You're as bad as he is. Don't want hot milk. Want whisky . . . I tell you."

Amanda pulled her to her feet, turning away from the smell of her breath. She had never before seen Bella in this state. She was very drunk—so drunk that she seemed scarcely to know what she was talking about. Did this often happen during the night? Was this how he often saw her?

Fortunately, she was not violent. She was sleepy, and Amanda was able to propel her towards the bed, to push her on to it and lift up her feet. She tucked her in as though she were a baby.

"Whisky . . ." murmured Bella.

"No more."

"As bad as he is. . . . But I have the key, haven't I?"

"Give it to me and I'll lock the cupboard door."

Bella smiled slyly. "Never give up the key. It's my key."

"You will have to remember to lock it in the morning."

"He'd like to get the key. He can lock up anything he likes as long as I keep my key. He's cruel to me, he is. He keeps me away from a little drink when I'm so thirsty. You're as bad. You and Hesketh . . . you're together in this. You're against me too."

Here was a well-remembered mood, the persecution mania. The whole world was against her. How often had she told Amanda that?

"We want to help you," said Amanda. "We want you to be as well as possible, and you can't be well if you drink too much."

"It wasn't too much. Only a little. Only a sip . . . please. Get me a sip. . . ."

Her eyelids were pressing down over her eyes. How terrible she looked now—decayed, no longer beautiful: her red hair was lustreless and hanging untidily about her face, her eyes bloodshot, her face flushed in blotches, her mouth slack.

"You won't . . . you won't give it to me? You and Hesketh . . . you're together in this." She seemed to wake suddenly. "Of course you are. You think I don't know. You think I'm blind. I've seen him look at you. He thinks: I wish I hadn't married Bella. Bella's no good. She's sick. She drinks . . . and she's terrible to live with. I ought to have married someone calm like myself, someone quiet and dull who'd think it was wonderful to be the wife of a rising doctor . . . who'd take an interest in my work. That's what he thinks. You can't fool me. I've seen it. He thinks, There's Amanda Tremorney. Pretty she is with that yellow hair and blue eyes . . . and soft too. No trouble. . . . I know him better than he thinks I do."

Amanda said sharply: "You must go to sleep. You must not talk nonsense."

"Nonsense? Nonsense. . . . Never mind. Give me a drop of whisky. . . . Just a little drop. . . . My legs feel queer. They wouldn't carry me to the cupboard. See . . . even they're against me. . . ."

"Go to sleep," said Amanda.

Bella lay back; her eyes closed. Amanda looked about the room, at the open cupboard, at the bottles and glasses, at the elaborate furniture, all the feminine things with which the woman liked to surround herself; and she looked at the door which led to the room which, on other nights, was occupied by the doctor.

Bella's head rolled to one side, her mouth fell open and she sent out a strangled snore.

Amanda went to the cupboard and shut the door; and as she went quietly out of the room she said to herself: "Yes, it is time I left this house."

* * *

The supper-rooms were flourishing. They were still called
Sam Marpit's Supper-rooms, but most people thought of them
as Sam's and Lilith's now.

Lilith did more than dance; she sat at the tables and chatted
and joked; she stood with Sam at the door to receive the most
distinguished customers. She appeared in her elaborate evening
dresses, friendly, welcoming and strikingly handsome.

She had hardened considerably, and life with Lilith, Sam told
himself, was not all anchovy toast and hot punch.

It was a funny thing, Sam thought, because he had imagined
that marriage would have softened her; he thought he would have
been the one to have had the upper hand. But that was not so.
She was as independent as ever. A little bit of trouble—and there
were, of course, a good many bits of trouble—and she'd fly off
the handle and talk about going over to Dan Delaney's, for all
the world as though she were not Sam's trouble and strife. Trouble and strife! Whoever first said that knew what he was talking
about!

Mind you, Sam often said to himself, I'd do the same all over
again, even if I could put the clock back. It was not that his
feelings for her had changed; it was just that marriage was a
disappointment. Then there was Fan. Put her nose right out of
joint, this marriage of his had. Well, you couldn't please all the
women all the time. One woman's wedding was another woman's funeral, so to speak. Not that Fan hadn't always been a
special favourite of his; she had. Fan was one of those women
who just could not say "No." Soft and yielding. Even though
he had married Lilith right under her nose, he knew that a little
bit of flattery, a little chucking under the chin, a friendly slap or
two and Fan would be as accommodating as ever. Perhaps he
ought to have got rid of Fan. Well, he wouldn't. Not unless he
found her another job. And why should he get rid of her? He'd
done enough harm there, he reckoned. Fan couldn't be expected
to lose her job *and* the fun she had had with him. Besides—Sam
winked at no one in particular when he told himself this—you
never knew!

Lilith hadn't asked him to get rid of Fan. If she had, he might
have been forced to. Oh no, Madame Lilith was too proud to
suggest that. That was where she was funny. Any natural woman
would have said, "Out she goes!" But Lilith just tossed her head

and made out to pretend that it was all one to her—Fan there or not.

So Fan stayed—for a rainy day, as you might say, Sam told himself with another wink.

That toff hadn't come to the Rooms again after Lilith. Sam would like to know what had happened to him. Well, Lilith had some classy friends. There was that cousin or sister-in-law of hers who came to see her now and then. A nice young lady. A sort of companion to some rich woman somewhere. He wondered why Lilith never went to see her. It was not like Lilith not to poke her nose in.

He had considered asking her, but there were some things you couldn't ask Lilith if you wanted to keep the peace.

Well, he mustn't complain. Business was good, and he had wanted to marry Lilith. Funny, though, how she could still torment him, make him feel he didn't know her very well in spite of what they called 'intimate relations.'

Behind the counter, Sam picked his teeth and watched her sitting at the tables. She brought the custom all right. She knew how to handle people too. Just a little bit flirty, and then Hey! Keep off the grass!

Lilith was All Right and she did more than sing her songs and dance the dance of the veils. She looked a bit queer to-night . . . a little bit thinner about the face. What would you call it? Thoughtful? No, that wasn't quite right. More as if she had some secret that pleased her. Uneasily, he hoped that she was not seeing that toff again. But how could she? He kept a pretty smart track of her movements, and she never seemed to want to go far from the supper-rooms.

Yet there was a change in her—no doubt about that. Lilith . . . but not quite Lilith. She threw off her veils one by one. He was glad she hadn't let him persuade her to use that cellar. Now he could puff out his chest; he could look down his nose when anyone mentioned Delaney's. It was the good, honest man who kept his Rooms respectable who won in the end.

What was the difference in her? She danced with the same movements. He knew every bit of the veils dance now . . . every gesture. Everything was the same, yet *she* seemed remote, no longer promising everything, no longer making them feel that when she cast off the last of the veils she would be really naked.

He followed her into the room, for that was still a habit of his. He had done it in the old days when he was courting her; he fancied that, in a funny sort of way, he was still courting Lilith.

"Oh, it's you."

"Well, that's a nice way to greet your old pot and pan."

She gave him one of her withering looks. She didn't like slang; she was trying to improve herself, trying to speak more like that lady-like sister-in-law of hers.

She was sitting down now, gazing into the mirror, and there was still that remote and dreamy look about her. He put his hands on her bare shoulders and she wriggled. He wished she was warm and loving like Fan.

"What's up?" he said.

She looked up at the ceiling with that gesture of exasperation which he remembered well.

"You're different," he said. "Something's happened. I know it."

She turned to him, soft suddenly and smiling. "Do you, Sam?"

She stood up then and sat on the dressing table, her back to the mirror. She was still smiling. He loved her very much at that moment. There was some power in her to make him hate her and then, with a sudden smile, turn the tables so that he felt like he was feeling now. Hadn't she affected him oddly right from the beginning, when she had made him pay her twelve and six and her supper instead of the ten bob he had offered her?

"Lilith," he said, a high note creeping into his voice, "what's happened?"

"I wasn't sure at first," she answered. "I didn't want to tell you until I was. It's a baby, Sam."

"A baby!"

"Well, don't look as though you can't believe it."

He took two steps towards her and put his arms about her. "Lilith," he said. "A baby, eh?"

"You're glad, I suppose."

"Well, and who wouldn't be? Ain't you?"

"Oh, Sam," she said, "so glad . . . I felt I wanted to kiss all the people in the Rooms to-night."

"Here, Marpit's is a respectable house, it is!"

Then they laughed and he kissed her; he kept on kissing her. She took him by the ears and shook him.

"It's what I wanted more than anything in the world," she said. "A baby. A real baby. Mine!"

Sam wanted to dance. He picked up the veils and wrapping them about him, danced . . . throwing them off one by one, laughing, or pretending to laugh, till the tears ran down his cheeks. But they were real tears. Fancy me, thought Sam, *crying*!

She leaned against the table. She was openly crying. Soft as Fan, yet far more beautiful.

"I shan't be able to dance a little later on, Sam."

He kept slapping his thigh tenderly, lovingly, as though it were the source of all his delight.

"No," he said. "Got to take care. Strike me with forked lightning if I don't stand champagne all round for the little fellow."

"Don't you say anything yet."

"All right, all right."

He smiled at her. He was glad they shared a secret . . . such a secret.

"When?" he asked.

"A long time yet. Six months at least."

"What's it going to be . . . boy or girl?"

"Boy," she said.

"Boy I say too. We'll call him Sam."

She did not answer; she had no intention of calling him Sam.

"He's got to have everything, Sam. He's got to have everything of the best."

"That's the ticket. He'll have a silver spoon in his mouth and diamonds in his napkins."

"They'd hurt," she laughed.

"Well, that's what you call speaking fancy like. What I mean is he's got to have everything of the best."

"We'll educate him, Sam."

"Educate him! What for? Education don't get people nowhere."

"I want him educated."

Sam thrust his hands into his trousers pockets, pulling back his coat to show the full glory of his waistcoat. He was picturing his son in a more glorious waistcoat, extending a diamond-studded snuffbox to his patrons at the magnificent door of the grandest supper rooms in London.

Lilith said fiercely: "He's got to have everything . . . everything. . . . He's got to have the best in the land, our son has. Nobody's going to turn round to *him* and say, 'You're not good enough!' He's going to be good enough to dance with the Queen."

"Lilith," said Sam, "I'll learn him the business. He'll have all the chances I didn't have. And when he's old enough we'll go into business together . . . Marpit and Son."

Lilith did not answer. The prospect of the child softened her. Sam did not understand, and she did not want to hurt him by telling him that his son would never run a supper bar. She, who had been so wretchedly unhappy because she was born in the wrong class, was going to make sure that her son did not suffer in the same way. Once she had wanted nothing but to share her life with Frith; now she no longer wanted him. Now she was concentrating all her passionate love on another being—the child who was not yet born. All her vitality, all her schemes and ambitions were for her child; she was determined that the stigma of lowly birth should never touch it.

It would be a boy, she hoped, and she was determined to make him a gentleman. She would allow nothing in the world to stand in the way of making him one.

Amanda was dressing for dinner in the black velvet dress to buy which she had borrowed money from Frith. She wore her fair hair piled high on her head, which was rather unfashionable, but she did not wish to outshine Bella, for Frith was coming and Bella was very fond of Frith. Amanda wondered if Bella believed Frith was in love with her. He paid her extravagant compliments which she accepted with pleasure. Everyone was grateful to Frith, for when he was expected Bella was in a good temper for the whole of the day.

Amanda went into Bella's room as she had been instructed to do before she went down. Her maid was there and Bella's toilet was just completed. She was dressed in mauve, which seemed to bring out the mauve of her complexion. Her eyes were bright and she had, Amanda guessed, already been to her cupboard.

"Ah, there you are. How do I look?"

"Very attractive," said Amanda, and it was true, for she certainly would attract attention in the mauve silk dress and the mauve velvet ribbon in her hair and the diamond ornament threaded on more mauve ribbon at her throat.

"Frith said the last time he was here that mauve suited me better than any other colour. Do you know, I believe he is right. He's clever about such things. Such a charming young man. I often wonder why he doesn't marry."

She was smiling complacently at her reflection. She saw Amanda through the glass. "How nice you look! Your black goes rather well with my mauve, doesn't it? Black goes with anything, of course. This dress reminds me of one I had years ago. Oh, we had real dinner parties in those days. Twenty of us sitting down to dinner. And now there will be just four. Well, never mind. Frith *is* so charming . . . and then if there were others he might not pay so much attention to me."

But she did not really believe that Frith or anyone else could be interested in others when she was about.

She had not made any further reference to Hesketh's interest in Amanda since that night some months ago when Amanda had found her intoxicated in her bedroom. Amanda was grateful for that; she felt that any further suggestion on those lines would have to result in her departure. No, Bella did not seriously believe that anyone could think of another woman while she was present. Perhaps, however, it was only when she was drunk that she saw herself as she really was; it seemed that when she was sober or half-sober she lived in perpetual dreams in which she played the part of a Helen or a Cleopatra.

It was for Amanda an uneasy dinner party, because all through the meal Hesketh was watching his wife. She talked continually—almost all the time to Frith—and she was drinking as heavily as usual.

Frith pretended not to notice that anything was amiss. He flattered Bella, deliberately putting her into a good mood. Dear Frith! thought Amanda. He really is very kind.

Bella dominated the table—just as she dominated the house—by making those around her afraid of what she would say in her tantrums. It seemed ridiculous that such a stupid woman could make herself so important for such a reason.

She was talking now of her father's house and the dinner parties he used to give.

"Hesketh foolishly thinks I'm not well enough for a lot of entertaining. I've told him that entertaining does me good. I love to be surrounded by people. But Hesketh seems to be more wrapped up in his work than anything else. It is nothing but Hesketh's work in this house. Frith, I believe you are the same. I believe if you *ever* marry you will neglect your wife as Hesketh neglects me.''

"Shame on Hesketh!" said Frith lightly. "But I don't believe Hesketh neglects you, for the simple reason that no one could possibly do that.''

"You are quite absurd. You remind me so much of a young man I knew once. I was eighteen at the time. He was—at least he said he was—in love with me.''

Hesketh was looking at his wife anxiously. Her voice rose at the end of her sentences into a high little laugh which could accurately be called a giggle.

"What is going to happen in the Crimea?" said Hesketh hastily in order to create a diversion.

"That," said Frith, "remains to be seen.''

"How will our men get on in that dreadful climate?" said Amanda.

"There'll be more dying of disease than wounds," put in Hesketh.

Frith said: "As a matter of fact, I was thinking of offering my services. I agree with you that the need for doctors will be almost as great as that for soldiers.''

"Oh, Frith!" cried Bella. "You're not going away?"

"I'm not sure yet. I can't make up my mind. Sometimes I feel it's sheer folly to leave London and go out to Heaven knows what. Things are going to be in a fine muddle out there. The French our allies! Why, it's not long ago that we were deadly enemies. Somehow I feel they'll be uneasy allies . . . and against the Russian Bear at that!''

"You must not go!" said Bella. "I forbid it.''

"Ah," said Frith lightly. "You have made my decision for me.''

"My dear," said Hesketh hurriedly, "do you think you should take another glass of wine?"

"Why not?" Her voice was querulous.

"Because I think that in your state of health you have already had enough.''

"And I think I am the best judge of that. You see, Frith," she went on, and the purple tinge was very evident in her face now;

it extended to her chin and the tips of her ears. "You see how I am treated. Like a child. I mustn't do this . . . and I mustn't do that."

Shackleton had turned to the sideboard; the parlourmaid was looking down at the carpet; that dreaded uneasiness was filling the room.

Frith came to the rescue. "It's for your own good. He's concerned . . . we're all concerned."

"You concerned! When you plan to desert me for a lot of people in some outlandish place!"

"As if I would ever desert you. That is why I join my voice with Hesketh's and say: 'Please, Bella, do not drink any more wine just yet.' "

She laughed, but she was only half-placated and her eyes gleamed dangerously. "You're all against me," she said mournfully. "You try to deny me every little pleasure. Anyone would think I was a drunkard. And it's *good* for me. One of my doctors . . . long ago . . . such a pleasant man . . . said that I should take wine for my health."

"I expect you twisted him round your finger."

Her good humour was restored. "Oh, you wouldn't be interested in him. Poor man! He never married. I often wondered why."

"Just another of those hearts you trampled on as you walked through life," said Frith.

She rose rather unsteadily and laid her hand on her heart.

"Are you all right?" asked Hesketh.

She nodded. "Come along, Mrs. Tremorney. You and I will leave the men together to drink their port in peace and to talk about wars and diseases and such-like pleasant things that they enjoy, I am sure, far more than our frivolous conversation."

When she and Amanda left the dining-room she went upstairs to her bedroom.

"I will be back shortly," she said.

Amanda stood by the fire knowing that she had gone to her secret cupboard to get herself the drink which she had been persuaded not to take in the dining-room.

When the men came to the drawing-room, Bella had still not returned. Hesketh looked alarmed.

"I will go and find her," he said.

When they were alone together Frith said: "Tragic! She gets worse. Poor old Hesketh! He has his troubles."

"I'm afraid so, Frith. Sometimes I think I'm not much use."

"You're wrong about that. He has just told me that she gets along splendidly with you."

"One of these days she will drink far too much."

"She does that already."

"I mean it will be fatal."

"Poor Bella!"

"Frith, did you mean what you said about going to the Crimea?"

"Certainly I am considering it." He frowned. "Sometimes I feel the need to get away."

"Wouldn't you lose all that you have built up here?"

"I've thought of that. No. I don't think I should. I think it would be a tremendous advantage to come back as a hero from the wars. My assistant will continue here in my absence. You see what I mean?"

"You might not come back."

"People like myself always come back. They turn up every time. Depend on it, I should return as a hero."

"I should miss you."

"My sweet Amanda!"

"Could I come with you? Oh . . . not actually with *you*, of course. But could I go there?"

"You, my dear Amanda! Women are not wanted in the Crimea."

"I thought I might help to look after the wounded."

"You! You would spend your days and nights in weeping. You cannot imagine the sights that are to be seen on the battlefields of the world. No. You stay and look after Bella. Try and make things more tolerable for poor old Hesketh. He declares that what you have done is a minor miracle."

"Have you seen . . . Lilith lately?"

"Lilith? I have not seen her since her marriage."

"There is a child now. A lovely boy."

"Lilith . . . a mother! How odd."

"She is a very good one. She dotes on the boy. She has called him Leigh. In honour of me, I think. I was godmother. I don't think I have ever seen her so happy since the days immediately after Napoleon found you."

"I'm glad she's happy. I would like to see her and . . . the son."

"Don't, Frith. Let her remain contented. Sam is a very good man. He loves Lilith, and I think the child will unite them closely. I am quite fond of Sam. He is amusing and . . . good at heart. Don't go near them, Frith. Leave them to themselves."

"Well, there'll be many miles between the battlefields of the Crimea and the supper-rooms of Sam Marpit."

"You want to go because you're restless, is that it? You want to put a great distance between yourself and Lilith."

He touched her cheek lightly. "Ah, how discerning our young Amanda has become! Listen. They're coming back. She sounds drunk. Poor old Hesketh! Does this happen often?"

"Not when there are visitors."

Bella stood in the doorway; the velvet band in her hair was crooked.

"Ah, there you are," she said. "I'm sorry . . . I deserted you. I just went to my room for a moment. We will have coffee now."

The parlourmaid brought in the coffee and brandy.

Bella sat straight in her chair; she was subdued, and Amanda recognized the beginning of the sullen mood, which was one to be greatly dreaded.

Frith took an early leave, and when he had gone Amanda retired to her room, but not to sleep. She took off the black velvet dress and hung it in her wardrobe; then she put on her dressing-gown and sat by the fire, thinking over the events of the evening. Bella must have forgotten she had a guest when she had gone to her room.

She pictured herself as a nurse in the Crimea. She had heard that a Miss Florence Nightingale was contemplating taking a company of nurses to the war. Frith was thinking of going, she believed, because he so regretted the loss of Lilith that he wanted to get away from everything that reminded him of her. She, Amanda, wanted to get away too.

She could hear voices in the next room. A quarrel was in progress. How often had she heard voices in the next room—hers angry and vituperative, his placating.

One of these days, she thought, he will not be so gentle. How can he go on enduring this? One of these days she will go too far.

There was a sudden silence; then she heard the sound of a door being closed. There was a light tap on her own door. She opened it and found Hesketh standing there.

"I wonder if you would be so good as to go in to her," he said. "She might respond to you. I'm afraid I merely irritate her."

"Yes. Certainly I will go."

She hurried past him. Bella gave a little laugh when she saw Amanda.

"So he has sent you. I was never so ashamed in my life. He almost told Frith that I was a drunkard . . . a secret drinker. . . . That's what he told Frith."

"He told him nothing of the sort."

"What were you and Frith talking about when I was upstairs? About me?"

"No. Not about you."

"I don't believe you."

"There are other topics besides yourself, Mrs. Stockland," said Amanda. It was rarely that she spoke with such asperity, and when she did so it never failed to be effective.

"What did he talk about then?"

"About his going to the Crimea."

"Do you know why he's going?" She laughed wildly. "It's because he's in love with me and I'm Hesketh's wife. That's what he said to you, didn't he?"

"Please, do be wise. Do go to bed now. You'll feel so much better if you do. Let me help you."

Amanda took her arm. Bella rose and tottered, catching at the chair as she slipped to the floor.

"Oh dear, the room's swinging round and round. I really am afraid that I'm just a little in . . . tox . . . icated."

"I am going to help you to undress, and then if I can't get you into bed I shall have to call your husband."

"Sometimes I think he'd like to see me in bed . . . in bed all the time . . . so that I couldn't have any friends at all."

Amanda undid the velvet ribbon at her throat and all the hooks and eyes of the mauve dress. It was difficult to get her out of the petticoat and the whalebone stays.

"You should not lace so tightly," said Amanda. "It's very bad for you."

"I had such a little waist . . . seventeen and a half. That is what I got it to. Seventeen and a half. . . ."

"That was when you were young. You can't expect to keep a young girl's figure for ever."

"You'd like to stop me doing everything I want. No more tight-lacing . . . no more drink. . . . Oh, I'm so thirsty. Give me a little drop of gin. . . . I fancy gin now."

Amanda slipped the frilled nightdress over her head. "Will you try to get into bed now?"

"When I have had a little drop of gin."

"Not to-night. . . . You've had enough."

"I shall sit here till you get it for me."

Amanda knocked on the communicating door. He opened it immediately.

"I can't get her into bed. I think we shall have to lift her between us. She's incapable of walking."

"I see. I'll give her a shot of something to make her sleep."

Together they went over to the bed. Bella's eyes were half-closed and she did not seem to be aware of them as they lifted her on to the bed and Amanda covered her up.

"I want a drink," moaned Bella.

"Wait with her awhile," said Hesketh. "I'll get her a sleeping draught."

When he returned he was carrying some liquid in a glass. This he put to her lips, and Amanda was surprised to see how meekly she took it.

They stood one on either side of the bed watching her. In a few minutes she was in a deep sleep.

"She'll sleep till morning," he said. "Let her sleep until she wakes of her own accord. Will you tell the servants that?"

She nodded, and thought how tired he looked as they came out and stood in the corridor together.

"To-night has been rather an ordeal," he said.

"I'm afraid so. Particularly for you."

"If only I could stop her drinking."

"Is there no way?"

"There are homes where cures are attempted. But she would not have the will to be cured, and that is very necessary."

"Has she been like this for long?"

"You have seen her grow worse since you have been here. In

another year . . . I dare not contemplate what will happen to her.''

"I'm very sorry."

"You are also very kind, Amanda. Oh, forgive me. I think of you as Amanda. It slipped out, I'm afraid.''

"It . . . it's of no importance. I can only repeat that I am very sorry. I do hope things will get better. It is so painful for you.''

"It has been more tolerable . . . since you came.''

"Good night," she said, and she turned away.

"Good night.'' And as she opened her door and closed it quickly she heard him say: "Good night . . . Amanda.''

Lilith lay in bed. Sam was beside her, and close to their double bed was the baby's cradle.

It was half-past nine, but they rose late. They did not go to bed until the early hours of the morning on account of the late closing of the supper-rooms; so naturally they slept on.

Leigh was playing quietly in his cradle. He seemed to know that he must not wake them yet, and now was deeply absorbed in the difficult experiment of trying to get his right foot into his mouth.

Lilith smiled as she watched him. How beautiful he was! How like her! There was hardly any of Sam in him. She moved slightly away from Sam. He looked coarser than ever asleep. There was a dark patch on his pillow where his greasy head had been, for his nightcap was askew; he was snoring intermittently, and every time he did so the baby would look round with a startled amusement.

To Lilith the man seemed gross, the child perfect. If only he had been born somewhere else! In a house in Wimpole Street, for instance.

Yesterday she had found Sam with the baby, lifting him up, holding him high over his head, singing a vulgar old song which he said his father used to sing to him. Since the child had been born, Lilith had been very sensitive to vulgarity.

> "A little old woman her living she got
>   By selling hot codlings, hot, hot, hot,
>   And this little old woman who codlings sold,
>   Tho' her codlings was hot she felt herself cold.
>   So to keep herself warm she thought it no sin,

To fetch for herself a quartern of
Ri tol iddy, iddy iddy iddy. . . ."

The baby had laughed and had pulled at Sam's hair. There
was no doubt that the baby and Sam, as Sam himself put it, got
on like a house afire.

He would be teaching him those songs; he would be teaching
him that life in supper-rooms was the life for him. And life in
supper-rooms was not the life for a gentleman.

Lilith saw many a battle ahead of her—battles for the baby.
Sam would do everything within his power to turn him into a
replica of himself; and she was determined to make a gentleman
of him. She had never been more determined on anything.

Sam stirred and put out a hand which she eluded.

She got out of bed and put on a dressing-gown. She leaned
over the baby's cradle; he took the finger she held out to him
and tried to put it into his mouth; and as she saw the little fingers
curl about it she felt weak with love and strong with determination.

She knelt down and embraced the baby, who wriggled and
crowed, thinking it was a new game. Sam snored and the baby
looked towards the bed with that expression of expectant bewilderment.

"You shouldn't be here, my little handsome," said Lilith.
"You should be in a fine room of your own . . . with no super-
rooms beneath it."

If I were to leave Sam, she thought, I'd have good reason.

She knew what had happened between him and Fan when she
had been in the last stages of pregnancy. She knew the meaning
of that repentant look of shame in his face when he had brought
great bunches of flowers and hot-house grapes to her. "Your
conscience worrying you, Sam?" she had asked ironically.

He had tried to look blankly bewildered, but he had not fooled
her. "Well, I'm sorry you've got to have all the pain, that's all.
It don't seem right somehow," he had mumbled. But she understood him too well.

Some wives might have made a scene, dismissed Fan, and let
Sam see what they thought of him. But not Lilith. She had a
feeling that she was waiting for something more important. It
gave her a sense of power to know that he had been an unfaithful

husband, while since their marriage she had been faithful to
him.

When she took the baby for his morning airing she wore her
new crinoline. She always dressed in the latest fashion and Sam
encouraged her in this. It was good for business. It let people
know they were prosperous. She stood in front of a glass, turning this way and that to admire herself; her waist looked more
tiny than ever, although it was not laced as tightly as before.
This was the effect of the crinoline. From beneath its flounces
her feet occasionally appeared, looking small and dainty. On
her dark curls she wore a bonnet of exaggerated size; it was dark
blue trimmed with pink ribbons to match those on the bodice of
her dress. She looked not only fashionable, but beautiful.

Sam watched her with the baby as she prepared to go out. He
had never been so proud in his life.

Lilith wrinkled her nose; a smell of smoke and drink hung
about the place. There was no escaping it; it mingled with that
of food; and how dreary the place always looked by morning
light! Children grew accustomed to the places in which they
lived; they could not be disgusted by what they considered normal.

"You look a picnic," said Sam. "And him."

She did not answer, and Sam leaned over the perambulator
and took the baby's hand. He began to sing 'Hot Codlins':

> "The little old woman then up she got,
> All in a fury, hot, hot, hot,
> Says she, 'Such boys, sure, never were known;
> They never will let an old woman alone. . . .' "

"Ba-Ba-Ba," said the baby.

"I never heard of a kid talking like that before," said Sam.
"He'll be singing 'Hot Codlins' in a week or two, he will. He's
a blinking marvel, that's what he is. He's a contented baby. So
he ought to be. Don't he have everything he wants? Never cries
nor nothing. He knows what's waiting for him. Marpit and Son,
eh? I tell you what, Sammy, we're going to have the biggest
supper-rooms in London, you and me. And all the best singers. . . . We're going to pack 'em in."

"Don't call him Sammy. His name's Leigh."

"The only thing I don't like about that baby is his name.

Leigh! Whoever heard of such a name? Sammy . . . that's what he ought to have been. Why I didn't have more say in naming him I don't know!''

"Perhaps you was too busy elsewhere.''

"And what do you mean by that?''

Lilith's eyes were dangerous. They rested as if by chance on Fan's apron, which was lying across a chair.

"Work it out for yourself,'' she said. "You're smart enough. And his name's Leigh and he's going to be a gentleman. Remember that.''

"He's going to be a gentleman all right,'' said Sam placatingly. What a fool he'd been about Fan! He didn't know how it had happened. Seemed so silly. Couldn't he have waited? But somehow he hadn't looked on Fan as 'another woman.' And Lilith knew! Trust Lilith. She was going to hold that against him to get what she wanted. She'd always been smart. "He'll be a proper gentleman, won't you, Sonny.'' Sonny instead of Sammy. He could not bring himself to call the nipper Leigh.

Lilith smiled. She had made him understand. She was almost fond of him at that moment.

"We're going out now. Come on, my little king.''

She was going to see Amanda. There were plans forming in her mind, and Wimpole Street figured in them. She believed that she could still love Frith, but not in the wild, abandoned way she had once loved him. She had the baby now. She looked at him in his perambulator, neat, clean and exquisitely dressed; with his dark hair—not as curly as hers—and his pink, plump cheeks, he was a model of a baby; and she knew that she would never again feel about any man as she had about Frith. This son of hers was more important than anyone else ever would be. She was primitive in her emotions. Her love for Frith had been all-absorbing, but now she was first the mother. It would be the boy first for evermore, she told herself.

How she enjoyed looking at him! She took him through some of the poorer streets on her long walk to Wimpole Street, but not too poor, for she was terrified of some infection touching him; she wanted to compare him with other children—those squatting on the cobbles, barefooted and neglected, those begging in the streets, those pale from work in the sweatshops; she wanted to compare him with those children standing outside the gin- and beer-shops, the babies in their wheel-carts sleeping the drugged sleep produced by a dose of Godfrey's Cordial. And she wanted to say: "Nothing of that for you, my king. You're a gentleman now, and a gentleman you're staying, while there's power in me to make you so."

She pictured him growing up. She would want a tutor for him; perhaps a governess first, then a tutor; then she would want him to go to Oxford, as Frith had done. She wanted him to have all that Frith had had. Frith was the yardstick.

But what was going to happen? She could see, in her mind's eye, Sam throwing the boy up to the ceiling, teaching him things on the sly.

She had to admit that Sam would attract the child. That was already obvious. Sam would dote on him, spoil him, teach him to be as sharp as Sam himself undoubtedly was, teach him to have an eye for making money and a contempt for education. That would not do.

She knew what she longed to do: it was to take him away from the supper-rooms altogether, to have him brought up in an atmosphere of gentility the moment he began to notice things.

That was why she was going to renew her acquaintance with Frith. If Frith still wanted her, if he talked about a little house somewhere, somewhere very genteel, she might consider it. It must be in a respectable neighbourhood where she could be known as a respectable widow of means, devoted to her only son. It must be somewhere where Sam could not find her. She would say: "Yes, Frith, find me the house and I will come. But if I do, you must help me to look after my son. I want him to be a gentleman, and you could make him that better than anyone else."

Those would be her conditions and, if he accepted them, one day she would quietly slip out of Sam Marpit's Supper-rooms, taking her baby with her, never to return.

That was why she was purposefully pushing the perambulator through the many streets between the supper-rooms and Wimpole Street.

She went hastily past Frith's house to that which was Amanda's home, and when she rang the bell a servant came to the door.

"I have come to see Mrs. Tremorney. Would that be possible?"

"Will you come in, madam? Let me help you in with the perambulator. Then I will call Mrs. Tremorney."

When Amanda eventually came into the hall she looked pleased and surprised to see Lilith.

"I've brought your godson to see you."

"Lilith! Why didn't you let me know you were coming? And how is Leigh?"

Leigh regarded her with his solemn stare.

"He looks so wise and important," said Amanda. "It's hard to believe he is only a baby."

"He *is* important, and he knows it." Lilith lifted Leigh out of the perambulator. "Is it all right to leave this here?"

"Yes. Quite all right. Come up to my room now."

"Come along, my precious," said Lilith; and as she followed Amanda upstairs she imagined they were living in this house— she and the baby—and that his future was assured.

"This is your room, then. It's beautiful. It's better than the one you had at Leigh House. And they treat you like a lady. Where is the mistress of the house?"

"Resting."

"Anyone would think *you* were the mistress of the house."

"You exaggerate, Lilith. May I hold the baby?"

She took him and kissed his hair. "He's beautiful, Lilith. How happy you must be!"

Lilith smiled. "I'm all right. I'd rather have him than anything in the world."

"I'm glad, Lilith, so glad for you." There were tears in her eyes. "How silly I am! Only it makes me so glad to see you happy. You did so much for me, Lilith. I feel I want to cry for joy because you've got him . . . and he must be the loveliest baby in the world."

"He's that all right," said Lilith. "But, Amanda, I'm worried about you."

"About me?"

"It ain't right that you should be *working* in a house like this. You ought to be its mistress. I'd like to see you married and happy . . . holding your own baby, that I would. You hadn't thought of getting married, I suppose?"

"No, Lilith."

"I was wondering about Mr. Young."

"He's a soldier now, Lilith. He's miles away . . . in the Crimea."

"So he went for a soldier. And . . . what about Frith? Do you ever think of marrying *him*?"

"Oh, Lilith, do you still think about him?"

"When you've got a baby there ain't much time for thinking of anything else. I just wondered if you saw him and . . ."

"I haven't seen him for a long time. He's gone away too."

"Gone away?"

"To the war."

"What, as a soldier?"

"No. He's gone as a surgeon. He thought he should go because, he said, they would be needing doctors as much as soldiers." Amanda spoke hastily. "He's coming back. His household goes on just as usual. His assistant is living in his house now and keeping things going. Napoleon is learning to be a groom. He's very happy."

Lilith felt stunned. She had cared for him more than she had realized. She was angry now because she had paid such little attention to the talk of the war. Names like Alma . . . Balaclava . . . Inkerman . . . came into her mind. They had been just names before. Now they were places—places where Frith might be.

"But . . . it must be very dangerous there."

"He'll keep out of danger. He said he would. He said that whatever happens, he'll be all right. Lilith, he loved you very much. I believe that was why he went."

Lilith laughed. "It makes me laugh," she explained. "He'd rather face death than marriage with me. That's funny."

"Lilith, he wished . . . I can't tell you how he wished . . ."

"I know. He wished I was a lady. I wasn't, so he would rather go to the Crimea than marry me."

"A lot of people get the feeling that they ought to go. I thought of going as a nurse."

"Do they have nurses there, then?"

"Yes. Miss Nightingale took a number out with her. I thought of going with her. It would have been a solution for me too. Frith said I shouldn't be any good. He more or less insisted on my staying here."

"Go out as a nurse!" said Lilith, her eyes veiled. She saw herself with Frith in a country which it was quite impossible for her to imagine. But, she thought, looking at the baby, what do

I care for Frith now? What do I care if he don't come back even? I've got Leigh now, and there's no one that matters but my baby.

She took him from Amanda then, because she could not bear that anyone else should have him at that moment. She kissed him and held him tightly against her.

"He's all my fancy painted him, he's lovely, he's divine . . ." she paraphrased an old song which she used to sing in the supper-rooms; and Amanda, looking on, smiled with relief. Thank God Lilith had her baby. Both of the lovers in that ill-fated affair had found their salvation: Frith in working with the Army, Lilith with her son.

As she held the baby tightly against her, Lilith was thinking that her little plan was not going to be of any use to her now. How could Frith provide that apartment? How could he help her make her baby into a gentleman if he was away at the war?

"Tell me about yourself, Amanda. Tell me what it's like here. The woman you work for . . . what's she like?"

Amanda hesitated.

"Ah!" said Lilith. "She's a bit of a tartar, is she?"

"No, not exactly. She's very ill . . . and that makes her a little odd at times. But . . . I'm all right. I do manage."

"Amanda, have you ever thought of what will happen when she dies?"

Amanda had flushed suddenly. Why did she flush like that? wondered Lilith.

"When . . . when she dies . . . ? Why . . . why should I . . . ?"

"Well you're working for *her*, ain't you? When she dies she won't be wanting your services, I reckon!"

"I should have to find something else to do."

"Would you be able to?"

"I think so. I've had experience now. The doctor would help me. He's very kind."

"Easier than her . . . to get on with?"

"I don't see much of him, naturally. My job is with her."

"Oh, Amanda, I would like to see you settled in a house like this . . . with babies of your own so that I could bring little Leigh along to play with his cousins. They would be his cousins, wouldn't they? Distant ones. That's what I'd like to see, Amanda."

"You mustn't worry about me. I'll be all right."

Lilith talked for a while of the supper-rooms; she almost told Amanda of her fears of what Sam would do to the baby, of her desires and hopes for him. But she restrained herself. There was no doubt that she had been a little shaken by the news of Frith. She must have been counting on his help more than she realized; she must have been more determined than she had believed to take the baby away from the supper-rooms and Sam's company before he was much older.

As she was leaving and Amanda was saying goodbye to her in the hall, the doctor came in.

What'll he think? wondered Lilith. Is it right for Amanda to entertain her visitors like this when she only works here?

"Good morning," he said.

"This is Mrs. Marpit," said Amanda. "I believe I have mentioned her to you."

The doctor took Lilith's hand. "How are you, Mrs. Marpit?"

"And this is Leigh," said Amanda. "Mrs. Marpit's son."

Amanda was holding up the baby for his inspection; and Lilith was aware of something which startled her.

When she left Wimpole Street, she was thoughtful.

So that man was in love with Amanda. What a situation for Amanda to find herself in: working for an invalid whose husband was in love with her! When the woman died, perhaps Amanda would marry him. Then she would have climbed right back into the class to which she belonged.

And although Amanda might not realize it—for Amanda had always been a little fool—it was clear to Lilith that she shared this man's feelings.

Lilith could scarcely sleep at night for thinking of it. Each day Marpit's looked to her a little more drab than it had the day before. Each day the odour of stale tobacco smoke, snuff and liquor seemed stronger. She no longer danced; she had given that up when Leigh was about to be born; but she would mingle with the guests; she would sit at the tables, resplendent in an evening dress of black and scarlet, with red roses in her hair. She was still a draw—dance or no dance.

There came a day when she knew that she could delay acting no longer. The night before was what Sam would call a gala night; it was the boy's birthday; he was a year old.

Sam, in his best waistcoat, his face tinged with the purple of gin and excitement, his hair glistening with Macassar oil, had gone into the middle of the room and held up his hand.

"Ladies and gentleman, this is a great—er . . . a very great occasion. It's one of the great occasions in my life. It may be that some of you ladies and gents know that a very important member of my family is not present with us to-night. For why? Is he far away? Indeed, he ain't. He's here. Just upstairs in his cot . . . fast asleep. Ladies and gents, I refer to my son. To-day he is a year old, and I'm going to ask you to drink his health with me . . . on the house . . . in best champagne . . . in Marpit's champagne, if you like, which I flatter myself is another way of saying the best champagne. Charlie! Jack! Fill up the glasses."

The patrons cheered, for there was nothing that delighted them more than free drinks all round, and they would be willing enough to drink Leigh's health providing it was in free champagne.

"To the boy!" he shouted, lifting his glass. "To young Marpit."

It would have been all right if it had ended there; but it had not. Lilith had been talking to some of the patrons about the child when suddenly she saw Sam with the boy, rosy from sleep, rubbing his eyes, looking with bewilderment all about him.

Sam said: "Ladies and gents, here's the little fellow himself. Now, it ain't right and proper to wake him out of his sleep, but he don't get a birthday every day of the year and I reckon once won't hurt him. It would take more than that to hurt you, wouldn't it, son?"

People crowded about the baby, and now that he was fully awake there was no doubt that he was enjoying his adventure, because there was nothing young Leigh enjoyed more than the flattering attention of adults. Dorrie Quinn, who used the supper-rooms as a meeting-place with her men friends, took the baby from Sam and kissed him.

Lilith watched, hot anger in her heart.

They sat him on a table. They gave him cakes and sweets. He laughed; he was the most friendly baby in the world, and he made it quite clear that, in his opinion, this was an exciting climax to an exciting day.

Sam was rubbing his hands; Sam was defying her, and Lilith

felt that this was a sort of initiation for the child; he was saying: This is my son as well as yours. This is the way he is going.

Lilith's opportunity came when Leigh began to cry suddenly. Someone had spilt champagne on his dressing-gown, and thinking to amuse the child, an ageing man with curled moustaches had put his face close to Leigh's and grimaced at him. Leigh's response had been to open his eyes very wide and emit a shriek.

Then Lilith went over to him. "What is it, my precious?" She took the baby, and he put his arms about her neck, hiding his face against hers. "It's all right. Mamma has you. It's all right now." She smiled at the company. "Over-tired," she said. "He's going to say good night to you all now. Say good night, my love."

Leigh lifted his face from his mother's and solemnly waved a hand.

"Good night, baby!" called the patrons.

Lilith hurried upstairs with him.

When the Rooms were shut for the night and Lilith and Sam were in their bedroom together, she turned on Sam in a fury; he did not guess that it was a regulated fury and part of a plan.

"That was a clever thing to do!"

"What?" he asked innocently.

"What! To take a child out of his bed into a place like that. . . . All that smoke. . . . All those people. . . . I wonder he didn't catch his death."

"It didn't hurt him. The little fellow liked it."

"Liked it! I suppose that was why he well-nigh screamed his head off."

"Oh well, that was after. Didn't you see him laughing?" Sam slapped his thigh, but a trifle nervously.

"Laughing! A nice thing! First you want your own wife to dance naked in a cellar. . . . then you take your son and try to make a drunkard of him."

"Look here," said Sam, "what are you working up for? I didn't want you to go into no cellar."

"Oh, didn't you? Then what made you talk about it?"

"Well, that was when you first came here."

"I see. Only trying to ruin an innocent girl."

"Not so innocent," said Sam.

"You judge everyone by yourself . . . and Fan."

That silenced him. She went on: "I won't have my baby taken down to the rooms again . . . never again."

"It was only because it was his birthday."

"I don't care what it was. It was bad for him, and I won't have it. I've told you I'm going to have him brought up like a gentleman."

"You've got big ideas."

"Better than having little ones."

"They're too big for you, Lilith."

"They ain't too big for him. I've got to look after him, because I see no one else will."

"Look here, Lilith. You've got to be sensible. I want the best there is for that boy. Nobody could want better for anyone than I want for him. But he'll have to work for his living like we do. You've got gentlemen on the brain."

"Sam," she said, "I think you're right. I've got gentlemen on the brain. That's why I'm not having *him* standing at the door of a supper-rooms, bowing to all the scum of London, just because they can come in and drink themselves silly."

She would say no more.

And in the morning she put on her best crinoline and dressed the baby in his best clothes and went to see Amanda.

Up in Amanda's room she said what she had been rehearsing all the way to Wimpole Street.

"Amanda, I'm in trouble." It was the right start. She knew her Amanda. The blue eyes were already wide with concern. "I shouldn't burden you with my troubles."

"But who else should you take them to? I should be hurt if you didn't come to me, after everything we've been to one another. What is wrong?"

"Everything, Amanda. Just everything. I've made a terrible mess of my life. I ought never to have married Sam."

"If you hadn't, you wouldn't have Leigh."

"No. That's true. I'd die for my baby, Amanda."

"Yes, I know. But tell me what's wrong. Do let me help."

"My married life ain't what you think it is. Sam hasn't been faithful to me."

"Really, Lilith! I *am* surprised. I . . . I thought he was so good . . . so fond of you."

"Fond of me!" Lilith laughed. "Do you know, when I was going to have the baby he took up with Fan?"

"You mean . . ."

"You know what I mean. They'd been going together before I went to the Rooms, and then . . . well, it started again. How do you think I feel, living in a house where that be going on?"

Amanda was very shocked. "I had no idea."

Lilith covered her face with her hands and was silent for a while. The baby, whom Amanda was holding, seeing his mother, as he thought, in tears, began to cry. He wriggled and tried to reach her.

Lilith took him and comforted him. "There, my precious, it's all right. Mamma's laughing . . . see."

Leigh nodded. He too began to laugh.

"Oh, what a little darling he is," said Amanda. "Whatever happens, you're lucky to have him."

"It's on account of him that I'm worried. I'd put up with things for myself, but Sam's harming him, Amanda, harming him terrible."

"You don't mean he's ill-treating him! But . . . he looks so bonny. He looks as if nothing is spared . . ."

"He doesn't beat him. In a way 'tis worse than that. He's trying to make him depraved. Do you know what he does? He brings him down to the supper-rooms and lets the women . . . you know the sort of women who come to the supper-rooms . . . well, he lets them hold the baby and fondle him and spill their drinks over him. He wakes him up at night to take him down and do that to him."

"Lilith!"

"Don't keep saying 'Lilith!' It don't help. What am I going to do? Am I going on living there, letting the boy know what sort of a home he's got . . . with Fan giving herself airs and those women hiccuping all over him?"

"It's dreadful. I had no idea. I wish I could so something."

"I want to get away from the supper-rooms. I can't let my baby be brought up in a place like that. I can't stay with a man who's not faithful to me. Amanda, do you think we could come here . . . the baby and me?"

"Come here?"

"Well, they seem to think a lot of you. Don't forget I'm your cousin. I was wondering if there was some little job I could have. They wouldn't mind me having the baby here, would they? I thought that doctor looked very kind, the sort of man who

would understand, who would feel for me, who wouldn't like to
see a child like my Leigh brought up in a place like Marpit's.''

''He *is* very kind,'' said Amanda.

Lilith smiled. ''If you were to ask, I reckon he might do
something . . . I do really. Just think what it would mean to me,
Amanda.''

''But what . . . could you do?''

''In a big place like this, they have a lot of servants. . . .
There might be a place.''

''Do you mean *you* would want to come here as a servant?''

''I'd do anything to take my baby away from Marpit's Supper-
rooms.''

''But, Lilith, you were so proud. You always said you would
never be a servant again.''

''I've got a child to think of now. I can't afford to be proud.
I'm afraid of what he'll grow up like if he stays at Marpit's.''

''And you think he would be better here?''

''Yes; I do. Oh, Amanda, you're more than a cousin to me.
You're as close as a sister. You and me . . . we'll never be parted
. . . no matter what happens. If I came here you'd be with me
and you'd help me to bring up Leigh. I want him to speak like
you speak . . . and like Frith speaks. I don't want him to be like
his father. If we were all together, you could give him lessons,
just like Miss Robinson used to give you. He'd grow up right
. . . as I didn't . . . and as I can't, by myself, help him to. Don't
cry, Amanda, just because I'm asking you to help me.''

Amanda wiped her eyes. ''Oh, Lilith, I can't help it. I see
exactly what you mean. How you have suffered!''

''Amanda . . . will you try . . . will you do something for
me?''

''I am only a sort of servant here myself, you know, Lilith.''

''But you're a lady, and they know it. They set such store by
ladies and gentlemen that, once you're one of them, nothing can
really cast you out. They'll listen to you, Amanda.''

''But they have all the servants they need.''

''Couldn't they do with another one?''

''It might mean waiting for some time. There is a chance of
the parlourmaid's getting married. If she does, she will leave,
and . . .''

''That's it. You speak for me. I'll be the parlourmaid. But you must tell them I have a child, and that he will have to come with me.''

"You'd find a difference working here as a servant. It wouldn't be the same as being mistress of Marpit's.''

"I've got to think of the boy.''

She kissed him fondly.

She pictured him growing up in this house. Amanda—Mrs. Stockland then—would teach him to read and write. He was such a handsome little fellow that he would be like one of the sons of the house.

It was the first step towards making a gentleman of the son of a supper-rooms proprietor.

Amanda knocked at the door of the doctor's consulting-room. She noticed the change in his expression as she entered in answer to his request.

"I hope I am not disturbing you?''

"Indeed no. I am very pleased to see you.''

"I wondered if you could spare me a few minutes. There is something I want to ask you.''

He received her almost professionally. He put her into the carved oak chair where his patients sat when they came to consult him. He sat at the table which he used as a desk.

Now that they were alone together thus, their manner was almost ceremonious; they were so acutely aware of their feelings that they felt the need to hide them.

He could not be with her without comparing her with his wife: Amanda was so mild, Bella so hysterical; Amanda modest, Bella ridiculously vain. Since Amanda had come to his house, he had realized how deep was his dislike and his disgust of the woman whom he had married. He was a man of high ideals, stern with himself, controlled, reserved; but he had undergone a change with the coming of Amanda. The ideals, the control, were less strong than they had been. He could not suppress wild thoughts which had come to him. Previously he had been resigned; now he could no longer be so. He had always been a man to analyse his feelings, and he could not break the habit now. As his hatred for what his wife had become deepened, so his regard for Amanda grew and he lived in a perpetual fear that she would announce her intention of leaving. He was aware that if she did, his reserve would break, and he would declare his feelings for her. He would put into words what he might have conveyed to her by a look, by a gesture, a tone of voice: Wait. I beg of you, wait. She cannot live for ever. She is a very sick woman. Wait . . . for, when she is dead, there is a future for us.

The waiting could be long; he knew that. How many similar cases had he handled? Bella's was not an uncommon disease. Hearts were strong. They survived against great odds. Their behaviour was incomprehensible; that was what had always fascinated him about them. He knew that Bella might die that week; on the other hand, she could live for ten or fifteen years.

Ten or fifteen years during which she would deteriorate still further! She would be more difficult to handle as the attacks became more frequent. But he knew how to help her, what drugs would prolong her life. How, therefore, could he ask Amanda to wait until he might speak to her of their future? How could he, a man of stern ideals, a man of integrity, admit to her that such ideas had entered his head?

At the same time he could not but be delighted with her company. The happiest hours of his days were those mealtimes when Bella was too ill to join them and he would find himself dining alone with Amanda.

As for Amanda, she could never be in his presence without immediately becoming aware of his feeling for her. Life was becoming difficult and dangerous; but if she left this house it would become intolerable.

She was more deeply sorry for him than she had ever been for anyone—even William; that was because she thought of him continually; every humiliation which his wife imposed upon him was suffered by Amanda; all his uneasiness was hers. She longed to comfort him. That was how it had started with Amanda. Afterwards she began to see him as a brilliant man, a great doctor, humble and unselfish; in fact, he seemed perfect in her eyes. She knew then that she loved him, and that situation in which she found herself was filled with a hundred dangers.

Now he smiled at her. They were alone together in the big consulting-room with its lofty ceiling, and its air of professional dignity. His smile was tender, as though he knew that here they were safe from prying eyes and that there was no need for him to conceal his feelings.

"If there is anything I can do," he said, "you know that nothing will give me greater pleasure."

"It is about Lilith—Mrs. Marpit. You met her with her son a little while ago. Poor Lilith! She means a good deal to me and she is in trouble. I want to help her, and I think that you and Mrs. Stockland . . . could help me to do that."

"Just tell me what you wish me to do."

"First I must explain. Lilith is unhappily married. She dotes on the child and she fears that the supper-rooms are not the right setting for him. She is in fact very worried about it. Apparently her husband is not faithful to her. There is a woman who works there . . . and Lilith says that she does not mind for herself. It is for the child that she is uneasy. He . . . her husband . . . takes the little boy out of his bed at night . . . down there to meet the rowdy people in the supper-rooms. . . ."

"It sounds as though she has good reason to be worried."

"She wants to leave him, and she has asked me to help her do that."

"How does she expect you to?"

"That is where I want you to help me. She has asked me to do what I can to get her work in this house. She would have to have the boy here. As a matter of fact, he is my godchild, and she wants me to teach him to read and write. One of the maids here will be getting married in a few months' time and if Lilith could take her place, she would be very grateful . . . and so should I. It would mean having the boy here, of course. But I think we could arrange that he causes no trouble. Oh, I do hope you will help me in this."

"I would willingly do anything you ask, but is it wise to take sides in this quarrel between a husband and wife . . . because that is what it amounts to?"

She thought how right he was, how eager to do what should be done, and she smiled.

"If it were an ordinary case, I would say 'No.' But this is for the child's sake. And I am afraid that if we don't help her she will find other means. She has set her heart on taking the child away and bringing him up, as she says, like a gentleman. She is very worried and she is not the sort to stay there meekly. I must help her. Leigh—the child—being my godson, I feel it is my duty to help them. I have promised to teach him. I must do everything possible. . . ."

She saw the panic leap into his eyes. He was afraid that if

Lilith did not come to this house, Amanda would leave it to be with her.

"I dare say it could be arranged."

"Oh . . . thank you . . . thank you. I don't know how to express my gratitude."

"Your gratitude! What of mine?"

They looked at each other across the barrier which must separate them. Bella was that barrier and only after her death would the path be clear.

Ten years, he was thinking. Perhaps fifteen! How can I wait as long as that?

She saw the weary frustration in his eyes.

"I have been very happy here," she said.

"I trust you will stay. I trust you will . . . wait."

She bowed her head, knowing his thoughts. She was trembling with longing and fear, because that for which they yearned had to be prefaced by death.

"I think," he said quickly, "that you should ask my wife about the maid. I am sure you will have no difficulty in persuading her."

"Yes; I will. But I wanted to get your consent first."

"Anything I can do for you . . ." he began, then broke off. "I am only too delighted to help, of course," he added.

Leigh was eighteen months old when Lilith escaped with him from Marpit's Supper-rooms.

Calmly and methodically she had gone to work.

Each morning when she took Leigh out she secreted some of her clothes and his in the perambulator and walked with them to Wimpole Street.

Amanda had not liked this method.

"Lilith," she had been fool enough to say, "couldn't you tell him? Wouldn't it be wiser . . . kind? Wouldn't it be more straightforward?"

"It might be straightforward," Lilith had answered. "It wouldn't be wise. As for kindness . . . well, we can't spoil everything for the sake of that!"

And then came that last morning. She awoke and looked with some small regret round the bedroom which she had shared with Sam. The regret surprised her. Perhaps it was because she knew that Sam was not a bad sort, and she had cruelly maligned him.

All he did he meant for the best. It was just that his idea of the best was not hers where their son was concerned; and she would consider no one but Leigh now.

She rose and took the baby from his cot.

"Come along, Master Leigh. You're going big ta-tas."

"*Big* ta-tas!" squealed Leigh.

That was silly of her. That might give something away to Sam. But why worry? Sam was still snoring. She hoped he would continue to snore, for when snoring he looked his most unattractive, quite unworthy to be Leigh's guardian. When she looked at Sam as he was now, she could say exultantly: "I'm right. I know I'm right."

She dressed herself in her second best crinoline, contemplating as she did so that she would have enough clothes to last her for a long time. She put on the blue bonnet with the blue ribbons and the red rose; there was usually a touch of red about Lilith's clothes. She certainly did not look like a servant! She was glad of that, for she did not intend to be a servant for long. The doctor's wife was an invalid, suffering from an incurable disease, and she could not last long. Then Amanda would become the doctor's wife and she would have to recognize Lilith as her cousin and her sister-in-law, and Leigh as her godchild. Lilith thought that then she would probably become a housekeeper for Amanda—a favoured housekeeper, a connection of the family.

She had planned it all as it should go, and had things not always gone the way she wanted them to, even though not always by the route she arranged?

In the perambulator she hid the jewellery which Sam had given her. Some of it was very good. Sam had liked to see her wearing jewellery in the Supper-rooms. It made them look prosperous, he said. That would be a standby, because you never knew what you would need.

She was very nervous this morning, hoping Sam would sleep on. She was terrified that he would discover that most of her clothes had disappeared.

She ate her breakfast with Leigh downstairs behind the public rooms, while Fan waited on them.

Poor old Fan! She was patient enough. This would be a blessing for Fan; she would be able to take up her old relationship with Sam now, and she was welcome to it.

Lilith could eat little; she was watching the clock all the time.

Leigh was a naughty boy that morning—blowing bubbles in his milk and nearly choking, telling Fan that they were going for big, *big* ta-tas that morning.

Lilith had asked Amanda to write a letter for Sam, and this Amanda had done. She would leave it for him, and she was afraid he might discover it before she was gone. He would not be able to read it very easily but there was no knowing what his action would be when he discovered what she had done. The letter was inside her bodice now; she could feel it scratching her skin.

"Now, Leigh, time to go out," she said.

"*Big* ta-tas!" he reminded her gleefully.

Sam came down just as they were about to leave.

"Hello! Off out? You're early."

"Same as usual," she said, bending over the perambulator and tucking Leigh in firmly.

"Then I'm the one that's late."

It was queer, but she felt just as though she could cry. She could not forget that he was not such a bad sort. He had meant well. He was vulgar but he couldn't help that. He was weak; he couldn't resist Fan. Perhaps he could help that, but she didn't hold it against him. He had been very contrite, very much ashamed of himself. And he loved the baby. What was he going to feel like when he realized that he was never going to see the child again?

She weakened. It was going to break his heart, for he doted on young Leigh.

For one moment of unusual weakness she felt that she could not do this to Sam; she would have to make some other arrangement. She would have to say to him: "Sam, Leigh has to be brought up as I want him brought up. But I don't want to stop you seeing him . . ."

How could she say that? He would be teaching the boy things on the sly, turning him away from his mother and gentility.

No. Leigh was not going to suffer as she had. Nobody was ever going to say to him, 'You're not good enough.' It was the most important thing in the world for him to learn to become a gentleman; and no matter whose heart had to be broken in the process, she must go on with her plan; if it was Sam's heart she was sorry, and if it was her own she would be sorrier still; but it would make no difference.

She wished she did not feel so soft and silly this morning; she wished she did not have these sentimental memories, such as first coming to these rooms and sitting opposite Sam and eating ham sandwiches and drinking hot coffee. She wished she did not remember coming back to Sam for comfort when Frith had wounded her so cruelly; she wished she did not remember how proud he had been on their wedding day and certain phrases in the halting yet moving speech he had made to the patrons. She wished she could forget his face when he had first looked at the baby.

But this was folly and she could not afford to be foolish now.

Sam said: "Looking lovely this morning . . . both of you."

He stood, legs apart, watching them, patting his thigh, rubbing his hands together. "So you're off out, are you, Son?"

"Big tats," said Leigh.

"Big 'uns, eh? That's fine."

"Goodbye, Sam."

On impulse she kissed him. It was a silly thing to do.

"Lord love us!" he said, smiling, smacking his lips. "What's up? The sky fallen in or something?"

Then he turned and embraced her warmly so that she was afraid he would hear the crackle of paper inside her bodice.

"You're knocking my bonnet off."

"And what a bonnet, eh? Everybody will know it's Mrs. Sam Marpit what's walking down the street. As for the nipper, he looks like a young lord or someone such."

"Goodbye, Sam. We must be off."

"Ta-ta."

She heard his whistling as he went into the supper-rooms.

On the way out, by way of the back entrance, she met Fan. She paused.

"You wanted me?" said Fan with some surprise.

"No . . . no. Not really, Fan. Look after him, won't you?"

Fan looked blank. "Goodbye," went on Lilith hastily, and she pushed Leigh out into the street. There she paused for a few seconds before taking the letter from her bodice and pushing it under the door.

She almost ran to the end of the street and only slackened her pace when she was some streets away from Marpit's Supper-rooms.

Furtively, she looked about her; she began to talk to Leigh as she pushed him along.

"Look about you, Leigh. This is the right place for you. See the carriage, my darling! One day you'll be riding in a carriage. That's where you belong to be. Never no more dirty old streets for you. You'll be turning up your pretty nose at them like the gentlemen do. Look at this house, Leigh. This is a great house. This is your new home. This is where you're going to learn how to be a gentleman."

Amanda met her in the hall.

"Oh, Lilith, I'm so glad you're here. I was afraid you might not be able to get away."

"We got away all right."

"I suppose I was wrong to worry. Come on. Let me show you your room."

Lilith, leading the boy by the hand, followed Amanda.

The first step was taken.

Leigh liked his new home. During the first few days he asked a good many questions about his father.

"Oh, he's all right, Leigh. Don't you go worrying about him."

"Home?" said Leigh when Lilith took him out.

"Not to-day, my darling."

He seemed to be aware of her fear during their outings, of her looking about furtively, of the cautious way in which she would turn a corner and scan a street. It seemed to Leigh like a new game; he would laugh and his eyes would shine.

In a few weeks he seemed almost to have forgotten his father and his old home.

Poor Sam! thought Lilith. What could he do? He did not know where Amanda was, for she had been careful never to mention Wimpole Street to him. He would guess that she and Amanda were together, but what help was that to him if he did not know where Amanda was?

And in a short time Leigh ceased to mention his father. The important people in his life were his mother and Amanda; the servants, after resenting his presence during the first few days, were quickly won over by his charm and now competed for the joy of fussing over him. There was another who won Leigh's interest. The little boy would stand at the kitchen window looking at legs and feet as their owners mounted the steps to the front door. He particularly liked those which belonged to the man.

Once he was in the area when the man appeared.

"Hello, Man," said Leigh.

"Hello," said the man.

Leigh ponderously mounted two of the steps which led from the area to the path on which the man stood. He laughed delightedly as he did so, because it was forbidden.

Then he solemnly took a biscuit from the pocket of his pinafore and, breaking it in half, gave a piece to the man.

"For you, Man," he said.

"That's very good of you," said the man. "Are you sure you can spare it?"

Leigh said: "Cook made it. It's nice."

The man put it into his pocket; then Leigh returned his half to the pocket of his pinafore. He laughed and went back to the area.

"Goodbye," he said.

"Goodbye," said the man.

Leigh liked the man, and tried to see him whenever he could. In the boy's mind the man had become merged with his father.

On one occasion he came out of the room which he shared with his mother and peeped through the banisters. He could see right down the stairs; miles and miles, thought Leigh. He saw the man and called: "Man! Man!"

The man heard him. He waved his hand as he looked up.

Leigh waved back.

"Be careful," said the man. "Don't you fall."

"Be careful, Man," said Leigh. "Don't you fall."

He often went to the landing and peeped down, looking for the man.

Once he saw him go into a room and shut the door after him, and then temptation came to Leigh. There was no one about, so he crept quietly downstairs and, when he got to the door through which the man had gone, he could not stop his fingers playing with the handle. He did not mean to turn it, because his mother had said that on no account was he to go into any of the rooms. But his fingers *would* turn the handle, and the door opened; and before he realized what he was doing, Leigh was standing on the threshold of the room.

It was a lovely room; the fire danced in the grate and made the poker and fender, which he thought were made of gold, all red and glowing. Everything seemed rich red and blue about

this room, and everything was so big that it made Leigh feel
very small indeed. He would have been a little frightened but
for the fact that the man was there, sitting at the enormous table
looking at enormous books.

"Hello, Man," said Leigh shyly.

"Why, hello," said the man. "Have you come to call on
me?"

Leigh lifted his shoulders, a habit of his which denoted pleasure. He shut the door carefully behind him and put his fingers
to his lips. He meant: Be quiet, Man, because I'm not supposed
to be here.

Leigh came and stood by the table. His head was just on a
level with it, so that by standing on tiptoe he could manage to
see the books and all the pens in the standish.

"What are you doing, Man?" he asked.

"Reading," said the man, "writing and learning things."

Leigh approached and laid a hand on the man's knee.

"Lift me up, Man. Want to see."

So the man lifted him up and he sat on his knee, looking at
the exciting things on the table. The man explained the uses of
pens, ink and blotting pad. He showed Leigh the inkpot, which
shone like gold; then he showed him the pictures in the big book.
There were coloured pictures showing people's bodies and all
sorts of odd things.

"What's that, Man?" Leigh asked from time to time, putting
a fat finger on the page.

"That's a heart. You've got one of those."

"You too, Man?"

"Yes. I have too. Everybody has."

The man showed him how to feel its beating and then how to
feel the pulse at his wrist.

"It's the engine that keeps you alive," said the man.

Leigh did not understand, but he liked to see the man's lips
move as he spoke.

Then the man showed him pictures of other men. There was
Dr. Jenner, said the man, who had saved people from the small-
pox; there was Dr. Paré, a very old French surgeon who had
lived a long time ago; and there was Dr. Harvey who had discovered how the blood in people's bodies behaved.

"I am a doctor too," said the man.

"Am I a doctor, Man?"

"No, but you could be when you grow up . . . perhaps."

"Like you?"

"I expect so. Better perhaps, because by that time a good deal more will be known."

Leigh could not take his eyes from the man's mouth when he talked; he also enjoyed listening to the words when they came out.

Lilith found them together. One of the servants had seen the child go into the room and had come to tell her. Lilith was worried. Leigh had been told not to go downstairs when he was up in his own sleeping quarters, and not to go upstairs when he was below with the servants. If Leigh started making a nuisance of himself, all her plans might be spoilt.

She hurried along to the library and knocked at the door.

"Come in," said the master of the house.

As soon as she opened the door and saw her son at the table with the doctor, she understood from his expression that he was enjoying Leigh's company as much as Leigh was enjoying his.

"I . . . I'm sorry, sir," said Lilith. "I had no idea that he was disturbing you. He has been told that he's not allowed in these rooms."

Leigh lifted his shoulders conspiratorially and smiled reassuringly at the doctor, as though to say: It's all right, Man. Don't be frightened.

He whispered: "Mamma's not really cross, Man."

"I'm sure she's not," said the doctor, lifting him from his knee.

"There are a lot of pictures in the book, Mamma," said Leigh placatingly.

Lilith took the boy's hand.

"You come along at once, and don't you dare go disturbing the Master again," she said reprovingly.

"You have an intelligent son, Lilith," said the doctor. "You must be proud of him."

Lilith looked at the boy and all her pride was in her face for the doctor to see.

"Thank you, sir."

Lilith hugged her son fiercely as she stood in the hall. He was so precious, so wonderful. Nobody could resist him; and with his natural charm and her immense determination, he would achieve all that she desired for him.

* * *

This household fascinated Lilith. She was beginning to think that she had never found life so exciting. Perhaps it had been more amusing, more colourful, but never had she experienced this undercurrent of wonderment, never had she felt so sure of her ability to succeed.

It was a house of strangeness. The mistress, with her illness and her secret cupboard full of strong drink, alone would make it that; but when you considered that her husband hated her and was longing to get rid of her, when you considered that he was in love with mild Amanda, you started to wonder what was going to happen next.

Lilith had made a habit of going to Amanda's room; she would lie on her bed and talk to her.

"What does this remind you of? The old days, eh? Do you remember, Amanda, how I would creep to your room when you were in disgrace . . . always bringing you titbits from the kitchen?"

"Yes. It does remind me of those days. Oh, Lilith, doesn't it astonish you to think of all that has happened since then?"

Lilith would lie, kicking up her legs as though she were a child again, her hair falling about her face; and she would smile slyly.

"Here we are, almost in the same position."

"Oh no, Lilith. You may be a servant here, but so am I in a way."

"Nobody in this house *thinks* of you as a servant, I'm sure. Particularly . . . the Master. I think he has quite forgotten you're nurse-companion . . . or whatever you are to his wife."

Amanda had flushed. "No, Lilith," she said, "he doesn't forget it."

Lilith merely smiled. "Listen. She's at it again. You can hear her at her cupboard. It's funny how you can hear so much through these walls. I reckon she drinks herself silly every night."

"It's very sad," said Amanda.

"She won't last long at that rate."

Amanda walked to the fire and unnecessarily poked it. She sought desperately to change the subject.

"I wonder we don't hear of Frith. I suppose it's very difficult to write from there. It must be terrible. Still, I do wish we could hear some news of him."

Lilith was subdued. She still thought of him a good deal. She had taken an interest in the war; in the kitchen they were astonished by how much she knew of it. When she had heard of the battles of Malakoff and Redan she had been very quiet for days.

"Anyone would think," Shackleton had said, "that you have a lover in the war."

"Would they?" Lilith had retorted. "Then if they said so to me, I'd thank them to keep their thoughts to themselves."

She could talk like that to Shackleton; he was eager for her favours and helped to lighten her duties considerably. Secretly she scorned him, but he was the head of the servants' quarters, and as he could be useful she gave him veiled promises which she had no intention of redeeming.

"I wonder if he'll ever come back," said Lilith now.

"I'm sure he will. Lilith. . . . If he does . . . what will you do?"

"How can I say?"

"He was deeply in love with you."

"Was he? Then he had a funny way of showing it. If I was in love with someone I'd want to marry him. I'd want to live in the same house with him, wouldn't you, Amanda? Wouldn't you?"

"Yes," said Amanda, turning back to the fire.

"Even you, Amanda. And you've never had a real husband, have you? I reckon that's a shame. I reckon that's quite wrong. I reckon you ought to be mistress of a grand house . . . a house like this with a lot of servants."

Amanda was staring into the fire; she dare not look at Lilith, and with a little laugh Lilith slipped off the bed and, kneeling by Amanda, put her arm about her.

" 'Manda." She called her that on occasions. It was Leigh's name for her. " 'Manda, if you ever were to, that wouldn't mean we'd be parted, would it? We'd always be together . . . us two, eh?"

Amanda dared not look at Lilith; she continued to stare into the fire. "Yes, of course," she said. "It must always be so. We'll always be together."

They could hear the low, monotonous murmur which came from the other side of the wall. The doctor's wife was indulging in one of her drunken monologues.

"She can't last long," whispered Lilith. "How can she? She's drinking herself to death. I reckon it would be a jolly good riddance, don't you?''

"That's not the way to talk," said Amanda sharply.

Lilith rocked on her heels. "You're right, Amanda. It's not the way to talk. It's only the way to *think*!''

Bella was very ill. Her skin was yellow through some ailment of the liver. Amanda sat by her bed at all hours of the day and night. The doctor had prescribed a certain amount of whisky to be taken each day.

"We will gradually decrease the dose," he said. "She has relied so much on alcohol that it would be dangerous to stop it altogether."

For a week Bella lay in her bed weeping frequently in her pain and the melancholy produced by her illness; then slowly she began to improve.

Her husband came to her room one night while Amanda was with her. He felt his wife's pulse and laid his hand on her clammy brow.

He said to Amanda: "She is a good deal better. I am going to give her a sleeping draught that will ensure a good night's rest. In the morning I think she will be greatly improved."

He gave her the sleeping draught; he stood on one side of the bed, Amanda on the other, as they had once before. They watched Bella slip into a quiet sleep.

Hesketh smiled at Amanda. "You look tired," he said.

"I'm all right, thanks."

"Have you been sleeping well? I know you have been up and down during the nights of the last week."

"I sleep fairly well, thanks."

"Shall I give you something to make you sleep? Something soothing and pleasant?''

"Do you think I need it?"

"Yes," he said. "Just this once. I'll prepare it for you."

"Thank you. I'll come down and get it."

"Come down to the library. I'll give it to you and you can take it up to your room. Take it last thing before you close your eyes.''

They went into the library.

"Sit down," he said. "I want to talk to you for a while."

He noticed the look of alarm which leaped into her eyes, and he said quickly: "There's nothing to be afraid of, Amanda. At least, only that I might say something which I should leave unsaid."

"Shall . . . shall I go, then?"

"No. We must talk some time. Do you know what is wrong with my wife?"

"I know it is her heart which is affected."

"Yes, the valves of her heart. They are becoming clogged so that it is difficult for the blood to pass through them. The clogging becomes worse as time passes; but the heart is a strong organ and it is amazing how it will recover again and again."

"This illness of hers . . . that must have made matters worse."

He lifted his shoulders. "She has been suffering from an illness of the liver. It was no doubt brought on by her excessive drinking. It astonishes me that she has the strength to recover from it. You see, we cut down her drinking and the effect was immediate. She is very strong. She has always been a particularly strong woman . . . apart from her heart."

"And do you mean that she will emerge from this illness and be as strong as she was before it?"

"I don't think that. She suffers a good deal of pain, you know. There will be more and more pain as the disease progresses. I anticipate other illnesses such as this one. The clogging of the valves will affect each of her organs in turn. Oh, Amanda," he said suddenly, "it would have been better if she had died of this. What good can we do by nursing her through one illness after another, seeing her gradually grow worse . . . watching the slow process . . . the deterioration . . . so cruel for her . . . and for us all?"

Amanda rose to her feet. "You . . . you must not say such things."

"Forgive me," he said. "I am tired. We are both tired." He came towards her and stood before her. He laid his hands on her shoulders and a tremor ran through her. "It's just that all this pain . . . all this misery . . . all this frustration seems so pointless."

"Not for her," said Amanda. "She wants to live."

"How can she? How can she want to live a life of pain . . . pain which gradually increases? Why does she drink so much,

do you think? Because she is tired of life . . . as tired of life as
I am.''

"Please give me what I must take," said Amanda. "I must
go. It is because you are tired . . ."

"I am saying now what I have thought of saying many times,
Amanda. If only I were free. . . .''

He put his arms about her and for a few moments she did not
resist.

"We must wait . . . wait . . ." she said at length.

"Wait?" he demanded. "How long? Sometimes I have
thought. . . . Sometimes I have thought how easy it would
be . . .''

She drew away from him and looked at him in horror.

"I must tell you all the thoughts which have come to me. I
have tried not to think of what I want. I have tried to think of
what is best for her. What can that be, do you think? What *could*
be best for her? To send her into a gentle sleep, peaceful, pain-
less . . . to use what skill I have to help her to rest? Or to keep
her alive . . . to bring her back again and again to wretchedness,
to frustration and terrible pain?''

"You must not talk like this.''

"I know. 'Thou shalt not kill.' '' He gave a laugh which was
quite mirthless. "There are times when I feel an urge to break
that commandment. There are times when I feel that laws are
laid down because they fit most cases. But, Amanda, do they
always fit *all* cases?''

"I don't know. I can't say. You are tired and overwrought.''

"No. I am thinking more clearly now. She is sleeping peacefully. To-morrow she will be refreshed. I have given her exactly
the right dose to make her do so. If I had given her a larger
quantity of the drug, she would have slept just as peacefully.
The only difference would have been that to-morrow morning
she would not wake up.''

"That would be murder!''

"Would it, I wonder? If I could satisfy my conscience that I
was thinking only of her, would it be murder, then? I have given
her drugs to ease her pain temporarily; what if I gave her drugs
to ease it permanently?''

Amanda seized his arm. "How could you be sure that you
had thought only of her?''

"I think I should know, Amanda. If she were not ill and if

her conduct were as intolerable as it is now, such thoughts would never for a moment enter my head. I would say to you, 'You must go away. It is not wise for you to stay. I am married to a woman whom I loathe, but I am married to her . . . and that must last as long as we both shall live.' I would send you away. I swear to that. Then my duty would be clear. But that is not the case. I watch her suffering . . . watch her sufferings increase. It is hardly likely that she will outlive us. We can wait, Amanda.''

''We must wait,'' she cried.

He walked to the table and seemed to recover his habitual calm.

''You're right,'' he said. ''I'm tired. I've been saying more than I should. I have betrayed my feelings to you. You know now that ever since you came to the house I have dreamed of another life . . . a normal life, reasonable and dignified. That child . . . Lilith's child . . . has made me realize that *I* want children. But I married Isabella and there is nothing more to be said. I beg of you, do not go away. I beg of you, do not be afraid. Stay here. Stay in this house. You are a great comfort to me. I swear to you that I would never do anything against my conscience.''

She answered: ''I am sure you will do what is right. I never doubted that for a moment.''

He gave her a powder in a paper.

''Just take it in a tumbler of water. You will sleep well then.''

''Thank you.''

''I will look in and make sure that she continues to sleep quietly.''

They went up the stairs together.

Bella was sleeping peacefully. Her face was less yellow than it had been and she half smiled in her sleep.

They came out, and at the door Amanda said good night.

''Forgive my wild talk,'' he said. ''I should never have burdened you with it.''

As she turned the handle of the door she said: ''I am glad you told me what was in your mind.''

He smiled. ''Good night. Good night, my love.''

Amanda went into her room and shut the door. As she walked across the room Lilith rose from her bed.

Lilith was smiling knowingly.

* * *

A few weeks had passed since Bella's illness, and she had now recovered and seemed to be her old self—garrulous, in turns aggressive and full of an almost whining self-pity. Amanda would shiver as she looked at the woman, at the plump white fingers that shook as she took up her teacup, at the furtive glances she sent towards the cupboard. Amanda could not help her thoughts. How long? she must ask herself.

Her greatest and most enjoyable recreation at this time was teaching Leigh his letters. He was only just past two years old and young to learn, but Lilith insisted and he was exceptionally bright. Every morning while Bella slept, Lilith and she would sit with the boy at the table in Amanda's room, and Amanda would draw the letters of the alphabet on a slate. Leigh, in deep concentration, the tip of his tongue showing at the corner of his mouth, his fat little hand grasping the pencil, would try to copy the letters. Lilith would watch in delight, enjoying the lessons with Amanda, learning with Leigh.

Lilith went about with her own secret thoughts, watching the progress of Leigh's education, of Bella's deterioration—for she seemed to be drinking herself into another illness—watching the affection between Hesketh and Amanda grow deeper and difficult to control.

There came a day when Amanda brought news to Lilith, who was in her room at the top of the house playing with Leigh.

"Lilith, the war is over."

Lilith looked over her son's head at Amanda.

"It means," said Amanda, "that Frith and David Young will be coming home now."

Lilith nodded. She smiled slowly. She would be glad to see him, but the news did not cause her the exultation which she had thought it would. She put her lips against the boy's dark head. He was the first, she thought fiercely, now and for evermore.

But when a few days later David Young's parents wrote to Amanda to tell her that their son had died of his wounds in Scutari during the last weeks of the war, Lilith was overcome with fear lest a similar fate, of which they had not yet heard, had overtaken Frith.

She was, as yet, uncertain of her feelings towards him.

* * *

Bella lay moaning on her bed. There was a purple tinge about her lips and her eyes were wild; to breathe was a continual struggle. It was late at night—a March night with the wind howling about the house. The doctor stood by the fire, watching his wife.

It had been an eventful month this, for the peace treaty had just been signed in Paris. Frith would be coming home, but that would take some months no doubt. He wished Frith were here now. He wanted to share his thoughts with someone. He could not talk to Amanda; as he saw it, she was too deeply involved in this. When he was with Amanda his emotions were uppermost. This was something he must think out calmly, with common sense and above all with the utmost honesty.

Hesketh was a religious man, but elastically so. He did not accept all the rules which were laid down. He knew from his own profession that it was sometimes necessary in cases of dire emergency to act contrary to all the rules which had been laid down, and which were suitable, for normal occasions. It was necessary often to take a chance, to act spontaneously, to say, "In all other cases this would be wrong, but in this case it happens to be right."

"Hesketh . . . are you there, Hesketh?"

He went to the bed. "Yes, Bella."

"A drink, Hesketh. Whisky . . ."

He bent over her. "Bella . . . no, Bella. It would be no good. It would excite you too much."

"I . . . I can't bear it, Hesketh."

"I know. I know."

He looked down at her and thought of her as she had been when he first met her—gay, young, pleased with life. He could think back to the gradual deterioration, the encroachment of pain which had laid its ugly mask over her beauty. Was she to blame for her stupid frivolity, her selfishness, her bad-temper? Poor Bella! She should have been fashioned differently; she should have been endowed with patience instead of vanity, saintly resignation instead of frivolity.

He remembered a day in his childhood which had been spent in a lovely Georgian house in the country. He had admired his father more than he had admired anyone; it was because his father had been a doctor that he had become one; if he had been alive now he would have taken this problem to him.

Hesketh's father had died in the cholera epidemic of 1848,

when he had worked among the poor and had eventually succumbed to infection because he was weak from constant hard work and too little rest and nourishment.

This day, which Hesketh now remembered, had been one nearly twenty years ago when his favourite horse, Ibrahim, fell and broke a leg. He saw the horse now instead of Bella, saw him writhing in agony on the ground. He remembered how his father had taken a pistol and shot Ibrahim through the head. He, Hesketh, had been a brokenhearted boy then, for he had loved his horse and had not understood why it had been necessary to shoot him.

"It was better so," his father had said.

"It is wrong to kill anything. You said so."

"Yes, that is so in many cases. But think how Ibrahim would be suffering now if he were alive. Imagine a horse like Ibrahim . . . dragging a leg all his life. No horse could be happy thus. He could only be miserable."

It was right, of course it was right. He knew that now.

And what was there left for Bella but a few years of suffering?

"Hesketh . . . Hesketh . . ."

"Bella, my poor Bella."

"A little drink . . . just a little . . ."

"I will give you something to ease the pain, to make you sleep."

"Oh, Hesketh, I wish I could sleep for ever . . . and never wake up."

She wished that. Of course she wished it. Who, in her sad case, would not?

I can't let her suffer like this, he thought desperately. It's too cruel.

A quick sharp pain, his father had explained to him, that was all Ibrahim would feel. A quick sharp pain and then peace.

And for Bella not even that pain—just a gentle sleep with no awakening in this world.

Had he the courage? It was said that it was wrong to take life. But there should be different treatment for different cases. Every case must be considered separately. He, as a medical man, knew that. And it was in his power to put her out of her misery.

Then suddenly he had decided. He was strong and he had the courage. He was not afraid to do what he believed to be right. If it were not for his love for Amanda, would he be ready to do this thing? That was what he must ask himself. If he could answer Yes to that question, the way was clear.

Would he do this for Bella if he loved her as he loved Amanda? Would he help *Amanda* out of this life if she were the one in pain?

He thought he knew the answer to that question.

"Hesketh . . . Hesketh . . ."

"I am coming, Bella. I have something for you, Bella."

His hand was quite steady as he mixed the draught.

"Take this, Bella. Take this, my dear. It will give you rest . . . and peace. . . ."

Lilith had been up to her bedroom to make sure that Leigh was all right. There he lay, his face flushed with sleep, his dark hair, almost as curly as her own, falling over his brow. He had thrown off the bedclothes. Gently she covered him and kissed his hair.

"Sleep well, my precious one," she said.

She stood at the door to look back at him. "Clever little gentleman!" she said softly. She shut the door and went out.

She heard voices on the lower corridor and, looking over the banisters and down into the well as Leigh did, she recognized the doctor's voice, although she could not see him. He was talking to Amanda.

"Don't go in to her. She is sleeping now. She is very ill, I am afraid."

"I'll look in later," said Amanda.

"No; don't. I will . . . last thing to-night. I am hoping she will sleep, and it would not be good to disturb her."

His voice sounded remote, almost as though he were not talking to Amanda. People betrayed their feelings in their voices. Usually, thought Lilith, I should have known at once that he was talking to Amanda.

She heard Amanda go into her room and she decided to go down to her.

"Hello, Amanda."

"Hello, Lilith."

"Are you going to the next room?"

"No. She's sleeping."

"That's good. A little rest for you."

"Yes. She is not to be disturbed, the doctor said."

"I expect he's given her something to make her sleep."

"I believe he has. Is Leigh asleep?"

"Yes. Kicked off all the clothes, of course. When will he be able to read, do you think?"

"Very soon, I imagine. It comes quickly. He's bright, and what is more important still, interested."

"I'd like him to be a doctor when he grows up."

"It's a great profession."

"Yes. And I'd like it for Leigh. I want him to be a doctor and a gentleman. What a wind there is to-night!"

"A real March wind! Never mind. Spring is on the way."

I'm sitting here, thought Lilith, making idle conversation, and all the time I'm listening for sounds in the next room. Why was he so cold when he spoke to her, so remote? Can it be that he has fallen out of love with Amanda?

Lilith said: "Good night, Amanda."

"Good night, Lilith."

Lilith came out into the corridor. The gas was turned low. It was nearly ten o'clock and the house was silent. Where was the doctor? In his library?

Lilith went to the door of Bella's room and listened. It was quiet in there. She opened the door stealthily. The fire had been banked up, the gas was turned low; the woman in the bed was lying very still.

Lilith advanced to the bed.

"Madam?" she whispered. "Did you call me, madam?" She looked at Bella. "I . . . I thought I heard you call."

She came closer and looked down at the pale face of the woman. Then she bent over her. She could smell something—a strange odour, faint but unmistakable. It was not wine or spirits. Where had she seen that strange look on a face before?

It was very difficult to see whether Bella was breathing.

Lilith felt a sudden panic. She did not want to be found in this room. In great haste, she tiptoed to the door and opened it. Looking furtively about the corridor, she assured herself that no one had seen her, and she hurried up to the room where her son was peacefully sleeping.

Lilith herself did not sleep until morning. Leigh awakened her by jumping on to her bed and shouting into her ear: "Mamma! Mamma! Wake up. It's morning."

She awoke startled, strange dreams still upon her, strange ideas burning in her brain.

"There's a lot of noise going on downstairs," said Leigh. "Everybody's up early."

She sat up in bed listening. She knew what the strange noises meant. The mistress of the house was dead.

It was evening of that day, and Lilith was putting Leigh to bed.

"Mamma, you're so quiet."

"Am I, my love?"

"Everybody's queer to-day."

"Are they, my love?"

"Didn't do any letters on the slate this morning. 'Manda said not to-day."

"Never mind. You shall do some to-morrow."

He knelt by the bed and said his prayers.

"God bless my mother and 'Manda and all my friends . . . and make me a gentleman . . . amen."

Lilith tucked him in.

"Now, keep covered up. There's a good boy."

"Why are you shaking?"

"Shaking? I'm not."

"You are. You are."

"Oh that? That's just for fun."

He started to shake his hand.

"No, no," she said. "Not you, Leigh. You mustn't shake. Now lie still and go off to sleep."

"Will you come up and see that I'm covered up?" he said.

"I expect so."

She sat by the bed watching him. Everything I do is for him, she thought. Everything is for him. I'd do anything for him.

When he was asleep she stood up and quietly went to the mirror. She hardly recognized herself; her face was pale and her eyes glittered. She looked, she supposed, very wicked.

And she was. But she did not care. It was for him . . . her darling. Everything she did from now on was for him, her beloved, her darling child.

She went downstairs and knocked at the door of the library. She knew he would be there, and she knew that he would be alone. As she stood waiting for his command, she knew that she was taking a risk. She was staking everything. He might be cleverer than she was. Love was the motive behind the actions of them both; people were strong in love. She knew that. He might say to her: ''You will pack everything and leave this house at once.'' But she was strong and bold, and if she could only be clever enough she did not believe she could fail.

He looked up from the table and she noticed how haggard he was.

''Lilith!'' he said with some surprise.

She advanced to the table. ''I must have a word with you,'' she said. ''It's about your wife.''

He was very startled, but she only knew this by the sudden whitening of his knuckles as he gripped a pen which was lying on his desk.

''About my wife?'' he said.

She nodded slowly; her mouth felt so dry that she was afraid she would not be able to speak. ''I . . . I don't think she died a natural death.''

She saw his face whiten now, and the look of fear in his eyes was unmistakable.

''*You* . . . don't think she died a natural death?''

''No. In fact, I feel sure she did not.''

''Why should you . . . imagine that? I am a doctor. I know the cause of her death.''

''Yes. I think you do,'' said Lilith. ''I went into her room last night. I was passing her door and I had a feeling everything was not right, so I went in. I think she was drugged.''

''*You* think she was drugged!'' He was, after all, a man of means, of substance, an important doctor; she was only a servant. He must feel that he had the advantage; but he did not know how strong she was, how clever. ''*You* are knowledgeable about these things?''

''Yes.''

''Oh?'' His voice was hard. He was preparing to tell her that he would not tolerate her insolence.

''I have seen babies under the influence of Godfrey's Cordial. You could always tell what sort of a sleep they were in. You could smell it too. It was some stuff in the cordial. Once I saw a baby who had had too strong a dose. It was dead. I remember the look of it . . . and the colour of it . . . and the smell. I've never forgotten the smell. I remembered it when I was in your wife's room last night."

"You were right to come to me, Lilith," he said. "And you're right about the drug. My wife was drugged. She needed sleep. That was very important to her. She died of complications due to congestion of the lungs, which brought about a stoppage of her heart."

Lilith was bewildered. He spoke so convincingly. He would never forgive her for this. She had been a fool. He would find some excuse to send her away. She would never have what she wanted for Leigh. He might be right. She realized now that she had built up her case on conjecture, on what she knew of human nature, on what she had discovered about his feelings for Amanda. She had one other step to take and she must be bold and take it, for she had gone too far now for retreat.

"They'll see that was what it was at the autopsy, won't they, sir?"

"Autopsy?" he said. "There will be no autopsy." Now he was on the defensive. She had been right; she knew it now.

He went on: "It is perfectly clear what my wife died of."

"Will they take your word for that?"

"Several of my friends have seen her, examined her, tried to do what they could for her. There will be others to confirm that she died a natural death . . . indeed, an expected death, one might say."

"But," said Lilith slyly, "if there *was* one of these autopsies . . . I remember there was one on the baby. They said there was no doubt that it died of an overdose. Well, its mother didn't know. She just wanted to make it keep quiet. She didn't know it was an overdose. It would be different with a doctor. He'd know . . ."

"What are you driving at?" he demanded sharply.

Lilith kept thinking of Jos Polgard and all the good that had come out of her encounter with him. Good was coming out of this.

"I think you gave your wife an overdose of a drug because well . . . perhaps because you didn't like to see her suffer, and perhaps because . . ."

"How dare you?" he cried. "How dare you say such a thing?"

"Because it's true," she answered. And she knew that it was, for he had betrayed it to her.

"You will pack your things and leave the house immediately."

"No," she said. "No. Listen to me. You've got to listen to me. I think you did right. I don't want anything . . . for myself. It was right to give it to her. It was wrong to let her suffer . . . and you suffer . . . and Amanda suffer. She was no good . . . not to herself or anyone. I know you're a good man . . . good enough for Amanda . . . and I know why you did it. But you did it. And if I had to leave this house and go away, I'd tell someone first. Then they'd cut her up and find out, wouldn't they? I don't want that. That would hurt Amanda. I love Amanda . . . next to Leigh, I love her best in the world. I don't want her hurt. I want her happy. I don't ask for myself. It's for my boy. I want him to live in this house always . . . not as the son of a servant . . . but just as though he were your boy. That's all I want. I want him to be brought up with the children you and Amanda will have. And I want to be here with him. I'm Amanda's cousin. I'm her sister-in-law. I could be a housekeeper . . . a companion . . . related to Amanda. You know what I mean. I don't want him growing up knowing he has a servant for a mother, and I want him educated. It's just for him, you see. I wanted him educated like a gentleman . . . so that no one will know the difference."

"I think," said the doctor, "that you are a little hysterical. Sit down here and try to be calm."

She sat down, lifting her smouldering eyes to his.

"You are overwrought," he went on. "You are a good mother, and the boy is fortunate in a way. I think you have been very worried on his account. You have seen a good deal of poverty and you are anxious to avoid that for him. That's praiseworthy, I suppose."

He was looking beyond her and his face was very white. She had to admire him; he had a control which she envied.

"I hope," he said, "that you will never mention these ridiculous accusations to Mrs. Tremorney."

"I've said nothing," she murmured. "I'll never say anything . . . not if you'll do as I say."

He lifted a hand to silence her. "You are anxious about the boy. Don't think I can't understand that. You feel that he is worthy of education and a settled upbringing. I myself have felt that.''

She nodded, sudden exultation filling her heart, mingling with a great admiration of this man, for she understood how he was going to deal with this situation.

"As you know, he and I have become friends. I have often thought of what I might do for him. Mind you, your absurd outburst has made me wonder whether you are a fit person to have charge of the boy.''

Her eyes glittered. "No one shall have charge of him but me.''

"That is a natural, maternal feeling, and I know you are the best of mothers. I had intended to make a proposition to you later on. It was that I should help with the boy's education.''

She said softly: "To let him live in this house? To bring him up like one of your own children?''

"I suppose it would amount to that. I feel, though, that I should send you away in view of your outrageous conduct.''

"I hope you won't do that,'' she said humbly, yet with a menacing look in her eyes which belied her tone of voice.

"I don't want to do that. I know what you have done for Mrs. Tremorney, and all that you have meant to one another. The boy is her godson. That in itself would make me wish to do what I could for him.''

Lilith nodded. She had won. However he put it, she had gained her point.

"I must tell you,'' he went on, "that if ever I hear any more of this ridiculous talk, and if it came to my ears that there had been such talk, I should immediately suspect and blame you, for I am sure that nobody but you would be guilty of such misrepresentation. Then you would leave my house at once. If you wished to take the boy with you, that would be your affair. If you left him, you could rest assured that I would look after him.''

Lilith said: "I will never whisper a word of it. I'll swear it. And he'll be here and I'll be with him; and he'll have everything . . . just as though he was your own son.''

He nodded slowly and, unexpectedly, Lilith covered her face with her hands and burst into tears. She did not know why she did this, unless it was from relief, from the tension and fear that had been hers ever since she had walked out of her husband's house.

The doctor laid a hand on her shoulder, she lifted her face to his and began to laugh.

"Stop that at once," he said.

She stared at him. She was the victor; yet he was so clever that it seemed as though he was.

He was quite calm now, calm and unafraid; and she knew that he believed that what he had done was right, for he was a good man. Only a good man, reasoned Lilith, could look as he did if he had done what this man had.

"Lilith," he said quietly, "there is no need for me to tell you that you have behaved abominably—in fact, criminally. Perhaps if I were wise I should send you away, even if I did not have you charged with attempted blackmail. But I want to tell you that I understand that everything you have done has been motivated by your love for your son and your desire that he should have a good life. I don't think you have been entirely wrong, therefore, though many people would say you were. It is motive that is important. You have tried to blackmail me, and that is a criminal action. If you had asked for money, I should, without hesitation, have handed you to the police; but the motive for what you did was the love for your son. You have been in fear for your son's future. I understand you. My own ideas are not necessarily held by others, but such as they are, they are mine and I believe in them. I judge you in a different light because I understand what prompts you. Have no fear. Your son shall have the best that I can give him; and as I do not believe in separating a mother from her child, you shall stay here with him. Go now," he added. "Go to your room. Rest and calm yourself."

Lilith went out with as little delay as possible. She hurried to her room and embraced her sleeping son.

Two

Amanda woke so early that May morning that she heard the first notes of the birds. Through her window came the fresh scents of the morning. She could just see the blossom on the chestnut tree, and she thought of the lawns of this old house with their pond and sundial; she pictured the orchards now beautiful with blossom; she imagined herself wandering through the rose garden and out to the small lawn with its border of tulips, to the summer-house, to the copse and the paddock; she heard the stable clock strike the hour. In this house and in these grounds Amanda had spent the happiest year of her life.

Yet it had been a year of waiting; but to-day the waiting was over, for to-day was to be her wedding day.

It was in this gracious Georgian house that Hesketh had spent his childhood and, as he had told her, had known much happiness; he had decided that she must wait for him here, wait for the passing of that year which the convention and respectability of the times demanded.

His mother had received her warmly, for, loving her son with a single-minded devotion, she had greatly deplored his unfortunate marriage, and she was ready to love anyone who could make his life happy again. Hesketh's mother had in one short year shown Amanda more tenderness than she had ever had from her own mother. Amanda often thought of Laura and wondered what was happening to her; she could not remember her very clearly now; when she pictured her she saw an ailing woman living under the shadow of a tyrant.

She had not been to London since she had left after Bella's funeral. Hesketh had spoken to her a few days after Bella's death and told her of the arrangements he had made. He had decided, he explained, to shut up the house, apart from his consulting-rooms. All the servants were going. He himself would stay at an hotel or rooms nearby so that he would be within easy reach of the house, to which he must go every day. After the year was over, they could find an entirely new staff and start afresh.

"I want you to meet my mother," he said. "She is very eager to know you. And," he had added quickly, "take Lilith with you. Take her and the boy. I shall visit my mother frequently."

Every week-end he came down to the country and they rode together. She would tell him then how happy she was in his mother's house, how the old lady had taught her to bottle the fruit and make the preserves, how they sat by the fire on winter evenings working on the trousseau and the household linen. Sometimes she felt he dreaded his return to London. She pictured his going to the house, opening the front door with his key and standing there in the hall listening.

Once she said to him: "Would you consider selling the house?"

His face had frozen suddenly. "Is that what you want?"

"I? No. I just wondered if you would be happier in another."

"It's ideal for my work. It belonged to my father. I think it would be difficult to find anything so suitable and in the right spot."

She said no more about the house, and it was he who spoke of it again:

"Are you thinking that there would be too many memories of Bella there? Are you afraid of that, Amanda?"

"No, Hesketh."

"Then I am not. We did everything for her, both of us. We have nothing with which to reproach ourselves."

Then she understood that, although the house was full of unpleasant memories, he wished to fight those memories. Did he feel, unconsciously or consciously, that there would be some cowardice in running away?

And now . . . the waiting was over.

She had dozed a little when she was aroused by the gentle opening of her door. Lilith glided into the room. She stood at the bottom of the bed smiling at her.

"Wake up," said Lilith, a thrill of excitement in her voice. "Wake up, Amanda. This is your wedding day."

* * *

Lilith was dressing Leigh in his white satin trousers. There was a blue jacket to go with the trousers. He was excited, full of the importance of the occasion; he was to be a page at the wedding of 'Manda and the Man.

"Do stand still," commanded his mother.

But how could he stand still? He must twist and turn to look at this strange little boy in the glass who was, surprisingly, himself. Huge dark eyes looked back at him disbelievingly.

"What's 'Manda going to be?"

"The bride."

"And what's the Man going to be?"

"The bridegroom. I told you before."

He nodded. Yes, he had been told, but he liked hearing about it. "The bride," he repeated. "The bridegroom. Shall I be a bridegroom?"

"One day, perhaps, when you're big enough."

He smiled, seeing himself grown as big as the Man. Everything the Man did he was going to do. He had long made up his mind to that.

"Tell me what I've got to do," said Leigh, pretending he did not know, just for the joy of hearing all about it again.

He was going to hold Amanda's train. It was easy. He had seen the train; he had held it in his hands; it was soft and beautiful.

Lilith talked to him, watching his animated face as she did so. How beautiful he was! How he fulfilled all her dreams!

And now he was going to be a page at a wedding; and when they went back to the house in London he would be like a son of the house. Everything was working out as she had planned. At first she had been embarrassed when the doctor visited the house; she had avoided him. But his manner towards her had been exactly the same as before—or did he look at her oddly at times, as though he could never like her, as though he distrusted her?

But he kept his promise regarding the boy, and kept it as she would have it kept. He was fond of Leigh; and as for Leigh, there was no one he admired as much as the doctor.

She heard herself saying: "And then when the organ peals out, you'll walk behind 'Manda right out of the Church."

"And the Man's a bridegroom, Mamma?"

"Yes, he's a bridegroom."

"I'll be a bridegroom one day . . . when I'm as big as the Man."

He laughed and nodded at the rosy-cheeked, black-eyed boy in the mirror.

"You shall be a bridegroom," she promised him. "You just wait until you're as big as the Man."

It seemed hot in the church. From her pew Lilith watched the pair at the altar. Her little boy stood there, and beside him another little boy who was a distant relative of the bridegroom. Lilith was not listening to the service; she could only see her son there, side by side with that other boy who had been born in the right station of life.

Leigh was as good as any of them. Oh, how lucky she had been! How clever! Looking back; there had been only one failure in her life, and when she considered it, she could not wholly regret it, for it had shown her clearly what she must do for her son.

Amanda was beautiful in her white satin dress that was made of a hundred tucks and frills. She was wearing the lace headdress which had been worn years before by Hesketh's mother. There was no doubt that Amanda was back in her rightful setting. That was not surprising; the miracle was that Lilith's son had followed her there.

Lilith believed she must be almost as happy as the bridal pair on this day, for their wedding represented triumph to her, the achievement of power. It was the outward sign of her success.

There was another reason for her happiness. Frith had returned. Only yesterday Amanda had told Lilith that he was to be Hesketh's best man. "I have been turning over in my mind whether or not to tell you, Lilith. I thought I had better warn you. It would be such a shock otherwise. He'll not arrive until the morning of the wedding."

Lilith had replied: "Shock! Oh, no. That was all over long ago."

And so it was, she told herself fiercely; yet she knew that the reason for her happiness was partly due to Frith.

She watched them—Frith, the best man, and Dr. Martin, that old friend of Hesketh's mother who was giving the bride away; she watched Hesketh's mother, Hesketh himself and Amanda. And with them was Leigh . . . her boy . . . her beloved son. He was one of them.

* * *

Amanda felt exalted as she stood there with her hand in Hesketh's. All her past anxieties seemed to have slipped away.

"I will," she said. And Hesketh slipped the ring on to her finger.

We shall be happy, she thought. There is nothing between us and happiness now. We shall go back to the house and I'll change everything. If anything of Bella remains to haunt him, I'll turn it out. It shall be *our* home from now on.

She was aware of Leigh, tugging at her train, and she slackened her pace to fit in with his. She could not resist turning to look at him, at his flushed face and his bright eyes; she could not help smiling at his determined concentration on the important business of being a page at her wedding.

Hesketh was thinking: All will be well. There is nothing to worry about; the house will be different when she is there with me. There will be new servants. There will be an entirely changed atmosphere.

There is nothing with which to reproach myself. Did she not say that she was tired of life? She had longed for escape. She had wanted to die.

How happy he was, now that the year of waiting was over. That year had seemed as though it would never end. There had been times when he had thought of asking Amanda to marry him quietly, when he had made plans for going away with her until the correct time had elapsed for them to take up residence in the house.

How often had he made up his mind to sell the house? How often, when he had finished his work in those lower rooms and the woman who came in to clean them had gone home, had he been unable to resist the opportunity of mounting the stairs to her room! How often had he stood at the door . . . looking at the shrouded furniture, the bed in which she had died looking ghostly under its covering so that he could almost imagine that she lay there, that she moved?

He had longed to sell the house, to make a clean break; but he could not rid himself of the idea that to do so would be to admit his weakness. If he had done right, he had nothing to fear; and if he had nothing to fear, why should he be haunted by fear? No. He was determined to live in that house, to bring Amanda

to that house. He would not let Bella drive him away as though
he were a man obsessed and haunted by a guilty secret.

He put the ring on Amanda's finger. How fragile she was!
How young and tender!

I did the right thing, he told himself as they went into the
vestry.

In the hall, which was filled with flowers for the occasion,
Amanda was cutting the cake.

Hesketh saw Lilith and Frith standing side by side.

There are some, he thought, who would say we are criminals,
Lilith and I. What strange criminals! Am I a murderer? Is she a
blackmailer? What terrible crimes are these—and yet are we so
wrong, are we so wicked?

She loves her son devotedly. Is that a good thing? She loves
him so much, and because she herself has suffered, she is ready
to commit a crime to make his way easy. I swear . . . I swear
what I did was for Bella, not for Amanda.

Leigh was pulling at his trouser leg.

"Man, I'm going to be a bridegroom one day."

"Are you, boy?"

"Yes, Man. I've got to wait though. Mamma says I've got to
wait until I'm as big as you."

Hesketh touched the dark head affectionately.

Blackmail? How could it be called by such an ugly name? He
loved this boy almost as though he were his own son. Murder—
Blackmail. Blackmail—Murder. No! He was being foolish.

The guests were drinking the health of the bride and bridegroom. Now the ghost of Bella *must* depart.

Frith smiled at Lilith.

"Well," he said. "I'm back."

"I see that," she answered.

She studied him. He had changed. He was in his mid-twenties,
but he looked thirty; the years in the Crimea had done that to
him, hardened him, battered him a little; but she realized in
those moments that nothing could ever take away that indefinable charm of his, that natural gaiety, that air of snapping his
fingers at life, the controlled excitement which he found in life
and which must indicate to others, as it did to Lilith, that any
who shared that life must share the excitement.

When she had last seen him, she had not had Leigh; and when the baby had been born she had believed that her feeling for Frith had grown less; now she was not so sure.

"The bride looks beautiful," he said.

"Are you jealous?" asked Lilith. "Do you remember that you once asked her?"

"I believe you remember everything I ever did and said."

"I remember what I want to."

Leigh had seen his mother. He left Hesketh and came to her.

"Hello, Mamma."

"Hello, darling."

"I'm being a page," he said to Frith.

"And carrying out your duties most correctly, I see," said Frith.

Leigh gripped his mother's skirts and looked wonderingly up at Frith. Lilith touched his head and looked at Frith; her gaze was almost defiant, as though she were telling him that no one mattered to her but this son of hers.

Amanda decided that there were too many memories of Bella in the house in Wimpole Street. She told Hesketh that she wished to make changes. He knew, of course, that the changes were for him. Continually she pondered how she might please him; and she thought she understood why he was uneasy in this house.

It would have been better to have sold it and taken another; she felt she understood that queer whim of his which made him prefer to endure this lack of ease. She believed that he felt guilty because he had loved her and longed to marry her while Bella was alive; and to a man of his integrity that seemed sinful; he could not forget it, and perhaps because he had been unable to prevent himself wishing Bella dead, his conscience worried him. He had, she felt tenderly, something of the saint in him. He wanted to do penance; he wanted to wear his hair shirt.

So, in altering this house she was going to remove all signs of Bella as far as that was possible.

Lilith helped her. Lilith was known to the servants as a distant connection of the mistress's; the position she occupied in the house was that of a very privileged housekeeper.

Amanda had listened to Hesketh's explanations about the boy. "He's an engaging little fellow and I'm quite fond of him. I want to help in his upbringing. Lilith is very anxious for him to receive an education, and I have felt that as we helped her in her escape from her husband, we are in some way responsible.''

She had smiled. ''Dear Hesketh! You don't have to make excuses to me. I know why you want to help Leigh and Lilith.''

He had looked at her in a startled way.

''It is because you are good that you want to help them,'' she had gone on. ''You are sorry for them. Even if you hadn't aided their escape, you would have still wanted to help them. What you are doing is making excuses for your goodness.''

He had held her against him so that she could not see his face.

''He is your godchild, Amanda,'' he had said at length. ''After all, you have a duty to him.''

When she had spoken to Lilith of Hesketh's plans for the boy, Lilith had smiled serenely.

''You don't seem surprised, Lilith,'' she had said.

''Well, maybe I'm not. My Leigh's such a wonderful child that it don't surprise me people should want to do everything they can for him''

Lilith wanted to make life as pleasant as possible for Hesketh and Amanda; she wanted the doctor to know that she was sorry she had to use blackmail to get what she wanted. It seemed to her that they had been foolish to come back to this house; however, there was nothing she could do about that except to help eliminate all signs of Bella, and this she set about with enthusiasm.

''The first thing I should do,'' she said to Amanda, ''is to take down that portrait in the drawing-room. It's so lifelike. It's almost as though she is up there, looking down at us.''

With the help of Padnoller, the new butler, they took it down and put up instead a painting of the village near Hesketh's mother's house; it was a gay picture of grey cottages in sunshine.

''And another thing,'' said Lilith when Padnoller had gone, ''I'd take away all the fussy bits . . . all the fans and dance programmes. The fire's the best place for them.''

So they made of the drawing-room a different place; they moved the furniture where possible and they filled the Japanese vases with flowers.

Their bedroom was now the one which had been Amanda's, and Lilith gave her opinion that they should have the big room on the first floor which had been the library.

"I think you'd like it," she said. "And it's bigger than this. You could make this room into the library."

"What about all the shelves and bookcases?"

"You could have them all fixed up here. Look, Amanda, *her* room is right next to this one. What you want to do is get all trace of her out of this house. Now you're shocked. The trouble with people like you is that they never say what they think. That's what *he* wants, if you don't."

"You think it's necessary for him, don't you, Lilith, to . . . to forget about her."

"I know it is. Let's talk sense for once. They were married, and it wasn't a good marriage, was it? Don't pretend it was. It was miserable. Why, mine and Sam's was a picnic compared with theirs. He wants to forget her. He don't want to leave this house because his father had it or something like that. All right. Alter everything. Get workmen in. Tell them what you want, and you and me will put our heads together and we'll make this place so he can't recognize it as the house he lived in with her."

Busy weeks followed. Each morning Amanda gave Leigh a lesson, and while Leigh was sent out with Annie, one of the maids who adored him more blatantly than the rest, Amanda and Lilith would be together, turning out cupboards, rearranging everything and, as Lilith put it, getting rid of Bella.

One afternoon Lilith opened the door of that room which had been Bella's bedroom.

They were both more silent than usual on that afternoon. Lilith could not help thinking of the last time she had seen Bella alive, lying there on the bed in a drugged sleep with that smell, reminiscent of Godfrey's Cordial, clinging to her.

Amanda was thinking of being here with Bella, of Bella's querulous voice, of another occasion when Hesketh had stood on one side of the bed with blank misery in his eyes.

She was afraid that, to her, this room would always be Bella's room.

She shivered and felt a desire to escape; Lilith felt it too, but she did not allow it to affect her. She sat on the bed, but Amanda noticed that even Lilith did that with an air of defiance, as though she were snapping her fingers at an unseen presence.

"I seem to feel her here," said Amanda, looking uneasily round the room. "It seems darker in here than in the rest of the house."

Lilith jumped off the bed and pulled back the heavy velvet curtains.

"Of course it's dark if you shut out the light. There! Now it's as light as anywhere else."

"Lilith, do you think that when people live in a room—I mean, live intensely as she must have lived—suffering so, do you think they leave some of their personality behind?"

Lilith opened the door of the cupboard and sniffed.

"Poof! *Spirits* certainly leave something behind. I mean the sort you have in bottles. You can still smell them in here."

Amanda came and stood beside her. "I expect a lot was spilt in the cupboard."

"That's about it," said Lilith. She turned to look at Amanda. In the sharp light her face seemed changed; there was an unusual pallor in her cheeks and a drawn look about the delicate contour of her face.

"You all right, Amanda?"

"Yes, Lilith."

"Here, sit down a minute." She pushed Amanda into a chair and stood over her.

"What's the matter, Lilith?"

"You wouldn't keep anything from me, would you, Amanda?"

"Well . . . not if I was sure."

Lilith bent forward and kissed Amanda as though she found the gesture irresistible and yet was ashamed of it.

"And have you told *him*?"

"No. I wanted to be sure. He will be so delighted. I shouldn't want to say it was so, and then find it was not true."

Lilith said: " 'Tis so. I can tell you that." Then she looked round the room. "I'll tell you what we'll do. We'll make this room into the nursery. There's the communicating door to make a night and day nursery. I reckon that'll drive old Madam Bella out of here . . . always supposing she's left more behind than the smell of spirits."

Lilith seemed to go wild with excitement then. She opened the door of the wardrobe and, taking out a handful of shawls and scarves, she threw them on to the bed.

She stood looking at them for a few seconds, her eyes kindling.

"Get rid of these," she cried. "Get rid of everything that was

hers. We'll make this house as though she had never lived in
it."

Frith called and Lilith received him in the drawing-room just
as though she were mistress of the house.

He had come, he said, to see Amanda or her husband; but he
should have known that Hesketh was at the hospital to which he
gave his services; and Lilith believed that, although he might
have come to see Amanda, he had hoped at the same time to
catch a glimpse of herself.

She dismissed Padnoller, who had brought Frith in.

"Are you the mistress of the house, then?" asked Frith, when
they were alone.

"Almost," she answered pertly, smoothing her hands over
her second-best dress with the velvet bows on the bodice.

"Almost! That means not quite. Are you satisfied with that?
Where is Amanda?"

"Resting. The doctor's orders."

"Indeed!"

"We are all delighted," said Lilith. "Please sit down."

He took a chair and drew it near to her before sitting down.

"I am sorry," said Lilith, "that you have been so unlucky as
to call at the wrong time. I can't disturb her."

"No, please, you must not disturb her. But . . . perhaps after
all I may not be so unlucky."

"All that going to the war and working with soldiers didn't
alter you much."

"Nothing will alter my feelings for you."

"Ah, the constant one, that's you!"

"And you, Lilith?"

"I told you once that when I change I turn right round."

"Then turn back, please."

With a rapid gesture he put an arm about her and, pulling her
round to face him, kissed her passionately.

"Stop that!" she commanded.

"You're the one to stop. Stop playing the mistress of the
house."

"I *am* the mistress of the house when Amanda is lying down."

He shook her. "Lilith, you must not make me laugh when I
want to be serious."

"I'll thank you not to laugh at me . . . or be serious over me."

"I can't earn those thanks, because it's something I can't help. You make me laugh and you make me serious; and all the thanks in the world won't alter that."

She stood up and moved towards the door, but he prevented her from reaching it; that was because she wished to be prevented.

"Lilith," he said, "you and I have a lot of talking to do. We can't do without each other."

"I've managed very well, thank you."

"You have missed me. Admit it."

She turned on him angrily. "All right. Just at first I did. When you decided I wasn't good enough for you, I felt I could have died. But people like me don't die for people like you. They've got too much sense. Then I married Sam and I got Leigh. I'm doing very well."

"I see you are, and I never doubted your good sense. But there's no reason why you shouldn't have me . . . thrown in as a sort of makeweight in all this satisfaction. The salt that savours the dish."

"I don't want no salt. It's all nicely flavoured without, thanks."

"Thanks?" he said.

"Are you laughing at me?"

"Laughing through my tears. I've not had a moment's peace since you so cruelly left me."

"We know where the cruelty was, so don't let's make no mistake about that."

"You're hard, Lilith. You're cruel. What happened to the husband?"

"I left him."

"He was just a means of getting a child respectably then? I didn't know you were such a respectable person, Lilith. And after that, he was dismissed. The drone, eh, no more required by the queen bee!"

"I'm not a queen, I'm a worker. I wonder you can bear to talk to me . . . in a drawing-room like this."

"It is a bit of a strain talking to you, I admit, when I very much want to make love to you."

She laughed. "Funny how I'm good enough for one thing and not for others."

"You take all this too seriously. You don't know how I wish I'd never let you go."

"Don't deceive yourself. You're as pleased as you can be. You're thinking: ' 'Tis safe now. She's married. Now there won't be no question of that sort of folly between us two!' "

"Lilith, I swear to you . . ."

"Oh, you gentlemen! Swearing comes easy to you."

It had been easy to banter, but he saw, of course, the flush in her cheeks, and the shine in her eyes, the softening of her lips.

"I assure you, Lilith, that I have never ceased to regret our parting."

"Well," she conceded, "it might have been so . . . in a way. You would have liked to take me to the house you offered so that I could have lived there tucked right out of sight."

"In what you call Sin . . . Secluded Sin. Do you know that what you did was far more immoral?"

"No, I don't then."

"You married that poor man just out of pique; and then when you'd got the child you left him. That's not sinful, is it? That's highly moral. It was cruel, heartless and ruthless. But let's waste no more time talking about each other's sinfulness."

"It was you that first talked of sin."

"Well, don't let's talk of it any more. I'm in love with you. Tell me frankly what you think of that statement."

"I think it's easy to say; meaning it's another thing. What do you want now?"

"You know very well what I want."

"Yes . . . but what else? Little houses, not too near and yet not too far away?"

"One little house."

"Well, I'm comfortable here."

"I'm sure you are. So Amanda arranged this for you, did she?"

"Perhaps I arranged it myself."

"That's more than likely. But if you do as I ask, you won't have to wait until the mistress is indisposed before you can take over the part. It will be yours by right."

"I'm staying where I am."

"Lilith!" He came to her and took her by the shoulders. "Are you really determined to have no more to do with me?"

She did not answer. When he was near her all her defiance deserted her.

He kissed her, and when he did that she forgot to be caustic; try as she might, every harsh thing she said seemed to be infused with tenderness.

It was a delightful summer evening in the gardens of Cremorne. Lilith sat in one of the alcoves. She was wearing a new bonnet of the very latest vogue; it was also the most becoming she had ever possessed, and it was trimmed with blue forget-me-nots and pink ribbons.

The light was fading and the ornamental lamps gleamed through the trees; in the distance a band was playing; and every now and then fireworks would shoot across the sky. This seemed an enchanted place to-night, but it was not the soft lights, the distant band and the fireworks that made it so; it was because Frith sat beside her—ardent, full of plans for their future, as he had been in the first days of their passionate love-affair.

They had come here that they might talk without restraint.

"How are we going to be together?" he asked now. "Where shall we meet?"

She did not answer; she stared at the lights in the trees.

"Don't be maddening," he said. "I know that it is as important to you as to me that we should meet."

"That's not true."

"Would you rather I said goodbye and went away?"

"No. I'd rather you stayed."

"You're always so honest, dear Lilith."

"I say what I mean. And if you'd like to hear more of what I mean, here it is: I don't want you to go away, because I like you. You amuse me and excite me. Love? I don't know about that. I ain't so soft as I was once. Once I reckoned you was all the world to me. Now I can say that you ain't. I've got my boy, and I'd say goodbye to you this minute if I thought that by doing that I could help him."

"Now please do step out of this maternal role. He's an engaging child; we all know that. I'll see that he has all you want for him."

"Now, that's very kind of you, but you're too late. The doctor's promised to educate him and give him a chance in life. That's why I have to stay at his house with Amanda. I wouldn't leave my boy for all your promises.''

He got up and took his chair round to her side of the table; they sat in the dimness and he kept his arm about her.

She thought: 'Tis queer. With him I'm as weak as water still. There's no one like him. Didn't I always know that?

She sat very still, sensuously delighting in him, yet exultant because she was in command through the knowledge that he needed her more than she needed him.

It was Leigh who saved her. Not for this . . . not for years of this . . . would she be diverted from her plans. The maternal role, which he had sneered at, was going to be the one she would always play. But it was pleasant to be with him, to think of nothing but the next few hours, and after that, other meetings. Leigh's mother could still be Frith's mistress as long as the latter role could not interfere with the former.

Frith began to talk of the days in Cornwall, the meetings in the wood, 'the beginning,' he called it, 'the idyllic beginning.' "Surely anything that began so wonderfully," he said, "must go on and on for as long as we live."

"Ah, you always did know how to do the talking. But it ain't talking that counts." She broke away from him. "When I think of what might have been. . . . He might have been your boy. You wouldn't like that, though, would you? 'Twouldn't be good enough for you, would it? You have to have the dark like this . . . and the secret meetings . . . with my sort."

"Look here, Lilith, I've made a mistake. I know that now."

She wanted to say: "And if you could have it all over again, would you marry me?" But she could not say it because she knew what the answer would be; and if he said it she could do only one thing—break away from him; and that she had no intention of doing.

She softened and turned to him. "I'm glad you're back. Glad. . . . Glad. . . . Don't never go away from me again."

They walked in the gardens and after a while took a hansom back to Wimpole Street.

When he took her hand she was reminded of another occasion just like this one. He opened the door and they stood in the hall where the gas was burning low.

"I told them to go to bed. Lilith, my love, does this remind
you?"

"Yes," she murmured.

They went upstairs together as they had that other time.

The entire household was waiting. The servants walked about
on tiptoe; they spoke in whispers. The midwife had arrived that
morning and the nurse was with her. They guarded the room in
which Amanda lay, like dragons set by a wicked fairy about the
apartments of a captive princess.

They alone were calm in this household, answering all
questions with superior smiles. "Everything is quite all right.
There is no need to fuss." They implied: And how could it
be otherwise, with *us* in charge!

To Hesketh the waiting was torture.

Up and down the library he paced, every now and then pausing to listen for some sound which would tell him that the waiting was over. When would he hear a step on the stairs? When
would he hear the cry of a child?

As he listened for these sounds, it seemed to him that he was
listening for another . . . a sound that came from the room next
to this one. That was ridiculous. That was fanciful. But he was
listening for a sound to come from that room which had been
Bella's bedroom.

Bella's room was now to be a nursery; but he would never
forget that it had been Bella's room. During these days of strain
and anxiety, he had often fancied he heard the clink of glasses
in that room, the low, monotonous voice which he had heard so
many times during the weary years, her soft, derisive laughter.

It was a great responsibility to take a life. And so he went on
and on over the same ground. He took up a book and tried to
delude himself that he was reading.

He went to that room which had been Bella's and stood outside the door; he opened it quickly and peered inside. A childhood fancy had returned to him; once he had imagined that
strange things happened in the dark or in an empty room, and
that when a door was opened or a lamp lighted, ghosts hastily
stepped back to the place whence they had come, and that if you
could only be quick enough you could see them.

He was ashamed to find himself opening Bella's door quickly

as though to catch her before she had time to hide. We are all children when we are afraid, he reflected.

There was the room, furnished now as a nursery, with a cot and all the accessories which would be required. It looked as different from Bella's room as it could look; but he would always remember her when he was here.

I did what was right. I did what was right.

How superstitious we all were, he thought. Even those of us who swore we were not! He was terrified that he would have to pay for taking Bella's life, and he knew that the most exquisite torture that could come to him would be the loss of Amanda. He was as superstitious as most people.

How long must he wait? What was happening in that room? He should be there. It was absurd not to be. He could not endure this suspense.

He thought now of the last year, when he had been happy, but during which complete happiness had eluded him. What was standing between himself and that happiness but his own conscience, which in his weak moments he called the spirit of Bella?

What I did was right. She had asked for peace. She had been a hopeless invalid.

Yes, said his conscience, but you wanted her out of the way. You killed her . . . killed her that you might be free.

And he felt that her spirit mocked him.

I am overwrought, he told himself.

If one of those women came to him and told him he had a healthy son and that Amanda was well, his superstitious fears would be quietened for ever. He would know that there would be no more punishment. But not to know. . . . To wait like this. . . . How could he endure it?

Now . . . footsteps on the stairs. Someone was coming. He rushed to the door. The nurse was coming up the stairs.

"Ah, there you are. . . . Longing for news, I dare say." Her face was red and beaming with pride. "A fine healthy baby girl," she said complacently, as though the child owed its existence to her cleverness.

He did not mind; he could have embraced her.

"And . . . my wife?"

"Doing very well indeed. You may see her. . . ." She lifted a finger, jauntily authoritative, which at any other time would have irritated. "Only, not for long . . . only a few minutes, mind."

"All right." There was a laugh in his voice. "All right, nurse."

He followed her humbly down the stairs—not a doctor, but a harassed husband and father.

They named her Kerensa.

"I want to call her Kerensa," said Amanda to Hesketh. "It's from the Cornish *Cres ha Kerensa*, which means peace and love."

She was vivacious from the first week of her life; she kicked more furiously than other babies; she screamed more violently when she was displeased; but she smiled more gaily when she was happy. From the first she was a person of sharp likes and dislikes, some of which were unaccountable, except in the case of her mother, whom she adored. Her father displeased her, and if he ever ventured to lay a hand on her he would be warned off with looks of dislike or even cries of annoyance. Lilith she disliked equally. Next to her mother, Frith and Leigh pleased her more than any other persons, although Padnoller was a close competitor for her smiles. She disliked all the female servants.

Kerensa's hair was dark like her father's, but she had her mother's blue eyes; they stayed blue and her hair grew darker.

Amanda was happy, but not—although she did not care to admit this even to herself—completely so. The cause was Hesketh, who could never enter the nursery without thinking of the room as it had been before it was converted. How she wished that she had insisted on their leaving this house! She knew that he thought often of Bella, and he could not forget that while she was still alive he had wanted to marry Amanda. Amanda knew that his conscience held him back from happiness, and while he held back how could either of them enjoy this life of theirs as they might have done?

When Kerensa was just over a year old she had had measles rather badly and for one night they had feared for her life. She had realized at that time that Hesketh was haunted by a superstitious fear; he was afraid for this new family of his simply because he had desired it so much when he had had no right to do so.

Then there was the behaviour of the child herself, which did not help matters; she would never go to him willingly, so that he had become awkward with her, unable to unbend, as he could so easily with Leigh.

But when the children recovered—for Leigh had had measles too and it was from him that Kerensa had taken them—Amanda forgot her uneasiness and it was only occasionally that she remembered it.

The children shared the nursery now. Leigh had his own little bedroom on the nursery floor, for he was too big to sleep in his mother's room now. Kerensa slept in that room which had been Hesketh's and which was connected with the day nursery by means of the communicating door.

As Amanda and Lilith sat in the nursery, sewing while the children played on the floor, they were both aware of a deep contentment.

To Amanda it was comforting to have Lilith with her, soothing all those fears which as a young mother she experienced, sharing with her the pleasures of motherhood. Lilith was naturally secretive, but Amanda knew that she and Frith had become lovers again; she knew that Lilith visited him in his house and that they occasionally went out together. It was a matter into which Amanda did not enquire too closely; and the Lilith who went to meet Frith was quite another person than the young mother who sat stitching as she talked domesticities, while she kept a maternal eye on the children.

Lilith was indeed content. She considered that she had managed her life very skilfully. There were times, it was true, when she thought of Sam with a shudder and despised herself for what she had done to him. There had been occasions when she had wandered dangerously near the supper-rooms, but she had never gone near enough to see them. She dared not. Sam had a claim on Leigh, and if he found out where they lived he might invoke the law against her; and laws were made for men, not for women who left their husbands.

She had two lives; one of erotic pleasure to which she must secretly steal—and that in itself was a fillip to her enjoyment of it—and the other was the life she lived as the mother of Leigh, whose sweet disposition enchanted her. Others saw these qualities in him, so it was not her maternal pride which made her imagine they were there. Each day she saw Leigh take his place more firmly in this household, becoming more and more like a son of the house.

She could not help but be delighted to see the indifference which the small Kerensa felt for her father, whom she called Man, following Leigh, as she did in all things. The doctor was hurt and bewildered by his daughter, and it was Lilith's son who showed him the affection for which he so obviously longed. It was almost as though Leigh was Amanda's child, Kerensa hers. Kerensa was wilful and wild, while Leigh was gentle and eager to please, kindly and thoughtful for others. Leigh was, in other words, perfect; and never had a woman possessed such a wonderful son.

As they sat in the nursery, she spoke her thoughts aloud to Amanda. "I was just thinking. . . . Leigh's more like you and Kerrie's more like me. Do you know, if we had had our babies together and it had been possible to mix them, I'd have thought they had been changed over."

The children played abstractedly with their bricks, knowing they were being discussed and immediately losing interest in the coloured pieces of wood since that topic—more interesting than any other—was under review.

"Leigh's a lot older than Kerensa," said Amanda. "He's had time to get used to life. . . . They're listening. I wish I was a good needle-woman. I have improved a good deal since my childhood, but I still would not call myself an expert."

"Look, Kerrie," said Leigh. "This is B. B for Bear."

"B for Bear," said Kerensa, knocking down the house of bricks which she had been making until the mention of her own name by the adults had made her pause to listen.

"And here's a K," said Leigh. "K for Kerrie."

Kerensa took the brick and held it lovingly. "Kerrie . . . Kerrie . . . Kerrie . . ." she murmured blissfully.

Then she stood up and tottered. Leigh caught her quickly as she fell. She put her arms about him and they rolled on the floor.

"She adores Leigh," whispered Amanda.

Lilith said: "Perhaps one day they'll marry. That's what I'd like to see."

"That's looking a long way ahead," laughed Amanda.

"Why? These things are decided when children are quite young."

"And often they don't make the matches which are arranged for them."

"I think," said Lilith, "that parents often know best."

"I don't," said Amanda grimly.

They stitched in silence for a while. Then Leigh came and stood by his mother's knee and Kerensa crawled to her mother and climbed on to her lap.

"Mamma," said Leigh. "When shall I marry Kerrie?"

"Listen to that!" cried Lilith. "He misses nothing."

And after that Leigh asked a good many questions about weddings.

Kerensa was eighteen months old when Amanda knew that she was going to have another child. She was delighted, but Hesketh's joy was overshadowed by a return of fear.

Amanda sat at the dressing table in that room which had been the library, and as she brushed her hair she looked over her shoulder at her husband and said: "Hesketh, you are glad about the child?"

"Yes, my love."

"You don't seem to be . . . entirely so."

He came to stand behind her and put his hands on her shoulders, hiding his face against her hair.

"Last time seemed so long," he said. "I was frankly terrified. The suspense was terrible."

She laughed. "But, Hesketh, women are having babies every day."

"They are just women," he said. "That's the whole point."

"I'm very strong, you know."

"Oh very. Another point is that you are also very precious."

She stood up suddenly and faced him. "Hesketh, I've wanted to talk to you so often. It's rather silly to have things in one's mind and not to say them. It's about Bella that I want to talk to you."

"Bella!"

She noticed the tightening of his jaw; he could not speak of his first wife or hear her mentioned and remain unmoved.

"What . . . of Bella?" he asked.

"It's just that she . . . haunts you . . . or seems to."

"My darling, what do you mean?"

"You can't forget her. In a way . . . you seem to feel *guilty*. I understand. We loved each other while she was alive and . . .

we longed for this life which we now have and to which then we had no right. You can't forget that, can you? Hesketh, my dearest, we've got to be sensible. She's not here any more. What happened was for the best.''

"Ah, yes. What happened was for the best," he murmured; and he put his arms about her and held her as though he feared Bella was there, trying to take her from him.

"So," she went on, "to feel guilty is ridiculous. We could not help loving each other. We were so suited to one another. Surely no two people in the world could ever have been so suited to one another as we are. Do you still believe that, Hesketh?''

"With all my heart," he said. "That's why . . .''

"What?" she prompted.

"When something seems so perfect, one is afraid."

"Not if one is sensible. Why shouldn't we be perfectly happy? There's nothing to stop people's being perfectly happy but themselves!''

"How wise you are, Amanda."

She laughed. "Sometimes I think I'm not so stupid as I appear to be.''

"Who says you appear to be stupid?"

"Lilith for one."

"Lilith is ignorant. Like a lot of people, she mistakes gentleness for stupidity, tenderness for weakness."

"Never mind Lilith now. Let's go back to us, Hesketh. Please answer me frankly: Why do you think of her so much? Why do you feel guilty?''

He hesitated. The temptation came to him to tell her everything. How absurd! How ridiculous that would be! Why should he burden Amanda with his guilt?

Then he said: "It's because I'm the foolish one. It's because I love you so much. I'm afraid. I'm a coward, I suppose. I think of the last time, and all I went through . . . wondering . . . listening. . . . I thought then of the old words, 'An eye for an eye, a tooth for a tooth. . . .' I had been guilty of mental infidelity to Bella. I wondered if that must be paid for. I was glad when she died. You asked me to be frank. Yes, I was glad, and I wonder whether I shall be punished for that gladness. So now I am afraid, as the greatest punishment that could be meted out to me would be to lose you. . . .''

"Hesketh, that is so unlike you. You, so wise . . . so calm, so practical."

"One is never wise or calm or practical in love, because love does not mix with these things, you know."

"Hesketh, when you come to see me, after the child is born, and if the child is a healthy girl like Kerensa or a healthy boy like Leigh, and when I smile at you and say, 'It is all over,' will you believe then that everything is all right, that it is as though Bella had never lived? Promise me, Hesketh, for that is what I want so much."

He kissed her. "I promise," he said.

"Kerensa," said Amanda, "I have something to tell you."

Kerensa loved to be told something. She sat on a stool at her mother's feet, her hands clasped about her knees.

"Go on," she commanded.

"You are going to have a governess, and I want you to love her."

"Why?" asked Kerensa.

"Do you mean why do you have a governess or why do I want you to love her?"

"Why both?"

"Well, you must have a governess because it is necessary for you to learn all sorts of things."

"Leigh teaches me letters. ABCDEFG."

"Yes, darling; but you must learn more than that."

"Leigh knows more than that. He said he does."

"But you need a governess all the same."

"What's a governess like, Mamma?"

"She's a lady who is very kind and will do all sorts of things for you."

"What things?"

"Teach you and give you your tea and your milk, and perhaps make clothes for you."

"I don't want a governess, thank you, Mamma."

"I thought you might say that. That's why I wanted to tell you about her. I want you to love her very much, because she needs loving."

"Why does she need loving?"

"Because she's lonely and has no little girls of her own."

"Has she got a lot of little boys, then?"

"No. Neither little girls nor little boys. So you must be very kind to her. You must remember that she is coming a long way just to be with you."

"Tell her not to bother to come a long way just to be with me."

"Now listen, Kerensa. I'm going to tell you a story."

"Oh yes, Mamma. Go on. Once upon a time . . ."

"Once upon a time there was a lady who was very poor. All her sisters had husbands and babies, and there was no place for her to go because all their houses were full up."

"With husbands and babies?"

"Yes; with husbands and babies. And this poor lady had no-where to go . . . nowhere to sleep."

"And no clothes to wear!" cried Kerensa. "Mamma, didn't she have even a little shift?"

"She was very poor and she was hungry."

Kerensa became solemn, because she knew now that this was going to be a sad story.

"Then," went on Amanda, "she said, 'I have no children of my own, so I will go out and look after other people's children. That will be the next best thing.' "

"And did she?"

"Yes."

"She was happy ever after?"

"Only when the children were kind to her. You know that every story has to have a 'happy ever after,' don't you?"

Kerensa nodded gravely.

"Well then, that's why children have to be kind to their governesses. Now when Robbie comes here you will be a good girl, because if you're not she'll be unhappy and I shall be unhappy."

"And Leigh and Padnoller and Frith . . . they'll all be un-happy too," said Kerensa; and at the thought of so much un-happiness, her eyes filled with tears. There were times when she seemed very like her mother.

Amanda kissed her tenderly. "We shall have to do everything we can to make them all happy," she said.

And Kerensa nodded vigorously.

Miss Robinson wrote exuberantly from the house of Lady Egger.

"MY DEAREST AMANDA—but I suppose I should say Mrs. Stockland,—It has given me great pleasure to hear from you. And so you are married, with a child of your own, and you are expecting another! That is excellent news. And there is a little boy with you! I have been here quite a number of years as you know, but my dearest Janet, who is the youngest, will be going to her finishing school in a year or so. I should, of course, stay with her for another year, but when I think of you with your little daughter and the adopted boy and the dear little baby not yet born. . . . I really think that you have first claim. . . .''

Amanda smiled when she read this letter, remembering vividly the worried eyes behind the glasses, the pathetic smile with its brave jauntiness and its false belief in Miss Robinson's importance.

This was the sort of power which Amanda wanted—the power to make people happy. She supposed that was what William and David Young had wanted. She was rather like them in her small way; the difference was that they thought of people as a mass, and she thought of them as individuals. She wanted to bring happiness to the few about her—Miss Robinson, Lilith, Kerensa, Leigh . . . and most of all to Hesketh. Hers was the small task which brought deep satisfaction; theirs had been the larger one which encountered perpetual frustration.

Miss Robinson arrived in Wimpole Street a few weeks before the birth of Amanda's second child.

This was an easy birth. Amanda rose in the morning without any idea that the child would be born that day, and by two o'clock in the afternoon her son lay beside her. Before she could rest she must see Hesketh.

She lay smiling up at him. ''A boy, Hesketh. A beautiful . . . healthy boy. Do you remember your promise?''

''I remember, Amanda.''

''You see? He is here and I am well.''

He knelt by the bed and hid his face against her.

''You were right, Amanda. You were right.''

There was contentment then. No more ghosts. Bella had gone and only Hesketh and his happy family remained.

Dominick was beautiful even as a very young baby. He was a contented child who hardly ever cried. His limbs were fine and healthy; but it was his beautiful blue eyes which attracted attention. They were large and serene and they seemed to look out on the world with unblinking wisdom. Amanda loved him passionately, differently perhaps from the way in which she loved Kerensa. Kerensa had been a fierce baby from birth—greedy, demanding, an angry baby who screamed at the least provocation; she had terrified her mother who had been constantly afraid that she was going to break or choke herself.

"It's different with the second one," said the nurse. "You know they're not so fragile as they look."

There never had been such a *contented* baby! said the midwife.

And even the nurse was guilty of baby-talk when she washed Dominick.

Leigh and Kerensa were brought in to view the baby.

"Mamma," complained Kerensa, "I wish you'd got a bigger one. This one is too little."

Leigh took the baby's hand. "Look, Kerrie. Look, how he holds my hand."

"He'll hold mine too. Won't you, Baby?"

Kerensa suddenly put her face close to the baby's.

"Careful, darling. Careful!" warned Amanda.

The baby seemed quite unconcerned.

"He's not afraid, are you, Baby?" said Kerensa. "Oh, but I did want a big one. I wanted one that could walk and talk. Now I suppose we shall have to teach him!"

Again she put her face close to the child's suddenly, almost roughly. The baby lay smiling.

A horrible fear had come to Amanda. Perhaps it had started when Kerensa had put her face so suddenly and so close to the baby's. She kept thinking of his unblinking eyes. After that she watched him closely, and often it seemed that he would hear a noise and yet would not see something that was held before his eyes.

Could it be that those beautiful and serene eyes were different from other children's eyes?

She waved her hand close to the baby's face. His eyes did not follow the movement. He lay . . . smiling . . . without blinking.

She was very frightened; but she said nothing . . . not even to Lilith, and certainly not to Hesketh.

It could not be. Why should it be?

Obviously she could not keep such a terrible fear to herself, and when Frith came to see the baby she realized that this old friend of hers, to whom she had turned before in a crisis, was the one to consult now.

"Frith," she said, "I'm glad we are alone. I want to speak to you. It's about the baby."

"Yes, Amanda?"

"I'm terribly worried. His eyes. . . . There seems something strange about them. He . . . he doesn't seem to see things. He doesn't seem even to be aware of the light. And when I wave my hand before his face he doesn't blink. He doesn't seem to be aware of movement."

Frith picked up the baby and carried him to the window. Amanda followed.

Oh Frith, she thought, say he's all right. Tell me I'm a stupid, fussy person who is looking for trouble. Tell me that.

But Frith was silent for what seemed a very long time.

"Frith . . . what is it? Why don't you speak?"

"I don't know what to say."

"Frith . . . he's not . . . *blind*!"

"Amanda, my dear, I can't say. I . . . just don't know."

"It's strange, Frith. You can't deny it. There is something strange about his eyes."

"It may not be blindness. It may be some slight thing . . . something that could be put right."

"Oh, Frith, what am I going to do?"

Frith walked away from the window. She sat down and he handed the child to her.

"First," he said, "we'll have to get expert opinion. I'll speak to Hesketh."

"No!" she cried.

"No?"

"I don't want him worried. I believe I'm just being silly. I am. I am. I must be. You know, I am rather silly. I always have been, haven't I? I always imagined things. I expect there's nothing wrong really. Don't you, Frith? Oh, don't you?"

"It may be so, Amanda."

"Frith . . . Frith . . . what *shall* I do?"

"You don't want to say anything to Hesketh yet? My dear, it would be wise to tell him at once."

"No. *No*! I want to be sure he's all right. . . . Hesketh wanted a son . . . more than a daughter. It seemed so perfect to him. Oh, Frith, I can't bear this . . . I can't. I won't believe it. Oh,

Frith, I can't spoil Hesketh's happiness with my fears. And they are only fears. I know they are.''

''Dear Amanda!'' said Frith, but he would not look at her. She was afraid, because all his habitual flippancy had dropped from him and his gravity terrified her.

''Speak to me, Frith,'' she pleaded. ''Tell me I'm wrong . . . tell me I'm a fool. Tell me I imagine things . . . torture myself. . . .''

He came to her and laid a hand on her shoulder. ''Amanda, have this child's eyes examined as soon as possible. Something can be done . . . if it is necessary for something to be done. So many wonderful things can be done nowadays. You must not despair so easily.''

''I do despair, Frith. I do despair.''

''That's not like you, Amanda. We don't know yet. His eyes may be perfectly all right. But . . . to satisfy yourself . . . we must get an expert opinion immediately. I know a man who understands more about eyes than anyone in London. I will go to see him at once and arrange for you to bring the child tomorrow. How's that? Hesketh need not know until after you've seen this man. You and I will go to him secretly, eh?''

''Oh yes, Frith, please.'' Her eyes were full of tears. ''You're a wonderful friend. You always were. You're a wonderful person really.''

That restored his flippancy and made him laugh.

''Ah, Amanda, unable to discriminate between the goats and the sheep! I'm a wicked sinner, and you know it.''

''No, Frith, no!''

He patted her hands.

''No tears. No worries. It'll be all right. I feel sure it will be all right. And if not, something will be done. I'll get along now and see this specialist friend of mine. Smile, please. I believe I can hear Hesketh coming.''

Hesketh came in.

''Frith! How good to see you! Are you admiring our son?''

''Just one of the wise men come to pay homage,'' said Frith lightly.

Amanda watched them. ''Oh, God,'' she prayed, ''not blind. Not *blind*!''

❈ Three

Of all the children—and there were now four, including
Leigh—Dominick was the best-loved. Even Kerensa was gentle
with him, and her voice changed when she spoke to her little
brother. It was touching to watch the children at play in the
nursery, to see the roughness of Kerensa and Leigh towards one
another, and the change which came over them when they
touched Dominick.

Dominick was a beautiful child—beautiful in appearance and
character. He showed a great eagerness to be loved and he had
his special place in the household. He was bright and intelligent;
and often it was as though a special charm, a special sense had
been given him to take the place of his sight. He would play
hide-and-seek with the others, feeling with his hands—his long,
delicate hands which were more sensitive than other people's
hands—listening, for his hearing was more acute. Even his
laughter was more gay, more infectious. From the basement to
the attic, everyone worshipped Dominick. He was the favourite
with everyone except Frith; but, as Frith admitted to himself,
he was unsentimental, and fond as he was of the little blind boy,
it was Kerensa—wild and naughty Kerensa—who had his affection.

She demanded it. She lifted her great blue eyes to his face and
asked for the truth. "Who do *you* love best? That's what matters
really."

"*Whom* do I love best? Claudia, I think." Claudia was the
baby.

"Liar! Liar! Liar!"

"Don't you know that that is a word which ladies are not
supposed to use? You ask Miss Robinson."

"I do know it and I don't care. Robbie says you go to hell if you say 'Liar.' We always say 'Rail.' That's backwards, see? And a fool is a loof.''

"How clever of you!'' said Frith. "I wonder if you succeed in deluding the recording angel.''

Kerensa hugged him. He was so delightful—grown-up and yet not grown-up; he was a man as unaccountable as a child, and a naughty child at that. So it was very important to Kerensa that Frith should love her best.

She brought him back to the point.

"All right. *Whom* do you really love best?''

"People always love the babies best. Didn't you know that?''

"They don't . . . and you don't.''

"As you know far more about the state of my feelings than I do, why bother to ask me?''

"Nobody talks like you, Frith . . . *darling* Frith. . . . And then we *call* you Frith. Most grown-up people have to be Mr. or Aunt. Nobody lets you call them by their Christian names, except you.''

"I'm lazy, I'm afraid. And very lax.''

"What's that?'' But she was not interested in words and always clung tenaciously to the point at issue.

"Really . . . really . . . whom do you love best?'' She put her arms about his neck.

"Shall I be strangled if I don't give the right answer? Will you choke the life out of me if I don't say 'Kerensa'?''

"Yes; I will.''

"There's nothing to be done then but to say I love Kerensa best. But you must know that admissions extracted under torture may be unreliable.''

But he meant it. She knew he meant it.

"*You're* right at the top with Mamma, of course,'' she told him. She kept a list of her loves in a round and untidy hand-writing which grew larger and larger as it reached the end of the page. "You and Mamma are first. Then Nick. Then Leigh. Then Padnoller. Then Robbie. Then Papa and Claudia. I don't like Claudia. She dribbles.''

"So did you once.''

"I didn't!''

Then she hugged him, and he said: "I feel very insecure. The list is never the same for two days running. One little misdemeanour and I'll come in between Papa and Claudia. I know it.''

She hugged him more tightly. "No, you won't. Because, however wicked you are, I don't mind. I like you wicked.''

So there was no doubt that Kerensa was Frith's favourite, and Frith Kerensa's.

Miss Robinson had been four years in Wimpole Street, and during those four years she had seemed to grow younger and quite lighthearted. She was no longer worried, and never reminded the children of all she had done for them. She talked often of their mother's virtues and what a good child she had been. Lady Janet had been a model pupil too, it seemed. In fact, most of her pupils had been. Kerensa was a sad exception. But Kerensa was no fool. She liked to hear stories of her mother's childhood, and she quickly discovered that Amanda had been as poor a hand with a sampler as she was.

"One must," said Miss Robinson to Amanda, "be continually on the alert with Kerensa. She is too sharp, and although she can be most inattentive at lessons, very little of what is not intended for her ears escapes her.''

Miss Robinson loved Dominick deeply. She thought of him as her special child, for he had been born soon after she had come to the house; she had suffered during those terrible weeks when it had first been realized that he was going to continue to be blind, and the family had not then understood what compensations for a lack of sight the blind receive.

The happiest task of Miss Robinson's day was Dominick's reading lesson. She had explained to him how a French gentleman, Monsieur Louis Braille, who had been blind like Dominick, had thought what a pity it was that blind people could not enjoy books like other people who could see. And now each morning Dominick sat with her at the nursery table, and his long, sensitive hands would wander over the raised letters which he had learned so quickly.

It was impossible to be sorry for Dominick, because he was not in the least sorry for himself.

Miss Robinson was very happy. It had been wonderful to come to Amanda, to think of the children yet to be born, all of whom must come under her tutelage.

Just before the birth of little Claudia, Amanda had said: "Robbie, even when the children are grown up, I shouldn't want you to leave us. That'll be years and years ahead, of course, but . . . I don't want you to think of going."

Then Miss Robinson had turned to Amanda with very bright eyes, and her reddish hands had trembled. Afterwards Kerensa, who noticed such things, said that Miss Robinson was now like Pilgrim when his burden had dropped away from him.

Miss Robinson took the children into the Park, as she did most mornings after lessons. Leigh and Kerensa would go ahead, and Dominick usually walked beside her, holding her hand. He was four years old, Kerensa six and Leigh ten.

Kerensa was skipping along dangerously near the Serpentine. Kerensa would fall in one of these days. It was almost as though she knew it and wanted to fall in.

"I can't think," said Miss Robinson almost peevishly, "where you *get* your naughtiness."

"I don't get it anywhere," said Kerensa saucily. "It's all my own."

She would dip the toes of her boots into the water and jeer at Leigh for not doing the same. She would taunt him until he did.

"Come away from the water," said Miss Robinson. "It smells horribly to-day."

And so it did. The heat brought out the foul odour of sewage which was carried into the Serpentine by the Westbourne stream.

Kerensa's reply to Miss Robinson was to run away from the water.

"Come back!" called Miss Robinson. "Come back!"

But Kerensa ran a long way ahead of them, until she paused to look at a bundle lying on the grass. She thought it was a heap of rags, but it was an old woman—a poor old woman; and as Kerensa tiptoed towards her, she seemed to move slowly—her hair moved, her rags moved; and Kerensa saw that she was covered with crawling insects, and it was they who moved, not the old woman. The smell was nauseating, worse than the grave-yards where Kerensa had seen the rats busy with the dead.

Kerensa was horrified, yet fascinated.

The woman looked at her, so she was not dead; her eyes were streaked with yellow and red. She looked at Kerensa as though she were asking for something, and Kerensa who, for all her wildness, was almost as easily moved as her mother was, found a penny she had been storing in her pocket and threw it towards the old woman. It was all she had, and how she wished that she had more to give!

Then she turned and ran, the tears blinding her, because she was so ashamed of herself for not breaking all the rules which had been preached to her and going closer and asking the old woman what she could do to help her.

She ran to the water, which seemed to dance through her tears. Leigh came and stood beside her.

"Look!" she cried to distract attention from her tears. "Look at my feet. They're going right in. Look! They're wet!"

Miss Robinson came up and pulled her away from the water.

Hesketh came in late.

"Amanda," he said, "I want to speak to you alone."

She faced him in the consulting-room, her heart beating with anxiety, for she saw that he was very worried.

"There have been one or two cases brought into the Hospital," he said. "I'm afraid they have . . . cholera."

"Hesketh! Oh . . . how terrible!"

"Yes. From the East End of London. I'm not surprised. . . . All the filth in the streets. The sewage and . . ."

She was thinking of the epidemic which had taken place not many years ago, when, he had told her, fourteen thousand Londoners had died. She remembered that his father had caught this dreaded disease and had died of it.

"Dearest," he said, "I must stay at the Hospital. I can't come here. You see that. If we can isolate the epidemic . . . keep it to the East End, we can deal with it better."

"Yes," she said slowly. "I see that."

"We don't know how it is spread so rapidly. But we've got to take every precaution. I'm going back to the Hospital now. It may be a little time before we meet again."

"Oh, Hesketh!"

"I know, my dear. But, Amanda, it has to be. I dare not come back here where you and the children are."

"I cannot help thinking of your father," she said.

"He didn't take care of himself. I promise you I will. I'll take every care. You know, don't you, my love, that doctors are generally immune?"

"But . . ."

"My father was careless. He went on unceasingly. There are

several of us, and we shall be reasonable. We've got to keep this down, and we've got to find out how to prevent these recurring epidemics. Oh, Amanda, my darling, I've been happier than I ever dreamed possible. I've got you . . . and the children. . . . I'll come back safely to you. Never fear.''

When he left she stood at the window that she might see the last of him.

The sun burned fiercely down on the pavements and the intense heat continued.

Kerensa came out of the house all alone. She was not allowed out alone, but something was happening in the house. Her mother had not been listening when she had tried to tell her about the woman in the Park. Kerensa felt peevish; she hated not to be listened to.

She made out a new list of her loves. Frith was first, Mamma second now.

It seemed suddenly very important that she should inform Frith of his promotion to first place. She felt sick and dazed and very thirsty; and she wanted someone to comfort her. She felt that she wanted to be naughty too, to show her mother that if *she* did not listen to her, there was someone else who would.

They said she was not to go out alone because she was a child; and that was absurd, for she was six years old; and everyone knew that that was quite grown up. Besides, Frith's house was only a few doors along the street.

She walked to his front door feeling very important in spite of the pain in her head and the fact that her lids seemed to be forcing themselves down over her eyes. She rang the bell and Napoleon answered.

''Hello, Napoleon,'' she said.

Napoleon said: ''Why, it's little Miss Kerensa.''

''It's Miss Stockland,'' she corrected haughtily. ''I'm not little any more and I'm feeling very sick.''

''Oh, you do want to see the master, I reckon.''

''Yes, I do, please, Napoleon.''

She followed him up the stairs and when he had knocked at the door and she heard Frith's voice, she ran past Napoleon and straight to Frith.

''Kerensa! What does this mean?''

"Frith, I . . . you're first now, and I feel sick and I've got pains . . . lots of pains. . . ."

He picked her up and sat her on his knee. She heard his voice from a long way, it seemed, saying her name. His hands were on her face and he pulled down the skin below her eyes. Then he stood up and held her tightly in his arms.

"Frith . . . Frith . . . where are we going?"

"You're going to bed here, in my house. Napoleon!" he shouted. "Go at once to Mrs. Stockland and tell her Kerensa is sick. Tell her I'm keeping her here because I don't think she should be near the others. Go at once and remember what I've said."

Napoleon limped off, and Frith walked up the stairs to his room and there he laid Kerensa on his bed, whispering to her, very gently, and more tenderly, she thought, than he had ever spoken to her before: "It is all right, Kerensa. Frith's here. I'm going to look after you, Kerensa."

Every bed in the Hospital was occupied; people lay outside in the courtyard awaiting admission, suffering from all the symptoms of the dreaded disease—thirst, severe diarrhœa, cramp and collapse. They were dying in hundreds as they sank down in the streets of the East End of London or tried to crawl into their houses.

The Asiatic cholera, probably brought to the Port of London by foreign sailors, spread rapidly through the narrow streets. In the stinking gutters, where the filth collected, the children played and the cholera germs multiplied. Infection rose through the ground under which were the vaulted sewers where the polluted streams ran to empty themselves into the river. In the 'rookeries,' where as many as ten people huddled in one room, infection was passed from one victim to another; the flies which were breeding rapidly during those summer weeks helped to carry the disease from street to street; the rats that leaped over the decaying bodies in the graveyards, and roamed tamely round the cesspools and sewers, came boldly into the people's houses to play their part in the grim dance of death.

Hesketh was working all through the day and most of the night, snatching a few hours' rest when possible. There were others like himself—noble, selfless men who went among the afflicted, fearlessly bringing comfort as well as healing to the sufferers.

Hesketh found satisfaction in his work, but he was critical of himself. Bella's death still lay heavily on his conscience, and whenever he felt he had done something to save a life he would think: There is a life saved. If I took a life, I have saved others.

He thought of his family constantly and longed to return to them. He was continually wondering whether Fate had some blow in store for him. He had a happy home, a family to care for; he had always longed for these things above all others. But he had only reached them through Bella's death. He could not forget that. If the boy Dominick had not been born blind, would he have forgotten by now? He often asked himself that. Surely he was foolish to consider for a moment that Dominick's blindness was a punishment for himself, a Heavenly rap over the knuckles. Yet every time he looked at the boy's sightless face he fancied he saw Bella lying on her bed, laughing at him, mocking him.

"You should sleep while you can," said the young doctor who lay stretched out beside him.

He turned and looked at the man—Tom Barnardo, a young fanatic for work, not much more than twenty and only recently qualified, a young man with a gentle, idealist's face and some indefinable quality which endeared him to the children.

"Sleep won't come . . . just when you need it," said Hesketh.

"You're overtired," said Barnardo.

"I suppose so. What is your opinion of the Budd Theory?"

"Probably right. But I don't think that's the entire answer."

"I feel, too, that Budd's right. It comes from the sewers. And we've got to make sure that the drinking water is not contaminated. That's where the trouble lies."

"Well, we have isolated it more successfully this time. There's hardly a case beyond the East End, so I hear. And when you consider the last flare-up . . ."

"Yes," said Hesketh.

"You know," said Tom Barnardo, "you ought not to be here . . . a family man like you."

"Don't you think more of us should be here?"

"Perhaps. But you have a family . . . young children, eh?"

"That's true."

"Ah! The children! That's the problem. I found another to-day, wandering the streets, homeless. Mother dead; father dead. I said to him, 'And what are you doing? Why don't you go home?' He said: 'Home? I've got no home, guv'nor.' I brought him along to the Hospital for a test. What else could I do? Leave him in the streets! There are hundreds . . . dying every day . . . not from cholera only . . . but from starvation. . . . Homeless children. . . . Think of it!"

"It's terrible. The poverty in this part of London should make people weep to contemplate it."

"If they looked at it," said the young man scornfully. "But do they look? No. They pass by on the other side of the road. All our lords and ladies . . . all our Church dignitaries. . . . I'm sorry. I get rather hot, thinking of it."

"You too should be trying to sleep."

"Yes, to sleep and dream. Do you know what I want to do when this is over? Start a home . . . a home where I can have these children . . . these homeless ones. I want to clothe them and feed them and prepare them for a place in the world."

Hesketh smiled at young Tom Barnardo as he went on talking, detailing the plans of his noble dream.

And so they talked until, exhausted, they slept.

They awoke to another day of steaming heat, of disease and horror . . . and dreams.

Kerensa came out of her illness, tall and thin, at times quiet and serious.

She could remember very little of what had happened after Frith carried her to bed; she had known that she was very ill and that the other children must not come to see her in case they became ill too. Only Frith must come near her because he was so clever that he knew how not to be ill.

For a long time she was too weak to want to do anything but lie still. Frith himself fed her out of a little tea-pot thing with a funny spout, and she pretended for a long time that she was too weak to hold the cup, because she wanted Frith to go on feeding her. She wanted him with her all the time. He was at the top of her list now for ever.

The days grew colder and there was a good deal of rain.

"That's good," said Frith. "That'll wash the dirt away. That's what we want."

"Why?"

"Well, it's been too hot and that's bad for people who are sick."

"Are there a lot of people sick?"

"Quite a lot."

"Sicker than I was?"

"Much. They hadn't me to look after them."

She laughed, very pleased. It seemed right that she, Kerensa, should have the best doctor in the world to look after her.

"Soon," he said, "you can have visitors. You'll like that."

She shrugged her shoulders. "I only really want you."

"Oh come, you've got too much of me already. 'Variety is the spice of life.'"

"I don't care. I don't want spice. I want you."

But they did come. There was her mother, who was very tender and had obviously been very frightened all the time that Kerensa was ill; she kept holding Kerensa's hand and kissing her. Kerensa was pleased with this attention; she realized that her mother was very near the top of the list, and that if there had not been such a wonderful person as Frith she might have been right at the top.

There was Dominick too, smiling and feeling her face. Clever Nick, who knew who you were by touching your eyes and nose!

"Hello, Nick."

"Hello, Kerrie. When are you coming home?"

"I don't know. I've been very ill. I expect I shall have to be looked after for a long time yet."

Leigh was there, looking at her almost shyly and trying to pretend he was not nearly crying because he was so glad she had not died. Kerensa knew then that if Leigh had had a list she would have been at the top of it.

Miss Robinson said: "We shall soon be coming back to lessons, shan't we?"

"You may," said Kerensa. "I shan't. I've got a lot of getting better to do yet."

When they had all gone, Frith stood by the bed smiling at her. "You need not look so wan now, my child. You've played the poor little invalid very nicely."

"But, Frith, I am still an invalid!"

"No. You're much better. Well, what's the matter?"

"Shall I have to go home when I'm better?"

"Of course you will."

"Then I don't want to get better. I want to live with you."

"The whim of the moment," he said. "Still, it's a nice thought."

Lilith came to see her the next day, and she came alone.

Kerensa sat up primly in bed to receive her visitor.

"So you'll soon be coming home now," said Lilith.

"I can't come till I'm better."

"Leigh has missed you. He's done nothing but talk about you. I expect you missed Leigh."

"*I've* been too ill," said Kerensa. Then she thought of Leigh with his solemn, dark eyes, and the many times he had covered up her misdemeanours from the eyes of her parents or Miss Robinson. She was very warm-hearted. "I have missed Leigh," she said. "I wish he could come here with Nick sometimes . . . when Frith's not here."

"Well, perhaps he could now you're getting better."

Frith came in. "Well," he said. "Another visitor."

Kerensa was suddenly alert. There was something different about his voice when he spoke to Lilith; there was something about his eyes when he looked at her.

"So Lilith has done you the honour of visiting you!" He pretended to be talking to Kerensa, but really he was talking to Lilith. He drew his chair up close to Lilith's and he kept watching Lilith. "How do you think our invalid is looking?"

"Very well. It was good of you, Frith, to look after her as you did."

"What else could I do? She just walked into my house . . . cholera germs and all."

"I didn't know," said Kerensa resentfully.

"She is a clever one, our Kerensa," said Frith. "She knows how to take advantage of her disadvantages."

Kerensa wished he would not talk like that; she felt he was talking to Lilith and excluding her.

She would have hated anyone but Frith for talking like that. She certainly hated Lilith for making Frith look at her instead of at his little invalid.

They were talking now . . . talking together and quite forgetting Kerensa.

She knew that Lilith was very pretty. She had not thought of that before. Lilith was wearing a big bonnet which Kerensa had thought rather silly when Lilith had come into the room. Now

Kerensa was not sure that it was silly. The ribbons on the bonnet were very bright; and Lilith's crinoline was enormous—much bigger than most people wore. You felt there was so much crinoline and so little of Lilith that you must keep looking to see what there was.

Go away, she muttered to herself. You're spoiling everything!

And eventually Lilith did get up to go. Frith went to the door with her.

"Frith," said Kerensa. "Frith, stay here."

He turned to smile at her, but it was not the same smile which he had for Lilith. It was a far-away, grown-up smile.

"Be back in a moment," he said; and he went out with Lilith. But he did not come back in a moment. Kerensa lay still, listening for the front door to shut; nothing happened.

They were together, laughing together, talking secrets; and they had gone out of this room because they did not want her with them.

She was flushed and angry; she cried a little. "It's because I'm so weak!" she said pitiably. But what was the use of playing the invalid when there was no one to see and hear her?

It seemed hours and hours before she heard the street door shut, and she got out of bed and looked out of the window, but she could not see the pavement without opening the window, and she dared not do that.

"What are you doing out of bed?" It was Frith standing in the doorway watching her.

He came over to her and picked her up.

"How hot you are! Get into bed at once."

"I've been left too long alone," said Kerensa.

Frith burst out laughing and threw her on to the bed just as though she were a bundle. He covered her up and she put her arms about his neck. She wanted to ask him if she were top of *his* list; but she dared not because she was afraid that, if he spoke the truth, the answer might not be "Yes."

Amanda's family was growing up around her. There were now two more children—Martha and Dennis. She was contented with her little family. Dennis, the baby, was a healthy little boy; as for Dominick, they would not change him for anything—he was the best loved of them all; Claudia was four and Martha—who called herself Martie—was two.

Lilith was contented too. Leigh was now fourteen—tall and darkly handsome, a credit to the house, so said the doctor; and Lilith believed that he was every bit as fond of Leigh as he was of his own children. Although this might have surprised some, it did not surprise Lilith. Her son still seemed to be everything that a son should be, and when she looked at him her eyes would shine, not only with pride, but with triumph. She had moulded him; she had fashioned him to her own desires; and everything that she had planned for him seemed to be coming about.

He wanted to be a doctor; that was because the man whom he now called Father, as the others did, was a doctor. They spent a good deal of their time together, and Leigh had made known his wishes to the benefactor who had also been a father to him. His education was being superintended with the utmost care, and if Leigh would never be a brilliant doctor—although Lilith fervently believed he would—he would certainly be a conscientious one.

At fourteen he had already gone away to school, and this meant that Kerensa had set herself in command of the other children.

It was a day soon after Kerensa's tenth birthday—a day she was to remember years later.

She was lying on the nursery floor reading to Dominick, who loved to be read to. He was sitting on the floor also, leaning against a leg of the table, turning his head about with that peculiar air of excitement which never failed to interest the others; for in Dominick's world, they had come to understand, there was much of which they were not aware. All the children liked to hear him tell of what he experienced when he walked in the garden and stood beneath the pear tree or knelt to touch the flower bed which Padnoller attended so assiduously in the small and narrow garden. He, in his turn, liked them to tell him what they saw, the colours and shapes; he liked them to lead him to things of which they spoke, that he might touch them and smell them as they spoke of them. It was a game which they often played and one which never tired them.

Kerensa had finished the story, and as she closed the book she looked at her brother and saw the rapt look on his face which always made her long to enter his sightless world.

"Nick," she said softly.

He put out a hand and she took it. He touched her face with the other one.

"Kerrie, what's strange about this room? It's different from the other rooms. Why is it?"

"I suppose because it's our room. It's untidy. There are things all over the table. There are Martie's bricks and Claudia's doll. And there's somebody's pencil box. . . . And on the floor there are us and the book now."

"There's something else about it too. Kerrie, tell me about this room, will you?" He stood up and held out his hand. "Take me round it and let me touch everything . . . and tell me all about it."

She jumped up and stood beside him. Then she picked up the book and laid it on the table, for one of the rules of the nursery was that nothing should be left on the floor in case Dominick fell over it. It was a rule which Kerensa—careless in all other matters—never forgot herself and made it her particular task to see that none of the others forgot it.

"We'll start at the window," she said. "These are the curtains. They're a sort of velvet . . . lines and lines of velvet, all sort of together. They call it chenille or something."

"It's soft. Is it pretty?"

"Yes, and it's dark red."

"Red," said Dominick.

"Apples are red sometimes," said Kerensa. "And plums are red.

"This colour is like plums more than apples. Your cheeks are red and so are mine . . . but that's another red. Red's a nice colour. I like it best of all colours . . . because it sort of comes out at you."

"Does it?"

"Well, not really, but it seems to. When it's with a lot of others it seems to say: 'Look at me, I'm red!' "

They laughed. Kerensa, better than anyone else, always made him understand things.

"Then there's the window," she went on. "You can see through it because it's glass. Down there is the garden."

"The thing's not out there," said Dominick. "It's in this room."

"Is it here only when Papa is here?"

"Yes, and sometimes when Mamma's here . . . but only if he's here too."

"I wonder what it is! Oh, I *do* wonder!"

"Take me round."

"You know the carpet. It's the same colour as the curtains."

"Like plums!" said Dominick, laughing because his teeth were on edge. The last plums he had eaten were very sour.

"Here's a chair. You know all about the chairs, don't you? You've sat on all of them!"

"Yes, I know the chairs." He felt one of them lovingly.

"Take me to the cupboard," said Dominick. She led him to it and he touched it. He felt the panels and the knob which had to be turned.

"Could a big man like Papa be frightened like children are of the dark . . . children who can see?"

"I think perhaps grown-up people *are* frightened sometimes," said Kerensa. "They're terrible pretenders, grown-up people are. Sometimes I think they're just like us . . . only big."

"Yes," said Dominick; "like us, only big. Kerrie, what's a skeleton?"

"Bones . . . dead bodies. We see them in the churchyards. Ugh! Horrible! Nick, you ought to be glad you can't see them."

"They put skeletons in cupboards, Kerrie. I heard Padnoller say so to cook the other day. He said, 'Now that's a fine old skeleton in the cupboard, that is!' Kerrie, is there a skeleton in this cupboard?"

"Oh, skeletons in cupboards!" said Kerensa scornfully. "That's just one of the silly things they say that are not real. There are no real skeletons. It means, I think, that there's a bad secret."

"A secret in the cupboard?"

"No, not in the cupboard . . . but anywhere . . . a secret that grown-up people don't want to talk about openly . . . but just whisper about when they think people like us are not listening."

"Kerrie, I think there is something in this cupboard." He opened the door. "There's a funny smell. Tell me all about the things in the cupboard."

"There's the paste and the brush on the top shelf with our scrap-books. Then there are other books on the other shelf with our exercise books. There's a pot of ink."

"Everything in this cupboard smells different from things in other places. Can you smell it?"

"No."

"These books have it . . . as well as their own smell. Put your head in, Kerrie. Smell. It's like orange peel."

"Perhaps they used to put oranges here."

"It's like apples too . . . apples that have got wrinkled and are going bad inside."

"They may have kept fruit in here."

"But it's only *like* them. It's not them. There's one of those skeletons here, Kerrie. That's why Papa is so different in this room."

"Nick, don't tell anyone about the skeleton. Let's find it and keep it to ourselves."

"Yes," said Dominick. "I think it's a bad skeleton, Kerrie."

"How do you know?"

"Because Papa and Mamma are sadder in here than anywhere else."

They shut the cupboard door and went back to their places at the table. Kerensa read another story and temporarily forgot about the cupboard. But she remembered later, and sought out Lilith.

She had never liked Lilith, but since her illness her dislike had grown. All Kerensa's emotions were violent; indifference was something she rarely felt. She knew now that there was another grown-up secret which had to be discovered, and this was far more important to her than the one in the cupboard because it concerned the relationship between Frith and Lilith.

Intuitively she knew that she was more likely to discover the secret of the cupboard through Lilith than through anyone else, so she sprung a question on her, hoping to catch her off her guard: "What was in the nursery before it was a nursery?"

She had the satisfaction of seeing Lilith start.

"Well, it was a bedroom."

"Whose bedroom?"

"What questions you ask! Why do you want to know?"

"Because I like to know what happened before I was born."

"I always thought you imagined the world didn't begin till you was born."

"Oh yes it did. In the beginning God made it, didn't He? And

there was Adam and Eve first. That was years and years before
I was born.''

"I wonder He didn't make a Kerensa instead of an Eve!''

Kerensa gravely considered this and agreed that it would have
been a good plan.

"Well," she said, "He didn't. But whose room was that?''

"It was your father's wife . . . his first wife.''

Kerensa felt a thrill run through her. The wife her father had
had before he married her mother! Here was a clue to the rela-
tionships between men and women. Might it not be that if she
discovered the skeleton in the nursery cupboard she might understand the relationship between Frith and Lilith?

"There's a funny smell in the cupboard. What was kept
there?''

"Shall I tell you? Whisky, brandy and gin. You know what
they are, don't you?''

"Yes. I know what they are.''

"Well, don't go talking about them, because it might upset
your Mamma if you did. You see, the first Mrs. Stockland was
so fond of them that she kept them locked in that cupboard.
Fancy you sniffing them out!''

"It was Dominick.''

"I see. Well, don't you go telling anyone I told you, will you?
It might upset your Mamma.''

"Why?''

"Why? When? How? How many times a day do you say
them?''

"You have to. How would you know anything if you didn't?''

Lilith looked at her almost shyly. She was a lovely girl, an
enchanting child, the most attractive of all the children except,
of course, Leigh, and some would say Dominick. Lilith wished
Kerensa was fond of her; she would have been ready to make a
pet of Kerensa. She could see so much in her that she understood
and sympathized with. It was odd that Kerensa seemed determined to be the least friendly of them all. Moreover, Lilith had
plans for Kerensa. Kerensa and Leigh were going to marry one
day.

"Of course you've got to ask questions if you're going to find
out things," she said placatingly. "Well, look. I'll tell you
something. Your father's first wife was in that room . . . day
and night she was there because she was very sick. And she

liked to drink, which was bad for her. She kept the drink locked away in that cupboard so that people shouldn't know how much she took. Now, not a word of this, remember. It wasn't a happy marriage, and your father wants to forget all about it, so don't you start anything with your hows and whys and whens, will you?''

"No," said Kerensa, more excited than she wished to show, "I'll not start anything."

She sought out Dominick and told him. "I've found the skeleton, Nick. The smell is brandy, gin and whisky. Papa had a wife before Mamma, and it was unhappy, so he wants to forget."

Dominick nodded slowly. "That's right. It's a want-to-forget sort of voice he uses."

"So we mustn't say anything, Dominick . . . not to anybody. I'm glad it wasn't a real skeleton . . . under the boards. I shouldn't have liked that."

"I'm glad it's something that's all over, Kerrie."

Kerensa nodded, but she was not sure that things like that were ever all over.

She was older than Dominick, and for all his wisdom she was sure he did not know quite so much about the strange world of grown-ups as she did.

For Amanda the years went peacefully by, marked by those gala days: the children's birthdays when there were parties in the library; Christmas, when there was a decorated tree bright with tinsel and presents, according to the modern custom which the Prince Consort had made popular; summer holidays spent in the country with Hesketh's mother. Her life was devoted to Hesketh and the children. She believed that Hesketh was happy now and that the qualms of conscience which he had suffered during the first years of their married life were quietened. The idea that Dominick had been born blind because of his father's sin in loving Amanda before Bella was dead, seemed to have been expunged. They had young Dennis now, a sturdy, normally healthy boy, not quite as lovable as Dominick it was true, but who could be as lovable as Dominick?

Amanda often thought tenderly of her children. None of them was jealous of Dominick towards whom no one could help showing extra tenderness. Claudia and Martie would squabble over a doll or a picture book; but none of them ever denied Dominick what he wanted. Perhaps the reason was that Dominick never demanded anything he thought the others wanted. Amanda had begun to think that Dominick's affliction was not an affliction after all, since the little blind boy seemed to instil the other children with kindness, toleration and responsibility towards the weak.

And so, apart from minor storms, slight worries, small differences, it was a happy household.

Even Lilith was contented. Her relationship with Frith was irregular, but it had gone on for so long that it merely seemed like an unusual kind of marriage. Frith had never married; he seemed satisfied with things as they were. He was not a conscientious worker as Hesketh was. She suspected now that his desire for a profession in those long-ago Cornish days had been merely a desire to escape from the restrictions of country life. He had a small but exclusive clientele of rich people—mostly women. He gave himself largely to pleasure and travelled a good deal, spending most of the winter months out of England and leaving his assistant to deal with the rich women. "They appreciate me the more," he said, "if I am not always with them."

He was selfish and lazy, he declared; he would never have interested himself in Dr. Barnardo's Home as Hesketh had done. Hesketh was so serious, so determined to lead a useful life. This he did, always working hard, never sparing himself, dedicating much of his time to charity.

Amanda had met Frith's sister Alice and Anthony, her cousin, when they had visited London. Frith said it was quite absurd of them not to meet. She had enjoyed renewing her acquaintance with Alice; they found they had much in common since Alice had now borne six children. As for Anthony, Amanda wondered how she could ever have been afraid of this plump middle-aged man. She fancied he bore her a little grudge for running away from him; but he soon forgot that. After all he had lost nothing by her desertion since he was now her father's heir; and Amanda was sure that Alice made him a more satisfactory wife than she ever would have done.

Alice said that Amanda's mother often talked of her and how she would like to meet her grandchildren. Perhaps, suggested Alice, when she and her husband next visited London they might bring Amanda's mother with them.

When Alice and Anthony had returned to Cornwall Amanda began to receive letters from her mother. That was comforting. It was like healing an old wound.

So the time passed. Birthdays, Christmasses, minor ailments of the children, watching them grow, worrying a little over them, loving them a great deal . . . this was the family life for which she had always longed.

With Dennis now four years old, and a nurse as well as Miss Robinson to help with the children, Amanda found she had time to help Hesketh in his charitable works. This had begun when she had gone with him to Tom Barnardo's new home in the East End and had seen the children whom this good man had gathered in from the streets, and had listened to the pitiful tales he had told.

This was the real charity, she had thought then. Men like Barnardo, who did the practical things, were the true philanthropists. David and William had had dreams . . . flimsy dreams. David's had been born of a rich man's conscience, William's of a poor man's resentment; but they had been merely dreams—the result of personal feelings. Now that she knew a true reformer, a practical man, she could see the difference. Tom did not say: ''These are the rights of the case and those are the wrongs.'' He said: ''Homeless children are starving in the streets of London; therefore I will give them a home; I will give them food; I will teach them a trade; I will arrange for them to emigrate and make a place for themselves in the world.''

And thus the children grew out of their childhood. Kerensa was fourteen years old and Leigh—whom Amanda had come to regard as her own as much as Lilith's—was eighteen.

Leigh came home for holidays. He was doing very well in his painstaking way. He enjoyed coming home for he was devoted to the family; quiet and reserved, he was happiest at home.

He loved his mother, knowing that he owed a good deal to her. He was fully aware of the great devotion she gave him—not that she stressed this—and the desire that he should know nothing but happiness and success. He was aware of his slight relation to this family, and this knowledge made him gratefully accept their unanimous inclusion of him. He was conscious, as Kerensa and Dominick had been, that there were secrets in this house which he might one day learn; but unlike Kerensa he was not eager to know these secrets. He accepted the fact that there was a place for him in this beloved family, and that was all that concerned him.

Homecoming was a joyful time. When the train steamed into the station he would eagerly scan the platform to see who had come to meet him. His mother was usually there with perhaps Amanda; he always hoped that Kerensa would accompany them. Lilith's eyes would shine as she noticed how much he had grown, and she would want to hear in detail—although understanding little—about the examinations he had passed. It was her dream that he should be a great doctor . . . and a gentleman. He never forgot that prayer she had taught him: "Please God make me a good boy and a gentleman."

That told him a good deal, because it explained how she had worked for him, planned for him, how she had longed to give him a chance in life which, but for the beneficence of the doctor, would have been denied him.

But most of all when he came home he wanted to see Kerensa. He loved Kerensa. He wished that she were older; and yet at times he was glad that she was not. As he was only eighteen himself it was better for Kerensa to remain a child until he was a little older. Perhaps when he was twenty-one and Kerensa was seventeen, he could talk to her.

If Kerensa had not been so beautiful, so enchanting, so different from everyone else, he might have wondered whether his mother had put the idea into his head as, he suspected, she had put many more. He knew that his mother wanted him to marry Kerensa.

He had not meant to speak to Kerensa during those holidays, but she had seemed so grown-up, much older than her fourteen years. She wore her dark hair tied back with stiff black ribbon and seemed quite a young lady now. She was glad he was home. He was her favourite brother, she thought, because, although she loved Dominick she couldn't be cross with him as she could with Leigh, and there were times when she wanted to be cross.

"Kerensa," he said, "I'm so glad I'm your favourite, because . . ."

"Because what?"

"Never mind. I'll tell you later."

But Kerensa was not the sort of person who could ever wait for anything.

"No. You must tell me now."

So he had told her. "In a year or two I want you to marry me."

"I can't do that. You'll have to marry someone else. You're like my brother. Brothers and sisters can't marry."

"But we're not brother and sister."

"I said it seems like it."

"Never mind what it seems like. We're not."

"All the same, I can't. I'm going to marry someone else."

"Someone else? Who?"

"Well, it wouldn't be fair to tell you, because he does not know yet."

"Kerensa! It's just a game you're playing. I'm serious."

"I'm serious too." And she would say no more.

Lilith noticed her son's depression. She asked him what it meant, but he did not tell her until the day before he went back to college.

"It's Kerensa. She's going to marry someone else."

"Don't you believe that!" said Lilith. "She's going to marry you."

"She's told me there's someone else."

Lilith laughed. "Kerensa! She's just a baby. You wait. Why, I've always meant you two to marry."

"But if she won't . . ."

"Leave it to me," said Lilith.

She looked powerful and confident, and Leigh felt as he had when he was a small boy, sure of her omnipotence.

Kerensa walked solemnly down the street and rang the bell at Frith's house. Napoleon answered the door.

"Hello, Napoleon. I want to see your master. At once, please. It's very urgent."

Napoleon looked alarmed. He remembered that other occasion when she had walked in rather like this and had been so very ill afterwards.

Napoleon hurried up the stairs. "Not sick, Miss Kerensa? Not ill again?"

"Oh no. But it's very important."

Frith was in his room on the first floor.

"Miss Kerensa be here, sir," said Napoleon, throwing open the door.

Frith put down his book and got up. "This is an unexpected honour," he said.

Kerensa advanced, still rather solemnly, and gave him her hand.

"How do you do, Miss Stockland."

She smiled delightedly. It was the first time he had ever called her that.

"I'm glad you realize that I'm grown up. Not just Kerensa any more . . . only to my friends, of course."

"So you've grown up overnight and I'm not to call you Kerensa any more, but Miss Stockland. Does that mean I'm not one of your friends?"

"Of course *you* can call me Kerensa as much as you like."

"I'm glad. I was beginning to think that some of my sins had come to your ears."

She laughed. He could always amuse her. He always had. That was what she loved about him—a grown-up man, not exactly wicked, she supposed, but very near it.

"I want to talk to you. I know this is very unusual."

"Not unusual at all. You talk a good deal. In fact, far too much."

"Frith, you've got to be very serious for a bit. I'm thinking of the future . . . yours and mine."

"Yours *and* mine?"

"Have you ever thought of marriage?"

"I confess I have hovered near the brink of folly once . . . or perhaps twice . . . in my long and adventurous career, but I have managed, as you know, in spite of many dangers, to steer a lonely course."

"But you don't want to go on steering a lonely course. Every man ought to be married."

"Kerensa, don't tell me you have found a wife for me!"

She smiled complacently. "Well, as a matter of fact, I have."

"What an amazing child you are! Once you burst upon me chockful of cholera germs, and now you would provide me with a wife. Do you know, I think I might consider the germs the more acceptable. But who is the lady?"

"She's hardly a lady."

"Oh, that's too bad."

"But she will be one day. She's a girl at the moment." She

hurried on: "I think you like her quite a lot—more than you pretend to—and I think you'll be very happy with her."

"How old is she?"

"She's fourteen, but a grown-up fourteen."

"She's not by any chance . . . yourself!"

"Of course."

"Oh . . . Kerensa!"

He sat back in his chair and began to laugh. She ran to him, sat on his knee, and, grasping his shoulders, began to shake him.

"Frith, stop it and be serious."

"I am. I am. I'm collecting my wits. I think the thing to say on an occasion like this is 'Oh . . .' very coyly, you know. 'But this is so sudden! I greatly appreciate the honour, but . . .' "

"*But!*" cried Kerensa fiercely.

"Well, you see, you are so very young and I'm so very old, and it was once said by one who was considered an authority on such matters that youth and crabbed age could not live together."

"What's crabbed age?"

"My sort."

"Well, it *can* live with youth, and the poet is wrong. Poets almost always are."

"Kerensa," he said, "you just don't understand . . ."

"Of course I understand. I want to marry *you*. Not yet of course. But in two years' time. Will you wait for me?"

He put his arms about her and held her tightly against him. But he was laughing again and his laughter angered her.

"You *must* be serious!" she said, wriggling free.

"I am, Kerensa. But do you know how old I am?"

"Stop talking about ages. That's not important. I've wanted to marry you for years. You must tell me frankly. Is there anyone else?"

"Anyone else where?"

"Anyone else you want to marry, of course."

"I'm not what is known as a marrying man."

"Not till now, of course. But you can be in two years' time."

"It's a very big step, you know, Kerensa—marriage."

"I know all about marriage."

"Then you're very knowledgeable."

"Do you love me?"

"Of course I do."

"Then that's all that matters. You'll have to love me best in the whole world, you know. There mustn't be anyone else."

"Oh, Kerensa, I adore you."

She put her arms about his neck and hugged him.

He said: "It was sweet of you to put on a black ribbon and come and ask me to marry you, but I think if I were you I wouldn't bind myself just yet."

"I want to bind myself."

"You see, when people are your age they get old so slowly, and when they're my age they get old so quickly. In two years' time you'll laugh at the thought of marrying me."

"I shall not. I didn't laugh at the thought of marrying you years ago. I always knew I would one day."

"Kerensa, you mustn't sweep me off my feet like this."

"Then will you marry me when I'm sixteen?" He was silent, and she stood up and stamped her foot angrily. "You can't believe I'm grown up. You keep treating me like a little girl. I won't have it. I won't have it. I want a straightforward answer."

"All right, Kerensa. In matters of this sort which can't be decided on the spot for some reason or other, people have what's called a compromise. Let's leave it like this: The matter stands in abeyance for two years. If at the end of that time you still consider me a worthy husband, we'll review the situation. How's that?"

"I should have preferred you to say 'Yes' now."

"You are a very impetuous lover, and as I said, I am in danger of being swept off my feet. That must not be. I insist on there being two years during which we shall go on as we are. And then we'll see what you want at the end of that time."

"But I must have your promise not to marry anyone else until I'm sixteen."

"I think I shall be safe for two years, since I have been for so many."

"All the same, you must swear."

"I swear."

"Thank you, Frith."

"Thank you, Miss . . . may I call you Kerensa? You said we might revert to the old relationship."

"You may call me what you like, but you mustn't make fun of me. This is a very serious matter to me."

He took her hand and kissed it.

''To me too, Kerensa,'' he said.

Lilith was quick to discover why Kerensa did not wish to marry Leigh.

Kerensa was fifteen, and Lilith remembered her own feelings at fifteen. She had loved Frith then; and Kerensa loved Frith now. It was true that there were more than twenty years between their ages—in fact nearer thirty—but Frith would be attractive all his life. Lilith, who had always been aware of that attraction, understood the meaning of Kerensa's withdrawn moods which were the exasperation of the rest of the family. She knew that Kerensa often called on Frith, and this, Lilith thought with unwonted primness, should not be allowed. She had been about to point this out to Amanda, when she had stopped herself. She fancied that this passion of Kerensa's for a man old enough to be her father must be dealt with by the subtlest methods.

Moreover she recognized a good deal of herself in Kerensa, and that alarmed her.

As to Frith's feelings for the child, she was quite unsure of them. *He* was not fifteen, to give himself away. He was inordinately fond of her, that much was certain. Birthday presents for Kerensa were chosen with the greatest care and were more magnificent than those presented to the other children. It was the same at Christmas time. He was also spending more and more time with the family, and Lilith had heard him ask more than once that Kerensa be allowed to stay up half an hour later; and she had noticed that he left soon after Kerensa retired.

Lilith would not have said that Frith was a vain man; yet she supposed such blatant adoration as Kerensa offered was irresistible—particularly to a man nearer forty than thirty. Kerensa was a budding beauty; she was reaching urgently towards maturity as though she believed she could outwit nature and catch up with Frith. It would be difficult to be indifferent to such devotion.

Once when Amanda had said, ''Oh, Frith, don't let Kerensa tire you. She just hangs round you all the time!'' Kerensa had given her mother a look which seemed to contain hatred. Kerensa was as single-minded as Lilith had been, and as determined, as capable of passionate devotion, of ruthlessness toward anyone who stood in her way; and Lilith was seriously perturbed.

Of course Leigh was the one for Kerensa. Their marriage was
to be Lilith's final triumph. Moreover, she herself loved Frith
and he loved her. She had never wanted anyone but Frith; and
she did not believe that he would ever want to discard her . . .
but she was afraid of the effect of this young girl's persistent
devotion. He pretended to treat this as though it were a charming
joke; but Lilith was not sure that he regarded it entirely in that
way.

On Kerensa's fifteenth birthday Frith gave her a fur muff, a
most expensive present, the sort a husband might give to a wife,
a lover to his mistress. And there was Kerensa in a new dress
of blue velvet that matched her eyes, carrying her muff at her
birthday party because she refused to be separated from it even
for a moment.

When she blew out the fifteen candles on her cake and thanked
them for their good wishes, she said: "I hope you all realize
that this time next year I shall be quite grown-up."

She had looked at Frith when she had said that.

At the party they had talked of the old pleasure gardens so
many of which had closed down.

"I don't think," said Frith, "that the children will enjoy the
lights and fireworks, the open glades as we did. Cremorne's on
its last legs, so they say."

Kerensa cried: "Oh, I've never been. I *do* want to go."

"We must see that you do before it's too late," said Frith.

"When, Frith? Will you take me?"

"Kerensa," said Amanda, "you must not ask to be taken,
my love."

"Oh, Frith . . . Frith . . . ask me quickly," pleaded Kerensa.

Frith said: "Kerensa, may I have the pleasure of conducting
you to Cremorne?"

"Yes, Frith, I *think* I could manage to fit it in. When did you
wish to go?"

"Oh, some time."

"Well, I want to go soon. This week."

"I am, of course, at your command."

If ever I saw a girl in love, thought Lilith, that girl's Kerensa.

Amanda was just the same Amanda who had never seen anything, even when it was right under her nose. She thought the
shine in Kerensa's eyes was due to a birthday cake with fifteen
candles and the elegance of a fur muff.

So they planned to go to Cremorne together, and during the days between the birthday party and the visit to the pleasure gardens, Lilith's jealous fears had grown to such an extent that she too must go to Cremorne on the afternoon that they chose.

She saw them, but they did not see her. They were, she imagined, too absorbed in each other, Kerensa openly so, Frith pretending to himself that he was indulging the child, though it seemed to Lilith that he was not so much indulging the child as courting the woman. Did he seriously intend to marry Kerensa?

Lilith sat some distance away, watching them: the jealous mistress and—more than that—the angry mother. Kerensa was going to marry Leigh. Frith did not care perhaps if he made Lilith suffer, and Kerensa did not care if she made Leigh suffer. But Lilith cared.

I shall never let it happen, swore Lilith.

And then, suddenly, she saw a strange sight which made her temporarily forget even Frith and Kerensa. A party of about a dozen was coming across the grass—a man in very colorful clothes and a fat woman who was obviously his wife with their seven . . . eight . . . no, nine children.

"Here's the spot, Fan," said the man. "The very spot. Now young shaver, you just set the 'amper down here and we'll see what your Ma's put in it."

"Come on, Sammy," said the woman. "You heard what your father said."

Sammy! And there was Sammy, the replica of Sam, well-dressed in gaudy garments, the lock of hair ready to lie across his forehead when it was adequately greased, just the sort of boy who would grow into the successful proprietor of supper-rooms.

"Now . . . what's this? Anchovy samwich, eh? Ham . . . and these here patties . . . *and* a nice little something to wash it down with."

Lilith got up and hurried away. Sam! Fan! And their children.

She wanted to laugh, because she was aware of an immense relief. She realized now how many qualms of conscience she had had since she had wheeled Leigh out of Sam Marpit's Supper-rooms. She might have guessed. It was the inevitable conclusion. Everything was all right at Marpit's then. Sam had his Fan now; he even had his Sammy.

She stopped short and almost turned back to them; she wanted to congratulate them and say: "I'm glad. I'm so glad!"

They were a happy family. She could hear their shouts now.

Then she remembered that her beloved boy was probably going to break his heart over Kerensa and that she herself was going to lose the only man she could ever love. She could not help feeling then a little envious of Sam and Fan.

But she would not allow it to happen, of course. She would stop it. She had tackled bigger problems with success. Chance had come to Sam's aid. Fan had been beside him waiting to comfort him, to open up a new life. She, Lilith, had made her own chances before, and she would do so again.

It was the end of January and in three months' time Kerensa would have her sixteenth birthday. She was solemn, serene and very sure of herself.

Leigh came home full of talk about what he was doing at college, closeting himself with Hesketh, talking of his future; for with Leigh, Hesketh had reached an understanding such as he had failed to achieve with his own children.

Hesketh never ceased to marvel that so much good could grow out of evil. He had been blackmailed into treating this boy as his own son, and it was this very boy who had given him more affection than his own children. Life was not the conventional thing it was reputed to be; bad seed was supposed to produce bad fruit. But life was full of a hundred odd twists and turns, a thousand complications. Out of Bella's death had grown a happy family; out of Lilith's blackmail, another son for him.

"You are glad you followed me in my career?" he asked Leigh.

"Indeed, yes. To be a doctor . . . to belong to this family . . . that's what I want almost more than anything."

"Almost?" asked Hesketh.

"Well," said Leigh flushing a little, "there's something else I want very much. It's to marry Kerensa. Would you . . . consent to that?"

"I can think of no one I'd rather have for my son-in-law. I know Kerensa's mother feels the same. It's only Kerensa's consent you have to get."

"She is so young yet."

"You are both young, but her mother and I would both be pleased to hear that you had made up your minds."

After that he could not resist speaking once more to Kerensa.

She looked quite the young woman now, with her black bow of stiff ribbon and the locket and gold chain which she almost always wore. She had the air of being impatient with her youth.

When they rode together in the Park he said: "Kerensa, how would you like to be married?"

She was alert, restrained and quite unlike herself.

"That would depend on the husband," she said after a pause.

"What sort of a husband do you think I'd make?"

"Very nice." He laughed, but she continued very quickly: "For the right person."

Then she began enumerating possible brides for him—the daughters of her parents' friends; she even suggested Claudia, if, she added, he was prepared to wait for her to grow up.

"And men ought to wait," she said. "They shouldn't marry too soon. They . . . they need time to look round and have experiences."

"Kerensa, what do you mean?"

"Just what I say."

"Kerensa, *I* don't want to look round and have . . . experiences."

"Then that's very unnatural and unusual."

"Kerensa, you'll be sixteen soon, and, a year after that, seventeen. That's a good age for a girl to marry. I've always wanted to marry you."

"Oh, Leigh, *don't*. I can't marry you. I told you so before."

"What is all this nonsense about someone else?"

"It is not nonsense."

"Who is it?"

"I won't tell you. I can't."

"There is not anyone. I should know if there was."

She was silent.

"Oh, Kerensa," he went on, "your father says he won't hold back his consent to our marriage. We could be engaged now. You do love me, don't you?"

"Of course I love you. I love you like Dominick and Claudia and Martie and Dennis. I love you more than the babies. They cry too much. I love you more than any of them . . . except perhaps Nick. But that's not the way you have to love for marriage."

"You're too young to understand."

"I'm not too young, and it annoys me when people say I am."

"You will marry me. It's a matter of getting used to the idea."
She said nothing; but he had never seen her look so stubborn.
He was seriously worried now, and his mother noticed it.

"Leigh, my handsome, you're not worried about college?"
"No, Mamma."
"Something's on your mind."

He did not tell her immediately, but she found out that it was
due to Kerensa who could not marry Leigh because she was in
love with someone else.

Lilith was furious. How far had this ridiculous state of affairs
gone, between a girl still in the nursery and Lilith's rake of a
lover?

She did not know which way to turn; she was waiting, brooding, watching, convinced that when the time came she would
know how to act.

"So you told the doctor that you wanted to marry his daughter
and he gave his consent, eh?"

That was wise of him, she thought; if he had not . . . She
was the old Lilith, the Lilith who had faced Farmer Polgard,
who had taken Leigh from his father, who had staked everything
on what she had to say to Hesketh after Bella's death. She was
not going to let a silly girl from the nursery take her lover or
break the heart of her beloved son.

Lilith was not really sorry when she heard that Frith was going
away on one of his jaunts to the Continent. Each year he took a
trip to Italy or the South of France, avoiding the worst of the
winter. Lilith had always suspected that there was some attraction other than the sun. She pictured a beautiful woman somewhere, easy-going, ready to welcome him when he came to her
on his yearly visits. He had laughed at her when she had chal-
lenged him, but he had not denied it; he had talked round it
cleverly, and she thought she knew him well enough to understand.

Usually she sulked a little when he prepared to leave. Two or
three months without him! How did he expect her to remain
faithful? He would watch her lashing herself into fury over the
beautiful unknown. He would tease her, describing the woman,
and the description was different every time.

Now she was glad he was going. It meant that he did not
consider Kerensa's devotion with any great seriousness; he saw
her as an amusing child, nothing more.

Kerensa heard of his departure first through her mother. She was infuriated to think that he had not told her himself. She went along to see him at once.

"Kerensa," he said, "don't you know that you should not call on me unchaperoned? At one time you behave like a sedate young woman, at another like a child."

She ignored that. "Why are you going away?"

"It has become a habit to go away at this time of the year. I don't like February and March in London."

"I would like February and March in Greenland if you were there."

"Now that's charming of you, darling, but you have never been to Greenland. I believe the Eskimoes never leave their igloos during the winter months. You wouldn't like that, I'm sure."

"It's just what I should like. If we were Eskimoes you'd have to stay in the igloo too."

"Alas! We are not Eskimoes!"

"Why didn't you tell me you were going?"

"Didn't I?"

"You know you didn't."

"I'm sorry, Kerensa, but you know, it is rather a habit of mine to go, and one does not speak of one's habits."

"In view of the fact that we are going to be married, I think you have treated me very badly."

"Oh, Kerensa!" He came to her and put his hands on her shoulders. He kissed her swiftly. "Do you still think of me as your future husband?"

"You're not going back on your promise, I hope."

"You're growing up, you know."

"Frith!"

"Darling, don't look like that. I'd do anything rather than hurt you. I'd elope to-morrow rather than do that. You know that."

"Elope? Oh, do let's."

"Let's be serious, Kerensa; really serious this time."

"I always am. It's you who won't be."

"You've got a romanticized picture of me, darling. See me as I am. Just look at my face. It's rather horrible with all the excesses of my misspent youth printed on it."

"You're very handsome."

"And you're very blind."

She stamped her foot. "I believe you're going back on your promise. You said we could be married when I was sixteen, and now I nearly am, you're pretending it's a game."

Her voice trembled and he put his arms about her, kissing her first tenderly, then passionately.

"It's not true, Kerensa," he said. "Listen. I'm going away. I shan't come back until you're sixteen. And then if you still want me . . ."

"Frith . . . you swear?"

"I swear."

"Then we're engaged."

"There's no need for an engagement. If you want to marry me when I come back we'll speak to your parents. It depends on them, you know."

"Of course it doesn't. We could run away."

"They have to give their consent."

"You could get anyone's consent if you wanted it."

"They might have other plans for you."

"Leigh!" she said. "That's just because they don't see."

"Leigh's very nice," said Frith. "Have you considered that?"

"Of course I have."

"And you still prefer this old rake to that handsome young man!"

"I don't want anyone but you, and it's no use pretending you don't love me. I know you do by the way you kissed me just now. It was a wonderful kiss. Nobody could kiss like that unless they were in love."

"Mightn't it be because they had had a certain amount of experience in kissing?"

"No. No, Frith! We'll be secretly engaged."

"You wait until I come back. Don't commit yourself till then. It's always wiser not to commit yourself, Kerensa."

He sent her home then. She wished she knew whether he really loved her as he ought to love her. You could never be sure of Frith. He had never quite meant what he said; he bantered; he joked. Sometimes you thought he was serious when he was joking, and sometimes you thought he was joking when he was serious. It was maddening, but perhaps it was just that which made him so attractive.

When Frith went away, several of them drove to the station to

see him off. There were Amanda, Lilith, Kerensa and Dominick.

They were all rather silent as they drove along.

"I hate saying goodbye to anyone," said Amanda, "even if
they are just going for a holiday."

" 'Parting,' " said Frith, " 'is such sweet sorrow.' How right
that is! It's sorrowful to say goodbye and so sweet of you all to
take the trouble to come and see me off."

He seemed to keep aloof from Kerensa. She had seen Lilith
come home late on the previous night; it was well past midnight
when she had come along the street, and Kerensa had known
that she came from Frith's house. Kerensa had seen her leave
and had waited at her window to watch for her return; she had
been stiff with cold when she had climbed into bed.

How dared Lilith keep him up like that . . . talking . . . talking, she supposed, because he was going away on the next day.

They stood on the platform. Kerensa was desperately hoping
that the train would break down and that he would be unable to
go. She looked at Lilith and knew that she was wishing the
same.

But the train did go and Frith had kissed them all round; and
while he kissed Lilith, Kerensa was watching him, and while he
kissed Kerensa, Lilith watched him.

When they were driving back, Dominick said: "Everybody's
quiet. Everybody's being rather queer."

"We're sad because we shan't see Frith for a long time," said
Amanda. "But it won't really be so long. Time does fly so."

Lilith did not hesitate when Frith had gone. She had not very
much time. She was fully aware of that.

She chose an evening three nights after he had left, and went
along to Kerensa's room.

Kerensa, in view of her increasing years, had had for some
time a room of her own. It was one of the things she had insisted
on when she wished to be treated as an adult; she could not, she
had declared, go on sharing the night nursery with a lot of babies.

And, as usual, Kerensa had had her desire granted.

To this room Lilith now made her way, her thick curling hair
about her shoulders; she was wearing a beautiful red velvet
dressing gown which Frith had given her. She took a candle and

examined herself in the mirror before she went to Kerensa's room. She looked very beautiful and rather wicked, she believed; and that was how she wished to look, for so much depended on how she played her part. She must remember there was nothing meek about Kerensa; she must think of herself at sixteen—bold, ruthless, fierce in love and hate. All these characteristics she shared with Kerensa, so she ought to understand her well. And she would remember also that Kerensa was nothing more than a child.

She knocked at Kerensa's door and opened it. "Kerensa," she whispered, "are you asleep?"

Kerensa sat up in bed, startled. The firelight played about the room. Lilith stood at the foot of the bed, holding the candle. She looked, to Kerensa, like an apparition, beautiful and wicked. She had never realized until this moment how very beautiful Lilith was. She looked exciting and alarming.

"I hope I didn't frighten you, Kerensa. I want to speak to you alone . . . very seriously . . . and I thought this was the best time to do it."

"No. You didn't frighten me. What do you want to say?"

Lilith continued to stand at the foot of the bed, holding the candle so that in its flattering glow she looked like a young girl, as young as Kerensa herself.

"It's about Leigh, Kerensa. He's very unhappy. In fact, he's heartbroken."

"I'm sorry."

"It's because he loves you and has set his heart on marrying you."

"I know, and I'm fond of him, but marrying someone is so important. You can't do it just because someone wants you to. You have to be in love. I can't marry Leigh."

"Why not? Is it because you hope to marry Frith?"

Kerensa drew back against the pillows, and Lilith leaned forward. Her eyes were gleaming and Kerensa thought she looked as if she would like to kill her.

"Is it?" said Lilith. "Is it?"

"Yes . . ." stammered Kerensa.

"Has Frith asked you?"

Kerensa hesitated and Lilith laughed suddenly.

"What a question!" cried Lilith. "Of course he hasn't. Or if he has . . . it's for a joke."

"It's . . . it's not a joke."

"Do you think *I* don't know what Frith feels?"

Kerensa had begun to tremble. It was as though Knowledge was rapping on her brain, as though Lilith held out a key to her, as though she said: "You want to be grown-up. You want to know about us. Here is the key. Open the door and step through to . . . Knowledge." And Kerensa knew, from the way in which Lilith was smiling, that she was not going to like such knowledge; she knew that it was a hateful, ugly thing which was going to make her unhappy.

"Do you know what a mistress is, Kerensa?"

"Yes . . . like Mamma . . . to the servants."

"Not that sort. It's a woman who has a lover. They are not married . . . so she is called his mistress. I am Frith's mistress."

"It's not true. Not . . . now. Perhaps it was . . . once."

"It's true now. It's been true for years. I am married to Leigh's father, and because he is still alive Frith can't marry me. But when I am free he is going to. In the meantime, we live together . . . oh, not in the same house, but I think you know what I mean. I'm a wife . . . who is not a wife because we have not been to church."

"I know that's not true."

"Did Frith tell you it wasn't?"

"No. But I know."

"You don't know, Kerensa. You know very little. You are only a child. You haven't grown up yet. You think you have, because you're a bit older than Dominick and Claudia and the others . . . but you're only just growing up. You don't know anything about life and what people are like."

"I know what Frith is like."

"Has he said he will marry you? You can't say truthfully that he has, can you? He thinks you're a charming child who's got a feeling for him. He told me so."

"Frith told *you* about me!"

"Of course," lied Lilith. "He tells me most things. Just as your father tells your mother. That's our sort of relationship. I'm sorry to have to tell you all this. Your mother wouldn't like it. She thinks you ought to be sheltered, but sometimes I think it's better for people—however young they are—to know the truth."

"Do you mean that Frith . . . laughed at me!"

"'That's making him seem unkind. He did laugh . . . but just like you'd laugh at something little Dennis said.''

"I . . . I don't believe it.''

"'That's because you don't want to, my dear. The night before he went away, I was with him. You know what I mean, don't you?''

"Yes. . . . I think I do.''

"And you believe me, don't you?''

"No,'' said Kerensa, but she heard her voice break.

"I slipped out of this house and went along to his. I often do. He let me in. We went to his room . . .''

"Stop! Stop! Go away. I don't want to hear any more.''

But Lilith went on: "It was long after midnight when I came back.'' Kerensa knew this was true, for she had seen her return. This was the explanation. Pictures flashed in and out of Kerensa's mind; she remembered the way in which Lilith looked at him, the way he looked at Lilith, the smiles she had seen them exchange. "You see, Kerensa, you've been rather silly. Oh, it don't matter. Frith said it was very charming . . . the way you threw yourself at him. He thinks it's amusing. He likes you very much. But for your own sake don't be silly about it. Don't imagine that it's anything more than a joke to Frith.''

"I don't know why you've come here . . . just to torment me like this. Go away.''

"It's not to torment you, Kerensa. It's to make you see sense. No . . . it's not even that. It's on account of Leigh. My Leigh's unhappy, and you've made him so. That's something I won't allow.''

"He wants me to marry him, but I can't.''

"Why not? I reckon it would be good. Your father thinks so. So does your mother.''

"It's for me to think . . . not for them.''

"Oh no, it's not. It's for them to guide you. It's for parents to say who their children shall marry.''

"I wouldn't allow that.''

"Now look. They've always been kind to you. They've let you have a lot of your own way. But this is a thing you can't decide on in your own way, and they want you to marry Leigh.''

"How do you know?''

"Because Leigh's spoken to your father, and your father has said it is his will you should marry Leigh.''

"Well, then, it's because he doesn't know that . . ."

"That you've been having a little joke with Frith! Do you realize how much older he is than you?"

"Yes; and it makes no difference."

Lilith came round to the side of the bed; she set the candle on the table and stood, looking at Kerensa. Kerensa felt she was in the presence of something evil; she shrank farther back against her pillows.

"It does matter," said Lilith. "You'd see it in a year or two, even if he would marry you. But I tell you he's going to marry me. We were discussing it only the night before he went away."

"I don't believe it."

Lilith laughed; she leaned nearer so that her face was very close to Kerensa's. "You don't know anything. You don't know about men and the things they want. You think it's all having little jokes together and nice kisses. You've seen your mother and father together and you think that everybody's like they are. They're good people . . . but you don't know everything about *them*. Frith's not good. Nor am I. We're different. I tell you he has to have change. He's got to be amused, so in the winter he goes to see this Italian woman, and then he comes back to me. And he thinks it's funny because a little schoolgirl's in love with him . . . or thinks she is. I'll tell you how I first met Frith, shall I? I wasn't much older than you then . . . but, then, nor was he. I mean, of course, the night when we were first lovers. There had been a wedding . . . my sister's . . . and there was a crowd joking in the bedroom of the bride and groom, putting furze bushes in the bed."

Kerensa put her hands over her ears. "I don't want to hear about you and Frith."

"Are you afraid to hear it?"

Kerensa turned and buried her face in the pillows.

"Afraid!" cried Lilith. "That's what you are. Afraid!"

But she knew that Kerensa was not afraid of her; she was afraid of knowledge. She did not want to be enlightened by Lilith; she did not want to hear Lilith's account of what Frith had done.

"You believe me now, don't you?" said Lilith. "You believe that Frith and me have been lovers. You believe that even that last night . . . after he'd been so loving and tender with you . . . you believe that that night . . ."

Kerensa turned and glared at Lilith. "I said, 'Stop!' " she cried.

Lilith was ready to stop talking about Frith and herself for the time being, because she saw that she had won the first battle. But she had not finished with Kerensa yet.

"You're going to marry Leigh," she said.

"No. I'm not."

Lilith laid a hand on Kerensa's nightdress where it buttoned across her budding breasts.

"Don't touch me," said Kerensa.

"You are no longer a very little girl. You're nearly sixteen, and that's old enough to be married. My grandmother had been a wife . . . a sort of wife . . . long before she was your age . . . and I can tell you that Frith and me . . ."

"I'm not listening."

"You're going to. My boy loves you. If you don't marry him, he'll be miserable for the rest of his life."

"He won't. He'll love someone else."

"Like you'll love someone . . . not Frith?"

"He'll love someone else," said Kerensa stubbornly.

"He's a good boy; he's the best boy in the world. He'd be good and kind. Do you think he's not good enough for you?"

"No. Of course I don't. I love Leigh, and if . . ."

"And if it wasn't for Frith, eh? I'll tell you about Frith, and it's no good saying you won't listen, because you will."

Lilith began to talk then. It seemed to Kerensa that words crawled from her mouth like toads and snails in the fairy story—horrible words. Kerensa was shivering, trying not to listen and yet fascinated in a way she could not understand and unable to shut her ears. Lilith looked evil, her eyes gleaming, her mouth laughing, and the firelight playing on her face.

"Go away from me," cried Kerensa at last.

"Do you want to marry Frith now . . . even if he would marry you?"

"I don't want to marry anybody. Go away."

"It would be different if you married Leigh. He's good . . . like your father and mother. People like Frith and me . . . we're not good. Nothing would change me. Nothing would change Frith."

"I don't want to hear any more."

"To-morrow," went on Lilith, "you're going to talk to Leigh. You're going to talk to him, soft and gentle."

"I'm not."

"You are."

"You can't make me."

"I can make you and anyone in this house do what I want."

"How can you?"

"I did once . . . and I could again. Can you keep a secret?" Kerensa nodded.

Lilith spoke quickly and softly. "You know your father had a wife before your mother. He hated her. She was a drunkard. Your mother came here to look after her. I know what happened because I was here too. Her bedroom was in the nursery. You know the nursery cupboard . . . it was full of drink, intoxicating drink. She used to keep it locked." Kerensa was staring wide-eyed now. "She was ill . . . and your father and mother couldn't get married . . . just like Frith and me can't now. Frith and me . . . we're different. We don't let things like that stand in the way of making love. But there's some that do . . . and your father and mother were among them."

"What happened? . . . What happened in the nursery?"

"Imagine a bedroom with heavy curtains drawn across the window. Imagine a poor, sick, drunken woman. Your father was young then . . . younger than Frith is now . . . oh, a lot younger. Your mother was young too. Your father was sorry for his wife because she was very ill. He gave her something to drink so that . . ."

"So that what?"

"So that after drinking it, she never woke up again."

"Do you mean . . . he killed her?"

" 'Sh!" Lilith put her hand to her mouth. "Don't say that. It's not quite true. He . . . helped her . . . helped her out of this life. That's what he did."

"If Papa did that . . . it was right to do it."

Lilith's face was now so near to Kerensa's that Kerensa could see nothing but her wide black eyes.

"You love your mother very much, don't you? And in a way you love your father. You don't want him to fondle you . . . kiss you and cuddle you . . . like you do Frith." Lilith's laugh made Kerensa feel ashamed of everything she had ever felt for Frith.

"No. But you love him all the same. You'd do anything to keep him where he is, I reckon."

"Where Papa is? What do you mean?"

"In this nice, comfortable house, being the respected doctor and father of you all . . . quiet, a little stern sometimes with those of you that need it, not easy-going like your mother, but somehow right . . . just what you feel he ought to be. You wouldn't like a lot of trouble and things in the newspaper about him, would you?"

"I don't know what you're talking about."

"Yes; you do. You're not all that silly."

"Do you mean that there'd be trouble . . . scandal?"

"Yes; I do. There'd be trouble all right . . . big trouble."

"But it . . . it must have been long long ago."

"That don't matter. However long ago . . . they've means of telling."

"I don't believe it."

"Don't you?"

"I don't believe a word of what you've been saying. I'm going to ask them."

"Who will you ask?"

"My mother."

"Ah! She doesn't know. It was kept from her."

"Then I'll ask my father."

"I wouldn't, if I were you. As you said, it happened a long time ago. He's forgetting it now. It takes a long time to forget a thing like that. A man like your father gets haunted by a thing like that . . . no matter how much he tells himself he'd done right." Lilith caught Kerensa's wrist suddenly. "You like Leigh, don't you?"

Kerensa nodded.

"Do what your father wants. Do what I want and Leigh wants . . . and nobody need ever know what happened all those years ago."

"Does . . . Leigh know?"

"No. Only three people know. Your father . . . me . . . and you. And we don't want trouble, do we?"

"You want to make trouble for others. You're wicked."

"Yes; I am wicked. That's why I get what I want. I'm good for a time and then my wickedness comes over me. It's always been like that. It's because I want something that only wickedness will bring me, and when I want something I want it more than other people want things.''

''And now you're determined I shall marry Leigh.''

''I won't have you break my boy's heart.''

''What about mine?''

''You'll be all right. You couldn't have a better husband than my Leigh. All the wicked things I've done have been good things really. I've done evil so that good could come—not only to me, but to others. It's always been like that, I reckon; and one of the best things I'll ever do is to stop you making a fool of yourself over Frith.''

''I won't be forced by you.''

''You will, because if you don't . . .''

''You wouldn't be so wicked. Even you, Lilith, couldn't be so wicked as that.''

''I would. You know I'll have my boy happy, no matter what I have to do.''

Lilith put her lips against Kerensa's forehead.

''Don't you worry. Everything's all right. He's safe. Your father's safe with us.''

''What if. . . ?'' began Kerensa.

''Don't talk about it, my dear. I don't like to think of what would happen if I had to do it. Don't make me. When I've made up my mind to something, it's got to be. So . . . don't make me. But you wouldn't. Of course you wouldn't. You're going to save your father and mother and my boy and your whole family from misery. That's a fine thing to do. It's a lot better than doing things I've been telling you about. . . .''

''Don't tell me any more.''

''I won't . . . not if you'll say you'll marry Leigh. Then it would all be different. You'd be happy and safe and comfortable with my Leigh. I want you and him married . . . soon. I want you to tell your father and your mother that you're going to marry Leigh next month.''

''They'll say I'm too young.''

''Nonsense! How many girls marry when they're sixteen? Lots of them. Why, they begin to call you an old maid if you reach nineteen without. They'll put nothing in the way, and if they do you've only got to be firm and stamp your little foot. You know how to do that. You've been doing it all your life. Good night, Kerensa.''

Lilith picked up her candle and went to the door.

Kerensa stared at the door long after it had closed behind
Lilith. She felt frightened and bewildered. It was too much to
have learned so quickly. She hated being alive, being a girl; she
hated Lilith, and she thought she hated Frith more than anyone.

She kept remembering things he had said to her, his laughter,
his joking way. He *had* been making fun of her. And all the
time he had been Lilith's lover . . . Lilith's horrible, obscene
lover!

She hated all grown-up people, including her own father and
mother. Yes, she hated them too, for Lilith had smeared them
with the slime. And they had loved—they must have loved—as
Lilith and Frith loved; and her father had done something even
more terrible.

But he was a good man—as good as any man could be. She
could never really believe he was anything else. Even Lilith had
said he was a good man.

She wanted to escape from this world of grown-up people;
she wanted to close the door which led to Knowledge and throw
away the key for ever.

She wanted to talk to somebody. To Dominick? He was too
young. How could she talk to him? She loved him, and he was
nice and clean, not evil like these grown-up people; but he would
not understand. There was Leigh, of course. Leigh was not one
of them. Leigh was kind, and she loved Leigh.

She would tell him everything. But she must not. It was a
terrible secret. She believed all that Lilith had told her, for she
had always known that something terrible had happened in that
room.

But even if Leigh did not know why he had to comfort her,
he would do so, and if she married Leigh she would save her
father and mother and her whole family . . . herself too.

Leigh was the only person older than herself of whom she
could bear to think. She was not afraid of Leigh. He had always
been so kind and he would help her now as he had helped her
so many times before.

Lilith had said that the only thing she could do was to marry
Leigh, and Lilith was right. She covered her face with her hands
and she dared not take them away from her face for fear she
would see the figure of Lilith standing at the foot of her bed . . .
Lilith, the symbol of all evil.

* * *

There were great preparations in the house.

"She is very young, of course," said Amanda to Hesketh, but she said it happily. She wanted this marriage. "It's not like her marrying a stranger, though; and when Kerensa makes up her mind, there's no stopping her."

"Kerensa is old for her years," said Hesketh. "After all, she'll be sixteen in a few weeks' time. I like these young marriages when the people concerned can be sure of themselves. They've known each other all their lives, and there's no one I'd rather see her marry than Leigh."

"How quiet she is! Almost solemn."

"Marriage is a solemn matter, my love."

"But you would not expect Kerensa to think that. She's so changed . . . so withdrawn."

Leigh and Kerensa were together every day. They walked in the Park and discussed the future. At first they would continue to live at home, just as though they had not married. When Leigh was qualified, Kerensa's father was going to take him into partnership.

"Papa is so delighted that I'm going to marry you. Anyone would think this was *his* wedding."

Leigh laughed. He laughed at everything she said. He was a darling, and she had always loved him dearly; she loved him more so now, because he represented safety in some odd way.

She said: "Leigh, I might be just a bit frightened about . . . things . . . at first."

He answered: "Don't worry. I might be too."

We're young, she thought. We're not grown-up really. We're not evil. We're just Kerensa and Leigh . . . the two who used to play together in the nursery.

"You used to say there was someone else," he said. "Were you just teasing?"

"I was silly, I suppose. You know who it was."

"Well . . . Frith, of course."

She nodded, and he laughed heartily as though that was a joke. It was a joke to everyone but herself.

"He's a real Don Juan, of course."

She tried to laugh. They all knew what Frith was. She was the only one who had been ignorant. She had been a fool.

"It's a pity he won't be here," said Leigh. "For the wedding, I mean. I'm sure he would have liked to be here."

Then she went to the edge of the Serpentine and stared into the water. A pity? If he were here she would never be able to marry Leigh, because whatever Frith was and however much he laughed at her, she would always love him. There were times when she believed she would not care about anything . . . however horrible . . . if only she could be with Frith.

"Do you remember when we used to get our feet wet?" she said.

He laughed. He was so happy. And she pretended to laugh heartily to explain the tears in her eyes.

Amanda said: "Here's another letter for Kerensa. It looks like Frith's writing."

Lilith held out her hand.

"It's for Kerensa," said Amanda.

Lilith felt dizzy. Nothing must go wrong now. In three days' time the wedding would take place. Three days and her Leigh would be a true son of the house.

What was in the letter? Lilith cursed herself for not having learned how to read. She could steam open the envelope, but what was the use if she could not read the contents of the letter?

She must take possession of it quickly.

"Give it to me. I'll take it to her."

Meekly Amanda handed it to her. Silly Amanda, who never changed in all the years. She still did not understand that Lilith must be furious at the sight of her lover's letter to another woman. Amanda did not think of Kerensa as another woman. She was blind . . . blind . . . blinder than Dominick.

Lilith thrust the letter into the pocket of her dress. She must make sure that Amanda did not mention the letter to Kerensa.

"I don't know what she'll say about his letter. Have you noticed she hates to talk of Frith?"

"Yes," said Amanda. "She never mentions him. Both her father and I have noticed it. A little while ago she hardly spoke without mentioning his name."

"You can guess how she feels. They're sensitive at that age. I reckon she fancies now she was a little foolish about him. Oh, all that's a joke to us . . . but when you're Kerensa's age, you take yourself seriously. Frith's a sore subject with our little bride.

I think I'll put the letter in her room and say nothing about Frith to her.''

"I think you're right," said Amanda with a laugh.

The bride who went up the aisle on Hesketh's arm was pale and beautiful.

Amanda, watching with tears in her eyes, thought she had never been quite so happy as she was on this day. Her husband and her eldest child! Hesketh was growing white at the temples, but how handsome, how noble he looked in her eyes! Willingly he gave their daughter to Leigh; she knew that he loved Leigh dearly, and that the marriage of the boy and his eldest daughter was something he had always wanted. And there was Kerensa, unusually subdued, in her white satin gown with the bustle skirt and the fine flowing lace headdress.

Lilith also watched, tense and triumphant. This was the culmination of Lilith's dream.

Leigh was putting the ring on Kerensa's finger and nothing could now stop this marriage.

Leigh, her son, was Amanda's son-in-law. They were linked now . . . more closely than they had ever been before.

She glanced at the bride and groom, and from them to little Dennis and Martie, so pretty in their wedding garments, and to Claudia, a self-important maid-of-honour.

She caught Amanda's eyes, and Amanda was smiling as though she read the thoughts of Lilith.

As they drove back to the house, Lilith said to Amanda: "There's someone who will be surprised when he hears of all this."

"Yes," agreed Amanda. "I do wish Frith could have come to Kerensa's wedding."

"He don't know," said Lilith. "Just think. They weren't engaged when he went away. It has all been so quick."

"That's like Kerensa," said Amanda with an affectionate sigh. "She can never wait once she makes up her mind. But there was that letter from him a few days ago, so I expect she knows where he is. I wonder if she wrote and told him. She was certain to. I didn't like to ask her. She seems so odd about him lately."

"It'll be a shock to him, I expect," said Lilith.

"Oh yes. He would have liked so much to be here."

"It'll teach him not to go away, and stay away," said Lilith grimly.

Kerensa was changing her dress. She was going away with Leigh on their honeymoon in a few hours' time.

Lilith came in.

There was a letter in Lilith's hand.

Kerensa did not speak as she entered; she went on fastening the buttons of her blouse.

"Here's something for you," said Lilith. "It came some days ago, but I forgot all about it with this going on. You'd better have it now."

Kerensa took the letter. "Frith . . . !" she gasped.

Her fingers were trembling as she opened the envelope. Lilith stood watching her, but Kerensa seemed to have forgotten she was there.

"Dearest Kerensa," Frith had written, "My best and most beloved Kerensa, Do you remember, as I do, that in a very short time you will have reached the important age of sixteen? I have been waiting for that day. I want to tell you, now that it is so near, how very much I love you, so much more than I have ever loved anyone in the whole of my life. In fact, I know now that I have never loved anyone before. I have seemed to laugh at your determination to love me, at your protestations of affection. I was greatly moved. I had to pretend to laugh, darling, because you were so young and I really could not believe that anything so wonderful could happen to me. You were always a queer little thing, an adorable little thing, so different from anyone else. I tried to pretend to myself that you were just a child, a particularly beloved child, as far as I was concerned . . . like a daughter. I never had one and cynically I told myself that all ageing men long for daughters. It seemed a new and compensating relationship when others were beginning to pall. That was not true, of course. I love you in a hundred ways. I've known it for a long time, and that was the reason I went away. I wanted you to think about me when I was not there, and to find out whether or not you really did want to marry me. Your happiness is more important to me than anything else. It's a queer thing, Kerensa, but I'm writing and thinking all sorts of things which, previously, I've considered trite and hackneyed. Perhaps being in love is rather trite and hackneyed . . . and perhaps all the most won-

derful things in life are . . . which is a comforting thought, when
you come to consider it.

"I love you, Kerensa. I want you to write to me at once and
tell me that you love me and that you still want to marry me.
But because I love you so much I want you to think of me not
as the sort of fairy godfather-uncle I may have seemed, but as a
man who is much older than yourself, and who is not a very
good person, who has done many shocking things, but who
wants now to reform because of you. Will you write to me at
once at this address and tell me you are waiting for me? Then
I'll come back immediately, and I'll talk to your father and
mother; and I think that in a little while I shall persuade them
that we ought to marry. Don't be frightened of anything, darling. Remember I love you.

                                        FRITH."

Kerensa read the letter and started to read it again while Lilith
watched her.

"What does he say?" asked Lilith.

Kerensa turned to her.

"You lied to me," she said coldly and slowly. "He loves me.
It wasn't a joke. He says it wasn't. I know he loves me. What
have you done to me . . . ?"

Lilith snatched the letter from her and looked at it in frustrated
anger. "What does he say? What does he say?"

"He says he loves me. He says, don't be frightened. I shouldn't
have been frightened. What have you done! You are wicked . . .
vile!"

"Be quiet. Leigh might come in." Lilith came close and
gripped Kerensa's arm. She was immediately overpowering and
as wicked as she had been on that memorable night. "Be quiet,
I say. Don't forget what you've got to keep quiet about."

Kerensa stood still, her throat dry with emotion. She could
not believe that she was married to Leigh. She felt now that she
was free from the spell which Lilith had cast upon her. She had
always known that Frith had loved her, that he accepted the
future she had planned for them; his tenderness had told her so.
Yet Lilith had made her believe otherwise. But now the letter
brought Frith back so clearly. He was a man, he had travelled
all over the world, he had done all sorts of things . . . things

which other people thought wicked because they did not know
him. Nothing he did was wicked; the mere fact that it was he
who did it made it not so. The real Frith had returned with the
letter; and the mythical one whom Lilith had created on that
nightmare occasion, when she had come in with her candle and
her red dressing gown, did not exist any more. There was nothing evil about Frith, nothing horrible; life with him would have
been sheer joy once she had learned what she had to learn; and
he would have quickly taught her that as she wanted to be taught.
She turned on Lilith in fury.

"You knew what was in that letter and you held it back. You
have had it for days. If I had had it, everything would have been
different. . . ."

"What does he say? What does he say?"

"He says he will marry me. It was not a joke to him. He says
he loves me."

"He is a fool!" cried Lilith. "He is too old. He is just reaching for something new . . . some new experience. He wants
your youth because he has lost his own. It's all wrong. You must
thank me for stopping you make an unhappy marriage . . . a
marriage that would be quite unsuitable."

"It would have been the best marriage in the world," cried
Kerensa fiercely, "and you have stopped it."

"You don't know him. He's charming . . . but his feelings
don't go deep like yours . . . like Leigh's . . . like mine . . .
like your mother's and father's. . . ."

"Don't dare to talk to me. I never want to see you again. I
shall always hate you. I shall always remember how vile you are
. . . how cruel . . . how wicked. . . ."

"Listen. You've married my son. You've got to make him
happy."

Kerensa looked sorrowfully past Lilith. "It's not his fault that
you're his mother. Poor Leigh!"

Lilith smiled. This girl was a child. She did not know what
her feelings were. She was emotional and inexperienced. She
did not understand herself, and Frith had temporarily bewitched
her. Leigh was the one for her, and Leigh was her husband now.
She would be grateful for that in a few years' time.

Lilith now tried to comfort her. She had been ruthless; she
was sorry for Kerensa as she had been sorry for Sam. She did

not want to hurt these people who were in her way; she only did so that good might come to the people she loved.

"In a few years' time," she said, "Frith will be forty. Think of that! And you'll not be twenty. You'll be just on the threshold, as they say, and he'll be old . . . old. . . . It wouldn't be right. There's too much difference. You wait. You'll see. And Leigh loves you. He's loved you all your life; you're his first and you'll be his last. You weren't Frith's first and you wouldn't have been his last. You're lucky, I tell you . . . only it don't seem so now. Kerensa, little Kerensa, I don't want to hurt you."

"Don't you?" said Kerensa. "Then I want to hurt you. I hate you. I'll never forgive you for this. You lied . . . about him. You made me see him falsely . . . as he wasn't . . . and I didn't know till now. And you've dared to interfere with my life. . . . You've dared to make me marry your choice . . . not my own."

"You'll be thankful for it, my little queen. Oh, don't you scowl at me. You're my Leigh's wife, and he loves you. You're Amanda's daughter and I love Amanda. We're close . . . all of us. We must help each other. And you and me . . . we'll help Leigh grow into a great man . . . you and me together. We'll both love him as he deserves to be loved. It'll be the three of us now . . . you . . . me . . . and Leigh."

Kerensa stared at Lilith, her blue eyes hard and glittering as sapphires.

"Yes," she said. "I'll help Leigh. He's my husband now. But you . . . you can't have a place with us. You can't read or write. You can't help him . . . and there'll never be a place for you in our home . . . nor with our children."

Lilith felt frightened. That was silly. What could a girl like that do to her! Kerensa was angry for a little while, but she would grow out of that.

"From now on," said Kerensa calmly, "I am the most important person to Leigh. You arranged that. You did it for Leigh's good. Very well. We've got to think of Leigh's good, haven't we? No matter how it hurts us, we've got to think of that. Everything's got to be done for Leigh . . . and Leigh's children. You'd agree to that, wouldn't you?"

"Of course . . . Of course. . . ."

"I don't think it would be good for them to know their grand-mother . . . a vulgar woman who can't read or write . . . who ran away from her husband . . . who is the mistress of another man.''

Kerensa's laughter which accompanied her words was very alarming to Lilith. Kerensa had turned to the dressing table. ''Go away,'' she said. ''I have to get ready.''

''Yes,'' said Lilith. ''You'll be all right, darling. You'll be all right.''

Leigh was at the door. ''Can I come in?''

''Yes,'' said Kerensa.

He came. He looked from Kerensa to his mother. Then Kerensa went to him and put her arms about his neck. It was a significant gesture. It delighted Leigh; but to Lilith it meant: ''Go away. You are banished. There is no place for you with us now and there never will be.''

Amanda bent over her embroidery, frowning a little; she had never been good at it and never would be.

''I wonder how the children are enjoying Italy,'' she said.

Lilith was silent.

''I've been thinking so much about everything lately,'' said Amanda. ''I suppose it's this wedding. It's one of those occasions . . . those important occasions . . . that set you thinking of everything that has led up to it.''

''Amanda, I'm a bit worried. Kerensa . . . she was rather cross with me before they went.''

''With you? Why?''

''It was that letter. It was from Frith, you know. I put it in my pocket and forgot it.''

''Well, there was so much to do.''

''You know how strange Kerensa was about Frith. She had a great affection for him.''

''Yes, I know—one of those youthful affections that children get. Only with Kerensa, of course, it was fiercer and stronger than it would have been with anyone else.''

''Amanda . . . children are so strange. I think she has some notion that Frith would have married her, and that I held the letter back so that she shouldn't have him, but Leigh.''

''What nonsense!''

Sweet silly Amanda! thought Lilith. The same now as she had been all those years ago in her father's house.

"Yes; but when you're young like that, you don't see it. I think that, at the moment, Leigh's a sort of second best to her."

"It can't be. She was so eager for the wedding."

"Young girls are often eager for weddings. It means just the fuss and the attention, the dress and the ceremony to them."

"But Kerensa and Leigh are so fond of one another. Don't you worry about that letter. Any of us might have forgotten it."

"When I think of some of the things I've done," said Lilith reflectively, "I'm scared. But it's nearly always been for the sake of others. Amanda, when they come back, you'll help me, won't you? You won't let them . . . shut me out?"

"Shut you out? What do you mean?"

Lilith got up and, drawing a stool close to Amanda, sat on it, leaning her head against Amanda's knee.

"Sometimes," she said, "I think you're the wise one. You've got a home, a husband, a family. You'll always have your place. It's firm. Nothing can alter that. What did you want? Just affection . . . and I suppose to do what was right. I seemed to be important . . . to myself. I wanted power. It's like the Bible story I heard Miss Robinson telling Martie and Dennis the other day. You built on rock. I built on sand."

"Lilith, what's happened to you?"

"Sand shifts, Amanda, and what you have built stops being safe. I wish I'd known these things. I wish I'd learned more. Then perhaps I'd have done different."

Amanda put down her embroidery, and, bending her head, laid her lips against Lilith's hair.

"Amanda . . . I'm the frightened one now."

"You . . . frightened! You were never frightened, Lilith. I have been thinking of all that has happened to us two . . . right from the time when we first became aware of each other. We had the same grandfather. You told me that, and always you have felt how unfair it was that I should have been born in the big house and you in the cottage. Then Frith—whom you loved— just stressed all that . . . that difference which you felt to be so wrong, so unfair. But, Lilith, you've done for Leigh what you could not do for yourself. Surely that's something to be proud of. I've listened to the words of those who talk, and I've seen the work of those who act. Lilith, you're one of those who act. You're not one of those who kneel in the pit and cry; you climb out."

Lilith stood up.

"Why, Amanda, who said you didn't know anything? Did I? I was wrong. You're the wise one. You're right about them that kneel and cry, and you're right about me. No matter what there is to hold me back, I'll kick myself free; I'll climb out of it."

She laughed, and her laughter was a challenge to Kerensa, to Frith and the future.

THE END

About the Author

Jean Plaidy is also Victoria Holt and Philippa Carr. Under the Plaidy pseudonym she has written over forty-five historical novels for Fawcett Books, including the Georgian Saga, the Plantagenet Saga, and the Queens of England series. Ms. Plaidy resides in England.